ALSO BY SUSAN ISAACS

NOVELS

Long Time No See

Red, White and Blue

Lily White

After All These Years

Magic Hour

Shining Through

Almost Paradise

Close Relations

Compromising Positions

SCREENPLAYS

Hello Again

Compromising Positions

NONFICTION

Brave Dames and Wimpettes:
What Women Are Really Doing on Page and Screen

Susan Isaacs

Any Place I Hang My Hat

Scribner

NEW YORK LONDON TORONTO SYDNEY

SCRIBNER
1230 Avenue of the Americas
New York, NY 10020

SCRIBNER and design are trademarks of
Macmillan Library Reference USA, Inc., used under license
by Simon & Schuster, the publisher of this work.

For information about special discounts for bulk purchases,
please contact Simon & Schuster Special Sales:
1-800-456-6798 or business@simonandschuster.com

Designed by Kyoko Watanabe
Text set in Stempel Garamond

Manufactured in the United States of America

1   3   5   7   9   10   8   6   4   2

Library of Congress Cataloging-in-Publication Data
Isaacs, Susan, [date]
Any place I hang my hat / Susan Isaacs.
    p. cm.
    I. Title.
    PS3559.S15A85 2004
    813'.54—dc22   2004049138

ISBN 0-7432-4215-7

To Robert Stoll
with love and admiration

Of what avail is an open eye if the heart is blind?

—Solomon Ibn Gabirol (c. 1021–1058),
A Choice of Pearls

Any Place I
Hang My Hat

Chapter One

I stepped off the elevator right into the entrance gallery of the co-op. Wow. It was oval. White marble floor, black lacquered walls, ringed with eight or ten white columns topped with marble busts, like a hall of fame for some minor sport. The hostess of the fund-raiser eyed my photo ID, which hung from a metal bead chain. "Well," she said, "*In Depth* magazine. I absolutely adore it."

"Tha—" I replied.

I didn't get out *nk you* because she cut me off: "Is the photographer meeting you here?"

"Sorry, we don't use them. No photos, no illustrations." She'd had her eyes done, so they couldn't open wider than they already were. Still, I sensed she was surprised. "Only text," I explained. "We're the serious, boring weekly."

"Right. Of course no photos. I don't know *what* I was thinking. But don't call *In Depth* boring. I think people are feeling

1

desperate for depth these days. Well, enjoy. Feel free to help yourself to hors d'oeuvres." Her dress, I noticed, was the 2003 New York noncolor, white. Ivory silk bands were sewn horizontally, making her look as if she'd stopped her own mummification to join the party.

Although the words *In Depth* on my press credentials were clear enough to her, I could see she couldn't quite make out my name. I helped her. "Amy Lincoln." A microsecond of hostess uncertainty: Lincoln? Her upper lip twitched. Should her first smile have been warmer? Her heretofore unlined forehead furrowed as she pondered asking: *Any relation to the —?*

If she could have seen the rest of the fruit on our family tree, she wouldn't have pondered. *Any relation to the —?* Please! So where did the name come from? Though highly unlikely, it's conceivable that Grandma Lillian Lincoln's explanation of the family surname was a misconception, not her usual flagrant lie: something to the effect that in the penultimate year of the nineteenth century, some Protestant clerk on Ellis Island with an antic sense of humor wrote down "Samuel Lincoln" when my great-grandfather—full of beard, dark of eye, and large of nose—stepped before him.

More likely, Great-grandpa Schmuel Weinreb heard the names Washington and Lincoln while hanging out around the pickle barrel in downtown Nizhni Novgorod listening to stories about the Golden Land. Flipping a kopek, he got tails. Could he truly have believed that by being a Lincoln, he could keep anyone in New York from noticing his six extant teeth and ten words of English? Probably. My family tended to prefer fantasy to actual thought.

Take Grandma Lil. She took the subway uptown a day or two or three a week to fill in as a substitute waxer, ripping the hair off the lips, legs, and random chins of the famous and the merely rich at Beauté, an uptown, upscale salon.

From the jet-set and celebrity clientele, Grandma learned about the finer things of life, information she felt obliged to pass on to me, mainly because no one else would listen. Inadvertently, she also taught me what not to do. Early on, I sensed that pointing out that one shouldn't wear white shoes before Memorial Day was not the way to endear oneself to one's neighbors in one's low-income housing project.

Anyhow, a hundred and five years after Great-grandpa Schmuel, there I was, Amy Lincoln, at a political fund-raiser hosted by some men's footwear magnate in his ten-room co-op on Central Park West. His wife, now high on the abracadabra combo of *In Depth* and Lincoln, murmured to me: "If you want something more than hors d'oeuvres, I can have our chef, Jean-Pierre, whip up a light supper." This time she aspirated the *hors* hard enough for me to get a whiff of the garlic in Jean-Pierre's *boudin blanc* terrine. I said no thanks.

Listen, I was there to do my job, to observe the most recently declared Democratic candidate for the presidential nomination, Senator Thomas Bowles of Oregon. Originally the scion of an old and still-monied New York family, Bowles had gone west and made a larger, eco-friendly fortune for himself by finding some new way to recycle tires.

Normally, reporters were not allowed into private homes for events like these, probably on the theory that they'd pick up a disparaging remark and use it as their lead. Or they'd glom a thousand bucks' worth of Beluga, leaving seventy-five potential contributors with two hundred pygmy buckwheat blinis and a surfeit of lemon wedges. The senator's campaign manager, normally a human piranha, had made an exception for me because *In Depth* was so dignified it never published bitchy observations regarding a candidate's dyed hair or ferocious temper. And naturally, any insinuations about unconventional sexual predilections, even really sick and/or fantastically interesting ones, were left to lesser periodicals.

Anyhow, I'd been traveling with Senator Bowles's campaign for a few days now. I'd watched him avoid probably thirty thousand empty calories by sipping bottled water, and was awed by his willpower and robust bladder. Politically, he was a little to the left of where I stood; the word *evil*—à la Reagan's evil empire and W's axis of evil—wasn't in his vocabulary, and *corporation* was consistently a pejorative. Still, going on this campaign swing had been a plus for me. I was impressed by the thoughtful way Thom Bowles spoke about his big issues. With eagerness, too, as though complex ideas were not to be recoiled from but enjoyed. I admired his I-dare-you-to-call-me-liberal American flag pin as well as his clarity: Two days earlier, in Story City, Iowa, his explanation of the social and psychological underpinnings of global terrorism had turned an audience of small business owners from thinking "pinko weenie tree-hugger" to "Hey, he really knows his stuff."

Bowles was in his second term in the Senate, and from the start of his political career, he'd been a frequent talking head on news shows. His depth of knowledge, aw-shucks persona, and seeming lack of self-righteousness combined with a bit of humor made his the perfect response to all those ranting right-wing babes with Alice-in-Wonderland hair and Jewish neo-cons so low-key they appeared anesthetized. Also, he could make ordinary voters comprehend the gravity of issues—the greenhouse effect, the crises in Social Security funding and in the penal system—that usually left them snoring.

Alas, his campaign had gotten off to a bumpy start. During his announcement of his candidacy, the senator proclaimed:

"Our penile system is in atrocious shape!" A single, nervous fluff in a career remarkably free of bloopers and gaffes. After cruel and hilarious coverage on *The Daily Show*, the other late-night talk show hosts kept it alive for two weeks. This had been Thomas Bowles's first penile-free week, but his usual fluency and light touch had diminished; he actually seemed rattled. Day after day, sprinkles of sweat covered his forehead. He couldn't seem to stop inserting *uh*s as if they were commas, so on guard was he against a "pubic policy" suddenly bursting forth.

I glanced toward the living room. I figured the senator must be in the center of the herd of Manhattanites standing between the marble-covered Italian console that was serving as a bar and a Louis-probably-XV chair so commodious that at least three Bourbons could have sat side by side by side on its gold-damask-covered seat. However, Thom Bowles was not easy to spot. While he photographed as Strapping Western Outdoor Man, with rectilinear jaw and skin the color of a sun-dried tomato, he was not much more than five foot seven and built along the lines of a gazelle.

Before I get to what happened to Thom Bowles at that fund-raiser (and after), I should return to me for a minute, because this narrative is only peripherally about the senator. His fund-raiser is simply a good place to start my own story of loss, love, passion, abandonment, social mobility, and Discovery of Missing Person—not necessarily in that order. I don't want to sound overly dramatic, but my existence has had a fair amount of *Drang*, if not bona fide *Sturm*.

Okay, so there I was, Amy Elizabeth Lincoln, journalist. With an A.B. (Harvard, '94) and an M.S. (Columbia School of Journalism, '96). The sort of woman who ought to be self-confident enough not to have to flash her academic credentials. I stood on the border of entrance gallery and living room in the headache-inducing heat and Saharan aridity of that apartment on Central Park West, wearing a too-woolly gray herringbone pantsuit under which—in thrall to some idiot early-morning sexual fog—I'd put on my one and only thong. So I'd had a day-long itch I could not scratch. Admittedly, I had a fair amount of self-discipline, both below the belt and above the neck. People usually make associate editor at *In Depth* in their mid-thirties. I'd done it at twenty-eight. I could be very focused.

A little more about the magazine: No Spielberg cover photos à la *Newsweek* for us. No cartoony drawing of some schmendrick on a cloud to go with "Does Heaven Exist?" à la *Time* either. *In Depth*'s cover was merely its contents listed on the front page. As for our readers, they were educated, the sort who did not have to be reminded of the difference between monetary and fiscal policy. They could nod knowingly at a reference to Keats's epitaph.

My beat was the Democrats, an assignment that ought to have gone to a staffer with a more mordant sense of humor than mine. However, a sense of humor and focus were necessary not merely to face Democrats, but also to deal with one's personal issues. Ergo, a brief step off the footwear mogul's seventy-five-thousand-dollar, creamy yellow and pink Savonnerie rug and onto the grimy, commercial-grade gray carpet in my cubicle at *In Depth*. The photos on my desk best introduce my family and my life.

My parents were framed in burled bird's-eye maple. It was the only photograph I'd ever seen of them together.

First, father. Charles "Chicky" Lincoln, a.k.a. Chaz Linconi, a.k.a. Dallas Armstrong, a.k.a. Charles Von Hamburg. In that picture, Chicky was sitting comfortably on a high stool—bar, not soda fountain—with Phyllis Morris Lincoln, a.k.a. my mother, albeit not for long, perched atop his knee. The photo, one of the few of my father that wasn't a mug shot, was taken a few months after I was born, probably in late '73 or early '74.

Except for Chicky's amiable expression, he looked like the sort of guy a teenage girl would go out with to frighten her parents. Tall: six feet two inches. Long black sideburns, longer hair. Not bushy like Woodstock guys' of that era. Chicky's hair was held in place by some kind of James Dean slime. His biceps looked so buff they stretched out the sleeves of his tie-dyed T-shirt. Back then, in the early seventies, he was working as a part-time driver for Frank ("Clockwork") Silvaggio, a *caporegime* in the Gambino family, who had originally hired my father in the mistaken belief that all Jews are smart.

My mother? From their size differential, it seemed clear she was somewhere between tiny and petite. That could have made her look like a ventriloquist's dummy on Chicky's lap. Except with her arms pressed stiffly against her sides and her lower legs parallel lines ending in espadrilles, she looked more rigid than any mere block of wood. The marriage had clearly gone south by then.

From the bits of information I'd gleaned over the years from assorted relatives, neighbors, and the random social worker, my parents' troubles began with the Housing Issue: Their love nest was a walk-up on the Lower East Side of New York, a few blocks north and west of Grandma Lil's housing project. At the time my parents lived there, it had been one hundred and fifty years since the neighborhood had gone from humble to slummy. It would be another twenty-five before it was rehabbed enough for cool Jews to move back—along with the hip of all races, creeds, and national origins.

The story went that Chicky tried to pass off their two-room

apartment as in a "happening" part of town. My mother told him it was a hellhole. Chicky once admitted to me that the three of us had shared the premises with a rodent. "It wasn't like huge. Sort of like . . . cutely chubby." He said he'd named it Mickey, "because Phyllis was having hysterics. So I made a joke about it." My mother, however, didn't laugh. She called it a rat.

There was also the Money Issue. They had next to nothing. That was because Chicky was paying off a loan shark from whom he'd borrowed to take my mother on an extravagant honeymoon to El San Juan Hotel that included gambling and pearls. "Amy, babes, you never saw pearls like that! Like from chickens instead of oysters."

Despite the pearls my mother was discontent. I can say that with great assurance because the week before my first birthday, she left me with Grandma Lil while she ran some errands. "See you later, sweets," my mother is said to have called out to me as she walked out the door. She never returned.

A couple of days after she left, she mailed a brief letter post-marked New York to say she wasn't dead. I suppose that was the good news. The bad news was her certainty that I'd be better off without her. She wasn't coming back. Eventually, through the George Washington Plunkett Apartments' grapevine — where someone knew someone on Bank Street in Greenwich Village who was the great-uncle of one of my mother's blabbier girlfriends — Grandma Lil learned my mother had been keeping company with a guy whose first name sounded like Maumoon. His last name was some variation of Hussain, and he was said to be a bodyguard for the Consul of the Permanent Mission of the Republic of Maldives to the United Nations. My mother sup-posedly met him at a hot dog stand outside a B.B. King concert at the Fillmore East. Whether she'd actually run off to Suradiva with him or ditched him was anybody's guess.

Getting back to my parents' photo: Despite its being an interior shot in a dark bar, my mother wore large sunglasses. Because she was on Chicky's lap, I couldn't gauge her height, but obviously I got my stature—or lack of it—from her. Also, since it was a black-and-white picture, she appeared to have shoulder-length charcoal gray hair and ivory lips. Chicky told me she was a "stunning redhead." Grandma Lil swore her hair was brown.

Through the years, I'd tinted the chiaroscuro photograph two ways. First, my mother has my color hair, red-highlighted brown; she's wearing a headband. Red-highlighted Mom isn't the least bit wooden. She's adorable, exuberant, doing such a fabulous adaptation of the Frug or the Monkey that all the other dancers have stopped to watch her. My other image is Sophisticated Mom, languid on a chaise longue in Cap d'Antibes, flaming hair dipping, Nicole Kidman–like, over one of her huge green eyes. (Mine are large and hazel, nice enough, but there has never been a sonnet extolling hazel eyes.)

I guess it's important to mention that just three weeks before my mother took off, Chicky also had to say his good-byes. He was making his first trip up the river, this time to the Downstate Correctional Facility, to serve four to six for grand larceny, to wit, stealing a five-carat diamond ring for my mother.

With good time, he returned when I was four. We moved out of Grandma's into a room with kitchen privileges in an apartment in the West Thirties. The bathroom only had a shower, so I had my baths in the kitchen sink. We stuck to each other like glue. Luckily, he loved *Fat Albert* as much as I did. I recall our TV had a screen so wide and luminous that it lit the entire room. I fell asleep most nights watching the colors flickering through my closed lids. I was convinced that if I concentrated, I'd be able to see whatever grown-up movie Chicky would be watching after my bedtime. How did we get such an extravagant TV? I suppose one of Chicky's high school friends—men I knew as Uncle Denny, Uncle Moose, Uncle Chuy—must have stolen the television for him as a Welcome Back, Chickman! gift.

"Amy babes," Chicky would ask every day, "what you want for lunch?" Naturally I was in on the joke, knowing that no matter what I said it would be macaroni and cheese—whatever pasta he'd gotten on sale plus half a can of undiluted Campbell's Cheddar Cheese Soup. We'd share it, eating from the pot. Sadly, my father was back inside a little more than two years later. Grand larceny again. This time, assault as well.

He'd committed this crime for me. Chicky had decided I needed a more stable environment. Instead of trying to get a job, not easy with a criminal record, he determined he should be self-employed. So he set himself up as a limo driver with a car that had his name on it. He accomplished that entrepreneurial coup by stealing a 1979 Lincoln Continental. Then he talked his old boss, Frank Silvaggio, into hiring him back. On one of my quarterly visits to the prison, when I was nine, he raised his right hand: "I swear on my mother's grave, Amy babes. That assault thing? I'm innocent."

"Grandma's still alive," I pointed out. "I live with her. Remember? They gave her custody again because you had to go away."

"Yeah. Sorry, Ame. It stinks for you, it stinks for me. So listen to what really happened." Chicky explained he'd merely been driving his new Lincoln. Yeah, yeah, it was stolen and he'd been a moron because he'd left the New Jersey plates on overnight thinking, Hey, the guy I'm gonna get nonhot New York plates from wouldn't want Chicky Lincoln knocking on his door at three in the morning, and also I didn't wanna leave you at Grandma Lil's overnight because I knew you hated Raisin Bran. But he swore all he'd done was drive the Lincoln with Frank and

Vinny DeCicco, along with some poor schnook of a restaurateur, to a remote section of Van Cortlandt Park in the Bronx. "It was Frank and Vinny that roughed up the guy. I was, you know, sitting behind the wheel, looking the other way, listening to my Temptations tape. On a stack of Bibles, babes, I was minding my own business."

"You call what happened to that restaurant guy 'roughed up'?" I demanded. "Chicky, he was in the hospital for three weeks."

"Yeah? And what did he prove in the end? Huh? He could've gotten his tablecloths and aprons and crap from Silvaggio's Linen Service and not wasted all that time in the hospital."

So my upbringing was pretty much left to Grandma Lil, not the brightest bulb on the menorah. However, it was convenient for me to have someone to blame for my preference for schmaltzy movies over exquisite literature, as well as my secret belief that Polyhymnia's muse-dom should be abrogated in favor of Estée, goddess of makeup. Also, Grandma taught me all the indispensable life lessons she'd garnered from her ladies at Beauté. The best skiing in the world is at Chamonix. The *only* permissible color for patent leather accessories is black.

Grandma Lil's photograph is in a tasteful russet leather frame. Even in my office's harsh fluorescence, her photo bore no resemblance to me or my father. (God is good.) As a kid, I thought she looked like a relative of the Potato Heads. She had Mrs. P's Oooh! thick ruby lips, Oh-my-God! eyes, and front-facing ears. Though not Mrs. P's sweetly dumb demeanor. Grandma could have been the start of a whole new product line, the Supercilious Potato Heads.

Whenever there was a camera around, Grandma Lil got grander than usual, as though she should be posing for Sargent and photography was a comedown. She'd perform her concerto of sighs, then shrug, acknowledging defeat. After that, she'd spit delicately on her palms and slick down her Dutch girl–style blond hair over her ears. She'd lift her chin, suck in her cheeks, and dilate her already-sizable nostrils. In the photograph, she looks not merely haughty, but also capable of exhaling two grapefruit. In all fairness, however, what look like arrogantly elevated eyebrows could be open to exegesis. Drawn on each day with light brown pencil, they never were in the same place. Their raised position might have indicated disdain or that the bulb on her magnifying mirror had blown.

Grandma Lil's blondness? Once every three or four weeks, she'd pocket a bottle of Beauté's Morning Sun formula. At our bathroom sink, she tried to duplicate the Look that murmured *New York socialite*. But whether because of ineptitude or some missing secret ingredient, her hair always turned out the brash yellow of egg yolk rather than the pale, high-fat-content French butter blonde of the Ladies.

Finally, one more Lincoln, Aunt Linda. Breaking stereotype, my father's sister was a beautiful but dumb brunette. She had married an amiable, handsome fireman who was her intellectual equal. I remember as a kid, whenever they took me somewhere for the day or had me over for a weekend, my jaw would be charley-horsed afterward from smiling. I suppose I was hoping that they'd be so enchanted they'd take me back to Brooklyn to live with them. They didn't. They never had children, so probably it wasn't anything personal. In any case, they were only inches from Grandma Lil, in the heart-shaped Lucite frame they'd given me for my twenty-first birthday: Aunt Linda and Uncle Sparky (actually Anthony) Napolitano.

Oh, my own curriculum vitae: By age fourteen, I sensed a change of scenery might be salutary. Chicky was still in the big house. With each visit, I grew unhappier about the lulls in our conversation. How come we couldn't kid around anymore? With each visit, I'd get more revolted by the stink of the inmates. Eventually, whenever I climbed onto the bus to go up to Sing Sing, I was already nauseated. With each visit, I'd get more leers, more tongues ostentatiously trailing over lips, more rasping queries—"You bad girl?"—from the prisoners and their visitors, to say nothing of the guards.

Back home, two of my good friends from school, Alida and Lucy, both smart girls, dropped out to take care of their babies. Another, Jade, left to support her family. She was earning fifty bucks a head performing fellatio on homebound New Jersey commuters who would have otherwise gotten peevish during the usual thirty-minute wait to get into the Holland Tunnel. Some other girl, a couple of years ahead of me, became paranoid from a crack overdose and wound up stabbing her sister to death.

Around that time, my social worker, Joan Murdoch, mentioned that some of the best New England boarding schools were looking for girls from poor families. "What for?" I demanded, immediately seeing myself on my knees in a scullery maid's outfit—minus the singing mice and a fairy godmother.

"They want their students to get to know all different types of people—"

"Like one of those *Rich or poor, black or white, Native American, Asian, we're all one big American family who accepts each other's differences* videos?"

"Partly, but—"

"They always play 'My Country, 'Tis of Thee' and show five million faces, but—I swear to God—they use the same Orthodox rabbi in every one."

"Don't interrupt me, Amy. They also know they're lucky to have such wealth. They think it's only fair to give some promising girls from low-income families the opportunity to get the same education rich girls get."

"What's the catch?"

"Well," she said slowly, "you wouldn't be living at home during the school year—" Sold!

My guidance counselor at Intermediate School 495 genuinely believed I could do well anywhere, but she asked: "How about Bronx Science, Amy? I don't know if you'd be comfortable at a place like . . . Ivey-Rush." Yes, that Ivey-Rush. Even I knew about it. But then, for years I'd been reading the copies of *Town and Country* Grandma Lil swiped from her job. I knew from boarding schools.

So I said to my guidance counselor: "Don't worry, Ms. Buonavitacola. If I get in, I'll be fine."

The brochure was printed on shiny paper so thick it didn't squeak: *Located in the serene and verdant Connecticut Valley, the Ivey-Rush Academy was founded in 1903 by Susannah Ivey and Abigail Rush. These two young graduates of Mount Holyoke College were determined "to provide young women with an education as rigorous as that offered to young men."*

Serene sounded good. As far as the verdancy business went, the only things not green in the brochure's photographs were Tuttle Chapel (redbrick) and the students (white and yellow, as well as browns ranging from beige to mahogany), although once I got there I realized that about two-thirds of the nonwhites in the photo must have been hired for the day from some *Diversity, Our Specialty* model agency).

Joan Murdoch helped me fill out the application. When we finished, I told her that if I were half as gifted as all my teachers raved I was, I had a shot. She agreed. Once Grandma Lil discovered she would still be my legal guardian and that my going away would not jeopardize her monthly check from the City of New

York, she signed her name to my application in the rounded, overlarge letters of the semiliterate.

With the application, I submitted a heart-wrenching essay about visiting Chicky in prison: "Father's Day" was full of shocking language—in quotation marks, to assure the admissions committee that I, personally, wasn't the kind of girl who'd say "cocksucker." Having the typical fourteen-year-old's penchant for the lurid, I filled it with graphic descriptions of disgusting smells, oozing sores, plus wails from junkie girlfriends begging for money. Ivey-Rush was thrilled with such a well-phrased account of degradation. And to show you how refined they were, when the first alumna interviewer discovered that Amy Lincoln, the leading candidate for the year's Fahnstock Scholarship—the school's guarantee of at least one black face in the class photograph—was white, not only did she do a reasonably good job of hiding her dismay, she recommended that the admissions committee let me in. Graciously, they designated me a "full needs" student, which meant all fees, room, board, and books plus ten dollars a week spending money were on the house.

But to get back to work, and to the Democrats: A waiter was offering tiny circles of pumpernickel overlaid with curls of smoked salmon, which in turn were topped by minuscule twirls of crème fraîche. Most of the guests appeared to be going through the predictable internal debate—*How much sodium how many calories how many carbs can this three-quarter-inch canapé contain?*—before wolfing down a few.

Senator Thom Bowles declined the hors d'oeuvres without a second's consideration and remembered to flash a fast, egalitarian, vote-for-me smile at the waiter. The candidate had been to enough parties like this that he knew even slightly salty salmon could cause dry mouth; caviar was also a no-no, not just because of its salinity, but because a really fine Beluga might turn his teeth gray.

By this time, it was a little after eight-thirty on a Monday night late in February. The sleet and hail beating against the windows sounded like hundreds of angry women tapping acrylic nails. I had spent the afternoon with the senator's top adviser on taxes, mostly in a dark conference room, drinking a dangerous amount of Diet Dr Pepper to keep myself from getting comatose as I studied her graphs and pie charts. My pantsuit itched and I was so tired I felt my immune system was compromised. Lichen could grow on the insides of my cheeks and over my tongue.

At that point, it occurred to me that I ought to get the hell out of the fund-raiser, get home, and go to bed. Any details I'd forgotten? I knew that the footwear king's name was Harlan Kleinberg, but I had to get his wife's first name, though it was dubious that I would mention them in the article. Still, if I did I wasn't going to be able to refer to her as the Missus. I headed toward her, figuring she was just the type to have an annoying name—Tawnee Blankenship-Kleinberg—when I heard a voice above the Manhattan murmur of the guests. I turned and saw a guy at the door. He was about nineteen. Clean-cut, but not overly so, not like those kids who try to grab you in airports. He wore jeans and a sweatshirt with CCNY, City College of New York, in an arc across his chest. His black hair was soaked into a tight cap from the weather and sparkled with flecks of hail that had not yet melted. Café-with-a-lot-of-lait skin. Built small, one of those mini-men who make the average woman standing beside him appear the size of a Thanksgiving Day parade balloon.

"I'm here to see the senator," the kid was telling the Missus and a man who looked like he might have difficulty spelling *cat*.

I assumed the latter was part of Bowles's security detail. Even though the CCNY guy didn't appear nuts, the Missus and Security seemed to be blocking his entrance. Their heads, however, were turned away from him, toward the living room, as if seeking instruction on what to do. I figured the kid might be a too-enthusiastic Bowles Brigade volunteer. "I said"—his voice got louder, though not aggressively so—"I'd like to see Senator Bowles, please." I strolled toward the front door until I was about four feet from him. He glanced at me, at my press ID, then immediately looked back at the guests. "Senator Bowles," he announced. Really loud.

Well, he caught the attention of everyone in that endless living room. Forty or fifty people in four-hundred-dollar shoes swiveled in a single direction: toward the door. They then spread out, opening up like a line of chorus cuties, with Thom Bowles having the star tapper's center spot. He stood still. Although I was too far away to really be sure, it seemed to me I could read something out of the ordinary in the movement of his eyelids. Flicker, flicker, flicker, flicker, fast as a strobe. CCNY, though unsmiling, had the pleasant expression of someone selling Boy Scout cookies. So what was the senator's blinking business? Fear? I couldn't stop thinking: *Wow! Could this be my dream? A sensational story?*

Sure, I worked for *In Depth*. Yet now and then I'd sensed in myself the instincts of a tabloid reporter. Any sign of Crash! Clash! Conflict! was music to my ears. Unfortunately, the magazine's unofficial motto was Shhhh! Anyhow, my gut began screaming out to myself: *Shit! Why can't you keep a disposable camera in that abyss of a backpack?* My intellect then reminded me that in this era of almost incessant visual excitement, only *In Depth* deliberately stayed away from the cutting edge.

Now all eyes were riveted on the kid except mine, which

were on Thom Bowles. From where I was, near the front door in the vast entrance gallery, the senator's sun-dried face was growing redder. Cut the crap, I told myself. He's not afraid, he's perfectly . . . And if he seems afraid, well, what candidate these days can endure even the pop of a champagne cork without a shudder?

Suddenly, Bowles's stick of an index finger began stabbing the air in a forward direction. Out! A vicious stab. Get that kid out of here! Except CCNY and I were probably the only ones who saw it, as everyone else's eyes were fixed on the kid. Out! Out! OUT! the finger shouted. I turned back to the kid. No twirling eyeballs. No threatening gestures. Certainly no weapon. Just another college guy who chose that moment to cry: "I am Senator Thomas Bowles's son!"

Which was interesting because Senator Bowles and his wife only had two daughters.

Chapter Two

Damn it, you're not from one of those square states, are you?" my best friend demanded.

"You know I'm not."

"So?"

"So," I repeated, "what do you want to hear?"

"Meaningful New York gossip might be nice. Or something street-smart." Charlotte's Yums, *the* Upper East Side haven for foodies, had the peachy illumination generally found in the ladies' rooms of restaurants catering to dames who were not only grande, but riche. Tatiana Damaris Collier Brandt stood in a terra-cotta-tiled aisle and looked back at a small flask of viscous golden liquid. It sparkled in her hand and resembled an extraterrestrial elixir from one of the old *Star Treks*—tranya or something, though Tatty had explained it was an essence of lemon and blood orange she was contemplating using in her work.

Having flunked out of three colleges and two marriages, she had turned a pastime, baking, into a career. She made and decorated cakes for her fellow bluebloods and in-the-know social climbers and charged anywhere from two thousand to eighteen thousand dollars. A single hundred would buy you one breathtaking cupcake, a minuscule Eden, although she insisted on hiding Adam's schlong behind a buttercream calla lily.

"That boy who broke into the fund-raiser," she went on. "What was his con or scam or whatever you call it?"

"His scam?" I asked. Tatty was excited, which in her case meant blinking twice in ten seconds and clearing her throat.

"Everybody's talking about it. You were near the door when he came in. Right?"

"Right."

"And you had no thought of impending danger?" she demanded.

"Danger from what? A surface-to-air missile?"

Tatty and I had been best friends from the evening of our second day at Ivey-Rush. She was seated down from me at the same long table in the refectory. In conversation with another girl, though looking right in my direction, she referred to me, not at all sotto voce, as the "poor little poor girl." Somehow I executed a Jackie Chan–type leap over the table and punched her in the mouth, knocking out her left lateral incisor and splitting her lip. This soon got the headmistress's attention. She handled the situation by promptly making us roommates.

"This boy could have been a danger," Tatty remarked. She was fond of drama performed by others.

"Give me a break."

When she thought she was being misunderstood or ignored, Tatty spoke with irritating slowness, each consonant distinct. Her next sentence emerged as if she were dictating to substandard voice-recognition software: "Didn't you get the impression something was wrong?"

"No." I was the fast-talking New Yorker. "Nothing was wrong. It was a lousy night, so he'd been rained and sleeted on. As far as I could tell, he seemed like a normal nineteen- or twenty-year-old City College wet person who, for all I know, will graduate, make billions, and become a perpetually dry person with an umbrella-toting chauffeur, thus underscoring the accessibility of the American dream."

"Your American dream, not mine," Tatty muttered.

"*Your* American dream dropped dead in 1929, but you're all too self-centered to notice."

The kid who'd crashed the fund-raiser had vanished, but his claim about being Senator Bowles's son was all over town. Country, too. The *Today* show had an exclusive with Bowles's wife, Jennifer, who, when pressed, conceded to Katie that she believed it was possible the intruder had been dispatched by certain political interests to tarnish her husband's reputation and silence his progressive voice. But which interests? Treacherous Democrats who wanted Lefty Bowles out now, more than a year before the Super Tuesday primaries? Unscrupulous Republicans who'd swoop down and attack any Democrat? Jen Bowles didn't know. And no, she wasn't making accusations. The intruder could have been a random unbalanced person. The senator's wife wore a peach-colored twinset, a peach and blue plaid scarf, and crystalline tears in her sky blue eyes.

The other morning shows had featured the senator's campaign manager, Moira Fitzgerald, a woman around forty built along the lines of a Hummer. In her trademark turtleneck of kelly green, Irish eyes unsmiling, she offered a more scathing version of the conspiracy theory.

"I hate to disappoint you, but the whole incident lacked

drama," I told Tatty. I followed her trench coat past the mustard department and around the olive oils as she moved into the produce section. Amethyst grapes, emerald mangos, and ruby plums were displayed and lit like gems in Cartier's. Any fruit larger than a strawberry rested on its own fluted, white paper cup.

"How could it be undramatic?" she inquired as she picked up some new, green fruit. A plum? A hairless kiwi? "You were standing in the entrance foyer. That person pushed his way in and made the accusation about Thom Bowles. Didn't you sense danger? Or at least feel any excitement?" I took the green fruit from her hand and bit into it. Plum-like and somewhere between mealy and mushy. I wanted to spit it out, but I was stuck. Tatty went on: "What I don't understand is why your nerve endings weren't twitching, you, who grew up in the bowels of this city."

I swallowed the plum glob. "Stop with the fecal imagery. I'm eating."

"The what?"

"Never mind. And trust me. If there was anything to report, I'd tell you." We heard a clip-clip-clip of rapid footsteps. A guy in a white shirt and narrow, black funeral-director's tie was galloping toward us. The store manager. "For God's sake, does he think I'm stealing his fruit? Tatty, you know I would never—"

Tatty turned toward the man and offered a barely discernible bend of her head. People bred like Tatty do not expend energy on broad movements. Still, the manager got her nod, which said *This woman is one of us.* Us meaning me and my sort, not you and your. She was always rescuing me, even though she surely knew I did not need rescuing. In any case, the man immediately stopped short and practically genuflected before her. He smiled hugely at the green fruit in my hand, then at me, all but saying *How fortunate for us that you deigned to taste our produce!*

Tatty's silence caught his attention. She waited a couple of uncomfortable seconds before demanding of him: "Could you possibly have thought—"

"No, no, no, Miss Damaris!" He smiled and turned his head from her to me and back again.

Tatty narrowed her dark blue eyes as he hurried off. "*Quel* jerk." A stranger would have difficulty sizing up such a woman: Sure, boots made from a better class of Reptilia, mink-lined trench coat, handbag from primo ostrich. But take away the wardrobe and accessories, and what was left was a tall, angular body, narrow oval face, and shoulder-length dark blond hair teased big. She might be taken for a country singer on a mediocre record label.

However, if the stranger knew his ass from a hole in the ground as far as the city was concerned, Tatty truly looked like what she was—old New York. A flawless ivory complexion, angel-wing eyebrows that had never been plucked, a somewhat long, angular jaw that resembled a shovel. Her 'do? Not 2003 Nashville. Strictly 1962 Manhattan, sprayed until it was no longer hair but a shoulder-length, monsoon-proof structure. While Tatty naturally understood that among Betty Friedan, the Beatles, Black Power, and Vietnam, hair had been liberated, women like her—and her mother and grandmother—turned up their diminutive though slightly beaky noses to such emancipation. They remained true to Mr. Roland, a society hairdresser who had clearly been granted the gift of eternal life. He'd teased Jackie's mother's hair and Jackie's and saw no reason to pay homage to the vulgarity of the late sixties, much less the begooped coarseness of twenty-first-century hair.

"I forgot where I was," I told her.

"The City College psychotic."

"Right. Anyway, he came into the apartment and hardly got past the door. Before the I-am-his-son stuff, and before Bowles's bodyguard grabbed him and frisked him and dragged him back into the elevator, all he did was try to speak to the senator. He is not a psychotic. The End." She looked skeptical. "Okay, so his voice was a little loud."

"Where were Bowles's Secret Service agents?"

"Secret Service doesn't kick in until a hundred twenty days before the general election."

This legality displeased Tatty. A single *tsk* emerged. After a moment of silence, she said, "About this boy, man, whatever. Was he believed?"

"Hard to tell. The party broke up with what is known as unseemly haste. Before I could get to Thom Bowles, he came over to me and muttered, off the record, that the kid had been stalking him whenever he came to New York. I asked if he'd gotten a restraining order. He wasn't sure. Said I should ask his campaign manager. Lovely Moira said the kid was a radical right dirty-tricks person, but they hadn't gotten an order because then the paternity charge would have inevitably become public. She also said she was relying on my sense of decency not to blow this out of proportion, which was her way of warning she would rip the flesh from my bones if I made it the focal point of my coverage."

"Did the boy *look* like a Bowles?" Tatty asked. Her intelligence was keen, but almost entirely visual. She could remember a painting forever, but even if she'd read *War and Peace* five times, to her it would only be an Audrey Hepburn film. Add that visual ability to the fact that she was related to, or a former schoolmate of, the New York affiliate of Everyone Who Matters—a self-designated group of patricians, i.e., families who managed to slog through the entire twentieth century without completely exhausting their inherited wealth—she might have actually known what features or mannerisms were peculiar to Bowleses.

"I have no idea what Bowleses are supposed to look like and, frankly, I don't give a damn." Having unburdened myself, I pictured the half-frozen kid in his sodden gray sweatshirt and the senator in his gray pinstriped suit tailored slightly on the baggy side so as not to look custom-made. "Well," I conceded, "if there's a petit size for guys, they'd both wear it. You know, they've both got butts the size of . . ." I held up my two fists side by side.

"You're still as cultivated as you were on your first day of school."

"My first day of school was at P.S. 97."

"You know I meant your first day of *boarding* school." Tatty's voice was pitched low. Dictionwise, she was fond of vowels, though not enamored. For a score or more years, alumnae and alumni of New England boarding schools hadn't sounded like the preppies of old who articulated as if auditioning for *Lady Windermere's Fan*. Still, her diction was different enough from mine that a non–New Yorker might find it hard to believe we'd both been born and bred on the same twenty-two-square-mile island. "Besides their butts," Tatty asked, "was there a resemblance?"

"I don't think so," I told her. "I mean, Thom Bowles looks like the Marlboro Man, except photocopied to three-quarter size. The kid could have been Italian, Latino, Jewish—your basic Mediterranean model. Or some other mix that results in beige. Listen, I may be semi-street-smart, but I can't look at a guy and say, 'Oh, yeah, Sri Lankan and Belgian.'"

"Did he have an accent?"

"No. Well, he didn't start reciting *Leaves of Grass*, so I can't vouch for his every word, but he sounded like a regular guy in a sweatshirt." I thought back to *I am Senator Thomas Bowles's son!* "Probably a guy in a sweatshirt from one of the five boroughs. Anyhow, the moment was sensational only in the tabloid sense. Honestly, I didn't think of him being a psycho or a drama queen." True, it had been a night of rain and sleet, with a bitter wind. It may have been mildly weird for the kid just to be wearing a sweatshirt. But he might have been wearing layers underneath. He could have been too poor to buy a jacket. Or maybe February 2003 was like my second winter at Ivey-Rush, when Tatty and I and all the girls ran around coatless with lips blue and fingertips fading from red to white as they went numb from frost-nip. We were all convinced we were so incredibly cool not to be wearing coats. "Tell me what you know about Thom Bowles," I said.

"Let me think." For some reason, she put her index finger to her lips rather than to her head. "Okay, I forget Thom's father's first name," she said slowly, "but I know he was big in banking."

"William Bryson Bowles," I informed her.

"Or investment banking," she continued. "Stock market. One of those."

"The father was an investment banker," I said. "I already know the senator's biographical stuff."

"If you've done so much research, do you know why he spells his nickname T-H-O-M?"

"No. Tatty, I don't know nor do I want to know. However, what I would like to know is this: Is there any dirt? Not that I could use it in my piece, but it would be comforting to know it's there."

Tatty picked up a lemon and squeezed it gently. Then she sniffed it and set it and five others in the country-cute woven wood basket Charlotte's Yums offered its patrons in lieu of red plastic with wire handles. "Dirt on Thom?" She ruminated for a second and a half, then shook her head. Naturally, her carved amber hair remained motionless. "Not that I can remember.

After college, he moved to one of those Washington, Oregon states and did something Sierra Club–ish but that made him tons of money. Not a whiff of scandal, as far as I ever heard. But I'll ask the parents tonight." After her divorces—both of which occurred around the time her monogrammed towels began to fray—Tatty had gone back to living in her family's palace of an apartment on Park and Seventieth. She claimed it was because the kitchen was the size of many commercial bakeries. "Naturally, I'll e-mail you if they have anything interesting to say, although such a thing has not occurred in my lifetime." Then she smiled. "I promise not to call. You *know* there's no way I would interruptus your coitus with John."

John Orenstein, my boyfriend, was a documentary filmmaker who had spent the day cutting five minutes out of a History Channel show about the Germans' summer offensive in southern Russia during 1942. Too much of a pro to protest that losing five minutes was commensurate with the excision of a vital organ, he was, nevertheless, not his usual easy self. For someone normally crazy about baked ziti and oral sex, he'd seemed less than wildly enthusiastic during dinner and after. "Do you have anything to drink?" he asked as he squished a pillow to his liking and put it behind his head.

"I've got Diet Coke, vodka, and orange juice. Oh, there's some milk. But I wouldn't drink it if I were you."

"Almost sour? Or curdled and gross?" I'd dimmed the lights to romantic candlepower. As long as the halogen reading lamp on the table beside my couch➔bed remained off, I could look like Venus on the half shell. As for John, while he probably wouldn't be asked to pose bare-chested for the cover of *Men's Health,* he wasn't bad. Not only did he have defined biceps, but actual, visible triceps. Add to that a solid torso with the perfect amount of chest hair: neither a half-plucked chicken nor someone with a shag rug over his pectorals. And while he was too big-featured and ham-handed to make anyone gasp and say *Stunning!,* or even *Handsome,* his broad shoulders, brown hair, caramel brown eyes, along with the gold undertone of his skin, always reminded me—if not the rest of the world—of the Oscar. Dressed, he didn't look like the archetypal doc filmmaker. He wasn't one of those vitamin-D-deficient downtown guys with black-framed glasses to match all-black, all-the-time clothes. His style was casual but cool, like an academic who got good consulting fees. Mostly he wore khakis or jeans with hand-knit sweaters and denim shirts that fit as though they were custom-made.

I got back to the milk. "If I had to guess? I'd say more than repulsive, but it won't be totally gross until tomorrow."

"Water's good," he said.

Before he could get up, I did one of those flying leaps that gets you from supine to upright in one fluid instant. "It's okay, I'll get it."

Over the years, I'd gotten enough compliments and seen enough of myself in those three-way mirrors while trying on bathing suits to be relatively confident about my rear view. This was not to say I would jog through Central Park bare-assed at noon, but I figured fetching a glass of water, high-butted and low-cellulited, was the kind of visual I wanted looping in John's mind after I dumped him.

Maybe "dumped" sounds a little harsh. Well, I suppose I was still angry and/or hurt from Valentine's Day. I'd been expecting a small, lightweight box. He'd handed me a heavy, medium-sized one. *Oooh,* I'd said, hoping I sounded more pleased than surprised. I opened it to find an electric appliance that produced heart-shaped waffles. It wasn't the fact of a waffle iron that had upset me so much.

It was that despite what I thought of as his apparent clinging—the same behavior he referred to as *enjoying my company*—our relationship was stuck in the mud. Yes, he wanted to be with me when I was buying groceries, and no, he didn't want to go off and pick up a roll of paper towels while I was checking out the green teas because *Wouldn't it be more fun if we did both things together?*

Yet he was perfectly capable of telling me he was going to the Fulton Fish Market the following morning, just to see what sunrise there looked like, then calling two weeks later to say sorry, he'd been out of touch. But hey, he'd been to a soybean-processing plant in Ohio, a pig farm in Georgia, and Safeway headquarters in California because he'd gotten backing to do a documentary called *Food Chain*. And what did I think of the idea?

One time, when I asked him how come he hadn't called, he'd replied, "Amy, the phone's a two-way instrument." It wasn't that John was undependable. I saw him as a man of enormous enthusiasms. He could become intrigued by a fly perched on the edge of a beer can, start to gather footage on houseflies, put together a film crew, set out a bowl of sugar, and wind up finding someone to pay for a documentary. And also make a profit on it. A small profit to be sure, but then he hadn't become a documentarian because he wanted to be rich.

After two years of seeing each other exclusively, I realized I'd become one of his lesser enthusiasms. No matter that we could talk about politics for hours, or even whole weekends, analyze the lives of our friends. No matter we both loved classic Hollywood movies, the Yankees, and walking for miles and miles all over Manhattan. He had never once said *I love you*. And after the waffle iron, I couldn't see asking him, *Hey, John, do you love me?* Because I knew he didn't.

Not that I loved John either—of that I was sure—but he'd taken me on such a damn long ride. Two years, two months. We'd gotten past his friends, then gone on to meet his family, then down to his assistant, his summer intern, and his professional pals at the History Channel and A&E. Naturally I figured: Well, he's revving up to ask the Big One. I've got to at least give it consideration, because John all but wore an identifying neon sign flashing *Hey, Women of New York! Great Catch.* After I wound up on New Year's Day minus a ring, I'd been positive February fourteenth would be the day he'd pop the question. Maybe he'd even have a ring ready. Instead, I got the waffle iron along with a small bottle of 100-percent-pure Vermont maple syrup.

"Since you're doing the whole hostess thing," John called out, "throw in a couple of ice cubes."

"If you want, but I have this theory why you shouldn't want ice."

"A theory on ice?"

"Yes. Jews have bad ice." I walked over to the refrigerator, not much of a hike as my apartment was a studio so small that I'd had to give a lot of thought as to whether a chessboard was too much furniture.

"You've been to my place a million times," he said. "Do I have bad ice?"

"Did I ever say anything negative about your ice?"

"Amy, this is the first time since I've known you that we're discussing ice, so you've never said anything either negative or positive." Although I didn't turn back to look, I could hear him shifting on the sheets, rearranging the pillow once again for our usual postcoital banter. Even after all this time, our lovemaking remained somewhere between passionate and wild. Yet it felt impersonal, or maybe desperate, as though we'd just been sprung after a decade in solitary. I guess we both needed the reassurance that after lust, we could have What-a-happy-couple! chitchat before we parted. "What's wrong with my ice?" John inquired.

"The same thing that's wrong with mine. Jewish ice cubes—okay, Ashkenazic, not Sephardic—always taste oniony. It's probably from bagels and bialys. Seriously, if you went to Tatty's freezer—any non-Jew's—you'd find totally tasteless ice. You get iced tea at Tatty's and it doesn't smell as if it had been stirred with a scallion. Do you still want ice?"

"Yes. Even more than I did before."

So how come I was getting ready to dump this not-bad-looking, smart, decent guy who probably didn't have a misogynistic bone in his six-foot body? Because together we had everything—except love. We were great at exchanging ideas and bodily fluids, yet there was a whole middle ground of transcendent emotion that eluded us. Plus I could see the writing on the wall, and it said, *He's going to be saying bye-bye pretty soon.*

Considering where my hands had been a few minutes earlier, I figured it would be genteel to wash them. I did that in the mini-sink in the mini-kitchen that took up three linear feet in my studio, a sublet on Central Park South that was mine until the apartment's owner, *In Depth*'s Asia editor, came back from Tokyo. It was stunningly cheap, as the owner's trust fund took care of the co-op's maintenance. Having gotten his colleagues' testimony that I was a neat freak, he'd decided it was wise to trust the place to someone who cleaned her keyboard with a Q-tip and precisely aligned her expense vouchers. The apartment faced West Fifty-eighth Street, not the park. All I could see from my window were other people's apartments and an old wooden water tower. I was too low for sky, too high for ground, so without watching TV or going outside, I could not tell what the weather was. But on good nights, the scent of flowers and trees and horseshit made it through my open window, the same smells that had wafted from the stables and grounds, across the quad and into the dorm at Ivey on spring evenings.

Anyhow, knowing John was watching, I bent over carefully. I didn't want to overplay the memorable butt bit, so I opened the minifridge and quickly grabbed a couple of ice cubes. That instant, I got this memory of the night we were standing on line to see *Adaptation*: I'd been babbling something to John about the consequences of the Democrats' loss of the House that November 2002, but I happened to notice the guy behind us.

He was about our age and was standing there alone with a sweet, dopey smile spreading across his face. I realized he was watching his boyfriend coming up the street, almost a block away. They probably couldn't see each other's face, but I was sure the boyfriend was smiling too. *They not only delight in each other,* I remember thinking, *I bet they can rely on each other.* If one of them decided to make a documentary called *Food Chain,* he'd call the other every day. Twice a day. When someone treasures you, you become a necessary step in his thought processes; he doesn't just miss you, he needs you.

"Hey," John said as I walked back, taking a different route, around a chair where the light was dimmer. Full frontal was acceptable, though not as good as the rear view.

"When did we stop saying 'Hi' and start saying 'Hey'?" I inquired. "We as a generation, I mean." He smiled and I handed him the glass. "Here's your onion water. The cubes are almost in meltdown." I retrieved my duvet from the floor and wrapped it around myself and sat at the edge of the couch➔ bed. "Why do guys like to stay naked after sex?" I asked.

"Why do women like to generalize about men? Or have you slept with a large enough sample—say fifty thousand—to know that all of us like to give it an airing?" He sipped the water. "It's perfectly good."

"For people without taste buds."

He set the glass down on the floor and took my hand. My hand being fairly small and his being big, I allowed myself a few seconds of self-deception to feel petite. Five foot three isn't gigantic and my weight was pretty much under control, yet if you noticed my shoulders and my leg muscles, you'd see why the soccer coach at Ivey took one look and knew she'd found her girl. John ran his fingers over the tips of my nails, that semi-conscious masculine tribute to a woman's manicure. I tried to think of a courteous way to say, *What do you think, I have all night?* I wanted him out. I wanted to floss, brush, say my prayers, get to sleep.

"Hey, Amy."

"Hey, John."

"Tell me something about yourself you haven't told me before."

"Is this some cute documentary technique?" I asked.

"No, this is what's called asking a question. Wanting to get to know a person better." I was about to ask him, *How could you not know me after more than two years?* when I realized I didn't want to hear his answer. "Sometimes I think we're in a weird dance," John went on. "We're facing each other, but not touching, and every time I take a step forward, you take a step back."

Even though I was tempted to pull my hand away, I let John fiddle with my nails. "I'll be glad to tell you something you haven't heard before, although I've never been able to figure out the allure of deprived childhoods. Nobody ever asks somebody who grew up in Scarsdale, 'Oh, tell me something you haven't told me before.'"

He gave me back my hand, patting it good-bye, and offered a small, no-teeth-showing smile, his being-patient smile. "I didn't ask about deprivation. I just thought it would be nice to know something new about you," he finally said. John did have a great voice. Had he been able to carry a tune, he would have sounded like one of those sexy, low-voice singers, like Julian Casablancas, that guy in the Strokes. But at that moment he simply sounded muted, as if he were already pulling out of my life. "Do you feel you know all there is to know about me?"

I could see that he needed something. "I know I can get a little . . . testy?" This did not come as a news flash to him. "Or oversensitive." No argument. I studied our path to bed from door to couch: his black sweater to white boxers, my blue-and-white-striped shirt to black panties. If John hadn't been naked at that instant, I sensed he would think *Fuck this lame attempt at intimacy*. He'd walk out, probably for good. Knowing him, very decent, very pragmatic, maybe he'd take me to one final dinner at a quiet restaurant, so he could feel safe that I wouldn't start wailing. He should have known he could have saved his money and picked a noisy diner, because I hated public displays of affliction.

As antidumping insurance, I began: "Okay, something about me I haven't told you before." Since he wasn't turning over on his side, getting ready to be rapt, I didn't let much more than a second go by before saying: "Joan Murdoch."

The next five seconds felt like minutes. At last he managed to say: "Who's Joan Murdoch?"

"When I was seven, the second time my father went to the big house, they assigned a social worker to me. I'm not sure why. I don't think it was routine with a grandparent as temporary guardian, but I like to imagine that Grandma Lil seemed either dumb or flaky enough to make the Department of Human Resources decide she was capable of taking me to Macy's, wandering off to see if there were any free makeovers, and forgetting about me. Not just for a few minutes. For good. Or maybe she had a record, too. Shoplifting. It was her hobby. The way some people read mysteries or crochet afghans. She'd swipe a couple of lamb chops, a potato, and voilà, takeout!"

John turned onto his side and propped up his chin on the heel of his hand. Good.

He was too caught up in the story to remember he was on the verge of taking a hike.

On the other hand, I had never before mentioned my grandma's habit of lifting goods she could not afford. Now he'd realize Chicky's criminality wasn't a genetic anomaly.

"Where was I?" I asked.

"Lamb chops and potatoes," John said. "And the social worker."

"Right, Joan. Well, she'd come by, like, I don't know, once a month or something. She'd always bring me a paperback. Kids' classics. *A Wrinkle in Time. The Phantom Tollbooth.* I mean, I was already the best patron the library had, but it was something else to actually own a book. So I was always excited when she came over. And all her routine social work questions were painless enough."

"Was there anything you didn't tell her?"

"Well, I wouldn't say, 'Yo, Ms. Murdoch, my grandma Lil heisted a big hunk of cheddar at Bloomingdale's food department and we've had great grilled cheese sandwiches three nights in a row.'"

"Anything else?" John asked. I almost asked him what was he waiting for. Some nightmarish story of abuse or neglect? But I didn't want to bring him out of my Scheherazade spell.

"No. There were no secrets. Joan knew my grandma did not exhibit Type A behavior employmentwise. I mean, she made just enough working at the beauty salon to supplement my government check. If that took two days, she'd work two days. If it took two and a half? After that fourth hour, Grandma Lil was out of there—probably even if she was in the middle of someone's bikini wax. But otherwise it was okay."

"Did you feel your grandmother loved you?"

I shrugged, but then realized I needed to say something. "I never really thought about it. She knew I could pretty much look after myself, but she did whatever she had to. And if something bad ever happened to me, she'd have been . . . I really don't know. Anywhere from upset to devastated. No, not devastated. I don't think she had that kind of emotional range. But genuinely sad. Listen, I was an easy kid. She never had to hit me or discipline me because there never was any reason to. Most of the time I was more mature and better behaved than she was."

I got off my grandma. "Anyhow, back to Joan Murdoch," I went on. "She asked my grandma Lil if she could take me to the Museum of Natural History one Sunday and of course my grandma said yes. I loved it. I wanted to live there. After that, every three or four weeks, Joan would come downtown, pick me up, and take me someplace. Usually to museums. Sometimes we went bowling. A couple of times she took me up to the Bronx Zoo. She handled it really well, as if we were two cordial acquaintances. Not overly friendly. And without *Oh, you poor little diamond in the rough* pity."

"She must have really liked you."

"I guess so. Well, I was a do-gooder's dream girl. One of those thirsty little flowers ready to soak up whatever culture or kindness came her way. And I wasn't bad company. When you're a kid who depends on the kindness of strangers, you either get nothing or else you learn to charm the hell out of people to get what you need. I know you find the charm business hard to believe."

"Cut the self-effacement shit," John said. "You are charming."

I figured he might already be regretting saying that, so I immediately jumped in. "Anyway, one year—I was eight or nine—Joan took me to see the Christmas tree in Rockefeller Center. I was, like, Wooow! So she talked to my grandma—she knew we were Jewish. Not that my grandma would volunteer information like that, but I'd told Joan. Anyway, she got permission to take me to her family's tree-trimming party at her parents' house on Staten Island. There were her parents, her sister, her sister's husband and kids. I went there every year, except later, when I'd go to Tatty's family's house on Jupiter Island for Christmas break.

"Anyhow, the Murdochs were originally from Scotland, so for Christmas they blasted bagpipe records and ate these oatmeal fried things called bannocks. And they gave me my own tree ornament. A Santa's elf in a green outfit with teeny green shoes with pointed toes, and a little loop of wire coming out of his elf hat for hanging. And year after year, they kept it for me and . . ."

Other than a mention to Tatty or maybe Chicky that I'd gone to the social worker's house for a trim-a-tree party, I'd never told anyone about the Murdochs. I always relied on my one-volume encyclopedia of the deprived childhood stories that I'd been telling since my first year at Ivey. My New York accent—"She's so genuine!"—to say nothing of stories featuring runaway mother and imprisoned father took me places where the F train didn't go. Like La Jolla. Jackson Hole. Ogunquit. One time to Rome and Capri. I learned to mesmerize a dinner party in Palm Beach with now-appalling, now-amusing vignettes of life in the projects. By the time I got to Harvard, I was a gifted guest. I'd go from Thanksgiving in New Brunswick to Christmas in Florida to spring break hiking on the Maine coast or riding bikes in Circleville, Ohio. My stories remained the same, though I altered my delivery to suit my audience.

New, unrehearsed tales of my past might be risky. I could be boring. Seem pitiful. Then what? Good-bye to my reputation for charm. Who knows? Maybe I'd get choked up. Then John would feel compelled to stay the night, comfort me. It was past eleven-thirty.

So I yawned.

Instead of sitting at the desk in my office and rereading Thom Bowles's alleged autobiography, a total snore full of paragraphs suitable for insertion in any Democrat's Earth Day or Martin Luther King Jr. Day speeches, I found myself staring at Grandma Lil's photograph. No one had ever said there was a resemblance between her and me, but I sat back in my chair wondering how much of her I'd inherited.

I had some notion of what I'd gotten from her before Ivey-Rush, Harvard, Columbia Journalism, Alzheimer's, and death separated us. Grandma Lil took home more than hair dye from Beauté. She brought home lessons about the finer things of life and insisted I master them whenever Chicky wasn't around, i.e., most of my early life.

She offered me these treasures not because I was an eager student, or even a polite listener, but because no one else was willing to hear her breathy communiques on gauche colors (teal, burnt orange), how to set a proper table (the water goblet is at the top and to the right of the knives), or the merits of a Parisian face peel.

"A lady is *always* nice to the help," she advised me one night, raising the water goblet she'd lifted from Bloomingdale's, which I later learned was a red wineglass. Holding the stem between her thumb and middle finger, her pinky a quarter inch aloft, she took a dainty sip through lips so puckered it seemed she was kissing the rim of the Baccarat.

I was around ten at the time. We were having steak for dinner. Dinner for two, due less to mutual delight than to our mutual shafting: my mother skipping and Chicky being otherwise engaged making license plates. That night, Grandma had "picked up" our steak at a Gristede's in the East Sixties on her way home from Beauté. She believed her luck at avoiding what she called "unpleasantness" came from never heisting from the same store more than once in any year. Ergo, the quality of the meals she tucked under her pilfered black cashmere shawl (Henri Bendel) varied considerably, from Upper West Side vacuum-packed Scottish smoked salmon to kielbasa.

"Amy, you listening?" I nodded, my mouth full of oversalted sirloin broiled until it attained rigor mortis. "I happened to overhear Silvana Feldstein today." She pronounced the *stein* the Teutonic way, "schtine." "You've head me speak of her. Her husband is in real estate. Old money." Probably 1979. "Well, Silvana was talking about this man—"

Grandma raised a finger in a hold-on-a-second gesture and leapt from her chair. With a fast hop-step that looked like the opening of a Latvian folk dance, she clunked her foot down on a bloated cockroach. I heard a barely audible crunch as insect became one with floor. The original red and blue flecks on the linoleum had darkened over the years, and the only way to distinguish between dirty dot and flattened bug was by size.

"—this guy named James," she went on, booting the squished half-inch corpse under the stove. "He owns a catering business—I told you what catering is?"

"Yeah," I said.

Grandma sat, picked up her fork, and pointed it at me. "Amy." She sighed, then wearily soldiered on. "Don't say 'yeah.' Well-bred girls don't say 'yeah.' They say 'yes.'"

"Yes. Hey, Grandma, I gotta go, I got a math test tomorrow."

"Anyway, this James guy is such a . . . I forget what word Silvana used. . . . But he's such a shit to his waiters—"

"I told you, I gotta study."

"Who's stopping you? So listen. James is such a shit to his waiters that one of them actually spit on the cheese straws! And half the guests at the hemophilia benefit saw him do it!"

"A cheese straw?" I inquired. I already knew what hemophilia was and could figure out *benefit*.

"Not like a straw, you know, for soda."

"Then what?"

"It's something rich goyim eat. So Amy, you listening?"

"Yes."

"What does the story tell you?"

"I give up."

"It's *Treat your help good and they'll be good to you.*" I angled Grandma Lil's picture until I could no longer see her staring at me, and turned back to my monitor with my notes on Thom Bowles.

Technically, my office was a cubicle enclosed on three and a half sides by wallboard and some hideous plastic meant to look like smoked glass. When I looked out, all objects and people appeared blackish-brown, as if saturated with pollutants. Still, I allowed myself tokens of pleasantness: a weekly rose for a bud vase, a Van Gogh *Summer Fields* mug, a tenth-reunion picture of my Ivey-Rush class on Lilac Day as a screen saver. A Rosie the Riveter mouse pad. The phone rang. I took out one of the foam earplugs I used so as not to hear muttered bytes of office conversation and the clicks of other people's keyboards. "Amy Lincoln," I said.

"Hi," a male voice said. "My name is Fred." He paused. "Freddy. Whatever." I said something like *uh-huh* rather than saying *Hi, Freddy,* thereby risking even a brief conversation with a telemarketer offering to manage my portfolio. "Actually it's Fernando. Fernando Carrasco. I saw you two nights ago. At the party for Senator Bowles on Central Park West."

Of all the men I'd seen at the fund-raiser, there was only one I was interested in talking to. "Are you the guy with the CCNY sweatshirt?" I asked, putting on a big smile. Some physiology-of-emotion grad student I went out with in my junior year swore doing that made you sound friendly.

"Yeah. I'm the guy."

"Are you okay? They didn't rough you up or anything, did they?"

"No. This big guy, I guess a bodyguard, went down with me in the elevator and kind of shoved me out the door of the building. He said, 'Don't let me see you again,' or something like that."

"Uh-huh. And how did you know how to call me, Freddy?"

"I saw Amy Something on your press thing. I got a copy of *In Depth* and found you on the . . . What's that list called? Oh, masthead. You were the only Amy."

"Glad you found me. Hey, do you actually go to City?"

"Yeah."

"Where exactly is it?" I asked.

"A Hundred-thirty-eighth Street and Convent Avenue. Why? Do you just want to see if I know where it is?"

I put back the smile and improvised. "Just trying to make sure you weren't that scrawny guy with the red vest who kept trying to show me what a brilliant raconteur he was." I grabbed a pen from my Van Gogh mug and jotted: *Fernando Carrasco, a.k.a. Fred/Freddy.* I never took notes on the computer; the clicks of fingers on keyboard reminded people this was not a conversation between friends.

"Not scrawny. No vest," my friend Freddy assured me.

"No paternity suit?" I inquired.

"No," he said evenly. "William Bowles, Thomas's father, paid off my mother three months before I was born. And then he sent my father out of town."

I knew what my editor, Happy Bob, would expect me to be doing at eleven-thirty that morning. Thomas Bowles had a radical tax proposal: a confiscatory inheritance tax. Of course it had a snowball's chance in hell of passing, but then again, those were the same odds as Bowles actually winning the Democratic nomination, much less the presidency. In Republican-right rhetoric, what he was aiming for was class warfare. Was it really? Could such a policy kill capitalism? Or could it be a revolutionary equalizer?

So I should have been calling a few congenial economists and sociologists, asking, Hey, what would happen if the right to pass along wealth went down the tubes? What would the world be like if Alfred and Preshie Demaris, Tatty's parents, could not bequeath to her the Florida house, the trusts, the house in Southampton, the collection of English garden statuary, Great-grandfather Kent's three Rousseaus and two Rodins, and other possessions ad (practically) infinitum. What if, instead of piping Cornelli lace or lilies onto cakes a couple of times a week, Tatty had to earn enough to pay for her own food, clothing, and shelter?

Instead, I was sitting in a Starbucks a couple of blocks down from my office on Union Square waiting for Freddy Carrasco to show. I felt fairly confident he wasn't a madman, but I knew enough from life and movies and Grandma Lil ("You'll learn when you're dead he wasn't Mr. Nice Guy") that the most successful kind of psychopath isn't the creep, it's the one with a sweet smile. Why I thought Starbucks would offer me protection if Freddy turned out to be toting an Uzi was a question I began pondering as I sipped my Espresso Macchiato. Except at that instant, he entered—this time wearing a blue fleece pullover. His hands were stuck in his pockets. His ears were such a dark red from the cold they almost looked purple.

After he sat across from me, we had a moment's negotiation before he agreed to allow *In Depth* to buy him a Toffee Nut Latte. When I came back to the table, he was nervously folding a napkin into increasingly smaller triangles. "I'm going to make a couple of notes as you talk," I told him. "But I'll be up front with you. We don't do scandal stories."

"So how come you're wasting time with me?" he asked, unfolding the napkin, putting it on his lap.

"I'm doing a long piece on the Bowles campaign. Maybe ten percent of what I learn will make it into the article. But the more I know, the more authoritative it will sound." I also figured if Freddy had a story that totally broke my heart, I could point him toward a woman from journalism school I knew at the *New York Post,* a reporter with few scruples and no shame when it came to Democrats.

"Okay," he said.

"Where do you live?"

"Washington Heights."

"Do you actually go to City College?"

"Yeah. At night." God knows I'd spent hours, days, watching Thom Bowles in person and on TV. I'd also seen hundreds of photos of him in all the background research I'd done. So searching for him in Fernando Carrasco should have been easy. Except it wasn't. Thom, blue eyes. Freddy, brown. Thom, lean, with a rugged, close-to-handsome, square-jawed lonesome-cowpoke face. Okay, Freddy did have a square for a jaw, but his face was fuller at the high cheeks and even broader at the temples, so the shape of his head was more flowerpot than telegenic rectangle. I wasn't sure if the vague resemblance I did see was in his face or my head.

"Have you declared a major?" I asked.

"Computer Engineering."

"What do you do during the day?"

"I'm a computer service tech at Widmann Financial."

"Are you cutting work?"

"No. I took this week as vacation because the senator was coming to town."

"Does your mother know you're doing this, Freddy?"

"My mother died a couple of years ago."

Convenient. "Sorry. Did she happen to leave any papers or records about the payment from Bowles senior?"

"No. She told me she signed something and gave it back to William Bowles. The senator's father. He's been dead for a couple of years."

"I know. So, do you have any reason to think William Bowles gave that agreement or whatever your mother signed to his son?" He shrugged and got busy sipping his latte. "Do you think Thom Bowles knew about their deal?" No answer. "What do you want out of this?" I asked.

"What do you mean?"

"Well, you're probably a logical person—a computer guy. So if step one was trying to get his attention at that party—or had you tried before?"

"I wrote him in Washington, just saying I was Nina Carrasco's son and would like to meet him."

"Any answer?"

"No. So I wrote basically the same thing again and put it in an envelope along with a letter to his administrative assistant asking him to please pass it along to Thom."

"Did that get an answer?"

"Yeah." Even before Freddy conveyed "'The senator regrets he does not have the time,'" I could read that rejection in the ridge between his luxuriant eyebrows, the inverted U of his mouth. "I guess I knew that would be the answer, but I was hoping, you know, that it was just a polite, routine drop-dead letter they send out to people who aren't important."

"And then?"

"So I saw on his website he was speaking to a group called Ecologistas en Acción"—as he was about to translate, I motioned for him to keep going—"at their annual meeting, in Washington. So I figured, Hey, that's a good place. Probably not thousands of people and I could pass as an academic, or at least an environmentalist. I took a bus down and got into the meeting. Zero security. Except after his speech, when I thought I could get to talk to him, he was already off to some other group. These guys can give twenty speeches a day or something."

"I know. So did you ever get to talk with him?"

Freddy nodded slowly. "Believe it or not, I was reading *The Paper*, the City College school paper, and there was an announcement that he was coming to the campus the next Tuesday. I went and there were, like, less than twenty people. At the end I went up to him and we shook hands. And I said: 'I'm Freddy Carrasco, Nina's son,' and he didn't faint or anything. He gave this little smile-nod thing and the next thing I know, some goon—not the one who threw me out of the fund-raising party—grabs my arm and drags me out of there. Like they had some secret signal that was a goon alert."

"I'm sure they did. But you still haven't answered my question. What do you want to get out of this? Your fair share of the family fortune?"

Either he was shocked or was giving a pretty good imitation of it. "No! I don't want a dime."

"So then what? To crap out his candidacy?" Freddy shook his head emphatically. "A DNA test?"

He took a deep breath and exhaled it slowly before saying: "Yes. I'd like that."

"What do you think the chances are of it happening?"

"Pretty low."

"So the night you came up to the fund-raiser and announced you were the senator's son, what were you expecting? A hug?" He set down the latte he'd been holding and clasped his hands. "I don't mean to sound harsh," I told him, "but what did you hope he would do?"

"Maybe . . . I was hoping for—I don't know—something or somebody to put enough pressure on him that he'd have to recognize me. Not love me or adopt me or even talk to me. Not give me anything. Just say, *Yes, he's my son.* How the hell can someone not have any feeling or, shit, even curiosity about a human being he was responsible for giving life to? What kind of a person is it who can turn his back on his own flesh and blood?"

That night I decided to call Chicky and ask about my mother.

Chapter Three

"Amy, would I lie?" my father asked.

"Of course not."

"Okay, so I lied a few times in my life. But not to you." Quickly, over his left pectoral, his index finger inscribed an upright triangle, then an inverted one to make a star of David. Apparently, he found nothing inconsistent in vowing "Cross my heart and hope to die" at the same time. We sat across from each other in a green leatherette banquette in the Royal Athens Diner in the borough of Queens, the sort of place with a menu longer than the complete works of Dickens.

He smiled at me. A nice smile, though jailhouse dentistry left something to be desired. His dentures seemed made up exclusively of front teeth. "So when I tell you, 'Hey, Amy, you're looking good,' trust me." Maybe he was right. I was wearing a lavender sweater, and for some reason any variation on purple made me unaccountably cheery. Had I been blown to Oz, my road would have led to Amethyst City. "You're looking A-plus in my book, babes."

Chicky himself looked very good. Having successfully stayed out of the hoosegow at that point for more than four years, a new record, he'd maintained his prison weight-lifting regimen. His neck was a massive, muscular cylinder that rose straight up from shoulder to ear. Not an ounce of flab could be seen under his long-sleeve shirt, which was made of some glossy green clingy fabric; were Ralph Lauren the expectorating type, this would be fabric he wouldn't spit on.

Chicky kept his long hair slicked back with Elvis sideburns. I hadn't seen him in nearly six months, but as every strand was now the glossy black of new Mary Janes, I figured he was dyeing it. A diamond stud twinkled on his left earlobe. He looked much younger than his forty-nine years, with the hooded eyes, long face, and full lips of the stereotypical gigolo.

And, in fact, that's what he was. He was being kept in Queens by a woman he referred to either as "my rich lady friend" or Fern. By rich, I believed he meant that she could afford to keep him in style. As he'd spent so many years incarcerated, his conception of style was probably not much beyond having the toilet in a separate room, and maybe cable TV and access to barbells.

I was not permitted to meet Fern. She accepted Chicky's story that he was an unmarried stud of thirty-six, which indicated either a permanent willing suspension of disbelief or the need for an ophthalmologist. It might have been awkward for him to have to explain the existence of a twenty-nine-year-old daughter. If I wanted to reach him, I had to leave a message on his cell phone saying I was Amy from the probation office. Fern's heart was not a trusting one. Indeed, she'd made him give her his PIN on the cell phone she was paying for so that she

48

could check his messages. Chicky would call back later and we'd arrange a time to meet in the diner in Elmhurst—a section of Queens several safe miles away from Fern. She rarely let my father out of her sight long enough for him to have time to get to see me in Manhattan.

"You like your ice cream?" he inquired.

"Good, really good. Thanks." I shoveled in an enthusiastic spoonful of mint chocolate chip. Then, knowing I always felt better dealing straight than oblique, I told him: "Chicky, I need to know the whole story. How come my mother took a walk?"

He'd already glugged down a coffee malted, so he got busy chomping on the top of the straw he hadn't used. I always wondered if he'd picked up his table manners in prison or chose them to rebel against Grandma Lil's *No, no, no. Chewing or swallowing must never, ever make a sound.* He dropped the straw back in his glass. "You know how I hate to talk about Phyllis. Give me a break, Ame. I told you once, I told you twice, I don't know how come she walked. Trust me, if I knew, I'd tell you. And it was so long ago. It's like I don't even remember what she looked like." He wiped away the drying malted residue from the sides of his mouth. "I mean, I know I thought she was great-looking way back when, but maybe I was under some kind of love spell, like they do with candles. For all I know, she could've been a real dog-face."

"Come on. She wasn't some girl you went out with in eighth grade, Chicky. You married her. You borrowed money from the loan sharks to pay for a fancy honeymoon. You had a child by her." I paused. "You stole a five-carat diamond ring for her."

"So?" A single barked syllable, but belligerent enough to demonstrate how he'd been able to protect himself in prison. Then a snarl, lip rising, a growl so low I almost felt it rather than heard it. He averted his eyes from me and stared at the diner's wallpaper, which depicted a scene that was probably meant to be the Parthenon, except it had Corinthian columns.

"So," I went on, "you and I both know that you don't forget about someone who was that important to you."

"Amy, leave me alone."

"I'm not out to make you miserable by bringing up unpleasant memories."

"Unpleasant?" Chicky countered, the bad guy banished, my father back. "How about like a hundred percent shitty?"

"Listen, Chicky, I'll make you a deal."

"You think I'm so dumb I'd deal with someone who went to Harvard, even if it's my own kid?"

"Hear me out." To show me he was being patient, my father puffed up his cheeks with a mouthful of air, then exhaled so slowly he almost whistled. I told him: "This is a good deal, Chicky. You give me your memories about her as an ahead-of-time thirtieth birthday present. Then you won't have to go out and buy something."

"Is this why you called me up to come out and see you? To pump me for stuff about her?"

"Talk to me. It's only conversation."

"It so happens I thought up a nice present. I got the money for it. A real silk scarf."

As I shifted in the booth, my pants squeaked against the leatherette. "I hate to pass up a real silk scarf," I said quietly. "But believe it or not, whatever you can tell me about my mother would mean more to me than any gift." He shook his head slowly as in *You're pathetic,* or maybe *You moron.* "You won't even have to buy a birthday card," I added. My father responded by staring at the froth at the bottom of his glass. Then he shook his head: No. "Come on." Another shake of his head. So I said: "I've never said this to you before, Chicky, but you owe me."

He grabbed the straw from his glass and pointed it at me. "Fuck that 'you owe me' shit, Amy. I was a good father to you whenever I was out. I never hit you. Not even once. And we had a lot of fun."

"I agree. You were a terrific father. Honestly, I never once doubted you loved me and wanted the best for me. But you gotta understand—" Too much emotion and, presto, my pre-Ivey diction took over. I began the sentence again. "You have to understand, Chicky, I love you. You did the best you possibly could for me. Bad times, good times, if a girl knows her father is on her side, it's a very big deal."

"I'm not stupid, babes. I know Grandma Lil wasn't any bargain and I'm sorry you got stuck with her. It must've been even harder for you than it was for me and my sister when we were kids. I mean, you being such a genius and my mother being—do I have to tell you?—dumb as shit."

"Grandma Lil did her best," I told him.

"Her best stank," he responded. "You know it. I know it. The smartest thing you ever did was get outta there. You know, when I was inside that time, when you were thirteen or fourteen, right before you went to that boarding school. You were getting to be a, you know, young lady, I kept worrying, *Jesus H. Christ, what if Amy gets herself knocked up or something?*" I must have looked surprised because he said gently: "Listen, those things happen. Or else I thought, *What if Amy runs off with some schmuck—or worse—just to get out of having to listen to my old lady's fucking stories about Mrs. Hoo-ha's yacht?*"

"Chicky, I knew your mother. I need to hear about mine." He shook his head. "What don't you want to tell me? What could be the worst thing you could have done to her? Beat her up?" His expression collapsed into a sappy, slack-jawed *duh* look. So I said kiddingly: "You arranged from prison to have a couple of your high school friends hide her under ten feet of landfill?"

"Shut up!" He was so loud I was startled. An older woman in the booth opposite us stopped in midbite of an oatmeal cookie the size of her head. The counterman turned his back to us and got busy scraping the grill. "I never laid a goddamn hand on Phyllis. Ask anybody. I treated her like a queen." Best, I thought, not allude to the fates of Anne Boleyn and Catherine Howard. "Like a goddamn empress, Amy. If you saw the pearls I bought her on the honeymoon you'd know how good she had it." He lifted his hand high and scribbled in the air. The international I-want-the-check sign. He couldn't wait to get away from me. "All these years, you think I had her killed?"

"Of course not!" Well, now and again, on long nights with too little homework, I had mulled over the possibility. "That was my point, Chicky. You didn't do anything so terrible that you can't talk about it. *She* was the one who took a walk on us. Believe me, nothing you tell me will make me think less of her than I already do." He was preparing his *no*. "Trust me," I continued. "And nothing I hear could ever make me love you less." His feet did an aw-gee-whiz shuffle.

"Let me tell you something psychological I learned, Ame. Before *Oprah*. Right after I got out the first time, there was another lady had a show in the afternoon. A talk show, except this lady was white. With a face to stop a clock and skinny legs. And if that wasn't bad enough, she kept interrupting whoever was on with a lot of dumb-ass questions." He caressed the diamond on his earlobe between thumb and index finger. "So she's talking to some guy about Children of Divorce."

"Were you and my mother ever divorced?"

Chicky cocked his head to the side, his attitude of intense cerebration. "Not really. But see, it was just the same because we didn't get married anyplace actually real. We went to this little dip-shit town in Maryland because she was sixteen and a half."

"She was sixteen and a half when she married you?"

"Yeah. We thought she was pregnant, but you know what? She wasn't. But by that time we were already married. By this weird guy with a long black hair growing on top of his nose. I kept thinking, *What's wrong with him? Why does he want to go around with a hair growing out of his nose?* I was dying to pull it out. So anyhow, he had a little office behind a drugstore down there. The whole thing didn't *feel* legal. You know? No 'Here Comes the Bride,' no rabbi or minister or nothing. So why pay a lawyer for divorce papers? Who was ever going to go poking around Maryland to see if I ever got married there? Anyhow, a couple months later, she got pregnant."

"With me?"

"With who else? Baby Jesus? So what was I telling you about?"

"A white woman on TV with skinny legs."

"Yeah, so she's talking to this psychologist guy and he says something like, Don't ever say bad things about the person you got divorced from even if they was a total shit because then, like, your kid could feel guilty about loving a total shit. Or get mad at you for putting your ex down and hate you unconsciously. So I said to myself then and there, I didn't want to make things lousier for Amy than they already was. And I warned my mother she better not call Phyllis a whore or anything in front of you." He rubbed his nose on the back of his hand, then wiped it on his shirt. "Did she?"

"No." Yes.

"So I did like what a lawyer does when he's plea-bargaining: I took Phyllis off the table."

"Put her back on, Chicky. It's time."

He peered down at his watch, a humongous thing of stainless steel that, like his diamond stud, had been a gift from Fern. "Amy babes, I really gotta go."

"Fern can wait."

"What can I tell her?"

I understood the truth was not acceptable. "Say your probation officer had a lot of questions about how come you're having so much trouble getting work. Now come on, Chicky. I need to hear about my mother."

Twice, he offered me a sorrowful sigh. Then he sniffled. When that didn't work he said: "Her name was Phyllis Morris." Not exactly news, but I nodded encouragingly. "She was a little bit of a thing. There was a song one time, 'Five foot two, eyes of blue.' You know? Well, she was just like that, except her eyes were green. And I think she was five three. And s-m-a-r-t, smart. She had a ninety-seven average. I swear to God."

"Was she in your class?"

"What? No. I was like nineteen. She was a kid from Brooklyn."

"Where did you meet her?"

"Washington Square Park. See, all the Brooklyn and Queens girls used to come on Friday nights to meet NYU guys. Or maybe poets. So a bunch of us from the project would go up there."

"Did she think you went to NYU?"

"You know, I told her I did. But she didn't buy it. She was smart."

"But she went out with you anyway, I mean, even though you weren't at NYU?"

"In my mind, she was a kid looking for excitement. A little, not a lot. So I was what you'd call perfect for her. I'm a nice guy. Basically. Anyhow, that first night . . ." For a second, his face softened until it was almost sweet. ". . . I hot-wired a '68 Camaro

RS. She watched me and was, like, That's *fabulous*! She thought it was so cool, stealing cars. I drove her back into Brooklyn and we parked near Coney Island. She didn't want to go home. But I made her."

"Where did she live?"

"You wouldn't believe it. The richest part of Brooklyn. In a gorgeous house! Huge. With a giant porch and a really giant tree in front. A four-door Chrysler Imperial in the driveway. Gold, with a white vinyl top. Her old man's."

"What did he do?"

"I don't know. Store or stores or something."

"What did he sell?"

"Bikes. You know, like what the little kids ride and regular bikes. I met him once and he wasn't even polite. I put out my hand. Guess what?"

"What?"

"He didn't shake it. He ignored me, like I wasn't even there. And he said, 'Phyllis, get in the house right now!'"

"Did she?"

Chicky's grin took years off him. If not for the dentures and the crow's-feet, he was a brash, young hoodlum with gooped-up black hair and a lot of personality. "Are you kidding? That wasn't after the first night we were together. It was maybe a week or two later. I was driving a blue Dodge Charger that day. So she turns her back on her old man, stomps away from us to the car and waits"—he crossed his arms over his chest and sniffed impatiently—"till I come over and open the door for her. And so we're driving away"—he laughed and shook his head—"and she rolls down her window and gives him the finger."

My ice cream was almost melted, so I swallowed a spoonful of green chocolate-chip-mint soup. "What happened then?"

"Nothing. I brought her over to my mother's. But Lil said something like, I don't want no jailbait staying here. Get her the hell out. So my friend Jesús, Uncle Chuy, remember him? His big sister was a shoe buyer at Macy's and had her own place. Phyllis stayed there a few days, till her old man cooled off."

"And then she went home?"

"Yeah, but she kept getting him super pissed by sneaking out to see me. And then we had that pregnancy scare. That's when we got married. But then she really did get pregnant, with you. I was thinking, Shit, I'm gonna have to get a serious job when the kid comes along, which, don't get me wrong, was fine, and then you were born. I got a good job doing intake and exhaust work at this garage on Tenth Avenue, specialized in Fords. Good garage, but you know I'm a Chevy guy: Chevys go, Fords too slow, I always say. But I didn't say that to my boss. Sometimes he let me drive his Torino GT. Nice, I gotta admit. 'Sky blue metallic' was what they called the color. But it was really more like turquoise. If you cared about cars, Amy, you'd go 'Wow!'"

"Wow!" I said, and began making two piles of sugar and Sweet'n Low packets, side by side. "So I was born and we were all living in that apartment with Mickey Rat. Then what happened? You stole the diamond ring for my mother?" He closed his eyes. "Chicky, did she ask you to do it?"

"No." His voice had a sandpaper edge. Then he looked at me. "I didn't steal any ring."

"Oh. I thought that . . ." All my life I'd been told, by Chicky, by my grandmother, by Joan Murdoch, the social worker: My father had taken me and my mother to the diamond district on Forty-seventh Street to look at rings "for fun." I, who questioned everything, had no reason to question the story that inside a store, while my mother was quieting me down, he'd pocketed a five-carat rock. "You didn't steal the ring. So where was it? How come you went to prison for grand larceny?"

He took so long it felt as if we were stuck in an eternity of silence.

My father leaned forward and grasped the edge of the table. "Tell me, Chicky."

"No."

"If I don't know, I'll always feel like I do now. Not empty, but always a little sad, knowing I'll never be full—a complete person."

"Fucking Phyllis stole the ring."

"What?"

He jabbed his finger toward me. "You wanted it, I gave it to you. Okay? So happy birthday." He swiveled his head searching for the waitress and when he didn't see her, roared, "I asked for the goddamn check an hour ago!"

Naturally, everyone in the diner stiffened, that terrified rigidity that comes with thinking, *Oh, God, he's a lunatic and he might have a gun and I want to live so should I duck or will that attract his attention*—

Years earlier I'd realized I could never be out in public with either my father or my grandmother without their acting coarse, tasteless, pretentious, or at least vociferously dumb. I couldn't afford to get embarrassed by them. My grandmother could come up for Chrysanthemum Day at Ivey-Rush in a getup she believed to be haute Wasp: heavy wool hunting jacket, pearls, tweed skirt. What she actually looked like was Mamie Eisenhower on a really bad day in 1953. But I was okay with it. She could say, "Awwwwfly glod to meet you," when I introduced her to my teachers. I did not die of mortification. My father could come up for commencement at Harvard and, after the academic robes came off, call my friends "sweetheart" while look-

57

ing them up and down like a pimp sizing up a new girl for his stable. And I could live with it.

But now, his terrifying everyone in the diner was something else. During the total of eighteen years and three months he'd served in the slammer, what might have been a native surliness had grown to rage whenever he felt under pressure. I had to stop it. I banged a fist on the table. It didn't make much sound, but it got his attention. "Chicky! Get a grip." He could go either way, I guessed: calm down or jump up and grab the shirt of the guy behind the counter, bellowing for a check. I glanced at the counterman, then back to my father. "If I were he, Chicky, I'd be thinking about pressing the alarm button under the cash register drawer and getting the cops here." All I got was the glare a bad-ass kid gives the teacher. "Calm down."

"I'm calm," he said, a little too loud. At that point, however, his slit eyes blinked. It was a minute before he spoke. "All right. I'm okay now."

"Good."

"Sorry if I scared you."

"You didn't," I told him. "I know you too well. Now, tell me about my mother."

"If that's what you want. It was like this." He paused, closing his eyes for a moment to look at the past. "Phyllis was big into platinum. For the Maryland thing, I bought her real gold, kind of a skinny little ring, but I told her, 'Listen, I'll get you, like, one of those really fat platinum wedding bands—' You know, Amy. Those ones that go from the knuckle up to the next knuckle. Anyhow I said I'd get it for her for a first-anniversary present. I mean, I already was into this loan shark Mitchy for two thou for the honeymoon and then I had to up it to three when we were in Puerto Rico because I got her pearls. So meanwhile, we were going out almost every night with this connected guy, Angie, Angelo was his real name, plus his girlfriend and some of their friends because Phyllis . . . she had this thing about, kinda mob guys. Like a groupie, except for the Mafia instead of a band. The only problem was I was working this legit job in the garage. The pay wasn't bad, but hey, like I told you, we were living in this dump with the mattress on the floor because who the hell had money for furniture what with pearls and cocktail lounges. Right?"

"Right."

"Plus we were staying out late and I overslept sometimes and my boss was getting hot under the collar about it. Said I was a damn good mechanic, but if I couldn't show up on time I wasn't any use to him."

I'd been stacking packets, and sugar was beating Sweet'n Low, but now I stopped. "What was there about mob guys that she found so attractive?"

"Who the hell knows." I waited. "Maybe a power trip. Like they could push people around." He looked dubious about his own explanation. "It could be the bad guy thing. Like the way at the beginning, when she got this large charge from me stealing cars."

"She wasn't concerned about getting into trouble with a stolen car if you got pulled over by a cop?" My father, I'd always thought, was somewhat unendowed in the superego department. I had hoped my mother was not.

He emitted a single *heh*, barely a chuckle. "Funny you should say that. With Phyllis, it was like she never ever thought anything could really happen to her. Even if we got pulled over, she probably would've figured the cop would arrest me and make a date with her. And the weird thing is, I bet you a million bucks that's what would happen."

Any second, Chicky's eyes could fall on his giant watch and he'd want to rush off, dreading the wrath of Fern. This probably would be the only time I could get him to talk about my mother, and I needed to get some sense of what kind of person she was. For two days, I'd been thinking about Freddy Carrasco: Let's say he wasn't psycho. Let's say he was what I guessed he was, a sweet, pathetic case, a motherless kid trying to make himself bigger by identifying himself with a rich, power-wielding guy. Freddy had picked himself a United States senator, a father figure he could study on C-SPAN or Charlie Rose. He could even confront him in the flesh, albeit unsuccessfully. All the information I could get on my mother, Phyllis Morris Lincoln, who took off before my first birthday with a guy whose last name might have been Hussain, resided in my father's brain. Not exactly a situation fraught with promise.

"Chicky?"

"Yeah?"

"What was my mother's ethnicity?" Even before the third syllable of *ethnicity*, I realized all I could get was my father's double blink of blankness. "I mean was she a Wasp? Morris is an English name."

"I can't remember. She didn't look Jewish or Italian or anything, not with her red hair. And she had a cute little nose. Up, but not like Miss Piggy. But maybe Jewish? I don't know. Irish? She was darker than that. Her hair. Very white skin. That's it. That's all I can remember."

"Did she have any special interests?"

"You mean like model cars?"

"Right. Or reading, knitting, cooking."

"She couldn't cook for shit, to tell you the truth. Not that I blamed her. She was only a kid. Like she really hated to talk about her family. She wouldn't say a word about them. But one time she said her old man made her old lady get a cook because the only thing she could make was cinnamon toast."

It was so odd, imagining that half my genes came from a family that had a cook and a porch. Just for a second, I pictured myself reading a nice, fat novel on a porch glider in the shadow cast by the great weeping willow. Probably *Great Expectations*. "Was there anything she liked to do?" The sudden right shift of his eyes away from mine was a clear sign of verboten father-daughter territory. It didn't take five and a half years of higher education to comprehend that the woman who was my mother liked to do it. "I mean, besides going out with connected guys and their girlfriends, was there anything she was enthusiastic about?"

"Like it pissed me off. She would do things for a week or two and then drop them. Sewing a thing for a pillow, where you go in and out of little holes."

"Needlepoint."

"Yeah, but then she forgot about that. So it was like one week futzing with her hair, then two weeks walking around downtown—the Lower East, Chinatown, the Village—then another week being friends with Lil, which was really funny because all the rest of the time Phyllis didn't want *nada* to do with her. Hate at first sight, the two of them." He made a big deal of glancing at his watch and looking horrified, but he must have understood I knew it was an act because he finally went on. "She read books and magazines sometimes, and don't ask me what ones because I don't remember. I probably never knew. Ladies' magazines and books from the library."

"What about when she did get pregnant? Was she happy about it?"

"Not at the beginning. To tell you the truth, she wanted, you know, to get rid of it. You. Sorry. I wasn't going to stop her, but then she was the one who changed her mind."

"She wanted to have me?"

"I don't know. Maybe more like she kept putting it off, and then it was too late. Listen, Amy, don't feel bad. She could have done it and she didn't. I'm not saying she was like Mother of the Year, but she didn't get an abortion, even though she was puking a lot and was panicked about . . ." he pointed to his chest ". . . sagging and getting those fat leg veins. For her, doing nothing was something."

"Do I look like her?"

"I don't know. Not really. You're kind of her color, but her hair was redder than yours. And you got her littleness. But it's like this. Once she took a hike, and Lil brought you up to see me on some visiting days, I made up my mind not to see Phyllis in you. Anyhow, you look more like my sister, which is better than looking like Phyllis. I mean, Linda's a good-looking girl."

That was true, but I looked nothing like her. Aunt Linda's hair was black and glossy, her eyes bittersweet-chocolate brown rather than hazel, her body willowy, much more supermodel than soccer defense. She had a peaches-and-cream complexion and I did not. I was passably pretty. My aunt was a knockout.

"Did Aunt Linda and Uncle Sparky like her?"

"Linda didn't marry Sparky till later. I guess he knew her though, 'cause they were going together since they were like two or something."

"So what did they think of my mother?" Chicky gave me his combination shrug and eyebrow lift that meant *Do I have to waste breath giving you an answer?* I looked down at my sadly chipped thumbnail in an attempt to calm myself. What if I couldn't get him to say any more? What if he got up and left? I was on the verge of panic. If my brain could have been depicted on *Nova*, viewers would have seen colossal bunker-buster-bomb-size explosions instead of the normal sparks of neural activity.

I wound up giving myself a pep talk like those cloying monologues in lousy young adult fiction in which the feisty narrator peers at herself in a mirror and begins: "Okay, Self . . ." I said to myself: Okay, I'm a journalist. I don't want to give my father time to ask himself, *What the hell am I doing here, giving the precise information I never wanted anyone to know?* I needed time to ask the questions that would elicit the information I wanted. "What part of Brooklyn did she live in?"

"The rich part."

"Brooklyn Heights?" I asked, although the house Chicky had described didn't sound like the elegant town houses of the Heights. Getting a blink as an answer, I went on: "Was it just on the other side of the Brooklyn Bridge?"

"No, it was like twenty, thirty minutes in. So maybe like somewhere in the middle. Who the hell can remember? It was a million years ago."

"Do you remember how you got there?"

"Yeah, Phyllis said, 'Make a right, make a left,' until we got there."

"What was the name of her street?" I got a shrug. "Do you remember the name of the neighborhood? Like Canarsie, Flatbush, Brighton Beach?"

"No, Brooklyn, the Bronx . . . they're Alaska. You know. Foreign."

"What were her parents' names?"

"Joe, Marty, Betty, Sue. I mean, those may not be the names, but they were probably names sorta like that. Nothing too weird."

"Do you happen to recall her mother's maiden name?"

"No. What are you? Sherlock or something?"

"No, I'm your daughter collecting on her thirtieth-birthday present. So tell me what happened the day you went to the jewelry store." My ice cream now was completely melted, and, having skipped supper (or dinner, as Grandma Lil would have corrected me), I was getting intoxicated by the aroma of hamburgers, sautéing onions, and french fries. I didn't want to order anything more because Chicky always grabbed the check. I sensed Fern kept him short on money, long on dependency. "What happened?"

"So Phyllis says she just wants to look at platinum wedding rings. So I said, 'That's stupid because then you'll feel bad I can't buy you one now.' So she swears she won't and it would be fun to just look and see what's there. Okay? We go to this place on Forty-seventh Street, that diamond street, right? Why she picks this place I don't know, they all look the same, but we go in. We have to leave your little thing, baby carriage, outside and some guy in the store says he'll keep an eye on it. So Phyllis carries you and we're looking at platinum rings. Then she sees like trays and trays of diamond rings. Her eyes get this sparkle and the sales guy, who I can tell thinks she's hot, even with a baby, says, 'Oh, Mrs. Lincoln, let me show you some of our finest diamonds.'"

I thought: *If he'd been planning on stealing a ring, would he have given his correct name?* "You gave your name?" I asked.

"Yeah. Why not? Well, now I know why not, but I didn't then. Anyhow, it's like this sales guy is showing off, but I bet he couldn't afford those rings any more than I could. Unless he's the owner, but he looks like a loser with that pukey wavy hair that kind of kinks. Like Nixon, I remember thinking. So she's trying on these giant diamonds and holding her hand out in front of her to see the lights in them, except she's holding you with the other arm, so I ask her if I should hold you and she says no, if we switch you'd start crying."

"Did I have a tendency to cry?"

"You were a baby. Babies cry. That's why they call them crybabies. But you weren't bad. So anyway, she's modeling the

diamonds—forget, like, the platinum wedding rings I couldn't
even afford—and all of a sudden you give out a scream and start
screaming your head off. You know what I think? I figured this
out one night after lights out, after I'd done a couple of months.
I think she pinched you good and hard to make you scream like
that. So anyway, you're bawling and won't shut up so finally we
said, 'Sorry, we gotta go,' to the sales guy and we leave."

"And?"

"Two, three days later, guess who shows up at work? The
cops. And they bring me in for questioning—I could see my job
at the garage going down the sewer. Then that night, a couple of
detectives go to the apartment with a search warrant. I say to
them, 'What diamond ring?' And they couldn't find it but the
next day they're back and say, 'You're under arrest.' Like, I swear
to God, it was the only time in my life: I blacked out. Just for a
second, but the next thing I know this detective is pulling me up
from the floor. Next thing you know, I'm in a lineup and being
fingerprinted and getting my picture taken."

"And then?"

"So Phyllis comes to visit me and swears it wasn't her. I said,
'I'll have you fucking killed unless you tell me the truth,' and she
whispers . . . I can hardly hear her, she's on this phone behind
glass. And she says yeah, she stuck it into your diaper when you
started to scream. She didn't mean to, it was in her hand. Then I
tell her, 'You take the fucking rap, you . . .' I'm not gonna tell
you what I called her. But she says to me, 'They can't prove it
was you. Please, let me sell the ring. Then I can get you the best
lawyer in the city.'" I waited. "So this little putz with a mouth
that's puckered up all the time, like he's waiting for the chance to
kiss someone's ass . . . he's my lawyer. I say to him, 'I hear you're
the best lawyer in the city.' And he says, 'Huh?' And I tell him
Phyllis stole the ring and put it in your diaper and he says, 'If

you give the ring back I can get you a deal. You won't even have to serve a year.' So I tell him to get the ring from Phyllis, so next time he comes he says she said: 'I don't have any ring. I don't know what Chicky did with it.' And you know what?"

"What?"

"She never came to see me after that. Never came to the trial. After that first money you give a lawyer . . . What's it called?"

"A retainer."

"Right. He got that from her, but then he started pounding me for the rest of his money. She probably sold the ring, gave him a couple of hundred, and kept the change. But a kid needs a mother. So I kept my mouth shut and got four to six years. I never saw her again in my life."

Chapter Four

As far as I can piece it together, shortly before Black Tuesday in 1929, Tatty Damaris's great-uncle Lemuel, a ne'er-do-well and know-nothing, yanked his inheritance from the Damaris New York Trust and handed it over to a slick piece of work with a pencil mustache from Toronto, who sunk it into an ailing aluminum company. Thus it was that the banking Damarises went bust and Uncle Lemmy became three times as rich as he'd been before the Crash.

Happily, he died after a long night of cocaine and a liquid his bootlegger referred to as brandy. He left his majority interest in the aluminum company to his boring brother, Alfred II. Thereafter, Tatty's family remained wealthy by investing conservatively and squelching any urge toward philanthropy.

Tatty and I sat in the library of her parents' Rhode Island–size apartment on a leather couch with buttons that periodically popped off, unsheathing teeny, butt-stabbing knives. Some earlier

Damaris had paneled the room in dark wood. Except for a desk with pigeon-toed claw feet, a couple of tables, and green curtains like the ones Scarlett used for her dress, everything was red leather. Red leather couch, chairs, ottoman, and the bindings of the hundreds of books no one in the family had ever opened. Alfred IV, Tatty's father, sat catercorner to us in a club chair so old that every time he shifted the springs emitted a deep *errrrg, errrrg,* though no guest would be tempted to titter at such sounds in front of a family who had transcended flatulence six generations earlier.

Mr. Damaris was sipping his customary vodka from his blue plastic freezer mug, a singularly unattractive method of keeping beverages cold. Periodically, he picked up a wedge of lime from the plate on his lap. He'd hold the lime aloft and squeeze it into the vodka and, occasionally, into his right eye. As always, Mrs. Damaris was sitting beside his argyle-socked feet on the red ottoman.

"'*Course* I remember Thom Bowles," he told me. "Blabber-mouth. Full of himself." A dribble that was either vodka or saliva meandered from his lower lip and down his chin. "Probably a communist, to say nothing of a pip-squeak. But a ladies' man, if you get my drift. And his ladies"—he restrained himself from laughing at his own upcoming wit—"weren't what one would call ladies!" Besides drinking and critiquing his brokerage statements, Tatty's father's great pleasure in life seemed to be thinking ill of people. "Went for cha-cha girls. Am I right, Preshie?" Preshie was short for Precious, his name for his wife, Louisa.

"Right!" Like her husband and daughter, Preshie was tall and spare. Well, in her case, gaunt. Her skin had the waxy sheen of malnutrition that comes when an alcoholic anorexic denies herself even the pearl onions in her martinis. "Thom to a T." She tweaked her husband's big toe, which seemed to be one of their little love signals. He beamed at her, the snaggletoothed smile of a man who believes orthodontia is for Jews and children of middle management in Ohio. "You never cease to amaze me!" his wife went on. "You remember everyone! Everything!" He smiled every month or so, and then only at Preshie. She smiled all the time.

I had known the Damarises since Thanksgiving Day of my first year at Ivey, when Grandma Lil forgot to turn on the oven to roast the turkey she'd lifted from a Food Emporium. I'd called Tatty to tell her about it and she'd invited me over. Way back then, when I was fourteen, Preshie's perpetual smile unnerved me. Now, pushing thirty, no longer awestruck by friends' rich mothers who wore high heels in the house and rich fathers who ate supper in jackets and ties, or by chandeliers, or the conspicuous nonconsumption of a platter of turkey and bowls of mashed sweet potatoes and oyster stuffing and haricots verts served from the left by a wrinkled family retainer, I found her smile merely unsettling.

"Amy, pet, have you come up with any . . ." Preshie paused for a frisson of anticipation ". . . dirt?" Her face was so tightly drawn that only the middle of her lips moved. Tatty claimed her mother always appeared to be doing a fish imitation. "I mean dirt on Thom, for your magazine?"

Tatty shook her head in annoyance. "M," she said to her mother, "*In Depth* is above dirt." Instead of saying Mom and Dad, Tatty called her parents M and D. The upper crust, I'd discovered at boarding school, squandered much of its intellectual energy thinking up nicknames for one another. Tatty, of course, was Tatiana and Alfred IV was predictably called Four, although he just as easily could have been nicknamed Puddles (had he been a bed wetter) or Quackie or Flip or Spike.

"I *know In Depth* is too . . . What's the word? High-tone. It's too *high-tone* for gossip." At her second "high-tone," Four laughed a single *har* from so deep in his chest it sounded like a pulmonary problem. Preshie did another toe tweak to show she was pleased by his appreciation, while Tatty did her standard gaze heavenward, her usual expression of disdain and embarrassment.

"Listen, Mrs. Damaris," I said, "forget what's acceptable at *In Depth*. I'm not too high-tone for gossip." I took a sip of my second glass of Gevrey-Chambertin (the family never scrimping on anything that contained alcohol) and turned back to Four, knowing he retained every sordid story he'd ever heard. "How well do you know Thom Bowles, sir?"

"Knew his father better. Andover, Bowdoin. Us both. Few years older." Four was only slightly more generous with complete sentences than he was with charity. I assumed he meant that William Bowles, Thom's father, had been older than he by a few years.

"Even if I were tempted to write about that young man who's claiming Senator Bowles is his father, your wife is right: *In Depth* wouldn't publish it," I reassured Four. "But just to satisfy my own curiosity, were there any murmurings back then as to why Thom Bowles left New York and moved out west?"

Four took a long sip from his plastic beer stein and hummed, "Hmm . . ." He hummed fairly often, probably to occupy himself until his neurons could manage to fire up in his alcohol-sodden brain.

"There *was* something!" Preshie said. Her eyes glinted from either excitement or her martini. "I remember, Four-y. You came home from the club and gave me an earful. About Thom and one of those girls."

Tatty avoided looking at me, as she usually did at times like these, after M and D had set sail on their nightly voyage from conviviality to stupor. What she didn't understand and could not explain was how come she'd returned home to this pair after both her failed marriages. Not for comfort. Although not overtly mean, they weren't particularly nice to her. She claimed she'd come back for the kitchen where she made her cakes. I'd often suggested she was still seeking the love these two ought to have had for her, being her parents. But maybe it was simpler. Everyone needs a place to hang her hat.

"Yes, yes. Something," Four replied to his wife. "Oh! The Puerto Rican girl."

"Hispanic," she corrected. "Unless you know for a fact she was from PR."

"Hush, Preshie. Thinking." Also slurring, but it was nearly seven and he'd been drinking for close to an hour. *"Thinking."* Tatty flashed me a *Time to get out of here* look. Since I couldn't pretend not to have seen it, I ignored it.

"Was Thom Bowles involved with a woman from Puerto Rico?" I pushed on. Four was either nodding off or studying the viscosity of vodka. "The woman from Puerto Rico?" I said a little louder.

"Right. Worked for Whitey."

"Thom's father," Preshie explained. "William. Everyone called him Whitey."

"Girl was a secretary. Bookkeeper. Something." Still gripping his freezer mug, he raised it high above his head. Then he put his left forearm across his belly and attempted to snap his fingers in what I guessed was a flamenco gesture. "Cha-cha-cha."

"Do you remember her name, D?" Tatty inquired. He moved his head once to the left, once to the right: No.

"So Thom got involved with this woman," I prompted as he took a long slurp. Finally his head went up, then down: Yes. "Did he get her pregnant, Mr. Damaris?"

"Worse."

"Worse?"

"Wanted to marry her, for heaven's sake!"

"Did he?" Tatty and I demanded together.

"Wanted to," Four repeated. "Don't worry. Whitey took care of that."

I hated leaving Tatty with M and D. But she had, after all, responded "Over my dead body" when, a month earlier, I'd asked if she wanted to go to an all-Mahler concert. Not that hearing *Das Lied von der Erde* was my idea of a fun night either. But John loved Mahler. Just four weeks earlier, before we'd somehow fallen from mutual enjoyment to unspoken dissatisfaction, I'd been positive he'd ask me to go. So positive that I bought two tickets. That way, when he did ask, I could say, *John, you're kidding! I already have two tickets!* thus exhibiting my exquisite taste, a necessity after I'd laughed uproariously when he'd inquired a few months earlier, "Wouldn't it be great to get to hear the Tuaregs from Mali play instruments they made from tools?" and then saw from his expression he hadn't been joking. Obviously, there were no limits to his enthusiasm for music.

But the Mahler offer never came, and John got lost in his research on Garth Brooks for *Biography*. So stuck with two tickets, I'd asked Gloria Howard, the senior editor of *In Depth* who was in charge of Europe. In the six years we'd been on the magazine together, I'd discovered she loved every art form I loathed. Thus, I was certain she'd be thrilled with the invitation, just as I would have bet a week's salary that she adored the novels of Alain Robbe-Grillet.

Alas, going to a New England boarding school had not classed up my intellect. I'd been immune to Harvard's transmuting power, which had been known to turn even dumbo jocks into contemplative souls. J-school, of course, did nothing to improve my taste. Being a journalist did not require aesthetic sensitivity. To ace any class, all I needed to do was demonstrate I could write a simple declarative sentence and also appear enraptured by any discussion of ethics.

Since P.S. 97, I'd understood mine was not a sensitive, artistic nature. My gift was being able to give back to my teachers what they wanted—and then some. A thirst for knowledge, an incurable bookworm, the Extra Credit Kid. The neighborhood being a little iffy, plus Grandma Lil not liking what she referred to as "the element," i.e., my friends, she never let me out after six o'clock. Thus, given the choice of watching *Falcon Crest* with her at the kitchen table as her stupnagel exegesis of the Channings' and the Giobertis' relatives drowned out the dialogue, or being alone in the bedroom reading the *Narrative of Sojourner Truth,* I opted for scholarship.

Sure, I was also smart. And yeah, I could express myself. But the finer things in my life were never esoteric or abstract. I wanted *Born on the Fourth of July* and *A Fish Called Wanda,* not revivals of *nouvelle vague* films. As my taste developed, I learned to love some accessible art: the Impressionists, Puccini operas. But I couldn't change my preference for American-style stick-in-the-knife-and-twist-it politics to the stuff of *Foreign Affairs.* I recalled reading Richard Hofstadter's *Anti-Intellectualism in American Life* during my last year of Ivey, and being unable to decide which side to root for.

But all along, the people I most admired embraced enthusiasms I not only didn't share, but couldn't comprehend. Joan Murdoch, the social worker, took me to the circus every year. I pretended to love the clowns, but thought them unreservedly unfunny; I couldn't understand this sensible woman's almost childlike delight in them. At Ivey, I didn't get what there was about the band Devo that made the hippest, smartest kids love it so. Or Philip Glass while at Harvard. I'd heard enough Mahler, read enough Donald Barthelme, seen enough Peter Greenaway films, and inspected enough Matthew Barney art to understand that a certain understanding was missing in me.

John was more high-culture than I for the simple reason that he was interested in almost everything. He really didn't need a remote. He could quite happily watch MTV, aerobatics, *The Grand Illusion,* or a performance of one of Schönberg's twelve-tone lovelies.

Somehow, while Grandma Lil was coaching me on how to eat asparagus, I'd missed Elementary Highbrow. Not that I was a total music lowbrow. I really liked Haydn and Mozart. But me going to hear Mahler was like a Cro-Magnon hanging out with a bunch of Homo sapiens hearing *12 X 5.* Sure, I could observe other listeners exhibiting signs not just of comprehension, but of pleasure. Except I couldn't get no satisfaction.

So there I sat, praying for release from recital-hall hell. Forget Eliot's "Hell is oneself" and Sartre's "*L'Enfer blah-blah-blah.*" Genuine hell was sitting in an overheated auditorium listening to the infinitely irritating, eternally long sixth movement of *Das Lied von der Erde* knowing I had done this to myself and, moreover, that John now would never think, *Hey, I was wrong. There's no limit to Amy's openness to culture.*

Gloria Howard, naturally, was leaning forward in her seat. Maybe she wanted to be the first to leap up and yell Bravo! though, more likely, she was being drawn to the orchestra by her passion for Mahler. Her profile looked beautiful, transformed by the music. Normally she wasn't even pretty, and with her new haircut and dark brown skin, she looked amazingly like Spike Lee minus facial hair. Of course, Spike Lee probably wouldn't be sitting in Rose Recital Hall in a navy dress with white cuffs and collar. Gloria put herself together in the way her mother's or grandmother's generation would have called ladylike. She always appeared perfectly groomed, feminine, and asexual in the manner of women who run for high office.

I longed to be as ambitious as Gloria. What she was going for was the executive editorship of *In Depth*. Now, at thirty-three, she probably planned to occupy it within two years. Besides being extremely smart (or possibly brilliant) and speaking six languages, Gloria was unique at *In Depth*. She did not posture. Nor did she lie. She did not fib, dissemble, or even pretend. Ever. If she hated Mahler, she would have told her boyfriend, *I hate Mahler. Find someone else to go with.*

At work, Happy Bob, the current executive editor, called Gloria "my conscience" and "my bullshit detector." Like a shark, there was something about Happy that let you know the perpetual smile he wore wasn't a sign of geniality. Still, one of the rare times he seemed in genuinely good spirits was at editorial meetings, when Gloria would respond "Not much" to his "What do you think of that?" His chest would puff with pride as she'd cogently explain why some particular idea of his sucked. It never occurred to him to view her directness as an attack. Too bad for him. Had he asked her, *Do you want to make me appear impulsive and unimaginative so you can get my job fifteen years before I plan to retire?* she would have answered, *Yes.*

Finally, *Das Lied* was over. After too many curtain calls for the tenor and the soprano (a bratwurst in basic black) and bows for the conductor and orchestra, the lights went up. "What did you think?" I asked Gloria before she could ask me.

"There are no words." Her sigh was contented.

"Gloria, there are always words." We moved along the aisle to get out for intermission.

"No, there are not always words. However, since you

wouldn't let me pay for the tickets, I'll give you words: 'incredibly moving.' It's clearly Mahler's most personal piece."

"Oh, definitely," I said. The crowd at the bar was pretty thick, but I was desperate for a Coke. A sugar high (if not general anesthesia) might get me through the rest of the program. Gloria kept me company while I waited on line. With her intelligent face and white-cuffed air of authority, she made me feel as if I were back at the circus with Joan Murdoch: grateful that superior people liked my company. But I was still smelling elephant shit while the uptown set was having a cultural experience. I looked into Gloria's satiny brown eyes. People talk about eyes sparkling, but that's usually more about vivacity than actual sheen. Hers were truly glistening—moist with feeling, reflecting the foyer's subdued illumination as tiny stars.

For an instant, I thought about scotch instead of Coke, but the two glasses of wine I'd had at the Damarises were enough for me. I didn't want to risk getting so plastered that I'd start making hostile retching noises during the second half of the program, thus forfeiting the not-quite-close friendship I had with Gloria. "What are you working on?" she asked.

"Thomas Bowles's campaign. I spent part of last week on the bus," I told her.

"I'm curious. Does he remind you a little bit of Adlai Stevenson?" Gloria inquired.

"Well, he's not bald. And no one ever accused him of a dry wit."

"He seems to take himself very seriously."

"He's not quite a heavy piece of furniture. He has a little humor, but you're right. He views every criticism as an attack. As far as your Stevenson comparison goes? He does believe in containment rather than preemption. But of course these days, that position will lead him to the same kind of landslide Stevenson got. Right now, Bowles is splitting the anti-war, anti-IMF/World Bank, pro-environment, uh, anti–death penalty, vegan blocs with Dean. Which only leaves both of them about a hundred million votes in the hole."

"You don't like Bowles," she stated.

"No. Not as a candidate and not as a human being. He's as close to an intellectual heavyweight as you can find in a presidential campaign, but I think a good president needs a balance of style and substance. Bowles is ninety percent substance. And lately, after the first few minutes of pleasantries and even humor, he's been getting ponderous, just as people were warming up to him. In South Carolina—in Columbia, where the university is—there was a decent crowd. Young, enthusiastic. So he spoke for forty minutes on how the Republicans are out to rescind the entire New Deal by bankrupting government. By the end of his talk there were three political science majors who were actually listening. If he were president and there was any kind of a crisis, he'd think about it a great deal and maybe handle it correctly. But he couldn't lead or inspire confidence." Gloria nodded her agreement. If I knew as much about her turf as she knew about mine, I could be Assistant Secretary of State for European and Eurasian Affairs. "Listen, Glo, you heard about that kid who crashed Bowles's fund-raiser last week?"

"Amy."

"What?"

"Don't waste your time."

"But what if it is true? Let's postulate that Bowles's old man paid off a woman young Thom was involved with and—"

"You're going to say it goes to the matter of the man's character."

"Right. He's Mr. Anti-War, Mr. Moral Man in an Immoral Society. Look, I'm not saying getting blow jobs in the bathroom of the Oval Office precludes an ability to—" I didn't finish the sentence because just then I spotted John Orenstein.

About twenty feet away. He stood beside a beautiful woman. Okay, maybe she wasn't beautiful, I couldn't be sure. But at the very least she was striking. Nearly as tall as John, with black hair pulled back tight. Probably into a chic chignon in the back, although I couldn't see. In an outfit by one of those magisterial designers who escort jet-setty women. I stared at them, him in a tie and dark suit, her in a silver dinner suit and a lot of tasteful, to say nothing of real, gold jewelry. What made me shake inside is that they looked like a matched set. Tall, elegant. And so stylish. His lush brown hair, his easy, graceful posture. Her olive skin gleaming warmly against the paleness of the suit.

"Something wrong?" Gloria asked.

He laughed at something she was saying. It didn't look like a forced laugh.

"No. I'm fine."

"You don't look fine."

"John is over there with another woman." Gloria's head swiveled. "He's the guy in the dark suit," I said. "She's the gorgeous one." They stood out because, unlike the dressy crowd that attends opera performances, most people who go to hear choral and/or orchestral music look as if they'd stepped out of the annual picnic photo of Ethel and Julius Rosenberg's communist cell.

"Maybe she's a friend," Gloria suggested.

I shook my head so emphatically that I messed up my hair. "No. I know his friends."

"Maybe a colleague."

"Of all the people here tonight, she looks the least like a doc filmmaker. Look at her dinner suit. That's not downtown retro. That's serious couture."

Gloria looked so sad for me I felt even lousier. She picked up my mood and tried to sound jaunty. "What do you think, Amy? Brazilian socialite?"

"Or some Jewish fashionista from the Bronx who knows her way around a sewing machine. And look at him. John's the guy who decided to be a documentary filmmaker because if he went to law school he could wind up wearing suits. Do you see him? He looks like his favorite hobby is wearing a suit." It was hard to swallow because my throat was so tight. "Gloria, do me a favor."

"What?"

"I know I'm being a pain, but please don't look right at them. He has a really good sixth sense." She had the grace not to say anything like John's senses, numbers one through a hundred, were completely focused on *La Belleza*, or however you say it in Portuguese or Bronx. "I hate to be adolescent," I told her, "but I want to get back to the seats so he doesn't get a chance to spot me." Gloria was the only person I knew who could raise one eyebrow without contorting her entire face. She raised it. "What's wrong with getting away from where he could spot me?" My throat got so tight I couldn't swallow, an allergic reaction to seeing John so happy with *La B*. Next I would break out in hives. "I don't want to be cowardly. But what else can I do? Grab a glass of red wine and throw it into her face?" My voice had become a croak.

I took a few sideways steps so that all John could possibly see of me (should he not be lost in the woman's eyes) was my back. Gloria was maybe two inches taller than I, so I couldn't rely on her to block me. Plus she was about my weight; I hoped if my shoulders and hips stuck out on either side of her, their configuration wouldn't be so familiar to him as to be recognizable. "I could start a catfight. Shriek, *Hands off my man, you ho!*" I forced myself to do one of those deep breaths—inhale seven, exhale seven—that are supposed to be calming. I knew I was sounding a little intense for an associate editor, to say nothing of immature. Casually, as though inquiring about button earrings versus dangling, I asked: "What would you do in my place?"

She shrugged. "Walk over, say hello."

"Just like that?"

"Absolutely. I'd let him be the one who's taken aback. I'd be cordial." Which of course was why Gloria Howard would be *In Depth*'s executive editor within three years, while it would take me another decade just to make senior editor. "Was it official, that the two of you were only seeing each other?" All I could manage was a shake of the head. No, not officially official. Just that we'd be sexually monogamous. We just did it. Still, even though the relationship was stalled—all right, going downhill— I'd assumed I'd get to say good-bye before he did. "Let's get back to the seats," she suggested. With a surprisingly gentle hand on my shoulder, she steered me back into the concert hall. As we sat, she advised, "Get lost in the music."

Goody. The house lights dimmed. More Mahler songs. I can't imagine what I'd been thinking in my junior year, but I'd taken one semester of German just for fun. So I kept getting distracted by a familiar word or phrase I was able to translate: "not in the songs" and "to watch their" something. And "bees," though I conceded there was a chance it could have been "beans." I tried concentrating on getting the gist of the lyrics to block out other thoughts. But the image of John and *La Belleza* kept coming back. I never would have believed he'd go for someone so soignée. I recalled his laughing at what she said. So utterly charmed. So man-of-the-world.

After the first time John and I went out, I'd gone home with this sense of *Here's a guy I could actually spend a lot of time with*. He was smart, funny, unafraid of a woman with a brain, and most of all, most rare, he was nice.

I wondered how *La Belleza* would fit in with his family. I fit in so well I couldn't believe it. Every one of the Orensteins had that niceness-smartness thing going: If they had a family crest, it would display an open book, a bowl of soup, and a motto like *benignitas et litteratus*. Could I see *La B* at their family Seder at their house in Connecticut with matzoh crumbs on her silver suit? Unfortunately, yes. But then again, she'd know not to go in silver. Whereas I'd show up in a twinset and faux silk slacks and feel uncomfortable because it evidently wasn't a silk slacks/twinset year, and the Orensteins would sense I was somehow ill at ease and fall all over themselves being kind to me.

What made it worse was that I understood fully what was up with me. The older I got, the more alone I was. There was a scene at the end of *Broadway Danny Rose* that was so lovely, but always caused me such pain whenever I watched it: Danny, the talent agent, is having Thanksgiving dinner for his clients—the guy with the parrot, the one-legged tap dancer, and all the other oddballs who have only Danny as their family. He's given them a family, a place to fit in the world.

I didn't have that place. There was no Danny in my life. I could only see my father on the sly. Aunt Linda went with Uncle Sparky to one of his sisters' houses for holidays—none of which was a Seder. And I'd started lying to Tatty years earlier so I wouldn't have to buy the sad Damaris holiday package: Thanksgiving (the usual vodka and martinis plus Gewürztraminer), Christmas (glogg or mulled mead and champagne), and Easter (tequila cocktails, looking like urine in highball glasses), with Four dozing off by the second course. With no one to carve, Preshie would stand up and angrily hack away at the turkey, goose, or ham.

I could fit in anywhere: With all the kids on the bus going upstate to visit their fathers in prison. With all the Ivey girls and the guys they hung with. In a government seminar at Harvard. Drinking with the Democratic powers-that-be in Chicago. Except when you could theoretically live a thousand different lives, how do you pick the one where you belong?

In any case, I was on my own. I remembered being at my desk on 9/11 when the planes hit. It being *In Depth*, there was only one TV in the entire place. We all ran from our cubicles and offices and huddled around it. I stood stupidly, watching the jumpers choosing how they would die, then leaping from the inferno. The circuits on our phones were busy and it was hard to get a dial tone. Those times, everyone kept punching numbers into their cell phones, some sobbing, some numb, all crazy to say *I'm okay.* A couple of times someone's phone actually rang—a Westminster chime, the first four notes of Beethoven's Fifth. On the TV, I gaped at the herds of people running up Broadway, screaming. The handheld camera recording their escape trembled. A few minutes later I realized: I'll be no one's first call.

Okay, maybe my father's, but it would take hours for him to invent an excuse to get away from Fern and get to a pay phone. Tatty didn't wake up until ten or eleven and, of all stupid things, my mind leaped back to the times after both her weddings, when I went from her best friend in the whole wide world and maid of honor to once-every-other-week pal for a girls' night out.

I'd been going out with John for a couple of months then, and I sensed he'd be calling his parents and brothers and college roommate; God knows what number I was on his list. Standing before the magazine's we-disdain-broadcast-journalism piddling twenty-inch television, I heard one TV reporter after another say *horrific. Terrible* and *horrible* were too small for this. "Dear God, save me from *horrific*," Happy Bob intoned. Since it would not have been politic to punch out his sneer, I left the building to go home.

I was pushed northward by the crowds surging up from the Trade Center and downtown. So many of them were coated head to toe with the ash of the buildings' collapse and the immolated bodies. They did, in fact, look horrific. Black, white, or Asian, they were all gray statues come to life, running uptown. Now I was part of the crowd, trying to outrun the stink coming from the Trade Center, the sweaty stench of hundreds, thousands of people fleeing from the terror. After a mile or so, sweat dripping into my eyes, I asked myself how come I was rushing uptown. Where was I running to? To get to my place, where there would be no one?

It was so weird: At that very instant my phone started vibrating. I was so grateful. I had trouble opening it. My hands trembled, even knowing it could be a wrong number, someone desperate to make contact with the person he loved.

It was John. "Amy? Amy? Are you okay? The fucking circuits kept being busy and I've been trying so long to get you. . . ."

"I'm all right. I left the office. I just had to get out and . . ."

"Can I meet you . . . where?"

"I'll meet you at my place, okay? It's closer."

"Okay, I'll park in front of the hydrant. But listen, are you sure you don't want me to come and get you?"

Later, blessedly free from Mahler hell, I lay in my bed in the dark, thinking about that terrible couple of days after 9/11. John and I stayed at his place watching TV, talking about what happened, what could happen. That was when I decided I loved John and truly believed he was in love with me, or at least was almost there. So what had gone wrong? Maybe I just thought it was love because, for those couple of days, I needed a future. Or if it had been the real thing, maybe our relationship just dragged on too long and exhausted itself. Maybe it was Love Lite. Or maybe John and I were on such different emotional cycles that we never loved simultaneously.

I curled up into a ball, too cold to get out from under the covers, close the window, and get a pair of socks. A horse's hooves clopped outside, probably taking its last tourists of the night. Poor, weary horses, so cheaply festooned with red feathers or plastic flowers, blinders on, unable to see they were giving an elderly couple from Kansas City the most romantic night of their lives.

John and I had been together for two years. We'd never talked about breaking up. Not even hinted. Two years. Seeing him with that sleek woman: What a shock! And what made it worse was that they didn't seem engaged in cosmopolitan chitchat. They looked as though they were having a wonderful time.

Maybe it had never been love with us. It was possible I'd simply taken the specs of John—Tufts, sexy, decent, smart, politically sophisticated, Jewish—and, building on them, created my own ideal lover. Or maybe it had merely been my biological clock.

No, it wasn't just some biochemical tic. My mind switched from John to my mother. Had Phyllis Morris Lincoln ever felt the urge for a baby the way I now did? Was that why she got pregnant? No matter what she was thinking when she took a hike, had she ever passed a playground and, with everything in her, yearned for a child to swing? Or had she just been a rebellious, middle-class teenager who'd gotten knocked up?

I was quite young, sixteen or so, when I decided I wanted a child no matter what. Even back then, I understood I might not be anyone's idea of a prize in the marriage sweepstakes. So husband or no, I would have a baby. Be in a family.

Except for the first time, lying on those cold sheets that would not warm up, I started wondering if that was such a good idea. Could I become a mother and then want out, the way my mother did? Could there be something innate in me so defective that I'd wind up abandoning my child?

For the ten millionth time, I wondered what my mother looked like. Curiosity, that was all. I didn't want to have anything to do with her. Why should I? I hadn't deserted her. But what if she were dying? Dying more painfully because she couldn't apologize or explain. All right, she knew my name, but I'd had my number de-listed three or four years earlier after the usual abusive calls from two or three crazy readers who didn't like something I'd written.

But she could find me on the web. My byline was on hundreds of articles. All she had to do was write, "Amy Lincoln, c/o *In Depth*," this woman who had a ninety-seven average in high school. But what if Chicky had been lying and she was a functional illiterate and my intelligence was a genetic fluke? Or what if she knew where I was, maybe even subscribed to *In Depth* or somehow saw my picture in the *Harvard Yearbook* and was too ashamed to reach out to me? Or too afraid.

All this nature-versus-nurture stuff. Lately, the news was that nature was trouncing nurture. I could give birth to a six-pound, six-ounce Grandma Lil. Or a baby Chicky. Did I have it in me to walk out on a kid? Or could I have a child who would grow up only to run away from me?

Chapter Five

In Depth was celebrated for allowing its reporters time to do, well, an in-depth job of reporting: You want to write on Turkey's changing relations with Europe? Take three weeks, maybe even a month. Fly to Ankara, Bratislava, Madrid on alarmingly minor airlines and stay at bathtub-on-the-third-floor hellholes—the only choice when the magazine paid your way. In the year leading up to the presidential primaries, however, with candidates jumping into the race or skulking away, reporters were given, at most, two weeks.

So it was no shock when the Beast, a.k.a. Bowles's campaign manager, called and rasped, "Hey, Hahhhvid, how's it coming?" in the lamest imitation of a Boston accent I'd ever heard.

"It's coming," I told her. "It'll probably make next week's issue unless Happy Bob has some problem with it."

"So tell me. If *In Depth* had an actual cover instead of that bullshit table of contents on the front"—she either got rid of some phlegm or chuckled at her own audacity—"would Thom be the cover story?"

This was Moira Fitzgerald's notion of repartee. She prided herself on her reputation for being, in her eyes, curmudgeonly. In my eyes, nasty. I figured her call wasn't really about the length or placement of the article. For that, she would have screamed at one of the kids working for her, *Get on the phone, you dumb fuck, and ask that bitch how long it is!* What she probably was after was whether I was going to write about Freddy Carrasco's drop-in at the fund-raiser without her actually having to bring it up, which of course would clue me in that they were worried about a substantive magazine such as *In Depth* considering a paternity charge legitimate news.

"I don't know. It's a nice-sized piece."

"How nice-sized?"

"Not enough to make me swagger, not enough to make me apply to *U.S. News*."

The Bowles 2004! website was already up on my screen, so while I waited for her next bon mot, I took a pass on Thom's Campaign Blog and clicked on Photo Album. Lots of Thom in crowds of college kids, having coffee with AARP types, and hanging with assorted real people—or an ad director's idea of real people, i.e., guys in caps advertising tractors and women wearing pastel pants and flowered blouses. Thom as Man of the Year in front of various banners, behind podia, seated at annual dinners for environmental, civil liberties, and labor groups, or organizations of African Americans, Latinos, Muslims, Jews, Koreans, Filipinos. There was also a despite-his-positions-he's-no-commie-atheist photograph of Thom, his wife, Jen, and daughters Brooke and April being greeted by their smiley pastor at the Little Creek Presbyterian Church.

"Can't you at least give me an idea of the *tone* of the piece?" Moira asked.

"The tone?" I double-clicked on the dinky little photo of the Bowleses at church and stared at dark Brooke and blond April, or perhaps dark April and blond Brooke, girls who evoked the lesser Dixie Chicks—except without discernable boobs or talent. No one could claim there was a family resemblance between either of the Bowles girls and Freddy Carrasco. "You know *In Depth* writes straight," I told her. "No nasty innuendos, but no adjectives that can possibly be construed as laudatory."

"You don't have to tell me that *laudatory* is a goddamn adjective. Believe it or not, I may not have gone to prep school, but they taught grammar at Cardinal Spellman High School. Anyway, Amy, as far as tone, you and I both know that even the most, uh, let's say objective journalist—"

"You and I both know, Moira, that you haven't gotten me that meeting you promised with Thom's Middle East person, to say nothing of that guy with the eye bags who's supposedly the monetary policy genius. I've read all your position papers. My editor is going to want more i-n d-e-p-t-h." I clicked back to the campaign's home page and went to Thom: A Short Biography. Naturally, not a word about fathering a child out of wedlock. However, there was a stamp-size picture of Thom Bowles in college, at a Princeton fencing team meet, far more hunky in his white padded gear than in life. With wire mesh mask off and hair sweated flat against his skull, he looked like . . . I squinted. Yes! Young Thom Bowles looked like Freddy Carrasco having a pale day.

"You've got that meeting! First thing tomorrow!" Moira promised, doing her best to sound enthusiastic. "I swear! Check your e-mail at seven tonight and you'll see where to go for the interviews. Or I'll get you their phone numbers if they can't physically meet you. Okay?" Enthusiastic was clearly exhausting, and she relapsed into snide. "You know, Amy, in this business, what goes around comes around. It wouldn't kill you to extend a little fucking courtesy."

Bowles's Middle East woman, the sort of policy expert who gets mocked on Fox News, was a pro-Palestinian, anti-war-in-Iraq Jew who occasionally appeared on PBS shows and who had thick glasses, long gums, and short teeth. She actually was in the Middle East. At midnight I called her in Amman and listened to her declaim for about fifteen minutes while checking for stray eyebrow hairs in my bathroom mirror and jotting down the occasional note on the pad resting on the sink.

The monetary policy guy with the eye bags, who'd retired from the Federal Reserve to make a fortune in international banking doing something that was, surprisingly, legal, insisted on a power breakfast in a luxe hotel dining room. So at eight a.m., I was in a Versailles-size room with a lot of guys and a few women in business suits sitting at tables with floor-length pale yellow cloths and getting croissant crumbs on their wool-cashmere lapels. I myself took a bite of whole wheat toast. The place had more silver-plated serving pieces—from toast racks to baby pincers for grabbing tiny, scalloped butter balls—than anyplace else in all Christendom and Jewdom. I also noted two other reporters; like me, their presence was given away by their tape recorders as well as their off-the-sale-rack suits.

"What really concerns the candidate and I," Matthew ("Feel free to call me Matty") Schwartz was telling me, "is the possibility of *de*flation." Without his eye bags, he might have qualified as cute. With them, two thumbs down. The bags weren't sagging skin; they were plumpish, as if filled with money. "Now, what is deflation?"

It was a rhetorical question he did not expect me to answer, but since I'd already stuffed myself with enough scrambled eggs and toast to last me through lunch and possibly dinner, I said, "A sustained decline in prices."

"Excellent. I see you've come prepared." Some men talk to a woman's breasts. Matty was talking to my mouth, and that didn't exactly take a high school diploma to figure out. He was in his mid-fifties, exceedingly rich, and apparently in the market for a fellating mistress with education enough to appreciate his brilliance. He went on about how Bush's proposed tax cuts could lead to a tanking economy, which could lead to people holding back on spending as they waited for even lower prices, which could lead . . . Actually, it was really interesting, so I relaxed from my I-gotta-get-outta-here position and had another cup of coffee.

Matty seemed ready to segue into lunch, but at nine-fifteen I told him I had to get to the office and finish my article. And also, I responded, noting the wedding band embedded in his flesh, I didn't need his driver to take me downtown. The subway was faster. But thanks. "By the way," I said, "are you a friend of Thom Bowles or just an adviser?"

"We travel in the same circles, run into each other every once in a while. I'd say friendly rather than friends." The eyes above Matty's bags were ice blue, but suddenly they took on a warm glow. He knew I was after something not monetary. Power guys like him, I'd noticed, ultimately lust more for slander than sex.

Well, the ball was in my court. I'd say something about the Freddy fracas, then he'd lick his lower lip and inquire, *Off the record?* "Were you at the fund-raiser at the Kleinbergs the night that kid crashed and started claiming he was Thom Bowles's son?" I asked.

Okay, no lip lick, though he did caress his chin. "Off the record?" he inquired.

"Totally," I assured him.

"I wasn't there. But I'll tell you one thing, Moira Fitzgerald is *beside* herself."

Nothing unusual about that, but I asked: "Is there any substance to the kid's story?"

"You're sure this is off the record?"

"Positive. Look, you know this isn't the kind of thing *In Depth* would print."

"The question, my dear, isn't whether your magazine would actually print it. The question is, if they would print it, *would you write it.*" I smiled my appreciation at his ethical acuity. "Now, you want to know if there is substance to that rumor?" he went on. "Who knows? I mean, what is Thom supposed to do? Go along with a DNA test to prove a kid with a criminal record is or isn't his biological child?"

"Criminal record?" I inquired.

"That's what I'm hearing," Matty said, no doubt from Moira, who had asked him to pass that information along to me.

"If he's not the father, why not have the DNA test?"

"Because," he replied, too patiently, taking an instant to point to the silver-plated bread dish and murmur "Brioche" to a passing busboy, "that would be acknowledging a candidate's personal life is fair game. Look where it got Clinton. From the moment that girl on MTV asked him about the sort of undershorts he wore and he didn't say, *I don't discuss that sort of thing,* he was a sitting duck. He drew no boundaries. And Thomas Bowles is too smart and far too refined to get near the mud, much less wallow in it."

After turning down Matty's car again, to say nothing of Matty or his suggestion of a little lunch someplace really nice any weekday except Monday or Friday, I got to the office and called Mary Sloane, a friend from college who was an assistant DA in Manhattan. Naturally, she spent twenty minutes bringing me up to speed on her wedding plans, which included invitations made of rice paper and a cake made by Tatty, to whom I'd introduced her. The cake was to be a garden of viburnum, tulips, and hyacinths to match her bouquet. I acted appropriately enraptured and pondered if it was just bitterness that kept me from getting excited about bouquets and china patterns, the way so many of my single and married friends did. I managed a convivial *Nice!* a couple of times when she mentioned a cheese course and illusion sleeves for her wedding gown.

For some reason, *wedding gown* brought to mind John and *La Belleza*. I pictured him in a morning suit, her in sleek ivory satin—in a delightful candid shot in *Town and Country*. From there I got to thinking about a) how I'd never rise above being a financially insecure single mother because I couldn't imagine life without a kid and b) why I was staring at my screen saver instead of the article I had to finish. Fortunately, Mary called back within ten minutes. "Amy, Fernando Carrasco has a juvenile record. It's sealed. Even if I wanted to do you more of a favor, I couldn't," she said.

"All right then: Did he serve any time in a whatever? Reformatory? What the hell do you call it?"

"A juvenile facility. I can't tell you anything."

"Okay," I said quickly, guessing she might launch into her flower girls and baskets. "I appreciate your trying."

"I'm assuming you're bringing John to the wedding."

"Unless he's in the Falklands making a documentary." Or in Brazil to meet *La B*'s parents on their fifty-thousand-acre coffee plantation.

When at last I was able to say good-bye to Mary, I left a message on Freddy Carrasco's voice mail: "This is Amy from *In Depth*. I need to talk to you."

Instead of writing, I swiveled back and forth in my chair trying to come up with a way to convince Happy Bob to let me put in something about the Freddy accusation. I mused that it would be cool to write about whether the simple fact of celebrity engenders defamation, though I doubted Happy would buy it. The magazine didn't do sidebars. But he might accept a couple of paragraphs on accusations about political leaders' out-of-wedlock offspring, or a précis of campaign dirty tricks since 2000. Or I could pitch him a separate piece, on how we, as a culture, became so publicly devoted to the prurient.

I finally stopped swiveling because it was making me queasy. Or maybe it was just gastrointestinal war, four cups of coffee versus God knows how many scrambled eggs. Except I had to admit to myself it wasn't that either. My five terms of a free shrink at Ivey-Rush had given me at least some self-knowledge. The Freddy story of a lost parent was so intriguing to me because it was mine as well.

Well, about me and my . . . At my good-bye session with the shrink, he'd said, "Amy, if ever something's bothering you, and you can't figure out what it is, let the first word that comes into your mind be *mother*. That will probably do it, but if not, you can always go on from there."

At college, if you wanted a shrink who wasn't a demented-looking graduate student, it cost money. So from time to time, whenever I was bummed, I'd taken to free-associating in my dorm room. Out loud. My theory was that articulation itself was salutary, as in talk therapy, as in the rite of confession. Except what I'd do is jump to third person and do my talking on the phone. That way, if my roommate came in or a friend stood outside the door, they'd overhear . . . *What's the matter with her? I swear to God,*

Aunt Linda, I don't know. I guess she feels that if she doesn't work until she's absolutely ready to drop dead with fatigue or on the verge of hysteria . . . she'll fall from grace. No not in a religious sense . . . Then I'd get busy pretending to listen and say, *Yeah . . . You may be right, Aunt Linda . . . Maybe deep down she feels—I don't know—that she could wind up back where she started from.* A tsk or a chuckle. And then a quick *I wish I could but I have to go.*

I suppose it was no coincidence that I conjured up Aunt Linda during my four years in Cambridge. I could justify my choice of her as imaginary confidant by saying "nonjudgmental" or "benevolent," words probably not in her vocabulary, but neither would sum her up. Aunt Linda was one of those good-hearted but not overly bright people who, nevertheless, were wise about life. So it was no coincidence either that I picked up the phone, actually dialed her number, and said, "You know, I haven't seen you or Uncle Sparky for ages. Let me take you out to dinner tonight."

"Amy, sweet pea, no taking us out. Come, six, six-thirty, whenever. Sparky just got me one of those new slow cookers and I threw in some lamb cubes. There's more than enough to go around. I'll make something nice to go with it. Now listen, I don't want you bringing anything, except if you see a couple of those nice vine tomatoes. No more than two because they'll just go to waste. I have a ton of other stuff to put in the salad."

Twenty-some-odd years earlier, soon after he became a New York City fireman, Uncle Sparky—Anthony Napolitano— bought my aunt, his new wife, a three-bedroom house a few blocks from the fishing boat docks in the Sheepshead Bay section of Brooklyn. Like most of its neighbors, the house was modest, a red-on-top, white-on-bottom cube. As I walked from the subway, I could spot it from a block away by the whale weather vane and the slightly pitched roof.

He'd bought it for her as a birthday surprise. Instead of choking him, as many women might have done, Aunt Linda said, "Oh my God, I love it!" They never moved anywhere else. I'm not sure whether they intended to fill the two other bedrooms with children or if from the beginning they knew they needed no one else and decided to devote the rooms to their hobbies—her needlework, his wood burning. In my apartment, I had their handmade college graduation gifts: her framed crewel design of the Manhattan skyline with *Home Sweet Home* arcing over the buildings; his eight coasters onto which he'd burned Harvard's seal, complete with *Veritas* on the three open books.

The table was already set when I got there, pale blue dishes on oval placemats that were straw or seagrass—one of those excessively dry, frizzy fibers. My aunt's blue-plate theory was that there is no food that looks bad on blue. The table stood in the breakfast nook, a tight area with a bay window. It looked out on a birdhouse that hung from a low, scrawny branch of an old oak. For decades the tree had been assaulted by car exhaust from the nearby parkway and the bay's salt air. The birdhouse had fared better. Modeled after the White House, it was one of Uncle Sparky's wood-burning masterpieces. Except when it was very windy, the incredibly detailed North Portico faced the kitchen window. True, it was actually a pale brown house with the black detailing of the burning plus a hundred coats of varnish, but it was, nevertheless, a great address for a sparrow. Beyond the birdhouse, the narrow backyard was nearly invisible. A shrouded gas barbecue and cushionless aluminum-frame lounge chairs glowed in the ghostly light of the fog.

"You know," Aunt Linda said as she sliced the tomatoes I'd brought, "if you got one of these slow cookers, you could go to work and come home to a delicious meal. Save a *fortune* from all the takeout you working girls live on. Someday, one of you will die from cheap sushi and maybe you'll all get smart." Somehow, my father's sister—to say nothing of Chicky himself—had managed to emerge unscathed from Grandma Lil's refinement lessons. They might have been raised by a blowsy, gum-cracking dame who wore glitter nail polish. "Like, what did you have for supper last night?"

"Peanut butter and jelly on whole wheat, uh, milk and a cookie."

"What kind of cookie?"

"Chocolate chip."

"Carb City, lambie. I'm not saying cut out all carbs—I'm not a fanatic—but you gotta choose. The jelly *or* the cookie. Not both. You got a cute, athletic little body, but the minute you hit forty, the weight starts piling on. And you're petite."

"Short."

"Whatever. God forbid you should look like a beach ball when you're fifty."

As always, indoors or out, rain or shine, my aunt was wearing form-fitting jeans with four-inch heels. That night, her black hair was pulled straight back and held by a leopard-print scrunchie in a ponytail that went halfway down her back. Her black sweater was so predictably tight it looked on the verge of unraveling if she inhaled too deeply. On each wrist, she wore a cuff of hammered copper that echoed her copper man-in-the-moon earrings. My aunt was pretty in the way my father was handsome: a bony Frank Sinatra face and piercing dark eyes softened by an awning of lashes. Her makeup (of the three-differently-colored-stripes-of-eye-shadow school) was flawlessly applied.

"Anything new with that guy you're seeing?" She slid the tomatoes off the cutting board into a bowl of dark leaves and a rainbow of chopped-up raw vegetables.

"Not really."

"You speak foreign languages, right?"

"Spanish and French. And I read a little Latin. But what—"

"So translate what 'not really' means."

"It means that the relationship doesn't seem to be going any-place. You know, after two years—"

"That time you brought him here and the two of you went fishing with Sparky? He's very, very cute. And a nice guy. We both thought so. You could just tell. So what is the 'not really' all about?"

"I guess we've got everything going for us except love."

"I don't buy that for two seconds. Every time one of you said something, the other one would look so proud, like *Isn't that, like, the most darlingest thing you ever heard?*"

"Look, Aunt Linda, it's as if we'd been matched up by a com-puter. Everything's right except . . ." I patted my chest over my heart. She shrugged, opened a cabinet above the sink. "The lamb smells fantastic," I said.

"You want to know my secret? Rosemary, yeah, sure. But also a teeny bit of cumin." The inside of the door was mirrored and she checked her lipstick. "How's Chicky doing with that old lady who's keeping him?"

"Have you met her?"

"You've got to be kidding." She closed the cabinet door. "He's passing himself off as twenty-six. No, wait, thirty-six, which is still a joke, but she's buying whatever he's selling. What name is he using with her?"

"James Madison." I sighed.

"Like the high school? Pa-the-tic. He dropped out of high school the beginning of his junior year."

"Aunt Linda."

"What?"

"What haven't you told me about my mother?"

"What are you talking about?" High heels squeaking on the vinyl tiles, she walked to the breakfast nook and sat down. "You think I'm hiding stuff?"

"No. But we haven't talked about her . . . God, it's been ages. I think I was still in college. So maybe in that time you thought of something else, but it wasn't important. I mean, if it had been, you would have called and told me."

With her index finger that ended in an apricot-colored nail, she pointed to a chair. I sat. "What? You thinking about if you get married? Genes and things?"

"Well, genes are an issue."

"Fine. You got your smartness from her. Ask Chicky: She had an A-plus average! Like she could've gotten into Harvard too. Well, maybe not Harvard, but one of those good colleges you can never remember the names of."

I picked up a napkin ring, with dark and light blue crystals sewn on, and twisted it carefully around the paper napkin. Aunt Linda hated laundry but loved accessories, both for herself and her house. "Okay, she was rebelling against her family. And I guess sex was a major item. But what else attracted her to my father?"

"If there wasn't any sex or rebelling, trust me, angel pie, they wouldn't have stayed together for two seconds."

"Was she bookish?"

"Reading? No. I mean, not that I ever saw. I mean, if Chicky hadn't said, 'You wouldn't believe how smart she is! A ninety-seven average!' I wouldn't have believed she was so smart at the beginning. She just seemed like a regular person. Quiet."

"How come you never liked her?"

"Did I ever say that? That's not fair, Amy, putting words in my mouth. Okay, she was kind of . . . not cold. Cool, I'd call it.

Like she never said anything nasty, but you felt she wasn't trying to meet you halfway because you weren't worth it—to her. She didn't say anything unless you asked her a question. Then she'd answer. Polite, but not . . . really with you. Like she was waiting for someone to come along and take her out of wherever she was. Which happened to be with us."

"She came from Brooklyn, right?" Aunt Linda nodded. "Do you know what part?

"No. See, Sparky and I were just engaged then, so I was still living at home. The grand duchess Lil hated him because of his being a fireman and Italian, I mean, she didn't care about him not being Jewish because if I'd have come home with a guy with a side part and a Wasp name—Sutton Van Schmuck or something—then it would have been fine. So me and Sparky didn't see Chicky and Phyllis all that much. We hung out with Sparky's family or other probationary firemen and their wives and girlfriends."

"Do you recall where she went to high school?"

"Hey!" Uncle Sparky sauntered in. "Two beautiful women in one room! How lucky can I get?" A guy can be described as a bear of a man simply because he is large, but Uncle Sparky looked like Smokey's cousin in an FDNY T-shirt. He was what is politely called hirsute, covered in every conceivable place a man can have hair; the hair on his neck and shoulders rose above the collars of his T-shirts, so he had a perpetual dark brown ascot. His nose had been broken during some teenage fracas in Little Italy and as a result was squished against his face, so his nostrils were on display, the way a grizzly's are. My uncle was so XXL that it was nearly impossible to picture him racing up a ladder to save someone from a burning building. But then again, it's hard to imagine a five-hundred-pound grizzly running thirty-five miles an hour. Yet Uncle Sparky was surprisingly graceful for someone so massive, whether simply ambling around the house or grabbing Aunt Linda and demonstrating the twirl and dip they did to their wedding song, "You Light Up My Life."

He put his arm around my aunt and tenderly kissed her cheek. Then, in his usual greeting, he pinched my cheek and tousled my hair. "So, what did I miss? I heard the doorbell. You think you can keep Amy to yourself, talking a blue streak and not fill me in?"

"We were talking about your favorite sister-in-law."

Uncle Sparky glanced up at the clock, which was shaped like a teapot; he was probably going through the list of his three brothers' wives. "Right. Gotcha," he said at last. "You mean Phyllis."

"Yeah. Amy was just asking me . . ." She pursed her lips into a rosebud. "What were you just asking me?"

"If you remember where my mother went to high school."

"God, I don't have the foggiest," my aunt said. "Sparks, hon, do you remember?" She and my uncle had been going out since eighth grade, so he had known my mother as long and as well as Aunt Linda had.

"No." He gave me a look just short of pitying. "Chicky was always bragging about what a brain she was, that she was, you know, college material. But I don't think neither of them ever mentioned where she went to school."

"Did you think my mother was smart?" I asked him.

"Yeah, come to think of it. Not like she hung around reciting poems. Most of the time she was pretty quiet, just doing lovey-dovey stuff with Chicky, like battering her eyelashes. But I always said to Linda, 'That girl knows the time of day and then some.' You could tell she was taking everything in."

My aunt got busy trimming the stems of the bouquet I'd brought, so that the flowers would fit into a glass pitcher for a centerpiece. My uncle observed her snipping as if it were some never-before-seen and quite marvelous technique. "How was she as a mother?" I asked.

Aunt Linda, holding a pink, daisylike flower between her thumb and forefinger, eyed me and said, "Amy, baby, I don't think there's anything me and Sparky haven't told you over the years. From all I ever saw, she was an okay mother. You know, not Miss Kitchy-kitchy-coo, but I never saw her do anything wrong. She was a kid, seventeen or something like that, and to be honest, I was surprised she was so responsible. If you cried she fed you, if you pooped she changed you. Like any mother would. Or should."

"Did she breast-feed me?"

Uncle Sparky did a sidestep of discomfort. Aunt Linda stuck a fern into the pitcher and then said: "I don't think so. I mean, there was always a bottle. She let me hold you and feed you." I could tell my aunt wanted to give me something to hold on to, and she added: "You were so cute! Your eyes were sort of greeny and kind of almond-shaped, even then. And you were bald. With the pinkest cheeks! You'd stare right into my eyes. And you made the world's loudest burps."

I smiled, then turned to my uncle. "Did you sense my mother's dissatisfaction?"

"Listen, if you'd have said, *Hey, this is someone who's gonna turn her back on her baby, to say nothing of her husband,* I wouldn't have believed it. All right, I didn't think she was matched up in heaven to Chicky. She was too shrewd and probably too classy. But I wouldn't have believed she would—Jesus, I hate to say it—that she would have dropped him like a hot potato, much less have abandoned you. Truth of the matter? If she hadn't mailed that letter saying she wasn't coming back, to this day I'd have thought she was dead, you know, murdered, or maybe had some freaky accident."

I let the subject drop. My uncle carried the salad to the table. Aunt Linda handed me three bottles of dressing—orange, white, and green—and I brought them over. We all sat and she dished out salad with a wooden fork-and-spoon set Uncle Sparky had whittled, then topped off with his wood-burned designs on the handles. As a kid, I'd always believed they were a cabbage and a penis and tried not to look at them when I went there for dinner.

I told them about following Thom Bowles around on a campaign swing. Then Aunt Linda filled me in on her technique for getting the seeds out of a cucumber with an apple corer so you got cute little cuke circles, and Uncle Sparky told me about how many guys in the fire department had taken up cigarettes again after 9/11 and were now in an antismoking program.

Finally I said: "Look, I don't want to take advantage of your hospitality—"

"But you're going to." My uncle smiled as he said it.

"Sparks, baby," my aunt responded, "put a sock in it. Go ahead, sweetie."

"I just want to be sure I have the right information. My mother's family name was Morris. Her given was Phyllis. Right?"

My aunt's mouth dropped open so wide that I could see a couple of tiny smears of her Copper Kisses lipstick on her bottom teeth. Finally she asked: "You're thinking of trying to look for her?"

"Are you kidding? No. I just want to know a little about her. Her background. Her genes, okay? I mean, every time I've gone to a doctor, it's always 'Is there any heart disease in your family?' and I only have half an answer. And just—I don't know—general information."

"What if she died or something?" Uncle Sparky asked.

"Forgive me for saying this, Amy," my aunt said, "but good riddance to bad rubbish. To leave a darling little baby who's not even a year old. There's no explanation good enough for that."

She might have gone on, but my uncle apparently thought she should put a sock in it, because he suddenly said, "Phyllis, right. That was her name. No doubt about that, unless she made that up. But Morris? My ass, if you'll excuse me. Morris was one of those made-up last names like Jews used to do all the time. Not that Italians didn't. Tony *Bennett*? Dean *Martin*? We still do. The guy who made up *The Sopranos*? Give me a break."

"What was the family name originally?"

My uncle's shrug brought his shoulders up to his ears. My aunt said: "Moscowitz."

"You're kidding," I said.

"Of course I'm not kidding. Who'd make up a crazy thing like that?"

"How do you know?"

"Chicky told me."

"He never told me. He always seemed positive—"

"Amy, honey-bunny, he told me *years* ago. Right when he married her, when they thought she was pregnant but she wasn't. You know your father. A mind like a sieve. In one ear, out the other."

"Moscowitz?" I murmured, more to myself than them.

"And I'll tell you the only other thing I know about her," Aunt Linda said. "My mother told it to me, so take it with a grain of salt. A whole box of salt, because my mother and the truth were never best friends, as you well know." I nodded. "A couple of weeks or a month after Phyllis left, my mother said she heard on the grapevine that Phyllis was living in Greenwich Village, like a couple of miles away. Talk about chutzpah. Okay, true, the Village is like another planet. She was supposed to be

living with some guy, but she wasn't Phyllis anymore. It was
something . . . I can't swear to this. But it was, I think, Veronica.
You know? Like the rich girl in the *Archie* comics." She gave me
a second helping of salad. "I wish I could help you more. But I
don't know a thing about Moscowitz heart disease, my sweetie."

Chapter Six

My article on Thom Bowles was published to accolades, or what passed for accolades at *In Depth*—the left side of Happy Bob's smile twitched slightly higher and he said, "Nice work." After that, I was on to the Democrats' possibilities with the Christian right, followed by a piece on the rise of populism.

Except my mind had other ideas about how to occupy itself. Disregarding the wisdom I'd received from Mary Rooney in seventh grade—*If you sit around waiting for a guy to call, he won't*—I worked halfheartedly, waiting to hear from Freddy Carrasco and John Orenstein, as a cold, damp March blew in.

The so-called real world was barely a distraction. It was the Axis of the Extremely Annoying countries—France, Germany, and Russia—versus the Axis of the Excessively Eager, i.e., us and the British. At work, I read six newspapers each day online, plus the usual four delivered to my desk. The war watch on the Internet occasionally distracted me as I waited for the phone to ring. At home, I surfed from CNN to MSNBC to PBS to Fox while periodically picking up the phone to check if the reason for its silence was that the line was dead. Naturally I got a dial tone every time, which then allowed me to agonize that my lifting the receiver had, in a second, cut off the incoming call that would have transformed my life.

As we galumphed toward war, I flew to Memphis for the three days of a convention of big-shot conservative Christian activists, men of vigorous handshakes and women of Jesus-makes-me-so-darn-happy smiles. As a group, they were far more cordial to reporters than, say, run-of-the-mill Episcopalians, and eager to explain their beliefs. I squeezed in six or seven interviews a day, toured Graceland with a freelancer from the *Gospel Advocate,* and engaged in much intense chitchatting at no-alcohol cocktail parties, trying to get the sense of their professed bipartisanship while I glommed a few of an astounding variety of cream-cheese-based hors d'oeuvres.

But I couldn't numb myself with busyness. In spite of the vow I'd made to myself years earlier, I became one of those women waiting for a man's summons to bring her to life, checking my voice mail almost hourly, flipping open my cell phone hoping for a message icon. Sure, I knew there was nothing stopping me from calling John, but the old double-standard doubts were creeping up on me; I'd gone with egalitarian behavior and what had come of it? A silent cell phone. Maybe even the best of guys, deep down, wanted a woman—colleague, friend, girlfriend—who wasn't eager. Forget eager: who played hard to get.

Daily, I left word for Freddy, pursuing him with the practiced ardor of a supermarket-tabloid reporter out for a scoop. I needed to know what his juvenile record was about. Homicide or aggravated graffiti? Was he mental? No matter what the truth about his paternity ultimately was, did he believe he was telling it? Why had it been important enough for him to pursue it so?

Time after time, I clicked on Thom Bowles's fencing team photo and swore I was staring at Freddy's face. Sure, I knew there was a good chance that if I saw Freddy again I'd realize I'd imagined the resemblance. And yes, having had my article published, I knew that even if I went back and yanked out one of Bowles's well-tinted hairs, got a perfect DNA paternity match, and wrote an insightful exposé, *In Depth* would not touch it. Still, I couldn't let go of Freddy's find-the-parent, win-a-prize fantasy.

But that was nothing compared with my waiting to hear from John. Fifteen days without a call: a new personal best. He, who had me on auto-dial on both his home and cell phones, who'd sometimes call twice or three times a day to discuss the Paul Wolfowitz testimony he was watching on C-SPAN, or to offer a factoid he'd discovered while researching Geraldine Ferraro for a *Biography* show, had not called since we'd last slept together, the time I'd told him about Joan Murdoch.

I spent what seemed like hours (and probably was) discussing with Tatty whether he had spotted me at the Mahler concert gaping at him and *La Belleza*. Had he said to himself, *Thank God! Finally, Amy knows. Now I won't have to go through a melodramatic mess with her begging me for one more night to talk things out*? Or had a new enthusiasm simply struck him—garbage trucks or turtles? Was he filming a landfill or turtle eggs hatching somewhere?

Reminding myself that John's decency would absolutely preclude his simply dropping me didn't calm me in the least. Whenever there was a message on my home phone or cell, I'd press the button and expect *Uh, Amy, I sent back the copy of* Kavalier & Clay *you lent me and, uh, obviously my cousin's wedding . . . I*

*asked you to go to with me, but I'm sure you can understand . . .
Listen, I truly wish you the best. You're a wonderful person.*

Ergo, I wasn't astounded that when I got off the plane in
New York and opened up my cell phone, there was a message
from John. Except it wasn't a kiss-off: "Amy, okay, I'm a total
shit for not calling, but I've been working day and night. That
PBS deal for Herbert Hoover finally came through! Can you
believe it? I thought it was dead in the water. Anyway, I'm sorry
I've been so . . . uh, negligent. This call is to say hi and let you
know I'm not a rat. Oh, and to remind you that we have my
cousin Laurel's wedding Saturday night. Give me a call if you get
a chance and are still speaking to me. Otherwise, be ready a little before six because we have to drive up to Westchester. Did I
tell you the invitation said black tie? Okay, see you."

So I figured John didn't think *La B* was, as yet, sufficiently
conversant with upper-middle-class Jewish mores to face a family
wedding during which strangers might grab her hand and pull her
into a circle for twenty minutes of "Hava Negila," followed by
"Shout" and then dinner music from a Tex-Mex klezmer band.

John actually double-parked in front of my apartment and
came to pick me up, the sort of behavior Grandma Lil would
have cooed over. With his latest haircut grown out and a black
tuxedo shirt, he'd moved up from good-looking to handsome.
Hip, too, the sort of guy who bounds up the stairs to the stage
to accept a Best Something award. "Hey, Amy. You look beautiful." His words had a warmth that contradicted his cool looks.

"You look good—" I was just about to say "too" when he
kissed me.

"Sorry about the not calling," he murmured. I jerked back
my head, but at least I managed a smile.

"At least it wasn't a shock."

"Do you want to discuss why you couldn't talk throughout

the entire 2000 convention in L.A.? Or the Bush-Gore business in Florida when the only thing I got from you was a message not to call because you were too tired to talk?" Before I could come up with an answer, he said: "Hey, great outfit."

My skirt was a hand-me-down from a fabulously dressed girl from Greece who'd been in the class ahead of me at Ivey. Before she'd graduated, she put a huge pile of winter clothes on the common room couch with a note saying, "Help yourselfs!" Three of us full-needs students, i.e., kids totally on scholarship, guilted out our classmates whose parents had money. We wound up with enough clothes to get us to parties from October through March for decades to come. The skirt was a black velvet so fine that it felt like a cross between silk and flesh. I wore it with an extremely scoop-necked white sweater and rhinestone chandelier earrings I'd bought from a street vendor one lunch hour for eight bucks.

All that day, out running, cleaning my apartment, getting a manicure, rewatching *Brazil,* I'd gotten whooshes of fear, those momentary waves of impending doom—the sort of fear that seizes you when you're late for a period and it's too early to test. I was pretty sure John wouldn't want to end things on our way to his cousin's wedding because there was always the chance I'd become hysterical and wind up red-eyed and sniffling as he introduced me to Aunt Gertie. No, he'd be affectionate, hold my hand—though not during the ceremony, which would give me the totally wrong idea. We'd dance. And when we were talking to his family, he'd put an arm around me and I'd feel the heat of his hand on the bare part of my back. He would tell me good-bye on the way home. Except what John didn't know was that I was going to dump him first.

So the trip up was predictably comfortable: too much traffic, but we had enough of his Herbert Hoover and my evangelical Christians to keep us busy for the hour and change it took to get from my apartment to the wedding palace. Its name was Allen-thorpe. It was a late-nineteenth-century robber baron's dream of a Norman castle, now converted into a chichi catering site. While the architecture was French, the name was English and the car valets were dressed like butlers in a 1930s Hollywood comedy about rich people.

I got through the ceremony without once—okay, without twice—noting that Cousin Laurel was three years younger than I and had parents who could afford to pay not only for her gorgeously understated, probably Vera Wang gown, but to feed and wow with flowers their upscale, ostensibly unwowable guests. Fortunately, I was sitting beside Dr. Orenstein, John's mother, who not only welcomed me with a kiss, but throughout the wedding procession whispered, "Did you see that cat tattoo on her back!" and "Isn't that Asian girl beautiful?" about the brides-maids, who were wearing eight different styles of gown, all in pink faille. Dr. Orenstein's asides were the kind of things a real mother would say to a daughter. I glanced at her profile. An unremarkable face, but appealing, browned and crinkled from her gardening, with a few moles. She was the human correlative of a just-baked oatmeal-raisin cookie. I could still feel her Hello, Amy! kiss, a brush on my cheek with her winter-dried lips.

Except I was going to lose her. I'd written the entire John-Amy breakup script in my head, but for some stupid reason, what hadn't occurred to me was that naturally I'd be breaking up with his family. So at dinner, when his father asked me to dance and twirled me around in a waltz in a graceful way you wouldn't necessarily expect from a history professor, I kept thinking: *I'm never going to see this man again.* It wasn't just that I'd never hear him talk about the Inquisition in Castile and Aragon. John's father was a born storyteller. He could even make a saga of having his tonsils taken out in 1949 come alive.

And though I didn't know them so well, I'd be losing John's two younger brothers, too. One was a landscape architect, the other in medical school. Both of them had their mother's sweet smile and round cookie face. By now I knew them well enough that I no longer needed my tortured mnemonic devices to distinguish them. Tall and thin like a tree was landscape guy; medicine was Mike, so landscape guy was Alex. I found myself glancing at John's watch too often. The later it got, the sadder I felt about being thrown out of their lives. Would Professor Orenstein become history department chair? Would Alex marry Nora? I'd only managed to see a frame or two when all along I'd assumed I'd be there for the entire movie.

Maybe I was a little too hearty in my good-byes to the Orensteins, knowing they really were good-byes. In the car, I recall watching John as he turned his head to check for traffic as we got onto the parkway, thinking how wonderful-looking he was. I suddenly realized that in the past two years my vision of my kids was Orenstein-ish children. Like John and his father, intelligent, decent, manly—or like his brothers and mother, with cheery cookie faces.

In the silence between us, family images—his, not mine—flashed one after another, snippets of Orenstein scenes from a documentary I'd put together in my head. John's little cousin lisping the Four Questions at the family Seder. His mother cutting a bouquet of flowers for me to take home after I'd spent a weekend at their house in Connecticut. Sitting in a dark editing room John was renting, watching his first documentary for the History Channel, reaching out to squeeze his hand because his work was so admirably done. The great sex and, okay, not one single I-love-you. And finally, seeing his face lit up as he talked to *La Belleza* during intermission.

I turned away from him, pretending to be mesmerized by the

wonders of the Hutchinson River Parkway. Except not only was I crying, I couldn't get the tears to stop. I know I couldn't have planned on it, even subconsciously, because if I had, I'd have worn waterproof mascara. Great, I thought: I'll wind up with racoon eyes, the ineluctable sign of a woman suddenly freed from her dependence on a man. I knew I had to stop the weepies and say good-bye fast. But first I'd have to sniffle to dam up the tears, to say nothing of the waterfall of snot cascading down my upper lip.

"So?" John suddenly asked. "I'm waiting for your critique of the entire wedding." I shrugged. "Amy, come on. You're the best amateur anthropologist I know . . . The only one, actually . . ." He went into a short monologue I barely heard, breezy, about how there had never been a social class I hadn't met. It was the kind of patter he was great at, that he'd used on all the distant relatives at the wedding. It said, *I know you only slightly, but it's really good being with you.* Easy, warm, disarming. John could always make interview subjects and third cousins from San Diego feel comfortable. He'd never spoken to me in that congenial, distant way, even the first time we went out.

It hit me then that he understood that simultaneously breaking up with me and driving safely back to Manhattan might be mutually exclusive. What he'd more likely do would be to get near my place, double-park on a side street, and then give his prepared speech. That way, he'd avoid all the agonies he could face if he actually escorted me up to my apartment: my pleading with him, my trying to seduce him into the Big Wow Final Fuck, my throwing my body against the door to keep him from leaving.

What other end-of-the-affair nightmare could he conjure? Oh, that I'd get suicidal and try a swan dive from the eighth floor. No, homicidal. Why in God's name had I told him that one of Chicky's imprisonments was for aggravated assault? On the other hand, maybe John was afraid he'd be overcome with guilt about leaving someone who was pretty much alone in the world and would, against his better judgment, take me back. "Amy." I wiped my nose with my hand and turned back. Grandma Lil told me a lady is never without a handkerchief; I didn't even have tissues. In all my rehearsals, I never considered I might cry.

"Hey, Amy, what's the matter?"

It took me a few long seconds before I could speak. "I saw you that night—the Mahler."

"What?"

Filtered through tears and a too-full nose, broken up by the occasional sob, my words were either inaudible or they hadn't hit him. "I saw you the night of the all-Mahler concert. During intermission."

"*You* went to hear Mahler?" Less than a second later, he added: "Oh. Listen—"

"After more than two years, John," I began. I didn't want to say, *How could you?* Except I couldn't think of anything else.

"Why the hell were you at a Mahler concert? You can't fake it, you know." His voice was getting tight, his charm wearing thin. He didn't like the timing of this. "Any composer between Beethoven and Gershwin is lost on you."

I looked away from him and stared down into those little brush things that line the track on a car's gear shift. A metal ring from a soda can was stuck between D2 and D3. I stuck my pinky in and fished it out. "The point, John, isn't my taste or lack of it in music."

He did the thing he usually did when upset, pulling in his right cheek and gnawing on it. Finally he snapped: "I know what you're thinking and you're wrong."

He gave me the briefest glance, then looked back at the road and checked his rearview mirror. Quickly, without signaling, he cut to the right and got off at the next exit. We drove in silence for a few blocks into some suburb. I stared out the window until he parked midblock between a Tudor that looked like a pub and its neighbor, a brick box with columns. Both had American flags that drooped in the windless night. The sky was clouding over into blackness, and on the entire block there was not a single light on in any of the houses.

John switched off the engine. I wasn't going to play the who'll-break-down-and-talk-first game. I knew I had to go first. "There are a lot of things to admire about you, John, but your sense of decency was always in my Top Ten. Couldn't you at least have said, *Amy, listen, this monogamy stuff isn't working so well for me.* Or *I met someone I really like, or have fallen in love with, and I want to be free to pursue a relationship with her*?"

He unlocked his seat belt and shifted to face me. "What are you talking about—*fallen in love with*? You saw me at Rose Hall listening to Mahler. Why are you assuming it's a romantic thing?"

"I've got eyes. And I've got sense. And I know how you look when you're hot for a woman."

"Amy, this is crazy!"

"You told me you were busy researching Garth Brooks for *Biography* that week!" For someone who was trying to sound rational, if not cool, my voice came out in almost a shriek. "Even though we never talked about the future, two years entitles me—"

He punched the steering wheel with his fist. "Fuck it, Amy! Talk about entitlement! Aren't I entitled to be believed? Do you want to discuss what I'm entitled to after two years? How about some closeness with you? Didn't you think I was entitled to that? But no matter how many times I tried, I always hit a wall.

The Amy Lincoln dance: I take a step forward, you take a step back."

"I feel as if I'm eavesdropping on some other woman's relationship," I responded. He was staring straight out the windshield, hands gripping the steering wheel as if he were driving somewhere in a storm. "I don't know what you're talking about! I never did a dance with you."

"How about after nine-eleven? When I all but begged you to stay at my place, and you practically ran out, saying, 'Oh, you must want your space'—"

"John, I honestly thought—"

"Bullshit! And I start talking about how I'd love to have kids, and you tell me you weren't sure you would because they all might look like your grandma Lil—"

"I was kidding!"

"Listen to me," he said, disturbingly calm. "Tonight is just the tip of the iceberg. The two of us . . . It hasn't been working. We ought to have been a wonderful couple, at least from my point of view. You're fun, interesting. Terrifically smart. Sometimes I'm awed by your analytical ability. And I admire the empathy you feel for anyone who's gotten a raw deal in life. But there's no life in our life together anymore—except for sex. And every time I want to talk afterward—that's prime time between two people—you either fly out of bed because a little cum is running down your leg or you make some wiseass remark that kills whatever mood there is. You never give me credit for caring. You never trusted me."

"That's so not true, John. How can you think that?"

"Because after two years you think I'm lying!"

"This is different!" My nose and/or eyes must have started up again, because he spent a couple of seconds searching his pockets for a tissue and at last came up with a section of paper towel from his door compartment he'd probably stuck there for checking his dipstick.

"The last time we were together," he said, more coolly, "you picked up I was pissed off at your pulling back. So you told me about Joan the social worker like you were bestowing some precious gift: *I hope this proves that I'm not afraid of getting close; I'm trusting you with my secrets. You're getting a special screening of my private, vulnerable self. So don't expect anything for your birthday or Valentine's Day.*"

"I can't believe"—I thought about his Valentine waffle iron and my voice went out of control again—"that you're being so unfair!"

"I can't believe we've spent, whatever, more than two years together and all I hear from you is the same story, over and over: that your father was in jail more often than he was out, and your mother ran off and your grandmother lived in a dream world—which incidentally, as I see it, you've spent your life trying to turn into a reality—and that's all I know. The story you'd tell anybody. A bare outline. Roman numerals one, two, and three. No capital As and Bs. Definitely not any regular numbers or anything lowercase. And don't tell me you're not doing a dance, because you've been doing that from day one. Tell me, didn't you ever hear the word *intimacy*?"

"Yes. It's a cliché. Did you ever hear the word . . ." I really couldn't come up with anything. Reticence wasn't right. Neither was *I didn't want you to think I came with a thousand emotional problems attached.* In one of the houses, a dog began to howl.

"Not believing me tonight is just another way of backing off." His tone had become disturbingly even, as if he were narrating a documentary. "What do you expect me to do, Amy? Hang around for five to ten years to see whether you can learn to trust me enough not to jump back whenever I get close?"

"You never said anything about this, goddamn it!"

"I said it all the fucking time. And on the rare occasion you decided to open up, it was in some half-jokey way that said, *Don't you dare take this too seriously.* What if you trusted me and you'd really opened up? And what if—for the sake of hypothesis—you'd stayed at my apartment for one week after nine-eleven? Or ten weeks, or whatever. Amy, I'm really sorry for all the sad stuff you had to live through. But for months now I've been thinking that I can't be with someone who's always coming up with preemptive strategies to avoid getting hurt."

"Are you sleeping with her?"

"No!"

"The one deal we had was to be sexually monogamous."

"How can you think I wasn't?"

"John, I never thought I'd see you try to weasel out of the truth."

"She's my producer at PBS. She's married, for God's sake."

"John, a married producer couldn't have brought out that glow I saw on your face."

"Listen to me. She's a business acquaintance—believe it or don't believe it. I really don't care anymore." His voice grew softer, like a doctor about to impart bad news. "You know what, Amy?"

"What?"

"I feel sorry for you. Do you want to know why?" I kept silent. "You'll never allow yourself to have what you've been looking for all your life."

"Tell me, John. What have I been looking for all my life?"

"Someone who will accept you and love you just the way you are."

⚊ ⚊ ⚊

So naturally the next morning, Sunday, I went over to Tatty's. She was in the kitchen finishing a sweet sixteen cake. "So that's it?" she demanded. "John was making pleasant conversation and you, with your genius for timing, brought up catching him with some cheap PBS slut—"

"Expensive. And how could she be from PBS? A public broadcasting woman wouldn't wear stiletto heels. That was his story and it was totally lame. And could you please stop with the Katharine Hepburn lighthearted banter. Be a regular Park Avenue boring person who listens."

"You listen. You have a nice time at the wedding and what do you do? Bring up catching him with a babe in a silver suit."

"You should have seen his expression that night. It said, *This woman is pure pleasure.*"

"Maybe the music gave him that expression."

"The music didn't have cleavage."

"You don't think it's possible that what he told you was the truth?" Tatty asked.

"I wish I could. But even the best music in the world couldn't give him that glow."

"Was her suit very nipped in at the waist?" With incredible care and sureness of hand, she pressed a piece of old lace onto the virginal blush-pink icing on the cake, then removed it. Still talking, she meticulously traced the debossed lace pattern with a fine line of ivory icing that exuded from the tiny opening of a tube on a pastry bag. "This girl must be a major loser to have a sweet sixteen on a Sunday afternoon," she muttered. "To have a sweet sixteen, period." Her head swayed back and forth and in figure eights, rehearsing the motions the pastry tube would make next. "Aimée, I can't look up to check you out. Are you crying?"

"No, I'm not crying, for God's sake." I ran my finger over a piece of waxed paper she'd practiced on and ate a blob of icing.

"Well, I cried last night. During, when I was with him. And after."

"Really?"

"Buckets. Now I'm just exhausted. But the weird thing is that when I finally stopped, I wound up sleeping like a baby."

"So was it nipped in at the waist?"

"The silver suit? Yes. What the hell difference does that make?"

"I'm wondering if it could have been a vintage Valentino. Did it have a narrow shawl collar?"

"Tatty, how can you go through life with your head continually up your ass?" I demanded. "We're talking about . . . a personal crisis. How about a little sensitivity?"

"You're getting it. All I'm saying—" What had begun looking like a deformed hand made of butter cream was taking shape, becoming an intricate lace pattern of flowers spilling over the sides of an urn. "—is that life goes on. You said the relationship was going nowhere. You *wanted* to get rid of him. So what's the dif if he beat you to it? Other than the blow to your ego, of course. Look, I understand catching him with another woman was a shock. And so was his beating you to doing the dump. A bruised ego is incredibly hurtful so close to your thirtieth birthday. But if he was on the way out, was it really so terrible that he beat you to the exit?"

"I don't know."

Tatty finished a squiggle in the middle of a fat rose or maybe a peony and set down the pastry bag. She turned to me. "You don't know *what*?" I didn't answer. "You don't know if it matters who left who or whoooom, as you're so fond of saying. Or are you having second thoughts?" She bent over to stretch. Her long body folded neatly at the waist. Touching the floor with her palms would have been easy, but she hated having to wash again after a work break, so she simply rested the tips of her nails on the tops of her kitchen clogs. When she stood she said, "Okay. I'm sounding too blithe about this no-more-John business, aren't I?"

My feet hurt, so I gave up trying to out-stand her and dragged over a chair. "Yes, way too blithe," I said, plunking myself down. "I mean, it lasted more than two years. I spent time with his family. I was crazy about them. I introduced him to Aunt Linda and Uncle Sparky. We were . . . whatever."

"Serious," Tatty said and quickly twirled a piece of paper into a cone, stuck in a different-size tube, and gooped in a spoonful of ivory buttercream. "He was your intended."

"Something like that," I admitted.

"I can't understand why you let it drag on for so long." We'd gone through this before, so I just compressed my lips, but Tatty was busy with a lace leaf and didn't see. "The staying power thing?" she asked.

"Maybe. I know you think it's my problem, not a guy's. But I can't afford to rush into anything without being sure, you know, that whoever he is really accepts me, my background, which is also me. Forget my probably having a lot of subnormal intelligence genes. I could have . . . I don't know what you'd call it. Predisposed-to-felony genes. And that's just my father's side. Plus I don't exactly come with a dowry. But all this is moot because John never came close to proposing. We went together and went together and everyone thought of us as a couple except him. Maybe me, too. But right around the time I felt really sure he had the staying power, the relationship got the air sucked out of it. I'm thinking, *Shit, something's missing.* And next thing, he's sleeping with a Brazilian socialite."

"You don't know if she's Brazilian or a socialite," Tatty said. "Maybe she's a très chic hooker who rents herself out for cultural events."

"He told me I'm afraid of intimacy," I told her.

Tatty set down the paper pastry cone and picked up her cloth bag. "Well," she said, "he wasn't wrong."

It was too late for a calming breath. My head felt as if it would split from the force of the anger I felt. "Fuck you, Tatty! You're not exactly the Queen of Self-disclosure." Unmoved, she squiggled out the contour of a ribbon and began filling it in with tiny grosgrain-like striations. The blood wouldn't leave my head. I wanted to throw that spoiled, rich high school kid's six-thousand-dollar sweet sixteen cake onto the floor. Instead, I picked up the paper cone, opened it, and licked off about six thousand calories' worth of sugared buttercream.

"You didn't put me in your article," Freddy Carrasco muttered. He kept his voice down because we were sitting in *In Depth*'s holding pen. Suddenly I was reconsidering the wisdom of having asked him to meet me at the office. Okay, I didn't have much time to devote to him, but my first meeting with him might have been a charm. This time around, he could show serious derangement, with tics and twitches and twirly eyes like Judge Doom in *Roger Rabbit*.

Except for the computer on the receptionist's rickety desk, the space could double for the front room of a sleazy funeral parlor in a noir film. Its beige rug was so old it had turned ashen and was flaking at the edges. We sat on two of seven extremely fake Chippendale chairs, perhaps from our Revered Founder's dining room during the years of his first wife; he'd probably smashed the eighth over her head, or vice versa. Periodically, the receptionist, Mrs. Snarck—who corrected anyone who called her Ms. Snarck—turned from her rip-roaring life on eBay to glare at me for daring to receive in a reception area.

I'd decided not to bring Freddy back to my desk on the off chance he'd start bellowing tabloid headlines the whole staff would hear: *I am Senator Bowles's son!* That alone could easily send my stock as prospective senior editor right into the toilet. (*Toilet* was one of many of Grandma Lil's proscribed words, a list that also included *mucous, vagina, penis,* and, if she'd known it existed, *smegma.*)

Anyway, I lowered my voice. "I told you right from the start there wasn't a chance in hell that *In Depth* would publish anything about a party crasher making a paternity accusation against a candidate."

"Did you even try to get something in?"

"No. Listen, Freddy, you seemed sincere when I met with you that one time at Starbucks. Not crazy. Maybe I would have called a colleague somewhere and said, *Hey, check this guy out. His story isn't for us, but maybe you guys could use it.* But then you didn't return my call for ages." Just in case I was emitting passive-aggressive, dumped-girlfriend rays by subconsciously equating Freddy's not calling with John's, I added: "I left a message saying I needed to talk to you. This isn't a leisurely business. The word *news* implies new information. By the next day or next week, it's nostalgia."

"It was spring break," he replied. A little shrug, a small smile: For just an okay-looking guy, he had confidence in his charm.

"Come off it, Freddy," I said. "You're going to a commuter college and you have a day job. Do you expect me to picture you leaving some dorm and heading down I-95 with a surfboard?" His head dropped a fiftieth of an inch, so I added: "I didn't mean to sound sarcastic."

"It's all right."

"Thanks." Though his head was flowerpot-shaped, with his

hair serving as a low, grassy growth, in the flesh he did look amazingly like that one photo of Thom Bowles on the fencing team. Even though each of them pretty much conformed to the coloring of their stereotypes—Bowles with blue eyes and leathery western white guy skin, Freddy with bittersweet-chocolate eyes and intermediate Latino brown skin—they could easily have been father and son. On the other hand, Fernando Carrasco could simply be a liar with a square jaw. "So," I said, "how come you didn't tell me about your juvenile record?"

He sucked in a shocked breath, then slowly breathed it out. "How did you hear about it?" he inquired, pretty equably.

"I can't reveal my sources," I said. That line was always invigorating, making me feel like Woodward and Bernstein instead of a writer at a self-important weekly. If *In Depth* had an escutcheon, it would bear the words *NULLA SCIENTIA SINE TAEDIO* on a field of bleakest gray. *No knowledge without boredom.*

"You heard about it from someone from Bowles's campaign," he stated. "It has to be." I kept quiet. "Okay," he said, "but I need to know that anything I say will be off the record or whatever you call it."

"I won't publish or quote anything you tell me. It will be confidential, between you and me."

"And you won't write something like *The twenty-one-year-old man, who has a sealed juvenile record, currently attending the City College of New York, wishes to remain anonymous....*"

"Of course not. So did you spend any time at a facility?"

"No. I was lucky. I had a really good lawyer. He made a case that I was a basically decent kid who got involved with a bad bunch of guys. That was pretty much true, although not an excuse. But I did have good grades and was potential college material. We did it late. Broke into an electronics store, I mean.

Nobody was at the store, nobody got hurt. The judge went for his argument."

"What did you take?"

"Electronics. Cameras, handhelds. A ThinkPad: That was strictly my deal."

"This was when your mother was alive?"

Freddy's shoulders tried a shrug, but wound up in more of a shudder. "Yeah. Two years before she died. The lawyer was five thousand dollars. She wouldn't have said a word about how much he charged if I hadn't asked."

"What did she die of?" I asked expectantly. Would he say *A broken heart*? I did have a weakness for tearjerking dying-mother scenes.

"Heatstroke. Can you believe it? All she was doing was coming home from work. She was an accountant, a CPA. After I was born, she used the money she got from William Bowles for day care and to live on while she finished college. She worked at a small firm, but it had a really good reputation. Anyhow, she had a seizure on the subway. By the time they got her out of there and over to the emergency room at Columbia-Presbyterian, she was dead." Freddy tried to change the subject by not talking, eyeing the back issues that sat on the glass-topped, stainless-steel-bottomed coffee table, scanning the indices that formed our covers. The *In Depth*s had been more tossed than fanned out. The table was probably an oddment from our Revered Founder's second marriage. "It's terrible not to be able to say good-bye," he finally said. His face fell into sadness, his brows drawing together, his lower lip pushing against the upper, which pressed down the corners of his mouth. I tried not to hope his voice would crack with lost-mother grief. "Her last words to me were 'I'll buy a nice piece of fish for supper.' Weird."

"A lot worse than weird," I said.

"Yeah."

Naturally I remembered that Freddy's mother had not possessed any evidence that she'd received money from Thom
Bowles's father, William Bryson Bowles, to shut up and go away.
And since the senator definitely wasn't up for a "Call me Dad,
son" segment on a Barbara Walters special, and if indeed the
paternity business wasn't a fantasy or scam by either Freddy or
his mother, I had to ask: "So what can I do for you?"

"Help me," he said. Maybe he thought I was on the verge of
saying *Get out* because he quickly added: "Look . . . Do you
mind if I call you Amy?"

"No." He'd probably heard the same squib I'd heard on Eye-
witness News, about how saying the name of the person with
whom you're speaking leads to a 38 percent increase in their
acceptance of you.

"So this is the thing, Amy. If I wanted to cause a real stink, I
could go to one of those right-wing guys' websites and post a
message. Trust me, in a few days it could build to something
really big and slimy. But I'm not looking for money. My mother
did okay and she left me enough that if I wanted to continue my
education, or even—I don't know—buy a studio apartment in
an okay neighborhood, I could. If I wanted to frighten the senator, I could follow him around the country and find a way to
speak to him one-on-one and say enough to scare the crap out of
him. All I want is for him to acknowledge that I exist and that
I'm his son. It's not that I want a daddy. Even if I did, I wouldn't
want Thomas Bowles because he's full of shit."

"Actually, even if you disagree with his positions, he's fairly
substantive—"

"Substantive?" Freddy demanded. "He sounds like an asshole
with too many advisers to me." He paused. "But who cares what
Thom Bowles is. It doesn't matter. My mother was a realist. She

knew that up against people like that family, she didn't have a chance. So after Thom Bowles dropped her when she wouldn't take money for an abortion, she heard from the senator's old man. I guess she scared both of them because suddenly what happens? Thom Bowles is gone from New York. She gets money. Besides being a realist, she was a serious Catholic. Abortion was out of the question. So you get the picture of her? Practical. Moral."

"Got it. But Freddy, are you going to tell me a woman of her fine character would never, ever sleep with two men in the same month? Are you going to tell me that if she once got too friendly with some quasi-lowlife—as many, many terrific women, including me, have been known to do in their tender years—that she'd tell you: *Fernando, your father's in Sing Sing serving two consecutive life sentences for murder?* Or would she say: *Your father's a Princeton graduate, a successful entrepreneur, and a United States senator?*"

"My mother would have told me the truth." He had the raised chin and the straight gaze of the true believer. "What I'm asking is . . . Look, I know I have a lot of strengths, including intelligence. But I also know I'm not sophisticated yet. From the way you act, and because you really understand the political world, you are. Without being snobby or condescending."

"Thank you. It's funny, though. I always think of sophisticated as being people who are waved in by doormen at clubs or who speculate in euro futures. Except okay, by your definition, I'm sophisticated in that I pretty much understand how the world works." I took out my cell phone, clasping it as if it were some enchanted amulet that would advise me what to do. I suddenly realized that admitting to sophistication was probably an unsophisticated act. "Give me a minute to think." He studied me as I thought. Flattering. Inhibiting. "Do me a favor, Freddy. Take a ten-minute walk and then come back up."

He left and I hurried back to my desk. How do you un-disown? How do you get a parent who wants no part of you to say, *Okay, kid, you're mine?* And would that satisfy Freddy Carrasco? Or would he also want *Hey, you look like a really good guy?* Or more? *Maybe we could go fishing or something, get to know one another. Brooke and April? They're like Snow White and Rose Red, cardboard characters, sweet but—just between us—boring as hell. I want to concentrate on you, Fred. I want to make up for all the hurt I've caused you.*

So I made a couple of calls. The old goy network. Alumnae of Ivey-Rush are, as our alma mater says, ever faithful, ever true. To the school, to one another. Well, it wasn't 100 percent, what with whiners, bitches, and the women who perpetually feel fucked. But I went back to my cubicle, typed my password into the Ivey website alumnae page. Moments later, I was on the phone with Margaret Jane "Mickey" Maller, '61, attorney-at-law, a grande dame of the New York family-law bar. Naturally, Mickey said she remembered me with perfect clarity from the meeting last April at Pucky Violett's place. Yes, certainly she'd be willing to listen to my nomination for her next pro bono case. He's claiming Thomas Bowles . . . ? Hmm. Hmmmm. Seems like a stable young man? Tell him to be at my office at five-fifteen on Thursday. No, no, Amy. No trouble at all.

Ergo, Mickey Maller was another name on my list of people I would owe big-time, forever. I can't say that when I met Freddy back in the reception area and told him about his upcoming appointment with her, his look of amazement, followed by a bar-rage of thank-yous, made my effort worthwhile. Well, I guess it did. His decision that it wouldn't be cool to kiss me as he left touched me, as did his near inability to stop shaking my hand and beaming. Mrs. Snarck, the receptionist, forsook what was prob-ably a major crackle-glass auction on eBay to observe us through the slits that were her eyes. "Freddy," I told him, "the cloud may not have a silver lining. Ms. Maller may tell you there isn't any case. Okay? God does miracles. Lawyers do not."

After another exchange of thank-yous and you're-welcomes, I went back to my computer. But instead of plugging away on my current yawner of an opening paragraph, I began searching for variations on Phyllis, Moscowitz, Morris, Lincoln, and—as per Uncle Sparky—Veronica.

Chapter Seven

I was that annoying perfect attendance type. All through P.S. 97 and Ivey-Rush, I never missed a day of school, slogging through the snow with bronchitis, sitting in class with chin pressed to chest to stifle the coughs that could get me sent out. Okay, I missed two days of college, succumbing to an E. coli sandwich masquerading as chicken salad, and a day of journalism school for Grandma Lil's funeral.

To announce I was taking a few days off for "family business" was a huge deal: for me. Not one eyelash blinked at *In Depth*. No expulsion from the magazine, with me cringing like Michelangelo's Eve departing Eden.

So on an unseasonably cold Wednesday, I began the search for my mother. Walking down to the Forty-second Street library, I told myself, *Relax. You're a damn good reporter,* in that excessively cheery way successful people buck up hard-luck friends.

I'd done a preliminary search on the Web and found a few Phyllis Moscowitzes. As far as I could ascertain, none of them would have been anywhere around seventeen years old in 1973, the year I'd been born. Chances were good that if her IQ was even slightly higher than double digits, my mother would have had the brains to change her name. To get anywhere in cyberspace, I would need something more: a date of birth, a Social Security number.

Also, I was a fool when it came to the allure of libraries. Most of the good memories of my childhood were set in two places, the playground and the public library. At Ivey, I'd gotten into the habit of working in the library, in part to get away from the constant presence of the other girls. Growing up on the Lower East Side, my zone of privacy outdoors was about two and a half inches. Inside, however, I was so used to escaping Grandma Lil—as well as reality—by saying I had to study that the mere physical feel of a book came to be pleasurable.

The library at Fifth and Forty-second was a researcher's dream, despite its nightmarish waits and the occasional churlish, book-banging employee. The Web was often too rich, offering 517,000 choices. I always had a sense that the best answer was lurking prohibitively far away, if only I had patience to scroll through eight hundred pages. Here, I had to rely on my own mind and intuition, although that assumed a productive search. There had been many days when all I had to show for my efforts were the specks of crumbly old magazines all over my shirt.

I had reassured myself I was a damn good reporter, but was I? No. Fifteen minutes after I got myself comfortable in the hardwood library chair, I was out of there. I dashed down Fifth Avenue, running the nine blocks to the library's business branch on Madison to check some factlette in their collection. Then back and forth, again and again. I, organized Amy Lincoln, who, since kindergarten, had never handed in a paper or an article late, who kept her nail polish bottles lined up according to their position on the color wheel, I, who could barely write a shopping list without first making an outline, had become scattered.

Running from library to library, I moved like a demented soccer forward, chunking past office workers, Arab pretzel men, Senegalese watch vendors, cops, tourists. My discombobulation added to my already off-the-chart anxiety and produced an all-over glaze of sweat that made me regret wearing wool as my first layer of sweater. Over the years, I'd become Total Sweater Girl. Coats can be a literal drag for a reporter; I learned that four layers was right for a cold day. Getting dressed I'd mixed lavender, orchid, plum, and violet. Hey, great combo, I commended myself before I left the apartment. But I caught a glimpse of my reflection in a store window. I looked like an out-of-towner trying to pass as a hip New Yorker.

I was worn out by ten-thirty. My feet throbbed and I was suddenly aware that the little toe on my left foot was begging for an intermission. I ordered myself to stay in one place for at least an hour. The sudden shift from frenzy to stillness made me hypervigilant. I felt four or five pulses thumping away in different parts of my body. My dry mouth tasted as if I'd been sucking on rubber bands. At some point, I realized, I had to deal with the pile of books sitting before me.

I took the one on top and began leafing through real estate records for 1970 to 1972. Those were the years just before I was born, when Phyllis Moscowitz Morris eloped with Chicky Lincoln. Maybe it was the feel of paper, the rhythmic turning of pages, but slowly the spell of the library came upon me. True, this particular research room was gloomier than Hell, but for me, any room filled with books was usually a balm.

Until I left for boarding school, my library was more home

to me than my grandma's apartment. When, at age nine, I recognized I was too short to beat anyone but a third-grader one-on-one in basketball, I headed to the Hamilton Fish Park branch of the New York Public Library every day after school. Within weeks, I became the librarians' pet. Sure, they'd say *Shush* to me now and then, yet they seemed so benevolent as to appear angelic. They actually wanted me to read. They kept telling me how smart I was. Best of all, unlike Grandma Lil, they made no demands on my patience. They did not want to confer with me for a half hour about the details of a photograph of Glenn Close in a 1984 Cadillac Eldorado convertible—as seen in a stolen-from-Beauté copy of *Harper's Bazaar*. Librarians truly wanted to know *What did you think of that book on Copernicus?* Until I was ten or eleven, whenever my grandma forgot to pick me up, one of them would walk me home.

The Hamilton Fish was a bland, tan brick building that looked like a generic library inside, yet my mind's eye saw the interior as grand, a high-ceilinged, glowing space. Starry pinpoints of light reflected off the protective plastic covers on the books. Objectively, I know the plastic was cloudy with fingerprints and sneezes, tacky from the caked-on residue of other people's Cheez Doodles. Still, I viewed the light given off by the books as celestial.

I put down the '70 to '72 real estate records and picked up the next book, and then the next. By one o'clock, my eyes were so dry I could no longer blink. My neck ached from hunching over to read tiny print. My stomach growled with resentment while I kept working to find who, from the masses of Moscowitzes in the borough of Brooklyn, could be my Moscowitz.

Finally, I had to admit I was famished. Huddling over a Kings County business directory printed in what must have been a four-point font, I did the pretend-to-sneeze bit, covering my mouth with one hand in order to sneak in a major hunk of protein bar with the other. Except just at that moment, I found myself staring at the names of my maternal grandparents: Rose and Selwyn Moscowitz.

My God! There it was! For once, Chicky hadn't made up some lame story when he claimed my mother's father owned bike stores. He'd been telling the truth. In 1970, a Selwyn Moscowitz had actually owned two bicycle stores in Brooklyn—one in Flatbush, one in Park Slope. Selly's Cyclery. Selly, along with Rose, also owned the buildings in which the stores were located. I tried to swallow the protein bar. It wouldn't go down. A big glob of protein—one of those chocolate, peanut butter, marshmallow things with the bitter undertaste of a low-end artificial sweetener that would shortly be declared a carcinogen—was leaning against my uvula. Not to panic, I calmed myself.

When I tried swallowing again, the glob glued itself to the back of my soft palate. Rose and Selwyn Moscowitz. I coughed hard. Nothing happened. I coughed harder. Zilch. Making hideous glugging sounds that a librarian and several patrons felt obliged to recoil from, I tongued the thing over to my back teeth. To hide my desperate chewing, I rested my jaw on the heels of my hands and covered my mouth. At last, the friction of molars against food generated enough heat to transform the glob from a lump to a liquid, and I was able to swallow.

Moscowitz, Selwyn & Rose. Except in that instant I realized I wasn't out of the woods globwise. Whatever I'd swallowed had congealed again and restuck itself in my esophagus, mid-breastbone vicinity. It seemed to be settling there for life. Or maybe death, because, as my eyes fixed on those two names, a lightning bolt of pain slashed upward from my heart to my jaw.

Talk about psychosomatic, I chuckled to myself, in the superior, humorless way of one who considers herself a summa cum laude graduate of therapy. Except this was genuine pain. Because I knew only half of my medical history, this could be It: the inevitable heart attack brought on by Morris/Moscowitz myocardial infarction genes. And all those years I brooded over cancer and schizophrenia.

Pushing back from the desk, I hauled myself up, or as up as I could manage. I probably looked like Quasimodo in a lavender sweater. But standing, I could drop dead and be noticed instead of quietly decomposing in the chair. My heart rushed on faster and faster, as it tried to make me understand: This is the Big Good-bye. They'd find my ID and call *In Depth* and Gloria Howard would volunteer to track down my father. How would Tatty find out? From Four, whose favorite daily reading was the obituaries? *Hmmm, looks like little Amy died Wednesday.* Would Gloria think to call John and let him know? Would Tatty? Would my father have the brains or the money or even time enough away from Fern to arrange a funeral? Would anyone think to call a rabbi?

I must have stood for three or four minutes, now drenched with sweat, fearing postmortem humiliation as well as death; a librarian filling out the "Dead Body on Premises" form would spot chocolate dribbles and note I'd been sneaking food. My mind went blank at that point until—who knows how many minutes later?—the pain began to abate. The pressure in my chest eased, too. Sixty grams of protein were finally moving.

I sat back down for a few minutes, just in case. I was okay. Psychosomatic. I moved on then, albeit gingerly, up the library's grayed staircase and into yet another research room. Not dead yet. I put my fingers on my wrist and glanced at my watch, but I was too rattled to remember my normal pulse rate.

I checked the shelves, and hefted a book of Kings County residential properties over to a long table. Selly and Rose, I discovered, owned a six-bedroom house on Wakehurst Road. In another book I read: "built 1898." I sat straight and motionless in the spine-hating discomfort of the wooden library chair.

Well, not totally motionless. Apparently, I was compulsively clicking my pen. I knew this because an old guy down the table from me was kind enough to hiss, "Could you ssstop with the pen?" I muttered, "Sorry," but before I could get back to "built 1898," I realized he was still glaring at me. I glared back. He was wearing an orange and brown plaid shirt, the loveliness of which was only enhanced by a bolo tie, that hideous string thing worn by antifeminist senators from the southwest. The bolo's fastener, in the shape of a steer's skull, was larger than the guy's Adam's apple, though smaller than his nose. As I knew he would, Bolo blinked first, then got up from the table and disappeared. I went back to the listings and reread "six bedrooms."

Had the Moscowitzes known about me? My God! All that real estate. All that money! Yet my mother—Phyllis—had turned her back on it and run off to be with Chicky. I waited for an insight into what had made her leave them, and later leave me. Maybe I'd have a genuine epiphany.

Not even an ersatz epiphany. Instead, my old sense of feeling fucked returned. It wasn't that John F. Kennedy, *Malcolm in the Middle* cosmic realization that life is unfair. Cosmic was never my style. As a kid, I'd focused all my anger onto my socks. I had two pairs—one to wear, one to wash out and dry. Sitting in the library, the socks came back. All I could see was the old bathroom sink in Grandma Lil's apartment. Its porcelain was worn off so the area around the drain always looked filthy.

Now that familiar picture joined with a new vision. Split screen. On one side, there I was age ten, tenderly soaping the back of the sock, so that the cat's cradle of cotton threads, all that separated Achilles tendon from sneaker, wouldn't rip. Beside it, the image of another girl's hand—young Phyllis's—trying to yank open a drawer that was almost impossible to open, overstuffed as it was with cashmere socks.

Every time I asked, Grandma Lil told me she didn't have the money for more socks. Nevertheless, she herself was in good shape, having heisted enough sheer and textured panty hose and knee-highs to take care of all the Rockettes. But she couldn't be bothered to lift a third pair of socks for me. Maybe she believed a well-bred young lady ought to steal her own footwear.

Knowing this train of thought would go no place fast, I shoved my notepad into my fanny pack and handed in the real estate records. Outside the library, in all my sweaters, I sat on the nonsmokers' side of the steps and stared at traffic, watching yellow cabs darting in front of buses, daring them to try something. I began wondering how come, closing in on my thirtieth birthday, I'd never before tried to find out whether Phyllis was still alive.

Tatty, had she been there, would have said it had been my fear of finding my mother and discovering she was a whore or an asshole, or even whore + asshole. No, I'd argue. What I'd really feared was not finding her, thus dooming myself to spend the rest of my life on a fruitless quest for Phyllis Morris Moscowitz.

Except, I told myself, that was unlikely. I was a pro. I did this kind of research for a living. The odds were I'd know in weeks, if not days, whether Phyllis was findable. So what had been the big deal? How come I hadn't tried before?

Sitting on the stone steps, my butt went numb with cold and my hands got so icy I stuck them in my armpits. I wound up hugging myself. The one person it would make sense to talk to about all this—John, trained in history, the compleat researcher— was out of my life. We used to speak to each other three or four times a day, the Hey–¿*Qué pasa?* call. One time, on a late afternoon, we'd both said *Bored!* That was when we started having mini–research races. Like who could come up with the most titillating fact about a president's sex life in less than sixty seconds. John won in fourteen with President Buchanan, who was reputed to have been lovers with Senator William R. de Vane King. Even if I couldn't find my mother, John could.

I could talk to Tatty. Her best-friend status should have made her the hands-down choice to confide in. Except I could write the script of our discussion before it occurred. We'd been going back and forth about our mothers since we were fourteen.

Who else to talk to? No one. I hugged myself some more, trying to find comfort in the conventional wisdom that no matter how alone I felt, most of the people in the world had it much worse—losing liberty, losing health, losing family, losing a village with the blast of one bomb. So I wound up not only feeling bereft, but guilty for making such a fuss with my good fortune.

Back inside, I trudged toward the library's telephone book collection. A ray or two of sunshine was sneaking in between an ancient shade and a window sash. Minuscule particles of disintegrating Cheyenne and Montpelier directories, suspended in the room's overbreathed air, twinkled in the brightness. I watched them until a kid who was having a bad dreadlock day handed me the 1970 Brooklyn phone book. Within thirty seconds, there it was. Not merely *Moscowitz, Selwyn, 925 Wakehurst Rd.,* but *Moscowitz, Phyllis.* She'd had her own phone. I waited until the kid whipped it up to find the directories for 1974 through 1980. Only Selwyn. Either Phyllis was dead, hadn't returned post-Chicky, or came home only to leave again, not staying long enough to get her own listing.

I got on a computer and did a reverse address search. By 1990, a family named Baptiste owned the house. In 1990, I'd been at Harvard, a freshman with four pairs of socks. One of them was a lamb's wool that some guy who'd been sleeping with my roommate had left on the floor. After a week of watching those abandoned socks sticking out from under her bed curled like two fat, friendly kittens, I'd picked them up, washed them, and adopted them.

According to what came up on the screen, the Baptiste family still owned the house. A few minutes later, I also discovered 925 Wakehurst in a street-by-street architecture guide to New York City. The listing called the house "a jewel of a Queen Anne. Shingled. Gabled." No photograph. But, God, my mother had lived in a jewel! I ran back to my apartment to shower, then stopped at an ATM. From there I got on the subway, the same Brooklyn-bound Q train I always took to Aunt Linda's.

People accustomed to journalists—politicians, legislators, performers—can be interviewed over the phone. But I assumed the Baptistes, now residing in the jewel, would require a face-to-face meeting if I was to get anything worthwhile. Fine. Face-to-face was my forte. For whatever reason—being short and therefore viewed as nonthreatening, or being someone whose New York accent made people think she had been born into a family unable to afford premium-package cable TV and was therefore an unassuming person—I could almost always get people to talk.

I got off nine stops before Sheepshead Bay and found myself in another Brooklyn, in another world entirely. This was not Aunt Linda and Uncle Sparkyville. This was comfortable country. *Comfortable* was a Grandma Lil word. According to her, refined people didn't talk about money, but if they did, they used *comfortable* for those who were well-off, but not stinking rich. Brooklyn's "comfortable" country was not dot-com-era real estate, as in some ten-thousand-square-foot loft in Soho.

And it was definitely not old money like Tatty's family's endless apartment on Park Avenue. This was a 'hood for successful hardware store owners and pediatricians.

Their homes were grand but solid Victorians, pleased—though not proud—to show themselves under the cold, brilliant blue March sky. As I went right, left, left again to get to Wakehurst, I noted they stood far back from the sidewalks, discreet, but not so distant as to appear snobbish. If you have legitimate business here, they announced silently, you may come up and ring our chimes.

But standing in front of 925 Wakehurst Road I couldn't be discreet. I said, "Holy shit!" and gaped—the whole jaw-dropping, eyes-opening-large business. What a house! Too simple to be called grand, too grand to be charming. Although a part of the facade was obscured by tall evergreens trimmed into large, breastlike mounds, it was clear a huge expanse of front porch must run the length of the house. The entrance was toward the left, but only slightly off, more eye-pleasing than eccentric. However, the door was so deeply shaded by the porch's green-shingled overhang that it was a leap of faith to believe there was a front door. The second floor was in four separate sections of differing heights. The part farthest to the right was a circular tower with three windows, topped by a cone-shaped turret. As a girl my mother could have played Rapunzel Moscowitz.

The house's facade was painted a warm shade equidistant between yellow and white. So were the architectural doodads, such as the scallops of wood running above all the second-floor windows. Two of the second-story sections had a third floor above them, but despite the varying heights of roofs, 925 had a unity, as all were covered with the same color shingles—a green several tones richer and darker than the overhang above the porch.

I did that inhale, exhale, inhale, squaring-of-the-shoulders business that female characters do in movies to show they're feisty or spunky—or some dimpled adjective never applied to men. I felt neither feist nor spunk. My palms were so drippy I kept wiping them on my pants until they looked as though I'd sent only the below-the-knee half to the dry cleaner. I loved this house, but I couldn't approach it.

Why am I scared? I asked myself. Certainly from my days at Ivey onward I had visited friends who lived in much grander homes, so I wasn't afraid of dropping dead from pleasure at the mere sight of a Persian rug. Maybe having always thought of myself as descended from people doomed to shtetls and low-income housing projects—to say nothing of petty crime and grand larceny—I couldn't assimilate the fact that 50 percent of me came from people who, long before I was born, had achieved such material success.

Anyhow, since the feisty/spunky thing was still not working, I trudged up the path, climbed the front steps, and rang the front doorbell. It chimed a complicated series of notes: Mahler, for all I knew. I wanted to run.

"Just a sec," I heard from somewhere deep in the house. Heavy feet clomped down carpeted stairs, across what was probably a wood floor, and to the front door. On either side of the door were long, skinny rectangles, panels of stained glass. I could vaguely make out a pair of eyes peering through an amber-colored petal of what was either a giant chrysanthemum or a zinnia.

"Hi!" I offered my adorable, I-almost-have-dimples smile and held up my *In Depth* credentials to the amber glass. "My name is Amy Lincoln. I'm working on a story."

With luck, the door would open about two inches, naturally with a heavy foot behind it in case I turned out to be an ax murderer. Instead, the door opened wide. A large, middle-aged woman smiled back at me. "Hi!" She was shaped like a packing crate, although a well-groomed one.

"Ms. Baptiste?" I inquired, handing her my ID. She studied it for a couple of seconds. "I'm a journalist."

"Amy Lincoln," she said. "Any relation to you-know-who?"

"Dubious."

"But who knows, right? Anyhow, I'm Judyann Baptiste. Capital J, no space, lowercase ANN. No E. I've heard of . . . What's its name again? Oh, *In Depth*. You work there?" I nodded. "Come on in," she said, and led me through a vestibule into a beige living room. Well, not totally beige. The coffee table was golden oak, a couple of side tables cherry, and the fireplace mantel mahogany. But the rest of the room looked done by a decorator who'd gotten a kickback on a few thousand bolts of beige silk.

I knew I had to say something, so I said: "A beautiful room."

"It's monochromatic," she said. Her voice was softer than she was, with the initial gentleness many heavy women present, unspoken amends for taking up so much space.

"You have lovely taste."

"Thank you. Please, have a seat." She swept her arm, giving me a choice of most of the furniture in the room. While her clothes—camel-colored pants and a beige twinset—also qualified as monochromatic, Judyann Baptiste was more vivid. Her hair and eyes were black, her skin a lovely pale olive, her lips bright red. It was a Mediterranean face that could have come from anywhere from Spain to Syria, though I put my money on Greece. Being a huge fan of any women's mag article or TV show that featured makeovers, I immediately wanted to make her toss out the beige and buy a new wardrobe in jewel colors: ruby, sapphire, emerald.

"Can I offer you anything?" she continued, her voice growing more confident. "I've got a full refrig. Tons of cheeses, berries like you wouldn't believe. Cut-up cantaloupe." I was on her turf now. She smiled, showing an endearing gap between her front teeth. "My husband likes to see a full refrig when he gets home, you know? He opens the door, grabs something Atkins-y, pours himself a glass of wine. I buy those half bottles, because for my money, you should throw out any wine that's more than two days old. More than one day old, if you want the truth. Oh, and you name the diet soda, I've got it. I could start a diet soda museum."

Knowing I'd be suspect if I didn't eat something, I asked for a small piece of cheese and a Diet Coke. Naturally, she came back with a rattan tray with four types of cheese, a fan of crackers, and a one-liter Diet Coke along with two hefty tumblers, one with ice, one without. I loved nurturing women like this, human cornucopias. I bit into a piece of cheddar and wished I'd grown up in this house. Not as a Moscowitz. They'd produced Phyllis. As a Baptiste, though I'd convert to Judaism, which would turn out to be fine with Judyann.

"Great cheddar," I told her. So she wouldn't have time to get a word in edgewise, I added: "I'm working on a piece, and the people who used to own this house—Moscowitz—may have some information that would be useful to me as background."

Her red mouth drooped. "It's not about the house?"

"No. God, would that be a dream assignment." To make sure I stayed in her good graces, I spread some goat cheese on a cracker. Maybe sheep cheese. "Did you ever meet the Moscowitzes?"

"A couple of times. You know how it is. You look at a house once, then you have to go back to make sure you're not reading the kitchen from another house onto this one, or whether the master bath is actually in the bedroom or if you have to go out into the hall, which would not be for me. Oh, and I think Gene—my husband—came another time with the broker, but that was to check the basement. What's the point of making a bid if a place is falling apart from the bottom up?"

"You're right."

"But it was a while ago. Let's see, we've lived here . . . whatever. Fourteen, fifteen years. My husband would know. I always tell him, 'You're math, I'm verbal.'"

"Do you know where the Moscowitzes"—I glanced at my notepad, which I knew was blank—"Rose and Selwyn—moved to?"

"Three guesses, but I'll give you a clue. Florida."

"Do you happen to know where in Florida?"

"I'm pretty sure Boca. But that was before half of New York moved there. People were still calling it Boca Raton."

"Did Mr. Moscowitz retire? I know he was in the bike business."

"Right. He retired. Emphysema, I think." Judyann put her index and middle fingers to her red lips as if she were holding a cigarette. She blew the imaginary smoke out slowly, through pursed lips, as though she herself still missed it.

"Do you have any idea if they're alive?"

"Well, the people next door, the Kleins . . ." she gestured toward the left with her chin ". . . kept in touch. I think they even visited them down there. Now they're in Florida too, but I don't think in Boca. Someplace else." Before she could go on, I got the Kleins' first names, Lawrence and Naomi, although I learned everyone called her Cookie. "But they only moved a year or so ago, so I guess I would have heard something. Cookie loved to talk. Talk, talk, talk. Not nasty gossip. Just— What do they call it? A yenta. Knows everybody's business, tells everybody's business."

"Before we get to what Cookie may have told you, what were your thoughts on the Moscowitzes, the couple of times you met them?"

"Nice. She was tall, on the slim side. A little clothes-horsey. I mean, who wears those cuff kind of bracelets in their own house? Blondish. Receding chin. He was short and dumpy. I remember saying to Gene, 'Can you imagine that guy riding a bike?' Well, I guess he didn't have to ride them, just sell them."

I made a couple of notes just to show how seriously I was taking her opinion, then asked: "What were they like in terms of personality?"

"He was friendly. Like you'd expect from someone who's essentially a salesman. But when it came to dollars and cents, tough. To be fair, my husband's that way too. I was so scared during the negotiations that we wouldn't get the place. I mean, this is my dream house. But at the closing, Selly Moscowitz and Gene were acting like old friends. Both of them probably thought they got the better of the deal."

"And Rose Moscowitz?"

"Smart. Even though she had a college degree, she told me she never stopped taking courses. At Brooklyn College and LIU. Philosophy, Italian. Or maybe Italian philosophy." She shrugged. "I guess Italians have philosophers." Petrarch came to mind, quickly followed by Pico and Pomponazzi, but I shrugged back the impulse to comment. "She was okay. I mean, not the warmest person in the world, but not not-nice. More than polite. Maybe it's that she really didn't have much of a personality. Oh, I think she may have had some work." She pointed both index fingers toward her chest. "I don't get it. She should have gotten a chin implant, not breasts. They looked so unnatural. And if she was so philosophical, why would she get plastic surgery? She had a modelish figure. It looked like she'd glued a couple of tennis balls to her chest. Well, bigger than tennis balls, but I'm not much for sports."

I opened the Diet Coke and poured it into the no-ice glass. "Do you remember if you ever got a forwarding address for them? Or a number to call if you had any questions about . . . I don't know. Air-conditioning or the plumbing?"

"Do you want some lemon or lime with your soda?" Judyann inquired.

"No thanks."

I was going to push her about a forwarding address again, but she stood, a somewhat slow but not undignified process: "Give me a couple of minutes," she said. "I wrote something somewhere. . . ." In a moment, she was out of the living room, climbing the stairs. I wanted to yell at her: *Hey, are you crazy, leaving a total stranger alone in your house?* Instead, I leaned forward and stared at the fireplace. The ceiling was incredibly high, so I figured the fireplace had to be nine or ten feet tall. The mahogany mantel was carved with flowers and birds and held up by columns. Above the ledge of the mantel, more carving framed a huge mirror. At the very top was a cornice with a long-necked bird—egret, heron, crane, whatever—rising, as if to fly off to Manhattan.

It was so easy to picture myself in this house. On a school snow day, stretched out before a fire, reading, now and then dipping into a bowl of popcorn. What had been so awful in this wonderful house to make Phyllis take flight, get into a stolen car, and drive off with a guy like my father? Sexual or emotional abuse, the contemporary justification for all antisocial acts in B movies and B-minus fiction? Had she been a reckless kid? An incorrigible? Clearly she'd savored Chicky's two-bit criminality. She'd enjoyed hanging with the mob guys he knew. And if he was telling the truth about her stealing the diamond ring and then setting him up to take the rap, then she was also a considerably more effective criminal than he was.

"I've got it!" Judyann called out. As I'd flown off to Moscowitzland, leaving the Baptistes behind, I tried not to look startled by her sudden reappearance. She waved a black-and-white notebook. "Everything about the house, including . . ." She sat beside me, riffled through the pages, and handed it to me. ROSE MOSCOWITZ, it said, all in tiny capitals so perfect they didn't seem handwritten. An address on Orchid Lake Drive in Boca Raton. A phone number.

I copied them down. "Thank you," I said. "This is a huge help. Just one more question." She nodded, happy to keep me there. She was either very friendly or very lonely: maybe both. "When you were looking at the house—When was that again?"

She chewed her bottom lip. Some red lipstick stuck to the bottom of her two front teeth. "Let me see. Nineteen eighty-something. My youngest, Karen . . . She's calling herself Kerri now, K-E-R-R-I. She went off to college in September of eighty-seven. Everyone thought we were crazy, buying this house after our kids were grown, but we loved it, so we said, 'Why not?' We started looking in the summer of eighty-seven, which means we bought it in . . . I think April of eighty-eight."

I calculated: If Phyllis had run off in 1972 at age sixteen, then she'd been born in 1956, which would make her thirty-two when the Baptistes bought the house. Well, it was worth a shot. "The Moscowitzes had a daughter. Phyllis, I think her name was. When you were here, looking at the house, did you happen to meet her?"

Judyann shook her head. "No. I don't think they ever mentioned a daughter." I clicked my pen and the point retracted. "That was why it was so funny."

"What?"

"About three or four years ago, the doorbell rings, and it's this woman. She says she was looking at her roots or for her roots or whatever and that she was the Moscowitzes' daughter."

"Phyllis?"

She shook her head.

"Veronica?"

"I don't remember. Her last name wasn't Moscowitz anymore, but I have no idea what it was. I invited her in. It was a weekend. Gene was off playing golf. Anyhow, I gave her the tour of the house."

"Did she seem familiar with it?" I asked.

"Oh, completely. It's funny. She even showed me—well, there actually is a secret staircase that you get to through the linen closet. It goes down into this little butler's pantry off the kitchen. I told her I never knew it existed. She said her parents never knew either. She and her friends found it one night."

I clicked the pen again, but couldn't think of anything to write. My mother must have been in her early forties then, when she rang the Baptistes' doorbell. "What did she look like?" I asked.

"Well, she wasn't tall like her mother. Petite, actually. Pretty. Wearing a shawl or something. A little artsy but very presentable. More than that, actually. Uh, red hair, what they call Titian, that dark red. I really can't remember anything more about her."

"Did she seem intelligent?"

"Yes. She reminded me of Rose Moscowitz in that way. I mean, they didn't look that much like mother-daughter. Except they were both a little too serious. Even when the daughter showed me the staircase, I remember, there wasn't any sign of . . . I don't know. Mischief."

"Did she say where she lived?" I asked softly.

"One of the suburbs," Judyann said. "I'm . . . I guess about seventy-five-percent sure. Maybe she didn't say it, but I have that distinct impression."

"A suburb of New York?"

"A suburb of New York."

Chapter Eight

I squinted, but still couldn't find Tatty in Blue J's. The place was an ersatz olde neighborhood saloon in the East Seventies. A brass foot rail ran along the long, dark bar, although it looked more like aluminum tubing in the dim lighting. The bar itself, the few tables, and the four booths in back were a blackened wood that had been either tap-danced on or distressed—a process said to involve beating wood with chains to give it age and character. The place had opened one balmy June night in 1990, just in time for a new generation of boarding- and day-school teenagers with fake IDs to claim it as their own. Outsiders called the place a preppy bar. Whatever the description, it was a place where privileged New Yorkers could get bagged and vomit with their own kind.

The same crowd was still there, only older, minus those who had either gotten married or serious. After the breakup of each of her marriages, Tatty headed right back to Blue J's and took up right where she had left off. All the old crowd did. In her case, it meant running into one or both of her ex-husbands whenever she walked in, but that potentially sticky circumstance was handled gracefully, if not painlessly.

Among the newly divorced, Blue J etiquette dictated standing at least five feet from a former spouse and going about your business as if he or she were not there. About a half year after signing the final papers, it was expected that the acrimony had diminished sufficiently that you both could manage the private school salute: jaw dropping in feigned wonderment/delight along with a How-are-you flapping of four fingers (thumb at a ninety-degree angle, at ear-canal level). The entire greeting could be executed in not more than a single second.

When I finally found Tatty, I asked, "Can you tell me why you claim to be supercautious about your drinking—"

"Hello."

"Hello. Anyway, your claim—"

"I don't claim," she replied. "I *am*."

"For once in your life will you let me get a complete sentence out?"

"You just did."

"Tell me why, Tatty, if you don't want to wind up like, you know, your parents—"

"You mean alcoholic?"

"Why is it that you're here four or five times a week?"

"It's where everybody goes. I have one, repeat *one*, Lillet au citron, see what's new, and then go on to wherever I'm going."

"But if you want to avoid the sort of people who puke on their coral suede Tod driving moccasins and make idiot conversation, why come here? Don't you think it's an odd coincidence that you, Ms. Almost-Temperance, met both husbands in a bar?"

"You know that Bobby was in my dance class when I was

eleven. And Roy was only tending bar here to support himself while he wrote his screenplay."

"Tatty, they both were serious drinkers."

"Amy, they could have a few drinks, but they weren't alcoholics. Trust me, I know better than anyone what alcoholics look like and neither of them was it."

I had never liked Blue J's and went there only to meet Tatty. I'd always worked three part-time jobs during the academic year—the usual: restocking library shelves, waitressing. For three summers I was a flagman with a Boston road construction company that paid union wages. Whenever I came back to New York, spending money on margaritas was not on my to-do list.

Also, early on, I recognized that the people in Manhattan I wanted to be with weren't frittering away their intellectual and financial resources at a bar, chugging Sam Adams or sipping martinis, attempting wit while describing their hangovers from the previous night's drinking.

I glanced around. From the end of their adolescences to the beginning of their thirties, Blue J loyalists only set one foot in the outside world. The other remained glued to the brass rail. No job, no lover, no cause could bring them the satisfaction of being one of the chosen who got the flapping fingers, the two-cheek kisses, the *I cannot believe how fucking fabulous you look* at Blue J's.

The only time half of them did anything—say, went to the theater or a ball game—was if a play or team was so hot that tickets were unavailable. Then they simply shelled out quadruple to a scalper. Charities got money, never time. I couldn't understand why their contempt for the city's real life got to me: maybe because I'd worked so damned hard to be something and the Blue J's clique acted as though being something was nothing.

Also, whenever I walked into the place—at age seventeen on

Christmas break from Ivey or now, at twenty-nine—I always got depressed by the women. At least half of them were tall and blond. While I was there, they made me wish I were too. I guess I could have been blond, if not tall, but even the slight temptation to be like them shamed me. Blue J's was something out of a horror movie in which aliens sucked out your essence and turned you into them. Tatty, meanwhile, patted the undercurled ends of her sprayed-stiff, dark blond hairdo. Being old money allowed her to use visible hair spray. Nouveau riche blond hair had to flutter—if not fly—in a breeze.

The only advantage I could see to Blue J's was that once you waved your hellos, you and the person you'd go in there to see could hang at a table or a booth way in the back of a long, rail-road-train-like space and talk freely, protected by the drone of other conversations, wrapped in darkness.

We sat at a table whose top was the size of the average apple pie. "Why are you in such a sucky mood?" Tatty demanded.

"My mother."

"Your mother?"

For the next hour or so, I filled her in about my research on the Moscowitzes and my interview with Judyann Baptiste. "You're getting someplace!" she exclaimed after I'd finished. "Then how come you're acting as if your best friend died? I'm still here."

"You were the one who always said trying to find my mother was a lousy idea."

"It *was* lousy when the mere thought of it put you in a snit for two weeks. But now I'm for it because you're for it. You're *engagé*. Not that I can tell it from the way you're acting. What you're doing is stuff that arises out of . . . whatever. An emptiness. It's sort of brave. Or maybe it's that you simply have to know one way or the other." She paused for a minute and toyed with a Plexiglass frame that held a card featuring dreadful cock-tails in garish hues, including blue, that nobody had ever ordered. The card's colors had dimmed over the years, not from exposure to light, for there was almost none, but because no one had ever bothered to wipe the thousands of accumulated finger-prints off the Plexi. "So with all this fabulously interesting stuff you're doing, why are you being so snappy?"

"Do you mean snappish?" I asked. "Like irritable?"

"Irritable? Either you have the world's worst PMS or it's still all about John."

"It is not about John. And PMS-wise, all I ever do is bloat up slightly. Two pounds' worth, tops, and you know it."

"You're lying about either PMS or John, but that's not my business." We sat in the noisy silence of the bar. "You're the one who always says talking helps," she tried.

"Oh, one thing more about my grandparents," I said. "Unless you'd rather discuss my bloating."

"Go ahead." Her shrug of indifference wasn't convincing.

"No Selwyn or Rose Moscowitz came up on the websites of either the *Sun-Sentinel* or the *Palm Beach Post*. Those are the two newspapers I figured would cover the Boca area. So I made a couple of calls down there to see if they had anything in their library."

"And?"

"And I spoke with two editors, did the professional courtesy waltz."

"What's that?"

"I know how busy you must be but I'd appreciate it if you could possibly . . . blah, blah, blah."

"Did either of them ever hear of *In Depth*?"

"Yes, Tatty." Because it wasn't about food or fashion, Tatty never read the magazine, although she subscribed and looked at my byline. Because she had no interest in it, she assumed nobody else did either and thought of it as an obscure periodical with a national circulation of about four hundred. "The *Sun-Sentinel* guy found something," I added.

"What?"

"Selwyn Moscowitz died six years ago."

"I'm sorry," Tatty said politely. Then she lifted the slice of lemon garnishing her glass and licked it. "The only thing bad about Blue J's is they use such ooky old lemons. Did you feel at all bad?"

"About the late Selwyn?" She nodded and put the garnish on the side of her cocktail napkin, then folded the napkin over it so we could be spared the lemon's decrepitude. "No, I don't feel bad about him. How can I feel bad about losing a grandfather I never knew I had?"

"Everybody has grandfathers," she replied patiently. In the fifteen years of our friendship, the notion had flitted through my mind once or twice that Tatty was dumb rather than droll. This was the third time.

"Everybody does have grandfathers," I agreed. "And everybody has a mother. Do you want to know what the six-year-old obit said about mine?"

"No. I deeply don't give a shit." She made a face as though she were still tasting the lemon, then said: "Of course I want to know!"

"It says, 'He leaves his beloved wife, Rose, and a daughter, Véronique.'"

The times I wasn't furious at Grandma Lil, or merely wishing her invisible and inaudible, I pitied her so much it was almost an ache. Here was a woman who was so conspicuous about denying what she was—brunette, working class, undereducated, Jewish, uncultured—that she hadn't a single friend among brunettes, working-class people, et cetera. That might have been bearable, or even a cause for celebration for someone like her, except among those she was trying to emulate, she was considered at best a joke, and at worst, beneath notice.

So whom did she have? Her husband, Grandpa George, a lox and sturgeon slicer at Ike & Myron's Smoked Fish Specialties, stopped embarrassing her when, at forty-two, he crossed against a red light and got hit by an M21 bus, which killed him instantly. Her son, Chicky, part-time grease monkey turned felon, couldn't even manage to get incarcerated at one of those nice, golf-course-y federal prisons where the better class of offenders go. Her daughter, Linda, had curved, two-inch nails polished Pussy Pink and a fireman husband who was, in Grandma Lil's eyes, unforgivably swarthy.

All my grandmother had was me. Yet early on, I understood I was not just a burden, but a disappointment. The only story she could ever come up with about my early years was one of vanquished hopes. "You were the cutest baby. You could have been beautiful, except you stayed almost bald." She'd elongate *baaaaaald* until about two seconds before I could act on my desire to strangle her. "Once your so-called mother ran off with—do I have to tell you?—the lowest of the low, I put a little hat on you every time I took you out so no one could see. They'd say, Oh, she's so pretty! Except you used to pull the hat off all the time. You should have seen their faces. Shocked! Then, I swear to God, you'd start to cry."

Still, nights when she came home exhausted after waxing the ladies at Beauté and stealing dinner, I felt obliged to keep her company. By age six or seven, I probably intuited the reason for her desperate loneliness was that no one wanted to listen to her.

For Grandma Lil, there was no reading romance novels or fil-ing supermarket coupons, all those other avocations of ordinary people. What she did do was obsess about Beauté's clientele, reading gossip columns and wedding announcements as well as committing to memory the photographs of their beautiful rooms and the personality profiles she found in tony magazines. Grandma Lil wanted to learn about what her idols wore to the opera, never what they listened to. *So Amy, you know what Mrs. Andrews's whole name is? Wait, let me try to remember. Uh . . . Okay: Leslie Jensen Arundel Andrews. Every one of those names is Old Society. You know how I found out?*

How, Grandma? In moments like this, she got so enthused she forgot her little rule, the one she recited to me at least once a day: *Back straight! Chin up, up, up!* She would hunch over, her neck thrust forward with eagerness. She reminded me of the sea turtle in the Central Park Zoo, sticking his head out of his shell, greedy for some exciting turtle business that never would hap-pen for him.

I overheard, because she was laughing about it. She was talk-ing to Elizabeth Stoll—you know, Mrs. Robert Stoll—how come she couldn't have her whole name printed on her informals—that's writing paper for, like, not wedding invitations. Little notes. Not letters.

So all the times I wanted to scream at Grandma Lil that she was repulsive or pathetic, I kept silent. I knew if I cut myself off from her, she would have nobody. She'd probably go mad and I'd wind up in foster care with a Hasidic family in Williams-burgh with eighteen children and they'd rename me something hideous, like Schmeel or Kroogele.

Tatty and I left Blue J's and had dinner at an Indian restau-rant. This was an off night; the chicken tandoori looked like an illustration of dermatitis. I came home feeling, as I sometimes did after being with her, starved for reality. I turned on my computer and read *Le Monde, ABC* of Madrid, the *Times of India,* and the *Irish Independent* online, and got that sitting-in-a-café worldly feeling, which, from experience, I knew would be gone by morning. Still, if anyone wanted to talk to me about Iraq for the next twenty-four hours, I wouldn't sound quite like the American provincial I was.

By the time I got into bed I'd succeeded in exhausting myself to the point where I was certain sleep was seconds away. But like all the other nights in the week, my head hitting the pillow was the cue for me to start worrying about what would happen if I never met anyone else who was right for me, anyone else I really wanted to go to bed with. If John hadn't been the most technically proficient guy I'd ever slept with, he definitely was the most passionate, and that brought it out in me. The whole time we'd been together I'd totally believed it was I who made him wild, that it wouldn't be the same for him with anybody else, either.

So as to not think about him, I turned off the lamp and decided to dwell on something I at least could do something about—the search for my mother. The first thing that popped into my mind was a question: How come Grandma Lil had hated Phyllis right from the start? It didn't make sense.

Okay, my grandma knew Chicky wasn't any prize, but at least he'd brought home a girl from a well-off family, someone academically competent—if that talk about a 97-percent average in high school was true. Here was Phyllis, whose mother was always in the market for education. Chances were, then, no matter what Phyllis thought about her own mother, she most likely hadn't been brought up to sound like a dese-and-dose, gum-cracking slut. Yet Grandma Lil had always vowed, *I couldn't stand her from Day One, that little* . . . Usually her voice would

157

trail off, but when she was particularly riled up or tired, she'd say *that little whore.*

Or did it take one to know one? Not a whore. A phony, someone trying to be something else and failing. Did my mother see through Grandma Lil faster than the two seconds it generally took most people? And did my grandma somehow comprehend that my mother wasn't some slut Chicky had picked up, but a faux slut, a girl from a background of tasteful bat mitzvahs, summer camp in Maine, bookshelves overburdened with hardcovers?

If Phyllis had failed at slutdom, was she or was she not now succeeding as Véronique?

Grampy Selwyn's obit didn't say where he was headed. A shady spot in a cemetery? An urn with a frieze of palm trees? I spent most of the day making phone calls. There were a multitude of Moscowitzes in south Florida, and for some reason, many of the places I called had them buried or entombed neither chronologically nor alphabetically by first names, but by some whimsical process I could not discern.

I was offered a Sherwin Moscowitz as well as a couple of Seymours in the Boca area, but it wasn't until four in the afternoon that I finally located him at, or in, Menorah Gardens in West Palm Beach. I wasn't sure if this move from Boca was upward, downward, or sideways on the social mobility scale. It was pretty much a wasted day, because Véronique was not the one who had paid for perpetual care of the grave site; it was Rose. However, my new friend Dawn in the Menorah Gardens office gave me my grandmother's address and phone number, and said she'd buy a copy of *In Depth.* I told her I'd send her one.

In the evening, I walked across the park and over to John's

neighborhood, West End Avenue, then up to Ninety-seventh for a dinner date I'd made weeks earlier. Erin Leung had been a friend at P.S. 97, though not a close one. Still, she was one of the few kids I'd hung out with back then who'd gone on to complete college. She'd gotten a graduate degree in math from the University of Maryland and now performed arcane manipulations of Asian stock indices for Citibank. She'd also become a total foodie, i.e., a person who thinks green cardamom is a subject for conversation.

The chances of getting a good meal at Erin's were fifty-fifty. It could be something elegant and delicious featuring shredded duck, or something horrifying based on the latest food fad. One year it was a vertical pile of frisée, smoked cheeses with a vague aroma of dead protoplasm, and roasted tomatoes. Another time it was some sort of lilliputian crab you were supposed to eat, carapace and all; I might as well have been chewing a fish-scented fingernail, although it wasn't quite that appealing.

This time, I smelled something garlicky and good. I rang the doorbell feeling hopeful. And indeed, Erin informed her five friends gathered for dinner that Neapolitan cuisine was making a really, really huge comeback. We had pasta and potato soup, and a meat dish I liked until I learned it was fried rabbit. We sat around the table, arguing about the war until ten-thirty. The three guys there, all single, were about as enticing as the fried rabbit. I didn't get all choked up saying good-bye.

With all the people I knew, from the projects through Ivey-Rush, Harvard, Columbia, and work, I could spend all the nights of my life having evenings like this. Little suppers in apartments and, as one or two of us got not only older but richer, town houses. Dinners à deux at restaurants with something low and tight to display cleavage and booberage. Or I could go to a play or concert or movie, with or without company.

I stopped to get some gum to get the remnants of rabbit out of my teeth, and walked home, not through the park.

The first thing I did each night when I got back to my apartment was call my voice mail, just in case someone had phoned in the fifteen minutes between the last check and turning the deadbolt on the door. Being a control freak, I had different venues for different phone tasks. Calls to Tatty, which tended to be late and long, were made while I was in the bathtub, with handheld between shoulder and chin, until the skin on my fingers started to pucker. Calls from her were received on my couch, or rather, the apartment's owner's couch➔bed, as were calls to and from other friends, regardless of gender or sexual preferences.

I talked to guys I was going out with lying back, my legs draped over the arm of the couch, unless I knew the relationship was doomed, in which case I sat on a pretty wood chair carved for slim-hipped people, which the owner had bought on a trip to Sri Lanka in his *Christian Science Monitor* days.

John was in his own category. Our conversations were under the covers, no matter what the topic, from phone sex to the clearly unromantic, like arguing over whether Bush's religiosity was profound or politically expedient.

Picking up my phone messages, however, had a business aspect to it, so I adapted a quasi-business posture, sitting on the edge of the couch and leaning sideways to write. I kept a pad and pen on top of a chest the owner used as an end table. Tatty had warned me the piece was antique, probably Korean, and to keep my soda cans off it. Anyhow, I made my call for my messages, expecting the recording to announce: *You have no new messages in your mailbox.*

Instead, I heard a familiar male voice say, "Hey, Amy." My God! I was so startled I slid off the edge of the couch. That sounds comical. It was not. As I went down, my side smashed into the antique chest. An instant afterward, the bottom of my spine slammed onto the floor with a bang that traveled from vertebra to vertebra until it resonated—*Boing! Boing!*—in my skull. Slowly, I touched my side to see if there was any blood, at the same time trying to catch the breath that departs with a sudden blow.

All I'd heard was "Hey, Amy," and then I'd dropped the phone. I tried to reach for it, but recoiled when the pain stabbed me again. With desperation, I drew back the phone with my foot. I screamed as the pain in my side sliced all the way to my center. Then I replayed the message.

The voice continued: "I had a meeting with the lawyer you sent me to, that Ms. Maller. She was so nice. She told me—" Oh. The physical hurt and the realization I'd sustained injury over Freddy Carrasco, not John Orenstein, made me groan, one of those terrible *aaargh!* sounds villains in comic books make when they get their just desserts. I touched my side again. No blood. "—some interesting stuff about, you know, about proving paternity. Give me a call if you get the chance. I'm in for the night and I'll be up till, God, two, three a.m. Otherwise, I'll leave this message at *In Depth,* too. Thanks." Then he gave me his number. As I dialed it, I tried getting up, but it didn't seem like such a great idea. So I stayed on the floor.

"You wouldn't believe how nice she was," Freddy began. "I mean, tea, coffee, mineral water—sparkling or still. I was so glad I wore a tie and jacket, because this is an office that never heard about dress-down Fridays. Or dress-down, period. I told her I could pay her something, maybe not her usual rates, but she just shook her head, like *Totally out of the question.*"

"Nice," I managed to say. "Did she have any advice?"

"Basically, there are a couple of ways you can make someone take a test to check DNA for paternity, even if he doesn't want to. If there's some written record that there was a connection between your mother and him. So I sat there, thinking and thinking." Meanwhile, I was thinking that when I touched my side, it was so painful that I could be bleeding internally. "I told Ms. Maller I doubted it. On the other hand, I never threw out my mother's stuff. How can you could throw someone's existence into a couple of Hefty bags? I guess after I have kids and die, they won't want to pay the fees at the ministorage place for a grandmother they never met."

"Uh-huh."

"So where was I? Oh, my mother's stuff. My girlfriend and I are going to go through every single one of my mother's papers over the weekend—or as long as it takes."

"Good."

"Except who knows if there was anything incriminating? My guess is, my father's father, when he heard about my mother being pregnant and all, he probably went straight to a lawyer."

"Forget probably," I told Freddy. I tried to shift my position, but that was too hard. Even breathing required concentration because inhalation hurt so much.

"So the lawyer would have told my grandfather not to put anything into writing, and he would have warned my father not to either."

"But if Thom Bowles is your father, he might have written something to your mother before she became pregnant." I recalled the phrase *contemporaneous notes and documents* from the Clinton investigation, but didn't have the energy to remind Freddy about it. Plus this was out of my hands now. Freddy was smart. Also, he now had a smart lawyer. I went on: "You said

Mickey Maller mentioned something about there being a couple of ways to go about—"

"Right. She told me that if I could prove my father provided for my support in any way—or possibly my grandfather—she wanted to look that up. So if there's some bank record somewhere with a check from William Bryson Bowles or Thomas Bowles to Nina Carrasco, I may be in good shape." I didn't have the heart to tell him chances were dubious to nil that a bank would keep routine records for twenty-one years. "I told Ms. Maller if I find anything, or even if not, I'd like for her to call the senator's lawyer to ask for a DNA test. I mean, I checked out her credentials: Vassar and NYU Law School. A class act. I can't imagine anyone thinking, *Hey, this is a veiled threat of blackmail* or something if she makes the call. And you know what? I think she was relieved I wanted her to do it, because that showed I wasn't trying to extort money, and I wasn't a crazy stalker."

It took a few seconds before I could say "Right" or "Good thinking" or whatever I finally said. I tried to come up with a way to extend the conversation so I wouldn't have to say goodbye. I felt scared. Phobiawise, after elevator fear, my number-two terror was dying alone, unable to do anything. Whenever I was in the mood to torment myself, I'd imagine choking to death on a piece of take-out dim sum. Or it could be blood pressure: It was low–normal, except it would plummet so much from the hot bath in which I was unwinding that I'd faint and— *glub, glub*—drown.

So it was predictable that I'd begin thinking if I had a broken rib it would pierce my heart or lung. Maybe I should just say, *Hey, Freddy, I fell and hurt my side and am having trouble getting up.* He might say, *Why don't you call 911?* Or maybe, *Oh, too bad. Gotta run.* Would he think I was some old lady, an almost thirty-year-old trying to lure him out in the night? Or would he feel guilty the rest of his life after reading my obit—providing someone remembered to phone it in to the *Times*—because I'd said something about having gotten hurt and he did nothing?

"Freddy, let me know what happens."

"Sure. And Amy, thank you again. No matter how this turns out, I know you could have kept your distance, and I'll always be grateful you saw your way to help me."

Once I hung up, I was able to haul myself up to a sitting position and then relied on my legs to get me standing. Between boarding school soccer, running in the park every day, and walking the two and a half miles from home to work and back again, I was a woman of iron calves and steel quads. I washed up, said my prayers, and got into bed, only to start a raging debate with myself: Was this pure hypochondria? If I went to the emergency room, would the triage nurse look at me with the expressionless contempt a whiner gets from medical professionals? If I stayed home, even if the broken rib missed my heart, could it have stabbed my abdominal aorta and make me bleed to death internally, like the guy who wrote *Rent*?

My usual cure for this particular brand of craziness was reading. Anything. Mark Twain short stories would divert me, as could back issues of *The Nation* or my collection of take-out menus. But lying there in bed, unable to turn and switch on the lamp, I decided to think about Freddy, mainly because I knew his hunt for his father had been the start of my search for my mother. For me, the night I'd seen him confront Thom Bowles was the equivalent of the assassination of the Archduke Franz Ferdinand in Sarajevo, the impetus for big-time action in my life that almost certainly would have happened anyway.

I'd taken the phone into bed in case I changed my mind and decided to give 911 a chance to save my life. It was late now, nearly eleven.

I tried to think of more parallels between Freddy Carrasco and me. But I hurt too much to concentrate, too much to even consider getting up and taking a couple of the pain pills I'd been saving since a root canal about three years earlier, although they'd probably degraded and would more likely give me diarrhea than relief.

And then I made a call. As I pressed the two numbers on my speed dial, I told myself, *You'll rue the day, asshole.*

"Hello." John's voice was clear and I thought, *Well, at least he wasn't expecting a phone-sex call.*

"Hi," I said. "It's—"

"How are you, Amy?"

"I'm okay. I just wanted to know how you were doing."

"I'm okay too."

"Good." I suppose I was waiting for an involuntary sob, then him saying, *It's . . . oh God, Amy, it's so lonely without you.* But if he was sobbing, he had his hand over the mouthpiece. I realized this second could grow into the Mother of All Awkward Silences, so I quickly added: "I've been busy doing some research lately."

"Uh-huh," he said, without any inflection. It did not sound like a lonely voice.

"The research has nothing to do with work." I waited, but got nothing. "I've been looking for my mother."

"Wow." A genuine *wow.* I smiled to myself. "Is there something I could do to help?" he asked.

"Not right now," I said. "If there is, I'll let you know."

"Good."

"John, can we talk? I mean, get together and talk?"

He took a deep breath and I told myself, *This isn't a good sign,* but then immediately went into self-protective mode and thought, *Well, he's got to consider it for a minute.* "Amy, I don't think it's a good idea."

"Why not?"

"Because whatever differences of—I don't know—philosophy, temperament, you and I have aren't going to change."

"You're not going to start with that business of me taking one step back every time—"

John cut me off. Quietly, without a hint of anger. "I think we're two good people who have so much in common but who happen not to be able to work as a couple. It was hard enough breaking up, breaking away from each other once. It would be worse if we tried it again." I wanted to tell him about how I'd hurt myself, sliding off the couch trying to get to that voice I believed had been his, but he said, "I wish you all the luck in the world looking for your mother. I hope it turns out well, happy for you, happy for her. And if there's any way I can help you with that research, please let me know."

"But otherwise . . . ?" I asked.

"What would seeing each other again do, except to start up the whole miserable breaking-up process again?"

"What would it do, John?"

"Right."

I couldn't come up with anything, so I just said good-bye. Then I managed to get up to take the pain pills.

Chapter Nine

When I awoke around six the next morning, I noticed two things: the pain was worse, and about one square foot of my left side was magenta. Also, I was hungry. Naturally, after dispatching a container of vanilla yogurt and half a navel orange, I pictured a surgeon talking over my near-dead body: *I have to operate. Pray she didn't eat or drink anything in the last twenty-four hours.*

Nevertheless, with a peach Snapple so I wouldn't have to drink from an emergency-room water fountain and a book of the Lewis and Clark journals for company, I took a cab to the nearest hospital, one of those places the sick rich favor, with private rooms featuring all-day/all-night snack service and phones with data ports.

No doubt they had a secret emergency room for the wealthy; I would have to ask Tatty. The ER waiting room I was in was decorated in the Soviet gulag style, what with a dead clock, its face veiled by shattered glass, a dying ficus with brown-edged, dust-coated leaves, and brown plastic chairs on rust-pocked metal legs. The TV was stuck on an in-house channel that kept rerunning a tape entitled "Neurocutaneous Syndromes."

The usual *New York, Crossroads of the World* types crowded in on foot or stretcher. Stabbings seemed to be mid-Manhattan's crime of choice. There were also gunshot wounds, convulsions, asthma and heart attacks, a carbon monoxide poisoning, a couple of attempted suicides, and assorted fits and fractures. Almost all the victims were accompanied by relatives and friends in various stages of hysteria and early morning dishabille, or by weary cops.

They were all triaged over me, so after three hours, I was more than halfway through the Lewis and Clark book, up to June 1805. I read a Meriwether Lewis journal entry twice: "When sun began to shine today, these birds appeared to be very gay and sang most enchantingly. I observed among them the brown thrush, robin, turtledove, linnet, goldfinch, the large and small blackbird, wren, and several other birds of less note."

I closed the book, then my eyes. The sweet echo of bird tweeting faded, only to be replaced by doubts over the usefulness of a life spent explicating Democrats' critiques of Republicans' fiscal follies. I don't know whether I doubted for seconds or minutes, but when I heard "Lincoln!" barked out, I stood automatically. As was invariably the case, several people glanced about, but not seeing a man in a stovepipe hat, went back to what they'd been doing.

An hour and several X-rays later, the emergency-room doctor corralled a meandering orthopedist, who took me into yet another vertical coffin of an examining room. He said, "Nice job," as he checked out the giant bruise on my side, which was darkening to purple. He poked at me for a while, then turned away to study the backlit film. "Three broken ribs," he finally said, a little too cheerfully for my taste.

"Cracked or actually broken?"

"Oh, definitely broken." He pointed to some pale, blurry streaks on the X-ray he seemed to believe were ribs. "See?" he asked.

"No."

"Here, here, and here." He poked his index finger toward the X-ray three times.

"Okay." Since I couldn't imagine why he would make something like that up, I took his word for it. "Do I have to get taped up?"

He shook his head. "No. We used to do that, but the constriction kept patients from taking deep breaths and coughing—which can lead to pneumonia. Time will do it. It's the best healer."

"What kind of time are we talking about?"

Shea D'Alessandro, M.D., as his name tag read, gave one of those manly bisyllabic chuckles—*hur, hur.* "You're an impatient patient," he observed. By the time I realized he expected a smile in response to his doctor drollery, he was writing something in my file. Just to have something to do, I retied the frayed white strings on the blue hospital gown and watched him.

Shea D'A appeared the flawless product of an Irish-Italian intermarriage, what with his eyes of choir boy blue, black crooner hair, and inverted triangle physique. I did my reflexive check. Loose slacks, ergo no detectable dick. No wedding ring. Ninety-seven percent likelihood heterosexual. On the down side, he was older, in the neighborhood of forty-five, used the kind of hair gel that retained visible comb tracks, and was acutely aware of his own desirability. "So, Amy Lincoln, what do you do when you're not breaking ribs?"

"I'm a journalist."

"Really?"

"Why 'really'? Do patients routinely claim to be journalists?" He did his double chuckle again and I immediately regretted not having given a direct answer. I always felt resentful during small talk with significantly cute guys who viewed their flirtation as their precious gift to you. Yet I always responded with some form of girlish gratitude, which for me usually meant a mildly sardonic remark. Plus I guessed Shea D'A's interest in me was minimal: He was probably one of those newly divorced men who needed to test what a hot ticket he was with every woman he met. Anyway, sitting upright on the examining table with my feet dangling was starting to strain my back, but whenever I slumped to relieve the discomfort, a bolt of pain went through my ribs. "I work for a newsmagazine," I snapped. He waited. "*In Depth*."

"You're kidding!" His long black lashes did a genuine *wow* blink. "I'm a subscriber!"

"Good." Meeting subscribers was usually disappointing. Most had messy hair and seemed the sort who'd memorized the periodic table for the fun of it while in high school and now liked to test themselves . . . *scandium, titanium, vanadium* . . . at cocktail parties.

"What do you do when you're not working, Amy Lincoln?"

First of all, I hated to be called Amy Lincoln. Okay, I understood the *In Depth* business sparked his interest, as well as his not wanting to call me Ms. Lincoln because the formality would undercut his perfectly pitched cool. I didn't care. Admittedly, being almost thirty and having no man in my life, I should have cared. But I'd never been able to stand guys, handsome or froggy, who posed routine questions—*Where did you go to school?*—in a smarmy tone, as if the real question they were asking was, *Do you like to fuck standing up while eating egg salad?*

Second, I was finding it difficult to chat with a stranger who had already gone eyeball to eyeball with my breasts. Third, I was never much for older guys who invariably made a huge deal over sex but really only wanted it every other night; fourth, he was wearing a double-breasted suit; and fifth, the pain was getting worse. Mostly, though, I was sick at heart for being such a fool as to have called John.

"Hmmm?" he prompted me, but I couldn't recall about what. "Flaked out?" he inquired with a tolerant smile. "Hospitals do that to people. I was asking what you did when you weren't working."

"I mostly hang out with my boyfriend," I said, and offered him a tolerant smile back.

Naturally, three hours and two Percocet later, it occurred to me I should regret having blown off Shea D'A. Among women, it is an article of faith that after the end of a relationship, especially when you are the dumpee, getting back into circulation is critical. Smile at men in Starbucks. Go to ball games. Call friends and relatives and plead, *Fix me up*.

Except blind dates never worked for me.

From my experience, I knew if I asked Tatty, I'd wind up with some ignoramus who'd ripped out a library in an apartment he'd just bought to make way for a plasma TV and his collection of model fighter jets. From college friends I'd get likable-on-first-date guys who would turn out to have insurmountable flaws—a Federal Reserve economist into stuffed-animal erotica, an agronomist at the Rockefeller Foundation who'd scratch inside his ear, then avidly examine the tip of his finger. From family? For a couple of months I'd gone out with one of Uncle Sparky's friends who'd become chief of a hazardous materials squad, but he wouldn't stop quoting Ayn Rand. Naturally, my father wouldn't have anyone to introduce me to. His one postprison reference to me and men was suggesting I marry a dentist so he could get a mouthful of free tooth implants.

Now though, on orders to stay home and take it easy for a few days, I toyed with the idea of calling the doctor, asking some idiot question. Maybe Shea D'A would realize I'd reconsidered and offer to pay a house call. As Aunt Linda had astutely observed several years earlier: "For girls like you, Amy, eligible guys don't grow on trees. Your motto's gotta be See and Be Seen. Go out with anyone. Okay, not a real creep or a pervert. But if you stay home, all you're gonna meet are delivery boys from the take-out place."

Except I couldn't make the call. Not for one of those Dr. God guys who was also so aggressively good-looking that he became unattractive. Not for someone who would get turned on by *In Depth,* but who would have rejected me utterly if I'd said I taught third grade. I glanced at my watch. Not even noon yet and my day shot to shit. Not just the pain: I had the one day before the weekend. Then I'd have to stop looking for my mother and research my article on the candidates' positions and records on the environment.

I got off my couch and went over to my computer. I walked stiffly, like one of the undead in an old zombie movie, so as not to jar my ribs. After two minutes on the Internet, I realized that if my father hadn't lied or simply repeated some overheard tale of an elopement, and if he and my mother actually did get married in Maryland in 1973, they would have to have gone to Cecil County. There were numerous references to its being the place young couples headed for back then. It had been the one jurisdiction close to the big eastern cities that had no residency requirements for either bride or groom: no blood tests, no waiting period, and a lot of motels.

A minute later, I was talking with Dan Summers, the deputy county clerk.

"Lincoln as in Lincoln?" he was asking.

Well, the name was Lincoln, so I said, "That's right."

From there it was a mere hop and skip to being phone friends with Dan. He told me: "Look, Amy, I'd like to help you, but the rules here say I have to *mail* a copy of a marriage license, providing there actually was a marriage." His voice had remarkable smoothness, like Fred Astaire's, and without the whiney O that people from Philadelphia to Baltimore get stuck with. "It means going through 1973 records down in File Storage, which would mean me leaving the office without anyone in it because my coworker's taking family leave for a month and we still don't have a temp to replace her."

Since speed and access to the generally inaccessible are often an integral part of getting a story, any reporter who can distinguish between her ass and a hole in the ground knows how to get other people to do her work. Depending on the reporter and the ethos of the institution she's working for, her persuasiveness can take any form, from making a doorman her best friend to offering an outright bribe.

The straightforward approach worked best for me, because I'd always lacked the patience necessary to sweet-talk some Democratic state committeeman in Kalamazoo into spilling his guts. Anyway, my last name elicited expectations of honesty. "Dan, normally I'd rent a car and be in your office in, whatever, three or four hours, but I'm stuck here in my apartment with three broken ribs. And I'm under time pressure."

"How'd you break three ribs?" he inquired.

"In the least exciting way possible. Sitting at the edge of my couch. I slid off and hit a table going down."

"Ooh. Bet it hurts like a son of a gun." A minute later, I was giving him my father's name and birth date plus Phyllis Moscowitz and Morris. Tempting as it was to toss in Véronique, I didn't want him to think he'd be doomed to File Storage for the rest of the day. "I'll call you back if I find anything," he said.

"Could you call me collect either way?"

"Sure thing."

I climbed into bed and watched the war. Normally, I had what was probably an unhealthy fondness for television news, but during those weeks, the end of winter and the start of spring 2003, I began to believe I was more like a normal person than a news-junkie journalist, more absorbed in my own life than in geopolitics. Still, when the fighting in Iraq began, I realized that not only could I immediately identify every network and cable news anchor, I also knew enough about the news analysts to write a brief bio on each of them.

Watching TV gave me something else to worry about while I waited for Dan Summers's call. Skies there were either cruelly bright or obliterated by desert sandstorms. Almost immediately, I got hooked on the high-decibel TV anxiety that drowned out my own. The anchors' voices escalated from consternation to near-hysteria at each commercial break. *We'll be right back with our military analyst, retired General Monte Bluchner, who, despite a lamentable problem with the letter S, will tell us all about Iraqi weaponsh of mash deshtruction that could con-sheivably kill thousandsh of our young sholdiers.* Or *When we return we'll ask Bernice Wollman in Basra if this* (camera pans from the reporter to the ground, revealing a six-foot-something blob resembling burnt marshmallow) *could be the remains of Saddam!*

However, Dan Summers called back in less than a half hour. "Charles Lincoln and Phyllis Morris"—so even though my father had at some point known her actual name had been Moscowitz, she must have come up with fake ID—"got married on February eighteenth, 1973."

"A thousand blessings on your head, Dan."

"It was nothing."

"Do you happen to have Phyllis Morris's birth date?" It was a leap, assuming that my mother hadn't changed her date of birth as well as her name, but a leap worth taking. With any luck, she would not have been sophisticated or prescient enough to know how important someone's DOB can be when it comes to tracking her down.

"June fifth, 1956. Which makes her—"

"A couple of months short of forty-seven," I informed him. "Dan, thank you so much!"

I didn't need a master's degree in journalism to take the next few steps in trying to find my mother. Providing the name of the someone you're looking for isn't hopelessly common, like Mary Johnson, any semicompetent Googler can track down a person she's looking for as long as she has a birth date, a willingness to pay for a couple of pricey databases, and a few hours.

I got out of bed and ordered in some sushi, which struck me as sturdy, rib-repairing sustenance. But I had to face the fact that although I could easily log onto *In Depth*'s network and use Lexis and Nexis, I needed a last name. All I had was Véronique. I'd try Lincoln and Morris, but I was sure she'd dropped both names. And I was willing to bet twenty bucks that she hadn't gone back to using Moscowitz.

Usually I was a whiz at this sort of thing, but after a couple of hours, yellowtail maki, and a salmon-skin handroll, I was on the verge of calling for help. I considered Gloria Howard, because she was the most efficient researcher I'd ever met—except for John. Or going back to the old school tie: Jay Polla had been in all my classes at P.S. 97 since kindergarten and was now a narcotics detective in the Bronx. We'd reconnected standing on a line buying tickets to a Yankees' playoff game and had one of those dinner-once-every-two-years relationships. Jay would not only have access to New York State motor vehicle records, he might also be sympathetic to me wanting to find my mother. His father had taken a walk a couple of weeks after he was born.

My apartment was starting to smell like cat's breath from the sushi, so I tossed out the remains and opened a window. A blast of cold air hit my face, and I got a whiff of winter. It was almost April, but no hint of lilacs, no spring rain. Just another day that made it seem as if New York were doomed to an eternal February.

From eternal February, it took me about a second and a half to free-associate warm weather, and from there, Florida. Florida made me recall the late Selwyn Moscowitz, Brooklynite turned Boca Man.

I needed help with Florida. Grabbing two more Percocet and downing them with the now-cold green tea, I returned to my computer and brought up my notes from the four crazy weeks in November and December I'd spent in south Florida in 2000 covering the presidential election debacle.

What I now needed was a Florida lawyer. Although my beat had been Democrats even back then, one afternoon in the shampoo aisle of a drugstore I'd started chatting about frizz control with a woman. She turned out to be a litigation associate at Greenberg Traurig, the law firm arguing for Bush. We'd had late dinner a couple of times during that month. I'd been fascinated that though Barbara Axinn was a registered Democrat who'd voted for Gore, she was so passionate in arguing the Bush case that she'd believed her cause was not merely just, but true.

We spent the first few minutes on the phone catching up. I was still covering Democrats and subletting a studio apartment. She was still at the same firm, but had become a partner. She'd taken up riding and bought a horse she kept out in the country. She'd also bought a condo on the ocean.

The condo got to me. There had been a weekend interlude during my junior year when I'd considered the law. I'd rejected it, mainly because I didn't want to be a lawyer. Why should I earn several hundred thousand per annum practicing law when I could make forty-three thou at *In Depth*? As Barbara talked, I pictured me in a condo with tiled floors and kilim rugs and a terrace overlooking the Atlantic. I decided we'd had enough pleasantries, so I asked: "Barbara, if someone dies in Boca and leaves a will, is it a matter of public record?"

"Sure." She hesitated. "Well, I'm pretty sure it's public. Let me double-check with our trusts-and-estates maven. I'll get back to you. Is there any rush on this?"

"Whatever you can do," I replied.

"I'll see if I can catch him before he leaves for the day," she volunteered. "Is this general info or are you interested in one person in particular?"

"Selwyn Moscowitz." I spelled out both names. "A wife, Rose. And a daughter whose name is probably Véronique—or maybe Phyllis. By the way, this is just the first stage of an investigation I'm working on." If Barbara chose to believe I was in hot pursuit of a scoop for *In Depth,* so be it.

"I'll get back to you as soon as I can," she promised. "And totally off the record."

"Off the record" was what I wanted to hear. Ergo, I was not to be surprised when she called back less than an hour later. I understood the attraction people have toward the media. Whether you're loved or hated, if you're a reporter from Radio Prague or

Asahi Shimbun or *Men's Wear Daily,* once you manage to connect with anyone short of a Colin Powell–level newsmaker, he would often blab on as long as you kept throwing out the questions. You, the journalist, by being attentive, are affirming his big-shot status and making him a part-time pundit.

"My partner had an associate down at the courthouse," Barbara reported. "He asked him to look up the will. The only two heirs are the wife, Rose Bernstein Moscowitz, and a daughter, Véronique Hochberg. *Accent aigu* on the first *e* in Véronique. H-O-C-H-B-E-R-G. If you give me your fax number, I'll have the associate fax it to you."

I'd called Aunt Linda at ten the following morning, ostensibly to chat, and offered a lighthearted account of me and my ribs. Her pause between "Oh my God!" and "Do you need me to help you with anything?" might have only lasted a second, but it was long enough to indicate a lack of enthusiasm, if not reluctance. Just as I was about to tell her I was fine, she said, "Give me a few minutes just to put on my face and call Sparky to say where I'm going and I'll be on my way."

Although the temperature was in the forties, Aunt Linda was wearing open-toed slides. Red, with a clear Lucite heel, to match her red pants. One of her fashion dicta was shoes must match pants, except for jeans. "Amy, I *love* how you keep your place. So neat!" She'd come with a tote bag of food and was bending over, putting stuff away in my midget refrigerator. She glanced over at me: "I'm going to have to let the chicken stew defrost in the fridge. There's only room for the meatballs 'cause your freezer's so teeny. I think you're going to love it. The chicken stew. I have a secret ingredient. Savory."

"Sounds great," I said.

"What do you think about my hair this way?" A red scarf, worn like a headband, pulled her dark hair away from her face. It hung down to the middle of her back. "Do I look too much like Cher?"

"No. You look like you. Fantastic. I love you in red."

"But not *all* red," she said, pointing to her army green, navel-baring sweater. "I got you two-percent milk because it's better for coffee and an extra one percent won't kill you." She closed the refrigerator door. "You're really a good housewife," she continued. "Not a wife. You know what I mean, like the way you wipe off the top of the ketchup. None of those little black gookies around the cap. You didn't learn that from my mother."

"You're not kidding," I agreed. "You know what one of my earliest memories is? Butter on a plate. It had melted and Grandma put it back into the refrigerator so it became a solidified blob with toast crumbs embedded in it. I remember staring at the butter—it was at my eye level—and feeling disgusted."

Aunt Linda nodded. "That sounds *so* like her. I used to hate going to the fridge. Even when my father was alive and he brought home day-old everything from the store, she'd keep bagels forever and wouldn't let us throw them out. Chicky used to run to the fridge every morning to see the green stuff—we didn't know what it was called, but we knew it was pukey . . . Where was I? Oh, he looked to see if the green stuff grew more overnight and then he'd report to me. And you know what she'd do? Cut the mold off and make us eat the nonmoldy part. Did she do that with you?"

"No. She was just careless, messy. When I was seven I was boosting myself up on the counter, so I could clean out the sink."

Once she was diagnosed with Alzheimer's, I looked back on

life with Grandma Lil and wondered whether, ten or even twenty years before anyone said *This is a disease,* she was showing signs of incipient dementia. As a kid, I recognized she was flakier than any other adult I knew. When she sprinkled scouring powder in the morning, I knew I'd be scrubbing when I got home from school. She'd meander through the apartment, admittedly a short meander, shaking a can of Ajax over tub, toilet, and sinks, then forget to clean. Even at eight or nine, I understood it was vagueness and not irresponsibility. Pots would burn as the water in them for her cup of instant coffee boiled away. There were occasional nights when she seemed to forget the existence of dinner and got annoyed, or maybe embarrassed, when I asked for money. Lower lip protruding in a pout, she would open the change purse of her wallet, then mutter *Shit* when I told her to give me bills, not coins.

I got up from the couch and walked to the desk, an over-dainty, overgilded thing with bowed legs and teeny balls for feet. My computer sat on it along with a wood box, a street find that I'd sanded and stained and used as a filing cabinet. I took a paper from the first folder.

"What's this?" Aunt Linda asked when I handed it to her. She held it at arm's length, pulled back her head, and squinted. "Some legal thing?"

"It's a fax. My maternal grandfather's will."

"Whose? Anyhow, I can't read it."

"Phyllis's father's will."

My aunt's persimmon lips parted and her jaw dropped. "Did he leave you something? Oh, God, it would be so great if—"

"No. I have no idea if he even knew I existed. He left all of it to his wife—except his cuff links and an Audemars Piguet watch."

"Never heard of it," she declared.

"It's an expensive Swiss watch."

"One of those thin ones? They make men look gay."

"Aunt Linda, he left the cuff links and watch to my mother."

"So?"

"Well, it could be because she's so rich money wouldn't mean anything to her," I countered. "Or maybe it was a way of acknowledging her existence without really giving her a share of his will."

"You think they were still on the outs because she ran away from home?"

"I have no idea," I told her.

Mechanically, Aunt Linda pulled out the desk chair and sat. "When was this?"

"He died in 1997. He and his wife were living in Boca Raton. She's still alive, or at least still has a phone listing."

"You *called* her, Amy?" I shook my head. "What about Phyllis?"

I took the will from her hand and pointed midway down a page. "Her name isn't Phyllis anymore. It's Véronique Hochberg."

"No!" She laughed. Then she asked, "Did I just get lipstick on my teeth?"

"No."

"Is that chutzpah or is that chutzpah? Say it again with that French accent!" I did. "Sorry I'm laughing," Aunt Linda continued. "I know this is serious for you, honey."

"It's okay." I refolded the cuffs on my sweater. I'd been wearing an Ivey sweatshirt that had been washed so often it had gone from its original dark green to the color of ash. But when my aunt decided she was coming over, I'd switched to my lavender sweater and put in my gold ball earrings. "So Phyllis is still alive."

"I guess so. I was so tired and strung out from the painkillers last night, I couldn't keep looking."

"So you're really going through with this looking-for-her thing?" She shook her head almost imperceptibly and made a near-silent *Tsk*.

"I think so."

"Let me ask you something, Amy. Say you find her and she turns out to be a total creep. What then?"

"I've thought of that," I replied.

"Besides the disappointment, you could start thinking: Half of me is a creep. Not that there's any creep in you. You know that. Even with Harvard. But you could *feel* that way. Or what if you find her and think, *What a loser!* and you don't want anything to do with her? Except she calls you and calls you—"

I cut her off. "I'd get my number changed."

Aunt Linda took off her scarf, pulled her hair back, did some fast winding, and made a ponytail. "You want the truth, hon? I know you're strong, you know you're strong. But strong people can still break."

"I know."

"And she's a bitch. Who else could do a thing like what she did?"

"A messed-up kid."

"You grew up without a mother, Amy, so what do you need one for now?"

"I need to see where I come from."

"You come from New York, for Christ's sakes!" She glanced down at her persimmon toes, then back at me. "You know, that's the one thing I can never say in front of Sparky, even after all these years. Like even though it's not making fun of Jesus or anything, I don't want him to think I don't respect his religion. He doesn't go to church, but I think he still believes it. Even the virgin business. Where was I? Oh, Phyllis. You got nothing of her except her brains, because we both know Chicky is no Einstein."

"But they're finding more and more personality traits are genetic—all those studies of twins separated at birth."

"What? Never mind, don't explain. You went to the best college in the world and I got out of high school with a seventy-eight average. What do you think, Amy, your genes will make you run away from your baby?" When I didn't answer she added: "Don't be stupid! You'll be a wonderful mother. What's with you and John?"

"Nothing. It's finished."

"Last time you were over, you sounded like things weren't going too good."

"They weren't. We broke up."

"*You* broke it off?" Her beautifully tweezed eyebrows lifted at the thought of such idiocy.

"It was mutual."

"So look, if John's out of the picture, all the more reason not to look for Phyllis. Who have you got to fall back on if she turns out to be weird? Or even not weird. I mean, she could be mature now. Say you find her and all she wants is to make it up to you. Can't do enough for you. A whole life without a mother and now you got Mademoiselle Véronique with a guilt complex 'cause she abandoned her baby and she can't do enough, which would be nice, except she's a total pain because she can't stop making you lace doilies or something."

Without asking if I wanted anything, my aunt walked over to the kitchen area and found the coffeepot. She measured out coffee and water and arranged what she said were soy cookies—two net carbs each. "They don't taste great," she observed, "but on the other hand, they don't taste like shit either."

"Do I look like my mother?"

"You've sort of got her eyes," she said reluctantly, turning from me to watch the coffee drip into the glass pot. "And you've got her height, but she was—I don't know what you'd call it—teeny-boned. She had a real long neck, like Audrey Hepburn. Except to me she always looked a little lollipop-ish because she had this big head, but Sparky always said she was a man's woman, not a woman's woman. Whatever that means." She shrugged. "Well, I know what it means, but I think guys liked her more because she was cold than for her looks. You know, guys have this big ego thing, thawing a cold girl out so she becomes a hottie, but only for them."

She grasped her bra straps between thumbs and forefingers and shifted everything slightly to the right. "Remember when we came up to visit you at Ivey-Rush on our way to Nantucket? It was right after you got into Harvard and that other good school but you were all upset about stupid Yale?" I nodded. "Well, that time, Sparky said you looked so much like Phyllis he almost did a double take, but then, after he kept looking at you, it was less and less. You know why? Because Phyllis was a cold bitch and you were a real person, even after hanging out with all those rich girls for three years." She took two mugs from the cabinet. "Do you think if you wanted to, you could get him back?" she asked.

"Who?"

"You know who."

"No," I told her. "I don't think I could."

"I bet you could. Whatever it is, apologize. You don't have to win every argument. Unless . . . Was it another woman?" I shrugged. "Men." She sighed. She reached over and took my hand. I noticed there were white blotches on hers, which I guessed meant she'd done something to get rid of liver spots. "Listen, angel pie, if it's over, it's over. You have to go out, find someone else."

"Aunt Linda, you know it's not that easy."

"You only think that because you think too much. There are thousands of guys who'd jump at the chance to marry you! Just go *eeny-meeny-miney-mo* with the best ones and pick somebody."

"You know, I never thought of marriage that way."

"It works, lovie. All over the world, what do you see?"

"Women without money or power dependent on men."

"No, Amy. You see arranged marriages. And you know what? When the husband dies, the wife cries."

Despite two mugs of Aunt Linda's killer coffee, I fell asleep the moment she left. I woke up a couple of hours later feeling so drugged that for a minute I had no idea what time it was or why breathing hurt. Recalling offered no particular consolation, so I trudged back to the computer. I had a vague notion I needed to dig deeper into the degree of John Kerry's commitment to marine ecosystems, but instead I watched my screen saver, a bunch of baby robins breaking out of their blue eggs.

God knows how many times I watched them. The room was dark except for the light of the screen, so until the phone rang that nest was all that existed. "Amy Lincoln?"

It was who I thought it was. "Dr. Shea D'Alessandro. How are you feeling?"

"Not too bad." My keyboard was almost noiseless, so I went online and started checking out old Kerry marine ecology stories in the *Boston Globe*.

"Not too bad considering three broken ribs." He chuckled. "I'd like to see you in the office early next week, check how you're doing."

"Okay. I'll call Monday and make an appointment." I bookmarked two articles, then moved on to the *Cape Cod Times*.

"By the way, I looked through a couple of old issues of *In Depth*. You're a political writer."

"Right." A piece written in 2000 began *Sen. John Kerry, D-Mass., has become the point man in championing a fishery management program that some compare to the fencing-off of the prairies and others hope will help end overfishing.* "Forgive me if I sound drugged, but I am."

"That's okay. If the pain eases, two or three ibuprofen should do the trick. That's like Advil, Motrin. But I guess you know what ibuprofen is."

I went back to Google and typed *Véronique Hochberg.* "Yes." I always hated it when guys didn't say anything—whether out of shyness or arrogance—and I wound up struggling to make conversation. Still, I added: "But you're right to be specific."

"Did you major in journalism at college?"

"No." I pressed Enter. "I got a master's in it at Columbia."

"Where did you do your undergraduate work?" he asked.

There it was. I double-clicked. A squib in *Newsday: Group to Restore Theater. A group of Shorehaven residents . . . former home of the Bard's Company . . . for years a movie house . . . Bring Back the Bard is headed by Janice Asher. Its members include Barbara Kiprik, Ken Warner, Véronique Hochberg.* "I'm sorry. I didn't hear what you said, Dr. D'Alessandro."

"Please, call me Shea. I asked where you went to college."

"Harvard."

"Oh. Now I'm doubly impressed."

There was a tiny photo with the article, the Bring Back the Bard committee. She was on the left. I copied the photo, then pasted and enlarged it. "Oh, sorry, Shea. My call waiting. Thanks so much for checking up on me. I'll see you early next week." If he said good-bye as I hung up, I didn't hear it.

It was the second picture I'd ever seen of my mother, the first without sunglasses. She was the shortest person in the group. She must have had long hair, because it was pinned on top of her head, although the photo was so indistinct it could have been a large sponge. She was wearing a tank top, a long skirt, and had on a bunch of necklaces. She looked casual and chic and so petite that the rest of the group looked like Goliaths. Smiling Goliaths. Everyone in the photo was smiling. Except for my mother.

Chapter Ten

I got to my office by seven Monday morning, because I guessed—correctly—that my eleven-thirty appointment with Dr. D'Alessandro would be no ten-second poke ribs/*You're coming along nicely*. Sure enough, I had almost an hour to check out the waiting room.

Right away I spotted a copy of *In Depth* there, along with a slew of high-end magazines. By merely hanging around to see one of the doctors at Park Avenue Orthopedic Associates, the average upper-middle-class New Yorker could gain such advantageous knowledge as why the director Aki Kaurismäki should have won the Palme d'Or for *The Man Without a Past* and in what sort of a mold to bake game pâtés.

From the look of the waiting room, Shea D'A and his partners were devotees of the Bauhaus aesthetic. Or perhaps they'd simply given a blank check to a decorator and said, *We want a guy office.* The waiting space was a long rectangle with six black

Mies van der Rohe–style chrome-and-leather chairs. There was also a square-armed couch, dark red, that looked displeased with its color. The rug, with its quadrilateral shapes, was also red and black. The space was cold, bringing to mind more "Nazi" than "Stendhal."

In Depth and the other magazines hung from the rungs of a narrow chrome ladder on a wall to the left of the receptionists' desk. With only a little shelf of mints, gum, and a couple of bags of stale nuts, they could have had a concession. The receptionists, three of them, were white-, black-, and brown-skinned, but all had black hair to coordinate with the decor.

I skimmed *Architectural Digest* for a couple of minutes and spotted a cappuccino maker that probably cost more than my net worth. Reluctantly, I put the magazine aside and spent the time reading the pile of material for my next article: where the candidates stood on environmental issues. I had to get beyond the customary Democratic stance: We'll-fight-polluters-and-all-those-who-don't-give-a-damn-about-the-Chittenango-ovate-amber-snail. I highlighted quotes and votes until a technician took me in for more X-rays.

When I was finally led back to the waiting room, I tried to get back to work. But my mother kept intruding. Same old story, latest revision of the one I'd been telling myself since I was a kid. In this most recent version, she was age seventeen, telling her ten-month-old daughter, *See you later, sweets,* knowing, even at that moment, there would be no "later," that she wasn't coming back. She probably didn't wait for the elevator—just ran down the stairs. Out!

I let myself experience her relief. Freedom! It was like being illuminated from within. *Thank God, no more terror-filled nights listening for the scratchings of rats' feet. No more worrying about what will happen when Chicky gets out of prison. He could kill me. Or worse, want me back. Freedom! No more wiping dribbles and shit off a still-bald baby. No more listening to dribbles and shit spewing forth from an imbecile mother-in-law whose IQ is half of mine.*

The story then skipped ahead, a few days, a few weeks. Phyllis was suddenly feeling low, realizing she was aching for the velvet of her baby's cheek. *How can I get her back? Sneak into the project at three in the morning, past sleeping cops in a squad car, open stupid Lil's door with my key and snatch Amy? Except what if I'm caught, charged with abandonment or something, thrown into jail? Calm down. Think. All right, I could get a lawyer, get him to do something for me, so I could keep her. Except a lawyer: His eyes would be filled with contempt for me. Abandoned her baby. Spoiled Brooklyn bitch. Maybe, being a lawyer, he'd even figure out that I should be the one in prison for snatching that diamond ring, not Chicky. He'd report it to the DA. But I want Amy back.*

The conflict in the Phyllis/Véronique story was always the same, her desire versus her dread. But there could be—was— only one way to finish the story, the true one. Dread always triumphed. The End. I lowered my head, closed my eyes.

When I opened them, I saw the stack of papers in my lap. For the five thousandth time in my career I wished that instead of being a writer at *In Depth*, I could be something else, something with emotion: an orthopedist (*Scalpel! Saw!*), a pollster (*Up four percentage points in Delaware!*), a soccer coach, the requisite short girl in the chorus line of a Broadway musical, tip-tapping and singing her little heart out.

Another fifteen minutes went by until one of the black-haired, white-bloused receptionists at the desk ushered me into Shea D'A's office. More black leather. In back of him, a black-and-white Ansel Adams poster of a desolate tree. The doctor sat behind a sleek black desk with curved sides, twirling a pen between his thumbs and forefingers. He gave me a blue-eyed glance, then looked off to the side, to a light box displaying two X-rays of ribs, presumably mine.

"They're what I expected," he said to the X-rays.

"Any restrictions on activity?" I inquired.

He turned back. Under yet another double-breasted jacket, he wore a blue shirt one shade darker than the hue of his eyes. Blue eyes had never done it for me. Growing up on the Lower East, I'd known mostly dark-eyed people. While I understood how some women could find light eyes appealing, I could never be drawn to a man from a culture that valued reticence and sweaters with snowflakes.

"Long walks are fine," he told me. "No weight training. No—"

"I run three to four miles a day."

"How does it feel now when you walk?"

"Now? It hurts a little."

"Wellll," he said, too patiently for my taste, "don't you think the jarring of running would make it hurt more than just a little?" I'd always made it a point not to respond in any way to condescending rhetorical questions. "Walk your route for the next six weeks. But build up to it slowly." He was still twirling his pen, either a nervous habit or a display of some trendoid writing instrument that made a Mont Blanc look like a Bic.

"What about travel?" I asked. "Flying?"

"Following the candidates?"

"I have to get down to Florida."

"Same as the running. Well, I'll let you decide: four to six weeks. If there's a problem with air pressure on a plane . . ."

I'd implode or explode. My ribs would crack into shards and stab me in the pericardium. But I said, "I fly all the time. I've

191

never been in a situation where there's been a problem with air pressure."

"Amy Lincoln, you are a very determined woman." He did that nodding-smiling thing, a display of amused tolerance that works in George Clooney movies but not in life. He glanced at his watch. "I've got to grab lunch. I'm in surgery all afternoon." I realized his last sentence was, according to tradition, music to female Jewish ears, but for me it might as well have been Mahler. "Interested in grabbing a quick bite?" he asked.

A quick bite? Imagine a chorus of every woman in New York, from Tatty to Aunt Linda to Senator Clinton. They'd have sung out in a single voice: *What have you got to lose? It's a half hour and a tuna sandwich.*

So I was on the verge of saying *Sure* when suddenly John popped into my head. Not the notion of John. Not a vision of John at lunch, halfway through an overketchuped burger, but John as I'd seen him that night at the concert, smiling and gazing with such pleasure at *La Belleza*. It should have been all the incentive I needed to say yes to Shea D'A. Instead I mumbled, "Sorry, I've got a deadline," and I was back at my desk before my next coherent thought. Of course that thought was of John.

I left the office around seven feeling as low as I could go. I was one of those season/weather/mood people: summer good, winter bad. Yet even though we'd just gone over to daylight savings time and the sun was doing its damnedest to brighten the cold dusk, all I could see was the coming dark.

I considered calling Tatty for a bracing *You'll meet someone and be happy in no time* pep talk. For her, all a person had to do to get rid of the miseries was snap out of it. *Psycho* plus *pharmacology* equaled a word that was hard to spell and a waste of time.

For serious blues, her prescription was lightening your hair a couple of shades and getting a deluxe manicure. Since I was okay with my hair and could not afford to have my nails done in one of those pricey places that employed breasty women named Svetlana, I stopped in at my usual, Jane Nails, around the halfway point of my nightly walk home.

The owner, Jane, greeted me with her usual "Amy!" Genuinely happy to see me, though appropriately short of ecstatic. Other than my teachers, the only other person in my life who had visibly brightened upon seeing me was John. Even when I was beginning to sense *Uh-oh, maybe this relationship isn't going to be the one and it's not only me thinking it,* I'd return to a restaurant table from the ladies' room anticipating the polite hoisting of cheek muscles that creates the dating smile. Instead, he'd light up. *Hey!* he'd say, with a genuine smile. Then he'd lean forward a bit, the vestigial remains of the old etiquette: a gentleman standing when a lady approaches a table.

Jane said, "Five minutes," while holding up five fingers. I sat in a plasticized version of a leather tycoon chair, set down my backpack, and pulled out my cell phone. I also dry-swallowed a Percocet because my ribs were hurting so much I was actually contemplating spending money on a taxi to get home.

I cradled the phone in my left hand and did that staring-at-keypad thing, trying to decide whom to call. I'd noticed that people like me, who lived alone, tended to fondle cell phones in those tough moments when it hit them that not only did they live alone, they were alone. Any human voice would do at such a moment—a friend, a relative, a Time Warner Cable rep.

Well, I needed a less-than-five-minutes person, so I decided on Freddy Carrasco. The last I'd spoken to him, I'd broken my ribs. Why had he called that night? Oh, about his meeting with Mickey Maller, the lawyer I'd set him up with. He'd been planning to spend the weekend with his girlfriend going through his mother's papers, looking for something that might tie her to Thom Bowles or to Bowles's father, William Bryson Bowles.

Freddy's "Hello" sounded upbeat. Had he actually found out something that linked his mother to either of the Bowleses?

"Hi. It's Amy Lincoln." No response. "Freddy?"

"Yeah. Hi."

"How are things going?"

"Not bad."

"Did you and your girlfriend find anything about—"

"Listen, can I call you later this week? I have a class tonight and I'm already late for it."

"Sure. I'll speak to you—" But that was the end of the conversation.

Had Freddy been in that much of a rush to get to class? I didn't think so. In fact, I was thinking he couldn't wait to get off the phone with me.

It was still cold enough for my nails to dry to diamondlike hardness by the time I got home. Ergo, I was unable to avoid opening my mailbox. I extracted a few envelopes that looked like actual mail along with catalogues offering such life-enhancing objects as an American flag copper weather vane.

Actual mail was a MasterCard bill, two invitations, and a pink-and-white gingham cutout of a butterfly announcing the birth of Zoë Hannah Duckworth Levine. It took me a few seconds, until I got to the elevator, but then I remembered Zoë's father was an astronomy major I'd gone out with briefly in college, a man with as many flakes of dandruff on his shirts as there were stars in the sky. All I could now envision of him were white specks on green flannel.

In the elevator, whose fine brass buttons had been replaced with a fingerprint-streaked digital pad, I opened a brunch invitation from Bunny Morales and David Vale. They'd both lived in my building in the project and Bunny and I had kept in touch. When I got to my floor, I opened the second invitation. It was from a Democratic pollster and a *Chicago Tribune* reporter I'd met at the conventions in 1996 and 2000 and spent—tops—twenty minutes each talking to them about subjects non-Democratic. I had no clue they knew each other, much less loved each other. I also drew a blank as to why they wanted me at their nuptials in Sonoma Valley, at Gray Acres, which sounded like a graveyard but was probably a winery. Since I'd no doubt see them again in 2004, I had to send a gift.

I let myself into my apartment and took out two slices of pizza from the back of the fridge, then threw them out, uncertain whether the randomly placed convex white circles were icy pepperoni slices or fungal growths.

Each birth announcement, whether a mini–*Sports Illustrated* cover spotlighting seven-pound, eight-ounce Max beside an actual football, or something pink and cherubic on vellum regarding the arrival of eight-pound, fourteen-ounce Jordana, was a reminder that the father of the child I was determined to have was most likely going to be an anonymous sperm donor—some medical student whacking off for a hundred bucks to thoughts of getting blown by Reese Witherspoon. Every wedding invitation made me feel as if eligible men were evanescing at an exponential rate instead of a merely arithmetical one.

I wound up drinking a glass of milk and eating a bagful of sugared almonds I'd gotten at a friend's wedding a half year earlier. An excellent custom, Italian. I'd been invited with a date, and naturally asked John. When the band leader called on all the single girls to catch the bouquet, I held back. "You're not going to join them?" John asked casually. I looked over at the gaggle of squealing, giggling women, muscles taut, ready to leap, as if in the final game of an Olympic volleyball match. Not wanting him to think of me as one of those shameless, desperate gigglers, I'd merely shaken my head and stood my ground, which was beside him.

I heard a sharp crack: an almond and not a tooth. But it was one of those instants when not only do you become hyper-aware—suddenly tuned in to every atom of nut and grain of sugar sticking to your gums—but also farsighted. You not only look at that particular moment with especial clarity, you observe your life. Okay, maybe there was no actual panorama, Desertion by Mother leading directly to Me on the Couch with Three Remaining Almonds and a Quarter-glass of Milk. But I found myself re-viewing that wedding to which I'd taken John.

Maybe my refusal to join the gleeful female New York twenty-somethings elbowing one another aside to catch that bouquet of peach and white roses hadn't demonstrated to John how cool I was, how not-desperate. "You're not going to join them?" he'd asked. Instead of a casual inquiry, might he have meant *Are you going to be one of those women, ready to declare herself for marriage?* When I stood my ground in my pale blue silk slip dress, my hair held up by two silvery combs, thinking how cool I seemed, did John see a woman who was interested neither in marriage nor in him?

Another time: after the planes hit on 9/11, when he called and I went to his apartment on the Upper West Side. We'd stayed watching TV for hours on end. I'd asked him, "Don't you want to go up to Connecticut to be with your family?" As in, *Are you crazy, not getting out of Manhattan when you have an alternative?* He'd shaken his head. No. The next day we went down-town, as close as the cops would let us get, and he filmed for a while, asking the people who looked nailed in place, staring downtown, where they'd been when it happened, how they'd gotten home. Good documentarian that he was, he got many long stories. "Do you have an idea how you'll use this?" I'd asked. He'd said, "No. I doubt if I'll ever use it. It's not really professional quality. I may never even look at it again. Maybe I'll save it for my great-great-grandchildren. Although when you think about it, how much does Pearl Harbor mean to our generation? Whatever. At least it will be a personal link between them and some dead guy who lived in the early twenty-first century."

A few minutes later he said, "You be the journalist and I'll be the cameraman." I didn't want to. All I wanted to do was get the hell uptown, away from that thick air with its stench of melted steel, vaporized printer ink, burned-up flesh. But I went over to a coffee shop owner washing his windows. As he talked to me he held his squeegee the way the farmer in *American Gothic* held his pitchfork. He told me about the people he'd watched jumping from the towers. Some of them held hands, he started to sob, but none of them made it all the way still together. He'd been up all night praying for God to give him some sign that they'd died before they reached the ground or their hands simply slipped apart. No, he hadn't gotten any sign as of yet. John filmed us until the guy sat down on the curb to weep. I asked him to stop shooting. I took the squeegee and finished cleaning the window while John turned off his camera, sat down beside the guy, and put his arm around his shoulder while the guy wept into his hands.

That night, I went back to my apartment. He kept asking me why, and I said, "Look, I don't want to be in your way if you want to go up to Connecticut." He told me, "That's crazy, if I wanted to go that badly, you'd come with me. Unless you wanted to go to your aunt's house in Brooklyn. Or see your father . . ."

I honestly felt he needed his space. John enjoyed being alone. He could keep himself endlessly occupied: reading, screening other people's work, listening to every kind of music, going to lectures on arcane subjects, playing pickup basketball. I didn't want him to feel he had to be polite. Or that I was being sneaky, using the nation's nightmare to slide into his apartment and his life. Because then he'd be stuck. How could he get rid of me?

Well, by asking. But back then, that thought never occurred to me. I can't say for sure what I pictured: not me at ninety, going out to buy dental floss for my two remaining teeth. I suppose I imagined John at long last (two weeks? two years?) sitting me down to explain why it wasn't working and how I'd have to go. Or just getting so disgusted living with someone who kept straightening out the forks in the drawer that he finally screamed, *Get the hell out!*

Yet John had been so clear on wanting to be with me. If I'd thought about it, I would have realized it was the time everybody was clinging to the person or people closest to them. And there he was, not going up to his family, but wanting to be with me. What had I been thinking when I left? No clear thoughts at all, just a need to leave. Why? Because I was the one who really needed space, but rather than admitting it, even to myself, I'd lobbed that need over to his side of the court? Or had my heart known something my head couldn't acknowledge, that having been a guest at everybody's family occasions had only reinforced my Véronique-genes' proclivity for avoiding entangling alliances?

I was, and probably would always be, alone. All those weddings that weren't mine. All those babies I wasn't having. Sitting by myself in the emergency room, no annoying relative or concerned friend by my side. Being the loner invited by people for Thanksgiving turkey or Hanukkah latkes so they could feel benevolent. I could remedy all that. A baby. But was it fair for me to have a child simply because I needed a family?

I sensed I'd gone over the line from a cozy melancholia into serious self-pity, but Passover loomed a week and a half away. When I'd said good-bye to John's parents at his cousin's wedding, they'd said, "See you at the Seder." Where would I go? Okay, almost anywhere, since tradition says a stranger has to be welcomed because of Jews having been strangers in a strange land. But the one place in the world I'd felt I actually belonged was with the Orensteins.

Well, not anymore. I thought of everyone I knew who lived alone, single, divorced, abandoned, widowed. Did they sit around staring at three candied almonds, thinking that at some point they'd better start amassing pills for that final night alone? Was that the alternative to a life spent with no meaningful connections? Or did they simply shrug, turn on TCM, and watch *Lady L*?

The only thing holding me back from Florida, from maybe getting to talk to Rose Moscowitz, was Happy Bob's okay. "Are you sure you don't just want a few days in the nice warm weather?" he asked. A phlegmy sound resonated from his throat: a chuckle, or perhaps a chortle. As usual, he masked his distrust of his own handpicked editorial staff behind what he considered an open smile. His teeth, mottled with brown, always reminded me of the Dead Sea scrolls. "Why can't you do this online, or at a library? Get some expert at Columbia or NYU. Spend a day in Washington and come back—"

"Bob, three-quarters of the authorities I want to talk to are in Florida."

"What's wrong with the phone?"

"They're not going to give me an hour answering my questions on Kucinich's program for alternative energy sources—solar and ocean. That's what's wrong."

Happy Bob tugged at the black hair between his eyebrows, his reflective gesture. Finally he smiled again: "Don't let me see you come back with a suntan."

By my second day in Florida, I knew I had almost enough information for a good piece. I'd assembled piles of data on the rising ocean due to global warming, and on sewage disposal for America's ever-increasing population of a certain age, one not known for great bladder control. I even watched C-SPAN at night in my hotel; John Edwards was charming a United Synagogue convention in South Carolina and I took notes. Best of all, I'd gotten a free ride to check out my maternal grandmother.

At high noon, coated with SPF 30, I let the sun roast my face while my final interview, a meteorologist from the Gavarian Oceanographic Institute held forth with such dire warnings about the rising oceans it sounded as if all Miami's Latinos and gays and Jews and blacks and Others would soon be frolicking on the sand in southeastern Alabama.

I'd taken her out to lunch on the theory I could get more out of her away from the distractions of the ever-changing line and bar graphs that kept flashing on the screens on the wall across from her desk. Anyhow, she was pencil-thin and had enough broken blood vessels on her face to make me suspect she was bulemic, so I figured she'd be easy on the expense account because she wouldn't gorge in front of a relative stranger.

"It's not just a question of sea level rise and increased precipitation," she was saying about global warming. "It impacts on everything. Weather-related mortality, farm yields, forest composition, and I'm just touching the surface here—loss of habitat and species." While she talked, I multitasked, breathing in the sweet, humid Miami air; wanting almost to cry, that such an outstanding woman could be in thrall to compulsive puking; taking notes on ecological Armageddon; brooding about how I should present myself to Rose Moscowitz. Normally, I not only planned ahead, I wrote everything down in outline form so I could critique my own strategies. Yet for some reason, when it came to approaching my grandmother, I hadn't figured out a thing.

So now I was free to worry. Rose M. might be senile and not even know she'd ever had a daughter named Phyllis/Véronique. What if she lived in a gated community? If she said no to a meeting, how could I get past the guards? Under what guise could I present myself? Should I use the name Amy Lincoln? Maybe she didn't know anything about her daughter and Chicky Lincoln. But maybe she did. I didn't want to use my name, put her on guard, and have her refuse to see me. On the other hand, how could I use a fake name? She might ask to see some ID.

"Precipitation has been consistently rising?" I asked.

"Over land at high latitudes in the northern hemisphere, yes. But there's been a decrease in precip. since the 1960s over the subtropics and the tropics. From Africa to Indonesia. They're both causes of, uh, great concern." We hadn't gotten any bread, but she kept glancing at a bread basket on the table next to ours. "Off the record?"

"Sure," I said.

"The Bush administration's position isn't just dangerous, it's primitive. They ignore accepted scientific evidence because it's not to their immediate economic benefit. They don't care about—"

Just then, the waiter came around. The meteorologist almost snatched the menu from his hand and began devouring it with her eyes. I got a little nervous because I knew *In Depth* wouldn't pay for a binge. Fortunately, she only had a cheeseburger, fries, and lemonade, followed by a rather long trip to the ladies' room. When she came back, her eyes were slightly bloodshot and I caught a whiff of vomit and Juicy Fruit.

After I was finished with her, I started feeling guilty about taking the afternoon off. So I drove from Miami to Miami Beach because John Kerry was in town. I watched him dump on the Bush tax cut before the Hardy-Schmidt Conduit distributors convention at the Fontainebleau Hotel. They seemed unable to comprehend supply-side economics or, indeed, Senator Kerry, though I thought he was in good form. His press person gave me fifteen minutes on the bus with him on the way to his next stop, a Guatemalan-American leadership organization, and I got enough substantive, quotable stuff on his environmental views to put a genuine smile on Happy Bob's face. Then I popped three Advils and took a taxi back to retrieve my rented car and go back to my hotel on the beach. Excellent. I'd worked two whole days. Now this night would be mine.

I recalled my talk with Judyann Baptiste. Rose Moscowitz was a woman who had a college degree. She'd continued her education: Italian, philosophy, whatever. Even if I wanted to do it, I doubted if she could be easily duped. I had to come up with some reasonable story so she'd not only be willing to see me, but to talk about her daughter as well.

How about the truth? I asked myself.

My hotel was two blocks from the ocean, one of those formerly decrepit Deco ruins restored to aqua and yellow razzle-dazzle. Once inside, I'd realized about two seconds after registering that this was not a place for cool fashionistas and music minimoguls. My room was about as large as a medium-size walk-in closet, and the building's electrical system seemed overwhelmed by the guests' insistence on turning on their air conditioners.

I sat in the only chair in the room, a director's chair covered in white canvas. Except for a taupe rug, the entire room was white, from pleated shades to bed linen to the little basket that held the CDs, an odd collection of classical guitar, hip-hop, and country music of the you've-left-me-and-stomped-on-my-heart variety.

The lukewarm breeze being exhaled by the air conditioner wasn't the only reason my silk T-shirt clung to me like a wet washcloth. I sat staring at the display on my cell phone, half hoping to find the battery on the verge of death. But it was fully charged. I stood to check out my notes for Rose Moscowitz's phone number in Boca Raton, but sat back down, realizing I'd memorized it. I dialed carefully, not wanting mistakenly to reach some random widow and cause so much confusion and pain that I would not have the heart to try again.

Oh my God! It was ringing. I was praying passionately to reach either her voice mail or a phone company recording that the number was no longer in service, when a woman answered: "Hello."

"May I please speak with Rose Moscowitz?"

"This is she."

I gave her an A for grammar and a C for warmth. Just from those few words I knew she wasn't the sort of grandmother who either baked or ate chocolate chip cookies. "Mrs. Moscowitz, I am a writer and associate editor of *In Depth* magazine."

"Yes." A cautious yes, but at least it wasn't *Huh?* or *Wha'?*

"Our offices are in New York, but I'm here in south Florida researching and working on an article. I was wondering—since I'm down here—if I can meet you. . . ." I swallowed, but there was nothing to swallow. My mouth was dry because all the moisture in my body was being utilized to manufacture sweat.

"Meet me for what purpose?"

"Actually, it's a personal matter." I was nervous that she'd hear the clack my tongue made as it attempted to unglue itself from my hard palate.

"A personal matter?" It wasn't a query, as in *I don't understand*. It was said superciliously—a *personal* matter?—the way a hoity-toity matron in an old movie would address a groveling plebeian asking for a favor.

Fuck favors. I would never have gotten into boarding school and Harvard if I'd been a person who knew her place. Nor was I the type who'd try to top a cold remark with an even icier one. I was not Rose Moscowitz's inferior. And I wasn't her better. I was her equal. People like me, the successfully upwardly mobile, behaved as if we really did believe that all men and women are created equal, despite the sad amount of evidence to the contrary.

Yet the weekend before I went off to Ivey-Rush for my first year, my aunt and uncle took me for a bon voyage brunch at a pancake house not far from where they lived in Sheepshead Bay. Uncle Sparky asked, "You scared, kiddo?" "Yeah," I said, "I'm scared." As if to prove it, my hand shook and three drops of syrup landed on my pink T-shirt. Aunt Linda dipped the edge of her napkin in her glass of water and handed it to me, but Uncle Sparky went on talking: "You should be scared. This boarding school business is a big deal. But when you get there . . . Okay, be scared. Just act not scared. They let you in because you're as good as they are."

"Yes, Mrs. Moscowitz, a personal matter. But before I go into it, please feel free to check my credentials. On the Internet, *In Depth* dot com. They have the masthead there." I decided not to explain the word *masthead* as I would have been obliged to for anyone on my father's side of the family. "Of course, it's also in the magazine." She was so quiet she could have died two sentences earlier. I sensed I ought to lay it on thick. "I'm a graduate of Ivey-Rush Academy, Harvard, and the Columbia School of Journalism. I know their registrars' offices aren't open in the evening, but I'll be glad to call you back tomorrow, after you've checked." As she still hadn't said anything, I added: "And I'll be glad to meet you in any public place and show you my photo ID."

"You haven't given me your name."

"Oh, sorry. Amy Lincoln." Naturally, at this very moment that I'd been dreading, saying who I was, the air-conditioning shifted into high gear for the first time since I checked in. My sweaty silk shirt turned into a cold compress. Cradling the phone between chin and shoulder, I rubbed my upper arms, but despite that they were soon covered with goose bumps. *Amy Lincoln* appeared to be a conversation stopper. My teeth started chattering.

"You did say this was a personal matter," Grandma Warmth said. "May I assume you're related to a . . . Charles Lincoln?" She said Chicky's name as if she were saying *cockroach*.

"Yes. I'm Charles Lincoln's daughter. But it's not my father I'd like to talk to you about. It's my mother."

"Your mother?"

"My mother. Your daughter."

Chapter Eleven

Like so many of the gated communities I'd seen in Florida during the Bush-versus-Gore mess, Hibiscus Pointe in Boca Raton had a security booth with an overlarge sign on the window announcing the security guard's name, so that even residents with fairly advanced cataracts could see RODRIGO. Rodrigo, actually, was worth seeing: noble head, manly brows, luscious lips that needed only a touch of ChapStick.

"Hi. I'm here to see Rose Moscowitz. My name is Amy Lincoln."

He pressed his computer monitor touch-screen two or three times, then flashed an Antonio Banderas knowing look that said, *You would find me wickedly amusing,* although his actual words were: "Yes, Miss Lincoln, she'll meet you at the clubhouse. Do you know where it is?" When I shook my head, he punched a key. A printer wearily exuded directions. The gate rose slowly.

Speed bumps every twenty feet or so along Hibiscus Boulevard made sure I didn't get anywhere at a New York clip.

I wondered if anybody from New York could truly love this life. Probably, because more and more people wanted to live this way. It wasn't only rich whites. And not just in Florida, either. All over the country, I'd noticed the haves of all races, colors, and creeds hurrying to get themselves guarded so that their have-less and have-not fellow citizens could not steal their botanical prints. I wondered if this wouldn't be the true Reagan-Bush legacy: not a return to the laissez-faire, invisible-hand capitalism of Adam Smith, but a slide into a tsarist state, where government existed to enrich the rich.

I was minutes from meeting my grandmother. Clutching the steering wheel as if it were a lifesaver, I drove at the prescribed fifteen miles per hour past single-family homes and blocks of two-story attached houses the signs pointed out as villas. There appeared to be three permissible colors for residences in Hibiscus Pointe: muted pink, pale apricot, and cirrhotic yellow. The development did not seem particularly Floridian. I had no sense an ocean was ten miles away. The Pointe was a fungible community with palm trees that, but for the humidity, could have been in Phoenix.

Rose Moscowitz: The more I thought about meeting her, the more my broken ribs throbbed as if my pounding heart were attached to them. I slowed to about ten miles per hour, fearing that in this unstrung state, I'd mistake the accelerator for the brake and run over a urologist in a golf cart. After a couple of wrong turns onto Orchid Circle and Bird of Paradise Way, I got to the clubhouse, large and apricot, with a red-tiled roof. I gave over the car to a valet named MIGUEL and walked inside, into a blast of air that could have originated in Antarctica.

No men waited in the marble-floored, crystal-chandelier-lighted frostiness of the clubhouse lobby. Chairs and couches, upholstered in dark green chintz decorated with pink, red, and yellow hibiscus, were mostly occupied by women of a certain age, i.e., the age that would qualify them to be grandmothers of people my age. I stood just inside the heavy glass door and gave the space my reporter's once-over, that 180-degree visual sweep to get a sense of the place, as well as the women in it. Actually, that makes me sound too relaxed. My heart was still thudding, and I half expected to wind up shrieking at the sight of myself morphed into a seventy-eight-year-old with jowls and an Hermès scarf.

I quickly eliminated the gossipy twosomes, then the lone women, eyes demurely lowered, deep in thought or checking out one another's shoes. Instead, I focused on the one woman who was reading. Her back was straight, her head bent so she could read the book resting on her lap.

Either she felt my eyes on her or she was periodically surveying the room because when she saw me, she slowly inserted a bookmark. In one fluid movement, she was up. No old-lady stiffness in her rise, no hands pushing against chair arms for leverage. She merely uncrossed her ankles and her legs took care of the rest. She was tall and quite slender, but with unusually long arms. Despite a super-femme watch with a pink leather band on one wrist and a Wonder Woman–ish silver cuff on the other, her build was more suggestive of a women's basketball forward than a fashion model. Still, she managed to look elegant. Her hair was pulled into a bun; it was the gray that gave off silvery glints, so the overall effect was chic rather than granny-ish.

She walked toward me until she was a couple of feet away and then asked: "Amy Lincoln?"

"Yes." My heart stopped pounding and started racing at close to the speed of light. I was relieved to see she wasn't as cool as she was trying to look either. Her eyes began blinking at about the same speed as my heart. I wanted to cry out, *You think I look like my mother!* but I just said: "Nice to meet you, Ms. Moscowitz."

"Would you like some lunch? They have good salads and sandwiches, but of course if you'd like something more . . ."

"A salad would be fine." She nodded, but seemed unable to move. Finally clutching the book against her chest, she led me through a doorway tall and wide enough to accommodate an Abrams tank. I couldn't tell if she was deliberately displaying the book's title, but from the bookmark it appeared she was nearly finished with *The Crisis of Islam: Holy War and Unholy Terror*. I had to admit to myself that was cool, especially since Grandma Lil's choice for stimulating reading had been columns with bolded names: "Among the guests were **Count Roffredo Gaetani, Maisie and James R. Houghton**, and raconteur **Howard Stern**."

If you loved looking at golf courses, then the view from the excessively green dining room of the Hibiscus Pointe club was for you. Before Rose Moscowitz could even offer me a seat, I slid into the chair with its back toward the windows. As a journalist, you quickly learned not to sit facing any source of light that might blind you to the expression on the face of the person you're interviewing. I could have used a glass or two of wine, but didn't want the word *alcoholic* to bubble up in Rose Moscowitz's semiconsciousness. "I appreciate your asking me to lunch," I said. "Though I can think of about a thousand more relaxed circumstances under which to break bread."

"I agree," she replied, although she didn't smile. Her drawn-on lips were slightly wider than her natural ones. Otherwise her makeup was subtle, not that heavy cosmetic veil many older women use to hide the flaws that come with growing older, the foundation that cracks along fault lines as the day wears on. Still, though well put together, she wasn't a pretty woman. Not even attractive. Her face was an oblong, and with her prominent front teeth pushing out her lips, she would have been called horsey had she been a Wasp. Being what she was, it was evident she'd been born in those years between universal suffrage and universal orthodontia.

"If it's all right with you," I said, "I'd like to get business over with." I reached into my handbag and pulled out my *In Depth* ID and set it before her, beside her bread plate. Then I extracted my wallet and took out my driver's license and, for good measure, my MasterCard. She looked at the photos, at me, then back again.

"Central Park South," she murmured to my driver's license. "Your magazine must pay you well."

"No. I'm subletting a two-hundred-square-foot studio that faces the buildings on West Fifty-eighth Street. The owner is our Asia bureau chief. If he ever comes back, the only place in Manhattan I'd be able to afford is an apartment in the low-income housing project in which I grew up." I supposed she was intimidating me since I felt pressured to give up colloquial English and go for the sentence that didn't end with a preposition.

As she handed my cards and ID back to me, the waiter came over. She ordered a chardonnay, so I did too. When he left, I put the wallet back into my bag, took out a file folder, and handed over copies of my birth certificate and Chicky and Phyllis's marriage license from Maryland.

This was not a casual woman. She studied the two papers for several very long moments. "The name on both of these is Phyllis *Morris*, not Moscowitz."

"Correct. Members of my family knew my mother had changed her name from Moscowitz. However, Morris or Moscowitz, the birth dates on the documents are hers. And when I mentioned my last name, you immediately asked if I was connected to Charles Lincoln. Obviously, you knew of him."

She brushed some imaginary lint from the bodice of her gray

dress and readjusted the silver clasp of her belt so it was perfectly centered. Her pink-banded watch had diamonds around its face. She said quietly: "There is no proof that would stand up in a court of law—"

"I'm not interested in a court of law." When the waiter—his name tag said BUZZY—came back with our wine, she reached for her glass and, without preliminaries, took a healthy slug. I had three fingers on the stem of my glass, but my hand was trembling so much I had to leave it on the table. "I'm not interested in getting back at anyone," I told her. "I don't want money. I'm not even sure that I want to meet . . ." I hesitated, then said, ". . . your daughter."

"What do you want?" I can't say her tone was dripping with honey. When I didn't answer right away, she twisted her watch to get the face right between the knobs of her wrist. However, she did not look to see the time.

I willed my hand to get a grip on itself and managed to bring wine to mouth without spilling any on my shirt or on the foam green tablecloth. "Did you have a mother who was around during your childhood?" I asked her. She nodded, a little coldly. "You asked what I want. Let me try to explain," I went on. "Think about adopted children: They always wonder about their biological parents, but mostly they know there was at least a shot that their birth mothers would have kept them had it been at all feasible. They also know that their adoptive parents wanted them, or minimally, wanted a child. But for me it's different. My mother didn't want me. This privileged and intelligent young woman couldn't come up with any alternative to abandonment. All my life I've lived with the knowledge that no matter how good I was, I wasn't good enough."

Rose Moscowitz leaned forward. "Look, I'm sorry about what happened to you and all that. But Phyllis was not a young woman. Well, these days they call everybody who's female *woman,* but she was a girl. A girl who'd gotten herself into a terrible—excuse me, into an untenable situation."

"You're right. She married a punk. She was living in a tenement that had a rat in residence." Her eyes widened and the blinking started up again. "You didn't know that?"

"I don't feel comfortable saying what I did or didn't know."

Here I was, outing my own vulnerability, and this woman's response was the deep freeze. At that moment, part of me wanted to get right up and call John and tell him, *See? This is what happens when you show that you're vulnerable. People back off.* Meanwhile, the other part of me said, *Fuck vulnerability: I couldn't have gotten to where I am from where I've been without being tough.* Also, as far as Rose Moscowitz's aloofness went, I was used to politicians, half of whom shut down the charm when I persisted in asking a question they didn't want to answer. So I'd developed an immunity to the cold treatment. "Ms. Moscowitz, the last thing I want is to make you feel uncomfortable."

She seemed a little flustered, but finally said, "Thank you."

"But I want to check out the other half of my gene pool. And I also have a need to know about a very bright seventeen-year-old who, with or without her parents' knowledge, chose to get out of an untenable situation by pretending to go out for a couple of hours. She never came back."

"Didn't your father take care of you?"

"My father was sent to prison a few months after I was born. That's where he was when she took off. When he got out a few years later, yes, he did take care of me."

Rose Moscowitz was silent for so long Buzzy came over and handed us menus. She put hers on the floor beside her handbag and book. Then she swallowed. "We didn't . . ." she began. "We had no idea. When Phyllis ran off, we assumed it was with the man who kept coming to pick her up and drop her off. Each time he'd be driving a different car. We only knew his name was Chicky. Or that was what my husband, Selwyn, thought it was."

"Everybody calls him Chicky," I told her.

"My husband hired a detective. When he couldn't track her down, he hired another one—from a big agency on Third Avenue."

"Did you call the police?"

"Yes, but the police sergeant told Selwyn that if it were his child, he'd employ a private investigator. The police would try, but they really didn't have the manpower to keep going on any one missing person case unless there was evidence that a crime had been committed, like kidnapping or homicide."

"Did you believe your daughter had been the victim of some crime?"

She lifted her arm and wiggled her index finger, for the waiter. "Please, order anything you want. I mean, I would stay away from anything that's too elaborate. The kitchen is good, but basic."

Buzzy returned. Although he was wearing a smile, I noticed his eyes had a resentful dullness. A fleshy man with a crew cut, he had a double chin that hung below his collar and partially obscured his bow tie. His face could have been in an old newsreel, one of the crowd spewing *nigger* when federal marshals escorted black kids to school. Then I thought that maybe his feet hurt. "Yes, ladies?" he asked. Rose Moscowitz ordered a salade niçoise and I told him I'd have one also. "Very well, ladies."

"I forgot where we were," Rose Moscowitz told me.

"I was asking if you thought your daughter had been the victim of a crime."

"My husband did. He was sure Phyllis had been, you know, sexually assaulted and killed. It took years off his life. Years.

Sometimes, late at night when I woke up and couldn't get back to sleep, all sorts of—oh God!—horrible, sick, violent scenes would play in my mind. But most of the time, I knew she would be all right. Selwyn used to say, 'I wish I was blessed with your naïveté.' Except I wasn't naïve. I knew Phyllis would not get into any relationship she couldn't control. Yes, she was a runaway, but there's a difference between being willful and being self-destructive. I suppose *willful* is too weak a word, but I can't think of anything else to call it." She started to stare at me again, and did nothing to disguise it.

"Do I look like her?"

"No. Not at all."

I took a sip of wine. When she didn't say anything, I took another. Then I said: "Do I look like anyone in your family or your husband's?" She said nothing. "Okay, let me change the subject then. Let me try to reassure you some more. At *In Depth,* my beat is American politics, the Democratic Party. One of the candidates for their nomination for president has been accused of fathering a son out of wedlock." She nodded. "I did some background on that story, enough to know what a claimant's legal rights are in that sort of paternity case." She gave me a single blink. "So I'm well aware I have no rights, no rights to financial restitution, no rights to ask for a DNA test. Of course, if you said to me, 'Go to such and such a lab and give them some skin cells or blood,' I'd be there in a shot." She was concentrating so hard at maintaining a neutral expression that I couldn't tell if she was listening. "I know you have no way of assessing my credibility beyond checking my bona fides and using your own judgment, but that's the truth."

"Who brought you up?"

"My father's mother. Lillian Lincoln. Grandma Lil. And, as I told you, my father—the times he wasn't serving time."

"You mentioned you grew up in a low-income housing project. So you were poor?"

"Not impoverished. My grandma had benefits from the city and the state and worked part-time at a beauty salon. Upscale. The salon, not my grandma."

"She was a hairdresser?"

"No, a leg waxer." She started blinking again, but I was used to people being flummoxed upon getting this information, so I went on: "When I was fourteen, I got a scholarship and went off to boarding school in Connecticut. By that time, I was essentially bringing myself up."

Her sigh had a little commiseration in it, or maybe pity, but I thought most of it was because she was on overload. When the bread guy came around, we both chose whole wheat, then, simultaneously, got busy doing the break-roll, pull-out-soft-stuff, eat-only-the-crust-with-a-micron-wide-schmear-of-butter business. My first thought was to make some remark about us sharing the same bread gene, but then I figured that might push her from overload to collapse.

After an uncomfortably long couple of bites of bread, she asked: "What was it like for you at a boarding school? You said you went to Ivey-Rush, didn't you?"

"Right. Before I went there the first time, for my interview, I was a total wreck. I was afraid I'd screw up, say something I thought was perfectly okay but they'd think was incredibly coarse. Or that I'd get there, and even though I wanted it more than anything, I'd realize I wouldn't fit in. But what struck me almost instantly was how at home I felt." It was weird, being with Rose Moscowitz, a woman who wouldn't win the cuddle-some award, talking to her as if she were somehow obliged to make the best of me. As if she were family.

"The interview was in February, and it had just snowed up

215

there. The trees had white icing, and the sun was out, so everything sparkled. It was the most beautiful place I'd ever seen. Not just the trees, because I'd been up to Central Park dozens of times. What thrilled me was the entire setting, the perfection of the buildings, redbrick and tons of ivy. I remember how the brightness of the snow lit up the dark colors of the bricks and ivy. That minute, it occurred to me for the first time that no matter how right Ivey felt to me, they might decide I wasn't right for Ivey. I was sick with dread for a whole hellish month and a half, until I got my acceptance letter."

Probably without being aware of it, Rose Moscowitz took the excess bread she'd pulled out of the roll, buttered it, and popped it into her mouth. When she was finished swallowing, she asked: "Was it easy to fit in with the other students?"

"Not at the very beginning, because most of them went so out of their way to be nice. It underscored that I really didn't belong, because a lot of them weren't particularly nice to each other."

"They were snobbish?"

"Only a few. The woman who's been my best friend since Ivey was perfectly awful at first. But I don't think it had much to do with anybody's wealth or social status. It's more the nature of fourteen-year-old girls. Cliquish, occasionally cruel. So if they're excessively kind to you, you know you're pathetic. You'd probably find the same thing today at any public high school in the country."

"But in the long run you liked it?" she asked.

"In the long run I loved it."

I needed a breather. As luck or God would have it, the two salades niçoises arrived at that moment, awesome creations in giant oval glass bowls. Tomato and potato wedges and black olives ringed the base of a mountain of lettuce. At the top, skinny string beans and anchovy fillets spilled out from a tuna volcano. Rose Moscowitz watched as I transferred five of the six anchovies to my bread plate.

"That's exactly what I do!" she declared. "I never say no anchovies, and I keep thinking, *Oh, the next time I should remember to order just one.* But I always forget. I can't believe there's somebody else who does the same thing." She sucked in her lips for a second, as if struggling to keep her mouth closed. When she opened them, she asked: "What do you do with your one anchovy?"

"Watch." I put my final anchovy onto my bread plate, cut it into dainty slivers, then placed the slivers randomly about my salad.

Her brows moved up in astonishment. Unlike Grandma Lil, who drew on her eyebrows in a bad imitation of the Jean Harlow-ish grease-pencil arch, Rose Moscowitz's were unplucked. "Could it be genetic?" she asked.

"You mean like a low-tolerance-for-anchovies gene?" She seemed so silvery, like a cold moon, that I was taken aback when she actually smiled.

Her smile encouraged me: I spent most of the salad asking her about herself, most people's favorite subject. Her mother had come from Poland as a child and her father's parents from Hungary. She was the first person in either family to go to college. She'd gone to Brooklyn, had majored in English. "In those days, women didn't work once they get married. It was like announcing, *My husband is unable to support me.* So I never even thought of working. I just went to college because I like to know things."

"Did your husband go to college also?"

"No. In fact, he had to quit high school to work. At a bicycle shop near Prospect Park. By the time we were married he was almost ready to buy his own store. But he was very proud of my degree. A lot of men of our generation wouldn't have been, because it was like the woman showing them up. But Selwyn wasn't at all like that. We went to the theater two or three times a month. The ballet. He was always buying tickets for something."

"He sounds like a wonderful man." *So what happened with Phyllis?* I wanted to ask.

"Tell me more about yourself," she said. "How was it at Harvard? Did you feel comfortable there?"

"Never completely. Even though I was getting good grades, it took me five semesters to convince myself I wouldn't flunk out. But ever since I knew about Harvard, I wanted to go there. I wanted its magic. I wanted to be able to say those two syllables anywhere in the world and, if not be automatically accepted, at least know I'd probably be at the front of most people's line. I could have gotten better financial assistance packages at Penn and Vassar, but I wanted the name. I felt I needed it. I know that sounds shallow, but that's how it was."

"Did you like it?"

"I guess so. I got a fine education, met some extraordinary people. Some nice ones, too. But Harvard's institutional reputation loomed too large for me. I wasn't able to love it. All I could be was grateful I was there."

"I'm sure you got as much out of it as anybody possibly could."

"No. I'm not brilliant. I'm definitely not a scholar. I'm just smart and hardworking. Probably manipulative, too. Kids like I was—intelligent, tenacious, and socially or economically challenged—tend to be very good at getting powerful people to help them accomplish their goals. Teachers, social workers, rich alumni, deans of admission. It's not that hard. People genuinely want to help. They love to have a success to brag about and also to do a good deed. What they don't want is a permanent responsibility. And they can't even think about the possibility of endorsing a failure. So out of all the deserving kids in the world, it's the assertive and, frankly, the facile ones who get helped. Like me."

Rose Moscowitz's town house, one of the apricot residences, was surprisingly pleasant. I guess my first thought after *I cannot faint* when she led me into her living room to look at family photographs was *Hey, this is really nice*. Her gray and silver chill had led me to expect white marble expanses with furry white rugs ripped off the backs of baby mammals. Instead, the floor was composed of large blue tiles and covered with brightly patterned, almost gaudy rugs that I hoped had not been woven by child labor. The furniture was a mix of heavy dark Spanish and light country French, plus a mosaic-tiled table here, a rough-hewn rocking chair there.

"This is so pretty," I said. "All these wonderful pieces work so well together." I tried to keep my eyes from darting about the room, searching for pictures of my mother.

"Thank you. A lot of this"—her arm made a sweeping gesture around the whole room—"is what Selwyn and I picked up when we traveled. Quite a few of the pieces didn't look right in our house in Brooklyn and wound up in our guest room or the attic. But when we bought this house, it all seemed to fall into place."

I wondered whether all the cheery objects were reflections of Selwyn's taste or choices she herself had made before she grayed with widowhood. I didn't wonder too long because she motioned me over to a long, narrow table that stretched between two windows. It was covered with framed photographs. Now that I was there, my grandmother was looking as if she regretted inviting me. She stopped short a good foot and a half before the table. I wondered whether she was afraid I'd barrel ahead, grab the frames, and fog the glass by heavy breathing. Or that I'd sweep the pictures off the table in a rage.

"I guess you want to see what your mother looks like." Her voice was flat. Before I could answer she reached out and handed me a photograph of a man and woman. "That's Phyllis and her husband, Ira. They live on Long Island."

"I know."

"How did you find us?"

I didn't answer. I just stared at my mother. Unless Ira was seven feet tall and four hundred pounds, Phyllis was as petite as advertised. And pretty. Liquid green eyes, red hair, a face like a valentine—high cheekbones tapering into a small, slightly pointy chin. "My father . . . I can't believe it. He said he couldn't remember whether or not she was actually a redhead."

My grandmother sighed. It was less an exhalation of breath than a vocalization of weariness that her own mother's family must have brought with them from Poland. "Actually, when she was younger her hair was somewhere between very dark red and reddish-brown." She picked up another photo and, before handing it to me, took back the one I was holding. "This was her a couple of months before she ran away. It's one of the ones Selwyn gave to the police and the private detectives. When we knew she was all right, I wanted to get rid of all those pictures, but Selwyn wouldn't let me. He said it was a lovely picture and that the pain of what happened would pass."

"Did it?"

"No. Not for me. Not for Selwyn either, although he'd never admit it." In the photograph, my mother looked so seventies I almost wanted to laugh: hair way past her shoulders, a purple velvet shirt with bell sleeves that ended about three inches short of her wrists, frayed bell-bottom jeans. A peace symbol hung from some sort of a metal necklace that looked as if it had been made from a wire hanger. "Once she started seeing, um, your father, her whole style changed."

"To what?" I asked. I couldn't take my eyes away from my mother's to look up.

"I'm not sure. Updated gun moll. Maybe motorcycle girl. All of a sudden, her clothes were too short and too tight. She went from looking so natural, like one of those girls who put daisies into the soldiers' rifles, to being heavily made-up with everything iridescent."

Looking at my mother at sixteen, I felt more cut off from her than ever. "Well, Ms. Moscowitz, you were right. I don't look anything like her."

"Please, you don't have to call me Ms. Moscowitz. Call me . . . anything you'd like."

I was afraid that if I called her Grandma, she'd clutch her chest and quickly take her place beside Selwyn. "Is Rose okay with you?"

"It's fine. Are you finished with that picture? If you'd like, I'll have copies made and send them to you."

"I'd like that very much."

"Let me show you something else," Rose said. She walked over to a tall, carved cabinet that said *Spanish* as much as a rose between teeth. She opened the doors on the bottom and took out a leather album, dark blue with gold tooling. At first I thought it was a wedding album, but then I saw it didn't have those stiff pages. *Rose and Selwyn* was engraved in gold script across the cover. Inside were pages and pages of pictures, held in place by the old-fashioned triangular glue-y things in each corner. She hurried through page after page, then stopped. "Look." A nicely rounded, well-buffed nail pointed to a black-

and-white picture of a bride and groom—Rose and Selwyn—and two other people I assumed were the maid of honor and best man.

The finger came to rest on the maid of honor, so I looked closely. "Oh my God!" I said, or more likely gasped. "She looks so much like me!" It wasn't just the woman's round face, the small cleft in the chin, the wide-spaced eyes. She had my broad shoulders. Posed beside my grandmother, it was clear she was around my height as well.

"That's Selwyn's sister, Carol."

"Is she still—"

"Alive?" Rose asked. "Yes. She lives in California, in Marin County. She and her husband moved out there in the mid-fifties. They built up a very nice business. They service boats. Whatever that means. I'm not sure. I suppose scraping things off the bottom, although I doubt if they do that themselves."

"Did she age well?"

"Very nicely."

Twenty or thirty photos later, I determined that when I got to be seventy-six, I could deal with looking like Great-aunt Carol, sans her natural look of chopped gray hair and sun-bleached lips. By that time, it was pretty clear to me that my grandmother was controlling what I could see in the picture albums—there were three more—and I was just along for the ride. We sat side by side at the dining room table while Rose, middle finger dampened, moved through the pages without actually opening them up. Obviously she had some sort of a system going because she'd go turn-turn-turn, lick finger, turn-turn, and stop at a page that, sure enough, had another picture of Great-aunt Carol, Great-uncle Mike, and Selwyn at the Monterey Jazz Festival, a decade later than the previous picture I'd seen.

I was wiped to the point of suggesting we both take naps, so after Rose said, "We went to Tuscany with Carol and Mike," I said: "After those pictures, I'd like to see some more of my mother." Her head bobbed down and up, which I took for a nod of yes. Still, I needed to feel more secure that she was simply avoiding telling me about Phyllis for a short while, not clamming up forever. However, I sensed she was one of those people who preferred to experience life obliquely rather than directly. So I got as oblique as I could: "Do Phyllis and Ira have children?"

Rose bobbed her head again. I kept quiet not because I was cool, but because I didn't want her to feel as if I were browbeating her. I couldn't risk leaving, then never getting copies of the pictures she'd promised me. I didn't want to discover that she changed her number to an unlisted one. So no pressure.

Also no answer. I was fantasizing about driving back down to Miami Beach, buying a somewhat whorish halter top I'd seen in a store window, and getting drunk at one of the bars on Ocean Drive. Or maybe popping a few Percocets, not that I had any. I took this train of thought as a sign that all was not well with me.

"They have two sons," my grandmother finally said.

"Oh." Either they looked like Freddy Krueger or Rose had put their photos away in anticipation of my visit.

"Nicholas and Ryan. They're both very bright boys. And polite. Good values, too. That's what I'm happiest about, their character." She closed the album and clasped her hands on it, then shut her eyes. She looked as exhausted as I felt. "According to my daughter, I'm not very emotive. Well, I grew up in an era when talking to near-strangers about your personal life was not thought of as openness. More that you had a screw loose." Then she fell silent.

I rubbed the heels of my hand along my quads, something I always did after a run or when, like now, I was a basket case with sweaty palms. Dear God, please don't let her get all schmaltzy and start telling me about her loneliness and crying about Selwyn. Or offer up some hideous tale of incest between Selwyn and Phyllis, or her and Phyllis, to explain my mother's intractable ways. Oh God, save me from emotive.

"Both times when Phyllis was pregnant," Rose said at last, "I was hoping for a girl. I'm happy to have a granddaughter." She took time out to inhale and exhale. "And I couldn't have asked for better."

"Thank you." I was getting choked up, so it came out a Rod Stewart imitation. "And vice versa."

"I suspect we share a not-very-emotive gene as well as the one for anchovies," my grandmother said. I nodded and we sat in silence for a time that didn't seem too long because this time it was bearable.

Finally I said: "We share something else. We were both abandoned by Phyllis."

"I was up most of last night," Rose said. "I have to admit I was reeling from the mere fact of your existence. The one thing I couldn't get over was that Phyllis is such a good mother."

"You never call her Véronique?"

"Only when I had to. Her first marriage—I should say her second—was very short, only a couple of years. His name was Preston Groesbeck." She spelled it for me. "That must have been around 1978. Of course by then we knew she was all right. The detective agency we hired . . . they tracked her down about a year after she ran away. She was living in Los Angeles. They found her because she'd used her own Social Security number. That's not supposed to be public information, but I suppose they have ways. She was living in what they called a group house. It sounded like they were a bunch of hippies or post-hippies who came and went. To make a long story short, we agreed to wire her some money and she agreed to call as long as no questions were asked. Well, we wired the money. And when she got it, she actually called. I was surprised. Anyway, she said she'd been in San Francisco and now was leaving L.A. to go to an ashram. She wouldn't say where, claimed she didn't know, that it could be anywhere, even India. But she did say that she would call us once she settled in to let us know she was all right."

"Do you have any idea why she was like this?"

"None," she said softly. "It's something I've never stopped thinking about. Before she ran off she was seeing a psychologist. When all was said and done, the psychologist was as shocked as we were. I mean, Phyllis was rebellious, but those were the years for it. Vietnam, what have you. Nice girls her age, Brooklyn girls, were using pot and some sort of mushrooms with hallucinogenic properties. And every other word out of their mouths was f-u-c-k. But those girls wound up buying prom dresses, or at least going off to college. It was a stage." She took off her silver cuff, set it on a side table next to the love seat, and massaged her wrist. "Runaway girls often ran away for only a day or two. That's what everyone said. Even if it lasted longer, they eventually reached out for their families. But if the detective agency hadn't tracked her down, I honestly don't know if we ever would have heard from her."

Sitting right beside someone, it's awkward to try to look her in the eye all the time because you're practically nose to nose. I'd gotten fed up looking at the hibiscus trees and the golf course just beyond them. So while Rose was gazing down at her long-fingered hands, I checked out the house. It was one of those town house affairs without defined rooms. On one side of the living room in which we were sitting was a TV-library-game room. In the center of it, a chessboard set up on a square table. On the other side of us was a dining area that opened onto a kitchen. It was the sort of place that would be good for a couple who couldn't bear to be out of sight of each other. Or as a sitcom set, so the camera could dolly along from room to room to room.

"You were talking about calling your daughter Véronique," I prompted her.

"We didn't even know she had changed her name. Well, we knew about Moscowitz to Morris. She called us periodically, a *This is to let you know I'm alive* phone call. But she didn't want to see us. We thought maybe she'd had an accident and something awful had happened to her face, or that she'd had plastic surgery so she couldn't be found. We didn't know.

"But then she called and asked us if we'd fly out to New Mexico. Santa Fe. She was getting married. Selwyn and I were on extensions, and he was saying, 'Of course we'll be there,' and sounded so thrilled. So I didn't say what I wanted to say, *Let me think about it.* Then she was on to how her name was now Véronique Morris and if we were going to reconcile, we could never refer to her as Phyllis. And our names had to be Morris when we were there. So from that time on, even after she walked out on Preston and met Ira, we always called her Véronique to her face. But I think of her as Phyllis."

"Did you ask her why she chose that particular name?"

"No. She's not someone who explains very much. When we were flying out to Santa Fe, I thought maybe Preston was some sort of socialite and that she felt the name Phyllis was too déclassé for him and Moscowitz too Jewish. He turned out to be a time-share salesman. Nice, ordinary. Good-looking, but the farthest thing from a jet-setter you can imagine."

"Does Ira think your last name is Morris?"

"No. He's a very nice man, but I'm always uncomfortable with him. I know he must be thinking, *What's wrong with her that she named her daughter Véronique Moscowitz?*"

"So the name Phyllis is a secret?"

"I suppose. I don't see her often. And I really don't see her alone, without Ira or the boys. Ira calls her Véronique. I usually don't call her anything, but when I do it's Véronique, and she's never corrected me." She stood, went to the cabinet, and took out the framed photographs she'd stashed away. "I'll show you Nicholas and Ryan."

About half an hour later, when I was leaving, she asked if I was going to contact Phyllis. I told her I still didn't know.

"Does she know I'm here?" I asked.

"No." Then she said, "It would be nice if you and I could see each other again."

She walked me outside to my rented car. Neither of us could figure out how to say good-bye, so we wound up doing one of those fast cheek-to-cheek air kisses. I got into the car and kept the door open for a minute, waiting for the hot blast from the air conditioner to cool. Rose turned to go back indoors, but then came right up to the door. "We should keep in touch."

"I hope we will," I told her.

"Call me whenever you want to come down. I'll pay your airfare. You can stay here. If you'd be more comfortable, I'll be happy to take care of a hotel room."

I reached out, took her hand, and gave it an affectionate squeeze. Probably even more than affectionate. My grandmother squeezed back.

Chapter Twelve

Having spent my first full day back in New York writing about where the Democratic presidential candidates stood on the diminished ozone layer and global warming, I was no doubt oversensitive to the chill of what was supposed to be a spring evening. The air was wet and bitter, waiting for snow that would not appear so late in April. But winter was hanging on and would not give in to spring.

I stuck my hands into the deep pockets of a cashmere sweater I'd had since 1990. It was thick and beautifully cable-stitched, though the sleeves were too long; it was also orange. The girl at Ivey who had gotten it as a birthday gift proclaimed she looked hideous in orange. That was why she was giving it to me. Since only five or six people on the entire planet actually looked good in orange, I was walking up Madison Avenue in full knowledge of how less-than-lovely I appeared but how wonderful I felt in cashmere.

"Do you remember who gave me this sweater?" I asked Tatty.

"Suzy Dalton. Don't ever ask me *Do you remember?* when it comes to clothes. You know I always remember." It hadn't been easy to get Tatty to go for a walk. The only way to get her to move was to promenade past the windows of expensive stores. She was not fond of the outdoors, though she was enthusiastic about weather because changes in climate required changes of wardrobe. "Amy, did you honestly think you could distract me, talking about a sweater?"

"I was the one who was telling you all about Rose Moscowitz," I replied. "What's in it for me to distract you? Did you ever consider that the reason you get distracted is that you're eminently distractible?"

"No, I have not considered." At that moment, her eyes were looking right, at a display of cane handbags with leather trim that seemed to have been inspired by the suitcases in *The Grapes of Wrath*. This particular homage to the migrant worker started at about five hundred dollars per. "And while we're on the topic of considering," she went on, "have you ever considered that I am not a typical *In Depth* reader?"

"Tatty, that is so obvious it's beyond consideration."

"Then how come all you're giving me is facts? Facts, and all that boring archaeology or anthropology about the different places that different kinds of Jews move to in Florida. If you're not in the mood to talk about the human drama of meeting a grandmother for the first time, you could at least tell me about what you were thinking." I picked up my pace and got her past a scented soap/potpourri store and across the street before she slowed again, this time to study an array of antique watches. "Give me one minute," she said. "I've never seen some of these pieces before."

I buttoned the sweater and lifted its shawl collar higher around my neck. I should have been working on a Monday night. The magazine closed Tuesday and I was only half through with my article. I'd done a pretty complete outline on the plane coming back, so at least I knew what I was going to write and in what order I'd write it. But by five in the afternoon, I was worn out, not so much from the work, but from the effort of keeping Rose, my mother, my half brothers—to say nothing about John—out of my consciousness. I'd called Tatty, then walked up to her apartment to take her for an airing.

"Are you ready for my thoughts and the human drama of it all?" I inquired. "Or are you going to stand in front of those watches for half an hour observing the march of time?" She began walking again, and with her long legs, it was at a fairly good clip. "Tatty, it's not that I'm avoiding telling you what I felt meeting Rose. When I made the date with her, I didn't think I'd feel anything. It was just a logical first step to see her, before the big emotional onslaught of meeting or even seeing my mother. I figured that if Rose wasn't senile or a vicious bitch, I could probably get some insight that could help me if and when I decided to approach my mother." I took a deep breath. The air was so cold I could feel it flow through my nostrils and make the plunge down into my lungs. I blew it out through my mouth and was disappointed not to see a frosty mist. "If I do decide to see her, I wonder . . ."

"What? You wonder what?"

"Would you please give me time to finish a sentence? I wonder if she'll look like a total stranger—okay, a total stranger I've seen a couple of pictures of. But I've read about a phenomenon called infant amnesia, that for some neurological or developmental reason, you lose all memories of what happened to you as a baby."

"Never heard of it," Tatty declared.

This was not a shock. "So I'm wondering, if I do see her, will it be an emotionally neutral experience? Or will I get this sudden rush of memories? All the Mommy business. You know, like her saying *This is your nose, this is Mommy's nose* or *I love you* or *Shut up or I'll beat the crap out of you*?"

"I wish I could tell you, Aimée."

"I keep thinking about that old saw, that you can't put back the genie once you open the bottle. Maybe I should stop now. What if she turns out to be a moral monster? Or something worse?"

"Like what?" She looked intrigued.

"I don't know. There are any number of appalling possibilities. I have to give you credit, Tatty. You were the one to tell me to leave well enough alone."

"It's amazing how you can be so smart and so dumb at the same time." She had been saying that on and off since our second week at Ivey. "The genie is already out of the lamp or bottle or whatever." She blew on her hands, then stuck them into the pockets of her vest. Sheared mink. Dyed dark blue. "As a matter of fact, the genie got out the minute you told Rose your name and that she could check you out at *In Depth* and Ivey and every place else you ever were for more than two seconds, you fool. *Au revoir, Monsieur Genie, 'allo Véronique.* Okay, there's no law saying you have to go and meet your mother. But what if she comes to you? And what about this nouvelle grand-mère? Nouveau? Isn't it odd that I think it's *nouveau*? Do you think you want anything to do with her?"

"Yes. It's kind of weird, because she seems like a tight-ass. But I found her thoughtful, honest—well, I guess she's honest. Maybe I was taken in. But no, I don't think so. For all that control, she has emotional depth. Clearly, she was in love with her husband and that's a terrible loss for her, still. And she loves her grandsons."

"Ugh, half brothers!" Tatty exclaimed. "What if you reconcile with your mother and have to be nice to them, too? What could you do except take them to the Planetarium? Boys are so unknowable between ten and fifteen. Pimples, braces, and constant useless erections."

"To continue," I said. "Even though Rose is a very restrained person, I think a lot of that restraint is centered around what happened with her daughter. The trauma of it. You know, I told her that she and I had something in common: Phyllis abandoned us both. But at the same time, I couldn't stop wondering what was so horrible about Rose and her husband that would make a sixteen-year-old girl take off and not get back in touch. Not for a few days. For years."

Tatty stopped in front of a window, but didn't look in. "Maybe nothing was wrong with them," she said. "Did you ever think that? Maybe Phyllis-Véronique was one selfish, hostile piece of shit. Maybe the really amazing thing is that her mother is still willing to have anything to do with her." Her back was toward the store window. She glanced over her shoulder for an instant at the full-sleeved white blouses and beribboned dirndl skirts for Upper East Side peasants, and blew up her cheeks in an about-to-vomit gesture. "Come on, A. Phyllis-Véronique is a type. You know, all those kids we knew when we were fourteen whose character wasn't forming but was already in cement. All right, some were sweeties for life. But some were bad to the bone. *That's* your mother."

Actually, I was thinking I was disappointed Tatty didn't like the skirts and vests, because I thought they were pretty great. I once told her I thought she was part of a cabal that met quarterly to decide what was chic and what ought to be sneered at. And whom. Some of what she and her fellow chic raved about was incomprehensible to me: coats that looked like Klan robes, hobo bags that looked like portable potties.

"Now *you're* the one looking in windows," she announced, in a voice half of Madison Avenue could hear. "You're sooo distractible!"

"Shush, Tatty."

She lowered her volume slightly. "Not only that, look at what you're looking at. I bet you don't know why. I know. Because you were poor and your grandmother could only buy you the little box, with ten crayons. Anything in those kindergarten colors is irresistible to you. As I was saying, Phyllis-Véronique was the *worst*. Walking out on you, not coming back, not ever trying to get in touch." I attempted to interrupt her but she was on a roll. "Compare her to Grandma Lil and Chicky."

"What are you talking about?"

"They were loyal," she said. "I, for one, completely adored Grandma Lil, even though she was a perpetual embarrassment to you. I'm not saying you shouldn't have been embarrassed, even though you pretended you weren't."

"Lay off, Tatty. I wasn't embarrassed."

"Please. That time she told me, 'Tatiana, I know it's not classy to call someone classy, but you, my dear, have class.' You wanted to die!" I nodded. Old friends have unfortunately long memories. "Did Lil want to take care of a ten-month-old baby?"

"I guess not. No. But she did."

"That is just my point. Lil was responsible. She probably even loved you in her own self-centered, clueless way. Even if she didn't, she did what was right. She stuck by you. And look at Chicky. He got out of jail and what was the first thing he did? Took care of you. How many—pardon me—fuckups like him in their twenties get out of jail and only want to do the right thing for a little kid?"

"I know."

"It's not just being responsible. Just think about them: a criminal and, with all due respect, a leg waxer/shoplifter. Isn't it amazing? I never thought of this before. Both of them had good character. *You* have good character. Where do you think you got it from? Phyllis-Véronique? No, you got it from the people who brought you up."

Tatty and I wound up at Chop Meat Charlie's, a dingy coffee shop in her 'hood that residents embraced because they thought it delightfully sincere. Among Charlie's offerings was a tuna salad that tasted so close to the glop we'd eaten at Ivey it became our comfort food. Objectively, we knew proper tuna salad should not be as sweet as lemon meringue pie. Nor should it be studded with chopped pickles. Still, this was what we yearned for. We hit Charlie's every few weeks. After the tuna, we split a dish of coffee ice cream, so by the time I got home I was feeling properly comforted.

It was only about eight-thirty. Naturally, before I even took my sweater off, I checked voice mail. Two messages. The first, from *In Depth*'s production department, was something between a plea and a demand not to go over fifteen hundred words. The second was from John Orenstein.

"Hey, Amy, it's me. John. Listen, I want you to know that if you'd like to come to our Seder, you're still invited. This invitation is from me and also my parents. I know with all that's . . ." He hesitated for a second, and tried to cover it up by making a big deal about swallowing. ". . . that's happened you might not think the invitation is still in effect, but of course it is. I promise you, you won't feel uncomfortable. Well, let me know if you can come. I'll probably drive up early that day. If you take the train, I'll pick you up at the station. Okay, hope you can make it. Bye."

"Did your mother put a gun to your head?" I blurted out after I slammed down the phone. I might have gone on a rampage for a few minutes, but I was so upset my digestive processes went into shock and I kept hiccuping tuna-pickle and coffee ice cream fumes, which not only made me nauseated, but hurt my ribs.

I said, "Go fuck yourself, John," more decorously, then sat in the middle of the couch➜bed and did some yoga breathing. This took a while since, besides my anger at being an Orenstein family object of pity, I couldn't get over being broken up about how our relationship had gone from great to stale to broken beyond repair. I was torn apart, too, at the thought of how much of the blame was mine.

Once I calmed down, I got myself all fluttery again when it occurred to me that maybe John was using the holiday as a means of getting back together, consciously or subconsciously. I immediately divided myself in two so I was able to have a heated debate as to whether or not John was too direct in his dealings to use such an adolescent—Aha! But was it adolescent?—approach.

Naturally, this got me nowhere. I picked myself up from the couch and found a pen so I could deal with my response in a rational manner. As a first, I decided to make a list of talking points in order to sound *compos mentis* when I spoke to him. However, after jotting down *appreciate offer/other plans*, I drew a blank. I realized the wisest course would be to sleep on it. Naturally, two seconds later I was on the phone.

By the third ring, I knew John wasn't home, which of course put me on the road to rage again, thinking: *He calls me relatively early in the evening. I return the call later in the evening, when he should be home, but of course he's not because, having offered the invitation, he also has to make it clear that it's in no way an opening to resume the relationship. At this very moment, he's probably banging La Belleza standing up, in her five-hundred-square-foot walk-in closet, so that if I call him on his cell phone, he can be out of breath—and she won't be able to repress a giggle.*

I had already altered my grip on the phone so that when I smashed it down again I wouldn't break my nails. That was the instant it dawned on me that even if I hung up before his voice mail clicked in, my number might still register on his caller ID and how pathetic it would look if I called back an hour or two later, obviously dying to speak to him in person. His voice mail said, "This is John Orenstein. Please leave a message."

"Hey, John. Amy. Thank you for the invitation, and please thank your parents for me as well." So what that my heart was pumping double-time and squeezing all the blood through my arteries to my head and that I could truly feel my once and future stroke coming on? "I love how your family celebrates Passover, but even though I know I'd enjoy the Seder, I don't belong there. I appreciate your wanting to include me. I hope you and your family have a great holiday. Oh, and just to let you know, the search for Phyllis Moscowitz Morris Lincoln Véronique Groesbeck Hochberg is going well."

The next morning, I was watching my cursor blink on and off, debating whether to call Thom Bowles the *bête verte* of the Bush administration's environmental policymakers, when my phone rang. It was Happy Bob: He wanted me in his office, "to talk about Thom Bowles."

I traipsed down the narrow hall without looking into anyone's cubicles. God, how I hated coincidences like that: I think Thom, two seconds later someone else says Thom. Normally a summons to Happy Bob's office meant he was too uncomfortable to do his usual drop-in: clomp into your office without a *May I*, squint at your monitor to see what page you were up to, sit on your desk, crumple your papers with his ass, and direct his breath up your nose.

Everyone knew what was wrong when he was unable to walk. His discomfort was due to either flatulence or shin splints. The former was evident when you opened his door. The latter became clear when he'd draw up his slacks and, with two fingers on either side of the tibia, massage up and down his legs, occasionally emitting a squeal when he tugged at one of the few hairs on them. Now, however, his request sounded ominous.

"Have a seat," Happy Bob said. I was sitting on the only chair he had by his desk, a ladder-backed piece he'd bought at auction and told everyone was Shaker. Everyone said *Wow* or *I love the stunning simplicity*. The chair was pitched in a way that it pushed you forward a bit, not a great position to be in after two bowls of Frosted Mini-Wheats. "The environmental piece almost done? It would be good if you handed it in before lunchtime." He was wearing his least luminous smile.

I decided to be brave and inhale through my nose rather than my mouth. No gas. "It won't be finished until three or four," I told him. "I did a lot of interviews, probably too many, and I want to give each candidate approximately the same space, going to the depth, or the lack of it, of their commitment, and also who their advisers are. And then I got a call last night telling me fifteen hundred words, which I took to be a twisted joke."

"Look, what with Iraq and what's going on internationally, you'd be lucky getting a mere five hundred words. But I'm generous. You want to make extra work for yourself and write more than fifteen hundred? I can't stop you as long as you get the piece in by five-thirty, but I can guarantee you it will be cut and there won't be time for delicate surgery." He was being his usual irritating self. My fears about a looming Thom Bowles–related disaster abated. Too soon. "What the hell has been going on between you and this kid who's stalking Bowles?"

I asked, "Do you want me to write about the kid?" with a great deal of amazement that I didn't feel.

"Now Amy, you know I don't." He said this with his really broad smile, which besides being repulsive, was an omen that his next sentence would be far worse than the previous one. "Have you been talking to this Fernando Carrasco on the sly?"

"On the sly?"

Someone from the Bowles campaign had learned that I'd talked to Freddy. For a reporter at *In Depth*, folly, but certainly forgivable. No one cared if you talked to a kid making a paternity accusation, as long as you didn't demand to write about him. But for me to have counseled Freddy, to have gone out of my way and gotten him a lawyer, was probably as much unethical as it was foolish. This wasn't exactly a news flash to me. I'd known when I gave him Mickey Maller's number that this wasn't one of my more stellar moves, but I hadn't cared. Freddy was a kid in search of a missing parent and I was compelled to help him. Also, I figured the chance of anyone's finding out about my involvement was close to zero. Not close enough.

"I talked to Freddy Carrasco, but certainly not on the sly."

"About what?"

I took a deep breath. With it, alas, I discovered Happy Bob had indeed said *Fill 'er up* at the gas pump. "About his claim that Thom Bowles is his father," I explained. "Listen, there are two types of interesting stories: the ones that are fit for publication in *In Depth* and those that aren't. Right? This kid didn't seem like a stalker or someone who's unbalanced. I wanted to hear what he had to say. I bought him a cup of coffee and I listened. There's a decent chance he's telling the truth."

"Why didn't you tell me anything about this?"

"Because it's the type of sleaze we wouldn't touch with a ten-foot pole or anything else."

"Isn't that for me to decide?"

"Trust me."

"No, I trust myself."

"Are you the Potter Stewart of sleaze, Bob? You know it when you see it?" True, this was not the polite way of resolving an issue between an associate editor and the editor-in-chief. I realized that I ought to make some move that could be construed as an apology for my big mouth. Except Happy Bob was one of those people in journalism who overvalued guts, probably from having seen *All the President's Men* too often and envisioning himself as the Golden Mean between Jason Robards Jr. and Robert Redford.

Since I couldn't apologize without being seen as a wimp, I kept talking. "Bob, I'd always taken you at your word. During Paula Jones and Monica Lewinsky, I let you be my guide. I learned a lot. Just as Greg"—the reporter who covered the Republicans and the right—"learned from you during the Gingrich and Livingston brouhahas. At this magazine, as you run it, there has always been clear lines between what's news, what's analysis, and what's crap." He tilted his head to the side for an instant, his 'tweren't-anything gesture. So I added: "And you're the one who drew those lines the staff doesn't cross over."

He swiveled back and forth in his chair. "Next time," he said, poking his index finger at me, "if anything like this comes up, I want to hear about it."

"Absolutely." True, he'd been pissed, but part of what he was saying was also *I want to hear the gossip*. It always amazed me how so many high-level newspaper and magazine editors, far from the street and their old sources, retain a mean-spirited cub reporter's insatiable appetite for dish, the nastier the better. "So," I began with a smile, "who from the Bowles campaign subtly designated someone not in the Bowles campaign to complain to you about me?"

A bigger smile, a display of more teeth, even a crinkling of eyes. You'd expect a smile like that from an editor at one of Rupert Murdoch's lesser tabloids. "Forget about it, kid," he said. "Get back to work."

"Are you busy?" I asked Gloria Howard. It was an unfair question, because it was Tuesday, the day articles were due to be edited and copyedited by Wednesday. No one was not busy. She swiveled from her monitor around to me and adjusted the clasp of her seed-pearl necklace so it was in perfect alignment with her cervical vertebra. The jacket of her dark green suit hung on the back of her chair. She wore a pink silk blouse and looked ready for a Junior League luncheon or an interview with the Dutch prime minister. In all the years I'd known her, in and out of the office, she had never dressed as if she were expecting a minor moment.

"Yes. I'm busy. I'm trying to explain in detail as well as in depth how Germany and France are trying to pound a silver stake into the U.S.'s heart. It's going slowly. My article, not the stake." Because she was a senior editor, Gloria had an actual office, not just a cubicle. Except for a bust of Cardinal Richelieu she'd picked up at a flea market, she had not embellished the room. The furniture, a blond wood desk and two chairs, along with a red ceramic lamp that looked like a fat derrière in too-tight slacks, appeared to be of the Danish modern school and probably came from one of our Revered Founder's later marriages. I always wondered if after accomplishing a successful *coup de rédaction* and becoming executive editor, Gloria would redecorate Happy Bob's ex-office.

"Can you give me two minutes?" I asked. "That probably means no more than five."

"Come in. Have a seat."

"It's Happy Bob," I told her. "Someone not in the Bowles campaign was told by someone very much in the Bowles campaign to give Happy Bob a message: that I was getting too friendly with that kid who's claiming that Bowles is his father. Too friendly in the ethical sense, not in the sexual. So I did my *Come on, Bob, get serious* song and dance and I think calmed him down a little. But he really, really never liked me and now he has more fuel for his fire. I'd even say he hates me if I thought him capable of any interesting emotion."

"And your question is . . ." Gloria asked.

"What should I do?"

"About . . . ?"

"Give me a break, Gloria. You're using up my minutes with—whatever the hell this is. Socratic dialogue. What should I do to get Happy Bob to loathe me less?"

"If it were I, I would do nothing." What I liked about Gloria was that she kept talking and didn't make you say, *Oh, tell me what you mean, Great Oracle.* "Why bother? No matter what you'd do to get him on your good side, he would view it as weakness, which would only confirm whatever negative view he already has—if in fact that's the case. You don't have to worry. He is well aware that you have what this magazine needs: a talent for writing in an incisive and interesting manner."

"Are you sure I shouldn't do anything?" I demanded.

"When have you known me to be in doubt? I'm not claiming certitude is my finest quality, but there you have it. If you want the total truth, Amy, and I'm assuming you do, it's that you are too sensitive. You want to be liked. Fine. Lovely. You're gifted at being likeable. But if someone doesn't like you, you don't necessarily have to do anything about it. Just keep a respectful distance and do your work."

I looked at my nails, an excuse not to see Gloria's inevitably self-assured countenance. When I finally did look up, I asked: "Not do anything at all?"

"Right. I don't think there's anybody on the staff who hasn't thought *Happy Bob hates me* at some point. When I first got here, I was convinced he hated me because I was black. That was somewhat pedestrian, but I couldn't think of any other reason why he wouldn't like me. Then, when he began to smile upon me, make me his protégé, as it were, I was convinced he was doing it because somewhere in the past he'd had an episode—don't ask me what—and therefore needed to appear Afrophilic."

"But now you know he genuinely likes you," I said.

"No, I know he likes my work. He likes my directness. I have no idea if he likes me personally, and what's more, I don't care. Neither should you. He hires and promotes on the basis of merit, that much I've learned."

"Thank you."

I got up, took a few steps, and was halfway out when she said, "I can't believe you're walking out! For God's sake, sit back down and tell me about the kid and Bowles. *In depth,* Amy."

Chapter Thirteen

Political campaigns generated such huge amounts of e-mail that even during the buildup to the primaries, you could sense cyberspace vibrating from overload. This did not mean the fax machine was obsolete. If you were on a candidate's media list, any press release was also faxed, reflecting the belief of press assistants that reporters ignored e-mail that did not have VERY URGENT as its subject line (URGENT by itself having taken on the new meaning of BARELY WORTH NOTICING). Thus, the four colleagues and I who shared a fax replenished the paper reluctantly because we knew the machine would spend hours spewing out all the outdated releases its tiny mind had retained.

Still, no matter how hard a journalist might try, there was close to zero chance for anyone covering a campaign not to be aware of an imminent MAJOR ANNOUNCEMENT. Unless a member of the media was lying in bed dead drunk, or on a candidate's shit list, or had lost computer, cell phone, and beeper, he or she could not avoid knowing when something big was about to happen.

In my case, it was the shit list. I learned Thom Bowles had scheduled what his press secretary, the lovely Moira, was billing as *The most important press conference of his career* when I saw some of my colleagues suddenly staring at their pagers or talking on cell phones seconds before a Chat with Dick Gephardt Informally! event. On one side of me was an *L.A. Times* guy with wavy Romeo hair and on the other a woman from *USA Today*. I asked her what was going on because he struck me as one of those newspaper types with a *His Girl Friday/The Front Page* getting-the-scoop mentality who had never learned to share.

"Bowles is going to talk about that paternity thing," she said.

I flipped open my cell phone and gave its minuscule screen the evil eye. "Damn. It didn't come through. Can you tell me where and when?"

Two hours later, at three in the afternoon—so the announcement could be shown on all the early evening news shows—I was standing outside the Pan American Press Club with just about everyone who had been at the Gephardt event plus an astounding number of nonpolitical reporters whose media embraced the sleaze as much as *In Depth* embraced the ponderous.

Better to stand outside the Pan Am Press Club than a lot of places, I decided. It was one of those double-width town houses that had probably gone from being a rich family's home to an embassy to its present incarnation, as headquarters of some tax-exempt, let's-get-democracy-throughout-the-western-hemisphere-and-all-be-friends group. When a political campaign rented its double-width ballroom/auditorium, it was usually well funded enough that it could pay extra for coffee and non-rubbery muffins, or even a pile of half-sandwiches. Having missed lunch, I was simultaneously thinking about roast beef on rye and recognizing there was a reason I had not heard about the big-time Bowles announcement.

Someone yelled out: "What the fuck is holding up this fucking thing?" Someone else closer to the door said, "They're *really* checking ID." I asked myself if all this meticulousness, beyond the usual security measures, was because the Pan Am required it or because Moira was nervous about having to deal with so many nonpolitical journalists, photographers, and camera operators.

As I got closer to the door, I noticed hired security guards checking ID. One of Moira's assistants was standing behind them, her head bobbing up and down as the final authority: *Okay, let them in.* She was a kid who spent too much time trying to be Little Moira, mostly by being discourteous and loud-mouthed.

"You can't go in," she told me when I got to the door.

"Why not?"

"Because."

Not only did I have limited patience for asinine behavior, I also wasn't about to miss whatever Bowles was going to say. I glanced behind me. A fair number of people were still waiting. Ergo, I had about thirty witnesses.

"Why don't you want me to hear what Bowles has to say about this paternity business?" I demanded. My voice, after all, had been trained to be heard over many square blocks of the Lower East Side.

"Shut up," the Moira-ette told me. "Do you think screaming your goddamn head off is gonna get you anyplace?"

"If I don't get in, this isn't going to be your story anymore," I told her quietly. "I'll turn around, start talking about my friend Freddy Carrasco, and bingo, all the cameras will be on me."

"Don't even think of trying to play hardball with me," she said.

"Your choice." I turned about halfway toward the rest of the reporters on line, but then looked back at her, as if she were an afterthought. "What are you putting on here," I asked, "amateur hour? You're barring a journalist whose magazine is unlikely to publish anything about this press conference. Do you think I'm going to shop my story around somewhere else?" I gave her my best exclusive-girls-boarding-school-plus-Harvard look of contempt—which didn't amount to much more than slightly raised eyebrows, probably much like my *Where is the ladies' room?* look. "I'm on the staff of *In Depth*. There is a difference between staffers and freelancers. You ought to get that clear."

Her eyes moved as far to the right as they could go. She was searching for Moira, but didn't want to be obvious. Still, it was just she and two security guards between me and the press conference. Before she could call for backup or simply say no on her own, I was inside. As I whooshed past her, I murmured: "Smart decision. Thanks."

The ever-lovely Moira Fitzgerald, looking like a Holstein in a green turtleneck, lumbered over to the podium and in her usual mellifluous tones bellowed, "Shut up and sit down." The TV and print media people in their early twenties chuckled, happy to be witness to such an unforgettable character, the archetypal tough dame—loud and rude. Those of us over twenty-five muttered some variant of *Fuck off, Moira* and took our seats in the velvet-covered chairs. Not folding chairs. I hid myself as best I could between the bulk of a hunky guy from the E! Network and a nonhunky Brit from Sky News who had the contours of a hot-air balloon.

The Pan Am Press Club did not have a formal stage, but

rather a bandstand on which a small orchestra might have played for some early-twentieth-century debutante. So instead of glancing offstage, Moira waited until a door opened and someone signaled her by sticking out his head and nodding.

"Everybody," she said, "I am happy to introduce Jennifer and Thomas Bowles."

They walked out holding hands. Jen Bowles was yet another American wife standing by her politician/athlete/clergyman/performing artist as he acknowledged an extramarital affair, siring an out-of-wedlock child, or stealing from the poor to make himself rich. She was perfectly dressed for the sweet-and-loyal-yet-no-schmendrick part in an American version of a Chanel suit, sky blue with red trim and brass buttons. She wore low-heeled black patent leather pumps so she would not dwarf the man she was standing by.

He took his place behind the podium while she took hers about three feet off to the side. "Ladies and gentlemen, I appreciate your coming on such short notice," the senator said. He paused long enough to prove to me it was a technique some speech coach had taught him. "I know many of you heard about an incident that took place during a fund-raiser here in New York. It was widely reported that a young man, uninvited, came to this event and announced"—he coughed quietly into his fist—"that I was his father. Well, he was packed off by security, not too roughly, but packed off all the same. I had my campaign organization issue a denial saying I had no connection with this young man."

He took a deep-enough breath that the shoulder pads of his charcoal gray suit rose, then fell. He glanced over at Jen and, yes, she smiled at him, no doubt to give him the will to go on. "I do not take family lightly. I am more than lucky in that regard. I am blessed with a wonderful wife and two fine daughters."

The choreography worked: April and Brooke, or possibly Brooke and April, walked out onto the stage and took their place on the other side of their father. The blond one was wearing a plaid skirt, short-sleeved sweater, and ballet flats, the kind of style girls in Oregon wear or, more likely, the style an older person in Oregon would think a girl should wear. She was either calm or sedated. The dark-haired Bowles daughter, who had grown considerably heavier than her sister with just a few weeks of campaign food, wore camel-colored slacks and a bright blue sweater with yellow suns and moons, the aggressively cheerful garment of someone who does not want to appear self-conscious about her weight.

"Obviously," Thom Bowles continued, "I'm not here to tell you that I love my family, even though I do. I want to talk to you about someone not in my family, someone who is no longer with us. Nina Carrasco." Either he had a fine ear for language or a Spanish tutor, because he said her name perfectly. "Nina was a first-generation American, an enormously bright, hardworking woman. Actually, she worked for my father. I met her when I was going to college and I can't tell you how much I admired her. It didn't take long before I fell in love with her."

He spread out his hand sideways. Jen took one hand and the blond daughter gave him her right hand while at the same time reaching for her sister's with her left. After what was presumably a supportive squeeze along the chain of Bowleses, he let go of the hands.

"Even though Nina and I were in love, it couldn't last. Those were the days before many Americans considered diversity the gift that it is. Both our families put pressure on us. It did not make for a happy time, and neither Nina nor I had the strength to defy some of the people we loved the most.

"About a month and a half later, Nina called me. She was

pregnant. I never asked, but she told me straight out—right away—that she would not consider abortion. I asked her about marriage, and she said no. I told her that I was proud to be her child's father and that I would take care of him or her and be the best father I could. Unfortunately, this didn't happen."

Bowles wiped his hands along the sides of his slacks. I couldn't tell if they were sweaty or if he was playing nervous. He looked around the audience of reporters, took another deep breath, and continued—without notes or teleprompter. "Nina did not believe that a marriage between us could work. As she so wisely put it, *You and I are too strong for that, Thom! It cannot work when it's forced.* She thought it was better that I be out of her life and out of our child's life. She was firm about the child not being pulled between two cultures that, at the time, had limited understanding of each other.

"If I had been more self-possessed at that stage of my life, I would have argued with her. As it was, although I was of legal age, I was a kid. I offered to pay child support. She asked me instead for a lump-sum payment, the better for us to keep our distance from each other. I borrowed money from my father and gave it to her. I asked her to let me know when she had the baby."

He tried to keep talking, but seemed to be choked up and lifted his index finger to say, *Give me a minute.* His gaze was now above the reporters' heads, as if checking out the plaster garland that was part of the room's ornate molding. I was too far back to see if there were actual tears or if he was trying to get the light bouncing off the ceiling to make his eyes look misty. "Months later I received a call from a friend of hers, someone I didn't know, who told me she'd had a son. He would not give me the boy's name. I could not see the boy. This is what Nina wanted."

I knew what would happen next. Thom Bowles would talk

about Freddy, saying *Fernando* with a flawless R and A. He would explain that he moved to Oregon because he couldn't bear to stay in New York and not be able to see his child. He would offer some two-sentence version of how he grew from a boy into a man in the west, so I figured he must be somewhat confident about the New York primary.

Thom Bowles would then say how terribly, terribly wrong he was to have kept all this from Jen. Because she would have understood. She would have urged him to try and make contact with his son. She would have given him the courage he didn't have when Freddy first approached him. Instead of reacting like a politician, he would have acted like the father he was. Then Freddy would appear onstage. The only question I had was whether he'd walk out the door and stand beside his siblings or their mother.

It went pretty much that way. Thom Bowles was saying, "I'd like to introduce you to my son. He is a brilliant young man, a computer science major here at the City College of New York. He is also a warm and thoroughly decent human being, a credit to his late mother. Ladies and gentlemen . . ."

When he enunciated "Fernando Carrasco," Freddy, looking great, came out. He passed in front of Jen Bowles. As he did, she reached out and squeezed his hand. They exchanged brief smiles. Then he stood beside his father. A candidate's suit and tie for Thom. Sports jacket, golf shirt, dark khakis for Freddy, most likely chosen by an older Oregonian and not by a hip New Yorker.

Father looked at son fondly. Fond look returned in kind. Freddy looked out at the media and said: "I have been welcomed into a wonderful new family. Ever since my mother died . . . I feel now I have a place to belong. This coming together is new for all of us. I know my father is a public man. I respect him for

that. I would have voted for him anyway." Light laughter bub-
bled through the tough audience. "I ask you to please allow me
my privacy. My father is ready to deal with you twenty-four
hours a day. I'm not. Thank you." Then the Bowles-Carrasco
family cleared out.

The E! Network guy sighed and said, "I can't believe it. I'm
honestly, wow, touched. How weird is that?"

The Sky News guy said, "Nice work, wrapping up the Latino
vote that way."

After the press conference, I went back to the office for a few
hours. When I got home, about nine-thirty, I ate half of a pint
container of chocolate-marshmallow frozen yogurt for dinner.
After that, I took a bath and began watching a special report on
CNN: two journalists had been killed and some others injured
after U.S. forces fired on their hotel in Baghdad. The Pentagon
explained that the commander of the troops believed the place to
be a source of sniper fire. I clapped my hand against my forehead, the Duh! gesture, thinking about how doubly awful the
deaths were. What kind of sick son of a bitch could have thought
up the term *friendly fire,* and why the hell did the military keep
using it?

But time after time, my attention wandered. I could not get
the image of Freddy Carrasco out of my head. Whenever I'd met
him in the past, he'd always looked like a Before picture in an ad
for Prozac, a sufferer of longtime sadness. Up on that polished
dance floor in the Press Club, his eyes had sparkled when Jen
Bowles squeezed his hand. Standing beside Thom Bowles, he
radiated high energy. It was as if a momentary paternal touch on
his shoulder had transformed him from a blah boy into a man
full of vitality.

When I'd first seen Freddy being escorted out of that ridiculously posh apartment on Central Park West after trying to claim a parent, I hadn't even bothered making a comparison between him and me: I was made of much stronger stuff. So if being taken into Thom Bowles's life had done so much for Freddy, what would I become if I reunited with my mother? Xena the Warrior Princess? What would it be like to have a parent really love you? Sure, I know Chicky loved me, but if there were a paternity court, he might be adjudged a father of diminished capacity.

This led me to remember something Gloria had said a couple of years earlier. A few of us were having drinks on Tuesday night after work and somehow the talk rolled around to what our families' expectations of us had been. She said she'd been in fourth or fifth grade and had used the words *horizontal* and *vertical* in describing something to her mother. Her mother was so overcome with joy that she immediately called her husband to announce even further proof of Gloria's genius.

When I had been older than that, I think in seventh grade, Grandma Lil told me that if I'd stop wearing blue nail polish, when I finished high school she would put in a good word for me at Beauté.

That was the best she could imagine for me, waxing legs or maybe someday giving facials. She'd had no concept of what I was. Forget calling someone to proclaim my genius. Even for a woman who lived for superficialities, she never once said, *Amy, you look great,* or *Your boyfriend's a cute guy.* Instead, it was *Your hair looks greasy* and *Do you have to go out with every spic in the neighborhood?*

What was Freddy doing now? I imagined him taking all the Bowleses and his girlfriend uptown to some little restaurant between his place and City College. The senator would grab for the bill, but Freddy wouldn't let him pay. *It's on me.* I was won-

dering what he would call him: Thom? Dad? It was all so touching it didn't take long before I could almost see the movie version on Lifetime cable starring Jenna Elfman as the brave and
loving Jen.

There was absolutely nothing wrong with Steve Raskin, criminal
defense lawyer. In fact, on the phone, he'd sounded better than
most potential blind dates, telling me, "I'm not one of those men
who meet for drinks. From what Greg Watson said about you, I
think we could probably stand each other for three courses."
The Greg in question was my counterpart at *In Depth*, the guy
who covered the Republicans, the right, and the radical right in
all its forms—East Coast moderates to neoconservatives all the
way to radical racist, homophobic, anti-Semitic groups. Greg
hadn't known I'd broken up with John for the simple reason
that he probably didn't know I was seeing anyone. We were
congenial colleagues, not friends.

"Are you and Greg Watson good friends?" I asked Steve
before I ate a forkful of mysterious appetizer wrapped in puff
pastry, which he'd recommended. I'd given up salads on blind
dates years earlier because of the baby-spinach-sticking-to-teeth
factor.

"Fairly. I met him when I was in the U.S. Attorney's office.
He was interested in a case I was prosecuting, a bunch of right-
wing crazies. Refusal to pay income taxes."

"I like him a lot," I said, "although I don't think we've ever
talked about anything except politics. I was surprised when he
came over to my desk Wednesday and asked if he could fix me up."

"Actually, I mentioned something to him about my girlfriend, my ex-girlfriend now, moving to San Francisco for her
job. I asked if he knew anyone nice . . . Greg is a pretty basic guy.

He probably thought single Jewish male, single Jewish female—it's a definite go. What's with the Lincoln, though? How did that happen?"

"The usual way. Ellis Island, wanting to be a real American, couldn't deal with three syllables so Washington was out."

Who was I to complain? Steve Raskin had taken me to a well-regarded, totally nontrendy restaurant with heavy white table linen and waiters in short black jackets, a place where we did not have to strain to listen to our own conversation. He had an easy smile along with one of those massive but solid construction-guy bodies I was often attracted to. I considered height an over-rated quality. Growing up in a neighborhood in which real men carried their lunch to their jobs had formed my tastes. On the basis of looks, I would always trade in a six-foot-two guy with fine bones and aristocratic posture for a five-foot-eight guy who looked as if he busted kneecaps for a living. Plus, having recently tossed aside a doctor, Shea D'A, I knew I'd be a fool to take for granted an eligible lawyer.

"So you cover all the candidates?" Steve asked.

"We aren't a weekly in the sense that we offer the news of the previous week. We interpret, explain, try to give the big picture."

"Okay then, give me the big picture on which Democratic candidate would have the best chance against Bush."

How could I object to this rara avis, a blind date who believed there was something else to talk about besides himself, a man who was actually intrigued by what I did for a living? I started telling him about the candidates' strengths and limita-tions, but I couldn't whip up my usual enthusiasm for politics and being the center of attention. I felt only half present. The rest of me was waiting for John to call.

Look, I told myself, this is a completely predictable, run-of-the-mill funk. What woman approaching her thirtieth birthday wants to go through that struggle of looking for love, or even companionship, yet again? Was I missing John or just missing having a real boyfriend? Was I missing him or his family? Steve listened closely and ate his salad, apparently not having baby-spinach-teeth issues. The Orensteins were special: good-natured, thoughtful, happy with one another, generous to outsiders. So different from the Lincolns. My father would have been happy with a minimum-security prison, while the Orensteins loved and tended an old colonial house on five acres. Was this all I really wanted, to be part of a family that preferred gardening tools to burglary tools?

It was John, I decided. His family was just another one of his assets. Except I couldn't have him. Even on the tiny chance *La Belleza* was a PBS producer, he'd said my distrust was just the tip of the iceberg. Fine, so I was a realist. No more John. Then how come I couldn't lighten up a little more, at least to be more appealing to a man like Steve? If you'd been dating in New York between ages twenty-one and twenty-seven and a half—when I'd met John—you knew a catch when you saw one. Like the guy across the table from me. Easy, smart. Probably tough, being a trial lawyer, but not mean.

Steve would be fine: I didn't have to date him for six months or a year to know that. I could marry him on the spot and start having babies. I didn't even have to worry if he would want to marry me: I knew he would, even though he might not realize it this particular night, although my guess was he knew I was a def-inite candidate. We would date for four months, pro forma, and then I'd be deciding between platinum and gold.

Go for it, I ordered myself. Don't be one of those women who mourn the death of a relationship for so long that by the time they recover their ovaries have shriveled and their spirit is dead. Here was the rare man, aside from John, who I could take both to my Ivey-Rush reunion and to the diner in Queens to meet my father. Even the guys I fantasized about as a kid, like River Phoenix, the ones I'd endowed with every amazing power, weren't this adaptable. Steve Raskin and I could be that *They met on a blind date* couple who would give other women hope. We could have hot sex on Saturday night, then laze in bed together on Sunday mornings and watch George Stephanopoulos and Tim Russert.

But men weren't plug-and-play. Steve was admirable, Steve was fine. Maybe I was just tired from work, or maybe from the idea of, yet again, having to meet a new guy's friends—no doubt most of them married—and feeling obliged to praise excessively their pictures of little Max, who would be either a son or a basset hound. But Steve wasn't John. Nevertheless, I gave him my best semidimpled smile and got a bright, wide grin in return.

It could work.

Another day, another restaurant. Uncle Tai's was the newest hot spot in Chinatown, which meant that within six months, Uncle Tai's heart would be broken by the mass desertion of the big-spending media and financial types who would pick up on an aside by one of those high-tone, suspiciously thin food writers that Uncle Tai's cha sui bow was less than authentic. Meanwhile, Frankie Watanabe, *In Depth*'s hippest editor—although there wasn't much competition for the title—had organized a Sunday noon dim sum brunch to celebrate Gloria's birthday.

Everyone knew Frankie was au courant because her hair was always cut no more than an inch and a half long and her entire wardrobe was by some designer whose work was said to be post-postmodern, i.e., unstructured, i.e., her clothes hung on her. For all I knew maybe her face could also be called post-postmodern, if that meant going without makeup despite having no discernible lips and eyebrows made up of many scattered hairs, like cilia that had lost their protozoa. She was a rising star at the magazine, an associate economics editor, a good writer. She frequently worked with Gloria, especially on articles about the European Union.

The waiter rolled around a rattling metal cart stacked with covered dishes of some new delicacy and said something in Chinese that caused the women at the table, everyone but me, to say, "Ooh!" It was an *ooh* in the happy, anticipatory sense. Except when he lifted the hemispherical cover from the dish, I realized we were not up to dessert. So I said no thanks to chicken feet in ginger sauce and ate some more rice. I wondered if John had spent the night with *La B.* Her place? His? Or were they already living together?

"What are you," Dana Jones asked me, "one of those picky eaters?" Along with me, she was the only staff member at the table who did not work directly with Gloria. Dana was sport editor. Our Revered Founder had not liked the word *sports*, and had chosen instead the multimeaninged *sport* for the department that covered athletics.

"I'm not at all picky," I told her. "I mean, I eat a lot of different things, but I tend to be leery about newfangled body parts." Also, the barbecued pork pie soon followed by pork ribs with black beans had unsettled me enough to give me new respect for the phrase *losing one's lunch*. "Anyhow, I'm enjoying the rice."

"You don't worry about carbs?"

"Sometimes. Not incessantly."

"Oh."

I suppose many people imagine women sportswriters—or in Dana's case, sport writers—as looking like Vin Diesel with lip gloss. To the contrary, I'd noticed many were over the top when it came to femininity, blond bombshells, brunette sizzlers. Dana was another type of femme. Fragile, like what Mammy wanted Scarlett O'Hara to be. Beneath the white skin of Dana's temples, you could see a network of blue veins so complex it looked like a map of Los Angeles. Her pale blue eyes were the sort that liquefied in bright sunlight. Her hair was the fine, near-white blond of Republican babies. She was so delicately built you feared her soul might be separated from her body with one good sneeze.

Since I'd already failed to get a comfortable conversation going with her about the Yankees or about whom she'd nominate as best American sportswriter aside from herself, I pretended not to hear her "Do you follow *any* specific diet philosophy?" and returned to the group's conversation. In the few seconds I'd been talking with Dana, the subject had changed from the question of Kofi Annan's diplomatic muscle to Caroline Braden, *In Depth*'s arts editor, a woman in her early forties who had quit the magazine when her husband, an architect, decided to move to London.

"Does she have a job there?" one of the women asked. I think she was an assistant editor covering the Iberian peninsula and maybe North Africa. Most of the women at the table worked under Gloria, and I was relieved they weren't involved in some European Union discussion I wouldn't be able to follow.

"No job. Not yet," Germany replied. She had been born and educated there. While she had no discernible accent, she was a bit too definite about the letter T. I guessed she was well into her fifties, because she had been at the magazine for over thirty years. With black hair and white skin, she always reminded me of Snow White, if Snow White had been a middle-aged, stocky German lesbian who wore men's suits. "I don't know what she's going to do. It's not as if they are desperate for arts writers in England."

France was the sort of woman who wore leather jeans and black fuck-me shoes with ankle straps and four-inch heels to an all-women Sunday brunch. "Not that I would particularly want to live in London, but what was Caroline supposed to do? It's not as if he'd moved to Boston, where they could have some kind of a commuter marriage."

"How could she give this up?" Eastern Europe began hesitantly. She was Polish. Her written English was fine, but speaking the language fluently seemed to require more RAM than she possessed. "At *In Depth*, she was powerful."

"How was she powerful?" a woman I thought might have been Benelux plus maybe Scandinavia retorted. "When Frank Rich was theater critic of the *Times*, he could make or break a play. Maybe even Brantley can." She spoke quickly, impatiently, like someone who has a more interesting date waiting uptown providing she can extricate herself from this one. "We may be a national magazine, but we don't have enough subscribers to sell out *The Producers* for two nights in a row. Well, at least we can't get thousands of people tying up the phones at the box office."

"But important people read the magazine," I said, wanting to forestall Dana reopening our conversation, perhaps by seeking to know my position on trans-fatty acids. "Cultured people. When Caroline made an assignment, or if she thought a particular director's movies were self-important and refused to run a piece on him, her decision could influence the movers and shakers. My guess is Frank Rich and Ben Brantley probably read *In Depth*. I don't see why they wouldn't give some thought to what we write about."

"Excuse me, but we were talking about whether we would quit to follow a husband or life partner," Frankie Watanabe remarked, "assuming he or she had to move far enough away that we could no longer be on staff. What does that say about women?"

"How can you generalize about what's going on with all

women based on a group of writers and reporters?" I asked. "Whether we do political analysis or dance criticism, we have a movable skill. We could write for an English-language periodical or be a contributing editor somewhere, work on a book. Or be like the rest of the world and write a screenplay. It would be different if Caroline had been a corporate executive or in a law firm or was an academic. Moving might mean that she was going someplace where she couldn't get a job." John would have moved for me, I thought. He could find a crew and write and edit almost anywhere. Would I have moved for him? *Yes* came to mind so fast I hadn't the time to think of even one reason why I wouldn't. Steve Raskin and I would stay in New York.

"No job would be that important to me that I wouldn't be willing to give it up for someone I loved," France said. "I mean, what is more magical than—"

Gloria didn't have to clink her glass with a spoon or even clear her throat.

Everyone sensed she was about to speak. France fell silent. "Fifty percent of marriages end in divorce," Gloria began. "Caroline and Tim always seemed to have a fine relationship and we'll all be toasting them on their golden anniversary. But for the sake of argument, let's say Tim runs off with Posh Spice, if that's what that girl's name is. Where does that leave Caroline?"

"She gets another job," France replied. I'd heard she came from that part of Pittsburgh where they spoke English with a Continental accent.

"As what?" Dana demanded. "Either in London or New York, how many top magazine jobs are open to a woman who quit her last job and has been freelancing or—I don't know—writing a book for two or three years? That's a long time to be out of the game."

Gloria held her chopsticks midair. "Here's another thing.

260

Other than for jobs like Supreme Court justice or college president, how many men are there who would pack their bags and move for the sake of their wives' careers?"

"I don't understand you," France said. "Every man-woman interaction cannot be a confrontation. Women are more giving by nature. And we are amazingly adaptable. I could go to Afghanistan tomorrow and make a life for myself." And fit right in with her four-inch-heeled, fuck-me shoes with ankle straps. "If you were with the person who was the love of your life, wouldn't you risk everything to be with him? Or her?"

Dana, the sport editor, cocked her head to one side. "I'd been working about a year and still going with my boyfriend from college. Dartmouth. This is when I was at *Sports Illustrated*. One night I was looking at his profile, a handsome, classic profile, Mark Antony, not Julius Caesar, but what I was really seeing was my future with him. I realized he'd got totally upset when I was going to cover the Super Bowl. I mean, what was I supposed to do, hand over my press credentials so he could get in to see the game? I tried to get him a ticket, but I couldn't and he got even pissier. Right then and there, I knew the relationship wasn't going to work. My work wasn't important to him. I mean, I had a great job, but to him, my main job should have been him. He saw what I was doing at *Sports Illustrated* as a cute postcollege thing. That's all I had to see. He was off my masthead like—" She snapped her fingers.

"What are you saying?" Germany demanded. "That a fulfilling life means being able to love *or* to work? Check only one box? What about Onkel Sigmund's *Fähigkeit zu arbeiten und zu lieben*? He said *und*."

"Forget *und*," Dana said wearily. "For ninety-nine percent of us, there is no *und*."

Chapter Fourteen

That Monday, I yearned for the flu, though I would have settled for bronchitis—anything that would not allow me to get out of bed. True, when I walked my usual running route through Central Park, I was somewhat heartened by the trees. Real spring at last. The cherries were in full white flower—though they could have been apple trees. I was not from the great arborists, since beside oak, maple, and the über-category of evergreens, all I could identify were crab apples. That was because some alumna had donated a grove of them to Ivey. Every spring when they bloomed we had the Grove Walk, during which we strolled along a path through the trees singing the alma mater. It was a tradition I cruelly mocked and secretly cherished.

Now, it was crab-apple time in the park. My second favorite tree was flowering as well, a short, stubby thing with crackly bark, arthritic branches, and cascades of small, hazy pink blossoms that looked like upside-down mops. So much for nature. Maybe I was in a lousy low-endorphin mood from not being able to run. But God, how I wanted to go back to my apartment and instead of showering, get back to bed with a cup of tea I was too sick to swallow beside me. It's not as if I was under pressure. I had more than a week to get out an article on the Democratic left's evolving position on the Middle East. Yet it was precisely the sort of piece I most hated writing. Foreign affairs.

Whenever anyone at *In Depth* did more than touch on an area outside his or her own bailiwick, the article had to be vetted by one of the editors with expertise in that particular subject. While intellectually I appreciated their input, correcting my errors and offering new insights, emotionally I wished they would drop dead, thereby leaving me free to write without petty qualifiers; I detested footnotes in any form. Gloria, of course, was excepted from this disfavor, as was the physics/earth-science guy who had gone over my environmental piece.

But the editor for the Middle East was another story. A former academic, he had an upper-class English accent. I guessed it was upper-class: Though his mouth moved, he sounded as if his nose were doing the talking. His hair was parted slightly to the right of the middle so he always looked off balance. Both in coldest February and the tropical heat of a New York August, he wore three-piece suits. *Ah, Miss Lincoln,* he would say, *luffly to see you.* He thought me a fellow Anglo-Saxon and thereby felt free to make contemptuous remarks about Muslims and Jews. With people like him, I was more direct than usual. But saying *Shut up, Philip* or *Philip, you moron, I'm a Jew* amused him. He seemed to perceive the former response as coquetry and the latter as jest. It was only Monday, I told myself. I didn't have to deal with him until Friday. Nevertheless, I felt like Frodo gazing upon a distant Mount Doom.

Body and soul, I was worn out. Usually my legs came close to being perpetual motion machines. I'd go for my morning run, then walk the two and a half miles to work and never tire. Maybe the discussion at Gloria's birthday brunch the day before had taken its toll. Love or work: a phony setup. No need to choose. Yet all I kept winding up with was work. Never a real, reciprocated love. I had no man. No family. No circle of beloved friends with whom I'd formed a clan to stand in for kin. No people or person I could be with and think, *I'm home*.

Trudging down Broadway toward the office, I was in such a fog that somewhere in the thirties I stood on a corner waiting for the light to change from red to green and began crossing only when the light switched back to red again. Instead of legs, I was ambulating on two logs sawed from a sequoia.

Spring had arrived for everybody else. Pedestrians promenaded with a tra-la-la gait. When I stopped by a deli near the office, there was a long, slow line of people requesting iced coffee and tea. I willed myself not to be impatient, but when I found myself focusing on a pile of grotesquely large apple turnovers, I asked the woman behind me to hold my place, telling her I had a quick call to make.

I found myself in the back of the deli, standing before a pay phone, clutching three quarters in one hand and, with the other, holding the receiver against my ear—a repulsive necessity I had been able to avoid since the advent of cell phones, thus limiting my chances of contracting some new hepatitis mutation spread by drug dealers, the only ones I'd ever seen using the phone. On the other hand, the pay phone was caller-ID-proof. Even if traced, the number would be the one for Nate and Molly's Delicatessen.

Two seconds later, I was dialing a number I didn't even know I had memorized. My heart pounded. I turned my head and saw that if I wanted coffee, I'd better make it fast. That would be easily accomplished because I had no intention of speaking. A voice said, "Hello." I stayed silent. I stuck my index finger into my free ear hoping to hear more clearly.

Was this my mother's voice at eight forty-five on a Monday morning? It sounded fairly deep. Could it be a guy? Maybe Ira Hochberg was a castrato or, okay, a tenor, who left for work late. Possibly one of her sons was home from school, celebrating his voice changing. My heart banged harder. My stomach contracted into a painful knot. "Hello?" The voice was louder, sharper, but I still couldn't tell, man or woman. I hung up, though unfortunately not quickly enough to avoid spotting drug dealer goop on the earpiece. My stomach went from a knot into a backflip and I decided to pass on the coffee.

Five minutes later, I was in the office. After some time disinfecting in the ladies' room, I went to my desk. The usual pile of newspapers was there, as well as the newsmagazines. I opened my bottom drawer and set them all there, then rested my feet on my desk while I listened to messages. Five or six from nearly deranged Democrats deprived of attention, one from *In Depth*'s bookkeeper wanting to know where my expense vouchers were for the Florida trip.

And one from Steve Raskin, the criminal defense lawyer who had absolutely nothing wrong with him. "Hi, Amy. Steve Raskin. Hope you had a good weekend. Are you free this Saturday night? I've got a client who's a ticket scalper, so I can get tickets to pretty much anything you'd like to see. I'm in court this afternoon, but I'll be around most of the morning. Look forward to hearing from you."

What a nice guy. Thoughtful. Objectively attractive. The last quality raised only the slightest issue, that after theater he might expect a fourth act. I'd left my days of this-will-feel-good-even-if-I-hardly-know-you sex behind around the time I turned twenty-five. Well, he could deal. I called him back, had a really good chat about whether Donald Rumsfeld's high-handedness with the press was a cover-up for insecurity or was simply unadulterated arrogance. I told him, untruthfully, I'd probably have to fly out to Iowa for a piece on the caucuses, so if I had to give him an answer today, it would have to be no. He was pretty cool, and suggested that if I didn't go I should give him a call. Meantime, if something came up for him on Saturday night, he might take it, but then maybe on Sunday we could have brunch, take a walk. Was I interested in seeing the Klee exhibit at the Met? If I could make it home by then, that would be great, I told him.

I liked Steve for many reasons, one of them being that he'd called right away. Tatty slept late, so I started making calls for my lefties and the Middle East article until I could get her on the phone and hear her say, *Are you absolutely insane to put a man like that on hold?*

Tatty pretty much said what I'd expected her to say, and at great length. Right before we hung up, she said, "You're still so sad about John."

"I am. Don't tell me to snap out of it."

"I won't. This is a rough one."

I got back to work, broke for a protein bar and a Diet Coke, and when I next looked up it was nine at night. I then had a moment of lunacy. I took a taxi home for the first time in my eight years at *In Depth.* How come I hadn't done it before? If I'd ever analyzed it, which I hadn't, I would have recognized that my budget could withstand the occasional cab splurge. Using feet and subway exclusively would not get my college and graduate school loans repaid years earlier.

When it came to money, I was conservative. Some might call it cheap. Saving the extra napkins from a bag of take-out food. Collecting tiny bottles of inferior toiletries from the third-rate hotels on the magazine's approved list, so I had two shoe boxes full of shampoos, conditioners, and body lotion I never wanted to use.

Maybe it was knowing that if anything happened to me, I had no one to fall back on. Asking Tatty for money would be the end of what we'd always had, a friendship between equals. True, if I were in desperate straits, Chicky would try to come to my rescue. Unfortunately, that would put him in the difficult position of having to figure out how to raise capital: *Hmm, armed robbery or burglary?* He wasn't particularly adept at either. Perhaps I needed a larger nest egg than most people of my age and income bracket because I worried that in time of trouble, I might not be able to resist taking the easy way out and going into the family business, felony.

As the taxi bumped and squealed uptown, I watched the driver's shoulders rising way up to his ears, falling, then rising again. From the back, it appeared an extremely French gesture, one that would go with saying *Je ne sais pas* with much fervor. Shoulders up, shoulders down, over and over. A man with a tic, I decided, not a schizophrenic responding to an auditory hallucination. I closed my eyes, but opened them again fast.

All that day and into the night, whenever I stopped work for even a minute—to get a drink of water or massage the muscles in my neck—I kept hearing the voice from that morning phone call. *Hello.* And seconds later, the greeting again as a demand: *Hello?* Had this been my mother? It hadn't been too deep for a forty-seven-year-old woman whose estrogen might be on the skids. I found myself analyzing that single word. An intelligent *Hello.* The speaker sounded calm. It had been minutes before nine o'clock, but no hint of gotta-get-to-work pressure. No sharp edge as if expecting some annoying acquaintance or a telemarketer. Certainly not the deadened *Hello* of a depressed housewife with expectations of nothing. On the other hand . . . I closed my eyes again. It had probably been Ira.

"Amy!" Rose Moscowitz exclaimed. "How are you?"

"Fine. I figured that if you felt as unsure of yourself as I did about—you know—this actually being grandmother and grand-daughter business, we'd both wait for months or a year before picking up the phone, and then we'd hang up because it would be awkward. Too much time would have passed." Naturally, the instant after I said that, I worried she might respond with *I beg your pardon* in a Queen Victoria voice.

"That's just what I was thinking," she said. "I didn't know your work hours, so I wrote on my calendar *Call Amy* for Saturday. Not that I'd forget." She paused for a moment. "I have a big calendar on the bulletin board in the kitchen. It comes every year with beautiful pictures of Utah. I have no idea why we get it. Why I get it. Maybe Selwyn made some investment out there. I love being in Boca and seeing all those snow and mountain and desert scenes. I'm sorry. I'm going on and on. Anyway, now when I look at the calendar, it's nice to see *Call Amy* in one of the boxes."

"Thank you."

"Can I call you back? You shouldn't run up a big long-distance charge."

"It's fine. The magazine pays for my cell phone, it's a flat fee. I'm constantly calling around the country." I had opened the window for a breath of spring from the park and to hear the clopping of horses' hooves, taking tourists in the hansom cabs on a ride to see how beautiful the city was at night. Unfortunately, one of my neighbors appeared to be cooking up a late supper of fried garlic. I got up and closed the window.

"Good," Rose was saying. "I'd hate to think of me chattering on and on and you being upset when you get your telephone bill. Tell me, are you working on something new? I bought the magazine Friday when it came out. Your article on the environment was brilliant."

"Readable, anyway."

"Don't be so modest."

"Well, just think of it as your DNA in action."

I gave Rose a three-sentence summary of what my Democratic left, Middle East piece was going to be about. Even though I knew she was intelligent, her grasp of the issues surprised me. Everyone in the country had the TV tuned to Iraq for the war, and it was not a huge surprise that a Jewish woman who had made the move from Brooklyn to Boca was informed about Israel. Still, her knowledge of geopolitics, from preemptive counterproliferation to a comparison of Thom Bowles, Howard Dean, and Eugene McCarthy really wowed me. I actually jotted down a note to check whether McCarthy had in fact run for president against George H. W. Bush and Dukakis in '88 as a candidate for some minor party.

We talked for almost half an hour. Just as I was about ready to wrap it up, Rose said: "I called Phyllis."

My only thought was *Oh shit, now she'll know who the hang up was this morning.* "You told her about meeting me?"

"Yes. It wasn't something I looked forward to doing, but I felt obligated. I hope you understand." She hesitated. "Were you planning to surprise her?"

I wasn't planning on anything. If I were someone very objective standing outside myself, I'd have said it was inevitable that I'd try to make contact with her. But right then, from where I sat, I saw myself juggling four or five conflicting emotions, everything from *What if I think she's terrific and she doesn't want anything to do with me?* to *What if I'm overcome by rage and want to punch out her lights?* "Oh, please don't worry. I wouldn't—"

"I know that." I heard her take a sip of something. I imagined chamomile tea.

"How did she react to the fact that you know about my existence?"

"Badly. Not that she got hysterical. She's not that type. When she was a teenager, part of the reason we were so shocked by her rebelliousness and then the running away was because we didn't fight. If we said, *You can't do this or that,* we knew she didn't like it, but we thought she was pouting. Not seething. Not running around with the worst kind of—" She cut herself off. "I apologize, Amy. I'm so sorry."

"Okay. Look, I really don't want to talk about my father, at least not now. Let's just say that his criminal record is probably longer than a single page. On the other hand, he loved me, he raised me during the times he had his freedom. To the best of his ability, he was a good parent."

"He sounds admirable."

"In some ways he is. In any case, I love him." I wished I had some chamomile tea. "Did your daughter say anything about wanting to meet me, or not wanting to meet me?"

"I couldn't tell. It wasn't clear. When I told her about meeting you, she gave out a gasp. Not a loud gasp, but still, hearing that much—I don't know—emotion from her surprised me. I wanted to talk about you, about how lovely you are and how you look like Carol. I mentioned Harvard, but she kept saying in a very quiet voice, 'Oh my God, Oh my God,' and really, I could hardly get a word in edgewise."

"She didn't ask anything else?"

"Let me think. It started out 'Don't you dare tell Ira' and

then, before I could say I wouldn't do a thing like that, she was being—how should I put it?—much less confrontational, much less emotional. More like her usual self. She said what a shock it was, how awful she felt that she never told us about you." I wanted to ask Rose if she thought it odd that her daughter had not said how awful she felt about abandoning a child, but I didn't. I wanted to ask what the hell was wrong in that family that my mother turned out the way she did. "Then she begged me not to see you again."

"And what did you say?"

"'Not on your life, Phyllis.' Then she made a threat."

My stomach did a somersault the way stomachs are wont to do at such moments. "What was it?" I asked in my gentle voice.

Rose's voice got softer, but not gentle. "She said I would have to choose between you and my grandsons. I don't think she meant it. I think she was just, I don't know. Beside herself."

I could hear her breathing faster. "Rose, if you had to make a choice, I know you would choose your grandsons. They've known you all their lives; I'm sure they love you and need someone like you. But I don't think you have to choose. Your daughter is probably beside herself about a lot of things, like having her past lives intrude on the one she's living now. And she's probably upset about not knowing what to expect of me. Oh, and one more thing: She realizes someone other than herself knows that she left my father but never divorced him. She's had two bigamous marriages. Trust me, she's not going to keep a loving grandmother with that knowledge apart from her grandchildren. All three of them."

Strange, after being on the phone talking to my maternal grandmother about her daughter/my mother, the woman I dreamed

271

about that night was Grandma Lil. Not Grandma Lil with a plastic-wrapped filet mignon in her coat pocket, and not Grandma Lil making me practice on our one unbroken chair how a real lady sits: *No, no, no. For Christ's sake, what's so hard about it? If you can learn your times tables you can learn to sit like you got refinement. Amy, pay attention. I'm teaching you stuff you can't get in books. All right, there you are, facing front, your back's straight—come on, straighter. Chin up a little bit. Okay, now this is where it gets hard. Knees together to the left, ankles together to the right, so like your legs are making the letter . . . Whatever. Z? V? You're supposed to be so smart? Figure it out.*

In the dream, as in life, she had Alzheimer's. Not in its early stages, when she got fired from Beauté after coming to work on the wrong days and not showing up on the right ones and burning clients with hot wax. I came home for a week in August after my summer job in Boston ended and found her sitting in a puddle of her own urine watching an oily-haired televangelist declaring, *God wants to be the center of your life!* That turned out to be the week from hell, taking her to doctors, calling Social Security, Medicare, and fifteen other agencies to start the paperwork that would get her help. I observed her trying so hard and unsuccessfully to get her lipstick on straight; she looked stricken, on the verge of tears. What chilled me was my sense that somehow she'd lost the physical ability to cry. I put on her lipstick for her and told her how elegant she looked.

Joan Murdoch, my old caseworker, advised me on how to go about finding a place for Grandma Lil. Thus, a potential drawn-out, bureaucratic nightmare lasted six weeks. Between Joan's help and a phone call by the stepfather of one of the guys in my house at Harvard—a man who had given up charity to take on serious philanthropy—I was finally able to find a place to take care of her.

The dream I had was set after that awful month and a half, in the institution where she wound up. *Institution* sounds pejorative, but it was an appealing sprawl of buildings in which the people who changed her stinking diapers had the humanity to treat her not just with professionalism, but with fond detachment.

Lilly, sweetheart, look who's here! one of the aides says in the dream. Grandma's wheelchair is pulled up to one of the long tables in the dayroom. It's a place filled with sunshine, although the dream windows are more Ivey-Rush chapel than Gurwin Jewish Geriatric Center. Long rectangles of yellow daylight slant across the dayroom floor, and are crowned with the reds, blues, and purples of stained glass.

Grandma Lil looks up and her face breaks into a smile the likes of which I never saw in all my years living with her. *I know you!* she says brightly. *What's your name?* I tell her it's Amy and she pats a chair beside her wheelchair and says, *I can't find my teeth.* She's fairly sanguine about it, smiles—oddly, with teeth intact—and hands me a spoon. As far as I can recall, the rest of the dream is me feeding her mashed bananas that she eats happily.

For a short while, reality wasn't that different. Until she dwindled into a mere organism, devoid of speech and personality, kept alive by a feeding tube, there were moments of surprising sweetness in her dementia. When I came home from college Christmas of my junior year, I had no home to go to anymore, so I stayed at Tatty's. I took the train out to Long Island every few days. I'd meet Grandma Lil in the dayroom or in her room. At the sight of me she'd break into an enormous smile. I knew she didn't remember me from one visit to the next, but there was something about me that delighted her. Once she called me *Ma. You like my dress, Ma?* She was in bed that morning, watching cartoons, wearing a blue hospital gown, one of those things that tie in the back. *Gorgeous!* I told her. *You look like a million bucks.*

All during that winter break, I couldn't get my father or Aunt Linda to come with me and visit her. I offered to pick them up. Nothing doing. I said, "You know, they really make it very pleasant for family members to drop by. It's very clean. It doesn't smell or anything." My father said he couldn't get away. He was busy. I offered to let him drive Tatty's Jaguar, knowing he couldn't turn down an offer like that. But he did. Aunt Linda said she couldn't handle it emotionally. I tried one more time with my father. "Chicky, she's your mother. Believe me, I know what she was like. But at least once, get out there. Show your face. Look, she's getting great care, but it's important for the people who work there to know she has family behind her." He told me sorry, he was tied up with a million things and that there was no point in going because with Alzheimer's, they don't even know who you are.

After she died, my memory, and nearly all my dreams of Grandma Lil, were mostly about the Lillian Lincoln with that dazzling smile. I wondered, as the disease progressed, whether it was stripping off the layers of her personality until she became her essence, a sweet girl with an eager smile who liked being fed mashed bananas. Maybe deep down I understood this was the true Grandma Lil, and that's why she appeared in my dreams.

Or was this tender child some entirely new person, one so far from snobbery and venality that the girl in the gorgeous blue hospital gown could never have been the woman who brought me up?

I am always irritated when a character in a movie, wakened by the phone, appears dazed and gropes for it through four or five rings. It's a performance by second-rate actors playing alcoholic cops, or actresses eager to display erect nipples under white satin. So when my cell phone and alarm clock went off simultaneously with dueling tunes, "Karma Chameleon" and the Muppets' theme, it took me less than a second to spring into a sitting position, grab the clock, and put an end to the Muppets. People do get weird about early-morning phone calls, thinking it's about dear Auntie Ethel, but my assumption was it was someone I'd interviewed who'd somehow gotten my number and been up all night worrying if he/she had blabbed too much. Or that Chicky had gotten arrested again, the thought of which frightened me, although it would not have made me reel in surprise. So, not in any panic, I allowed myself a full second to flip open the phone and say "Hello" to whoever would be calling me at six o'clock in the morning.

"Hey, Amy. It's—"

"Hey, John." I was too shocked to try for cool. On the other hand, I would have liked to avoid awkward. Unfortunately, that didn't happen because I squawked *John* rather than said it.

"I know you get up around now." And are still sleeping alone. "I don't want to cut into your running time, but I wanted to talk to you. I was sorry when I got your message that you wouldn't come for Passover. But it's great to know you're getting someplace in the mother search. Look, I'd like to hear a little about it. And also, I thought that the last time we spoke . . . I hope I didn't sound rude or—I don't know—mean. I didn't want to end things on a sour note."

Even if I said, *My search for my mother is none of your damn business,* and hung up on him, there was no way I was going to have a day without thinking *John* and practically getting the vapors, so I made the decision to talk. Briefly, courteously, determined not to drag it out. Besides looking pathetic, it would also be futile. What the hell: I wasn't going to make my last note a sour one.

"Well, to cut the long story about my research mercifully short," I told him, "I came up with the address of where my mother had lived in Brooklyn."

"You know you're talking to a pro here. Don't cut it short. I want to hear all about the research. In as much detail as you remember. How about dinner one night?"

I didn't go through any of that *Oh, this must be a dream,* but his words sounded awfully light for a request that ought to have sounded important. "Dinner?" All those books about how men and women react differently in similar circumstances: I could not believe his heart wasn't beating like the kettledrums in *2001: A Space Odyssey.* "I'm going to be direct, John."

"How unlike you."

"What does dinner mean, and don't give me appetizer, entrée, and dessert."

"It means that I was glad when I heard your message. I'd like to hear what you found out. And to offer to do anything I can to help."

"You offered that before. Is it still the same friendly offer, emphasis on the word *friendly*?"

He hesitated for a couple of seconds, and I knew that the answer wasn't going to be what I wanted to hear. "As friends," he said.

"All right," I breathed. "I need a minute to think about what I want to say."

"Now that doesn't sound like you at all," he said. "Where is the Amy Lincoln of the instant comeback?"

I knew he was trying to avoid having the conversation get heavy, but it was my turn to talk. I didn't want to toss the repartee back and forth like a game of Hot Potato—moving fast, not thinking, trying only not to get burned. I didn't have the inclination and I didn't have the energy. It may have been only a couple of minutes after six a.m., but I felt I'd already lived an all-nighter. Just being on the phone with him wiped me out, to say nothing of hearing him say *As friends*.

"Are you up for ruthless honesty?" I asked.

"Do I have a choice?"

"Sure. You can choose to hang up." He didn't, so I gave it to him as straight as I could. "It's like this, John. The breakup was awful for me, maybe even the worst thing that ever happened to me."

"I don't know what to say to that, Amy. You've had some rough times in your life."

"My mother taking off, my father going to prison, maybe even taking the rap for her—all that was objectively traumatic, guaranteed to make any semirational person feel like shit. But you were on the other side of the universe from all that. You're funny, kind, intelligent, interesting, all sorts of things. You don't like sour notes. And you're a hot guy."

"Thank you."

"I guess that's a compliment, but I mean it as an explanation. I loved you. I lost you." I pulled up the covers to form a hood over my head. I didn't know why. I'd always talked to John in bed, under the covers, but I'd left my head outside. Maybe I was trying to shelter myself from the realization that there would be no future under-the-covers business with him. If I got it going with Steve or with some other guy, I'd have to carry on our conversations from a different venue.

"Do you think I was in the relationship just for laughs?" he demanded.

"I know you weren't. And I know there were plenty of times I let you down or hurt you. Being so close-mouthed, which I guess was a way of saying, *I can't trust you with this information.* Leaving you so soon after nine-eleven. I was afraid you'd get

277

tired of me or need your space, and I couldn't bear to hear it. Instead I ran—without regard for what you wanted. I'm sorry for all those times. I'm sorry if I hurt you. I'm sorry I wasn't a big enough person to trust you."

"Don't take it all on yourself. I should have spoken up. I shouldn't have dumped all of that on you the last time we were together, after my cousin's wedding. It wasn't fair." I could hear in the flatness of his voice that he was seriously upset with the conversation and trying to maintain self-control. When he'd called, he probably saw himself as being a nice guy, possibly an interested friend, and he was getting more than he'd bargained for.

"John, I can't be your friend. Friendship would only extend the pain."

"You're still not over it?"

"I'm not sure." I was tempted to add, *Don't worry, it's no big deal* . . . but realized it would sound sarcastic, or even bitter. "Well, probably not over it yet. Look, if I were in your shoes I'd want to know what happened with the Great Mother Search. And I think you should know. So when I get some distance from all this, from you, from whatever happens or doesn't happen with my mother, I'll write you and tell you about it. At length. But here's the deal. You can't acknowledge the letter in any way. I don't want to spend a week or month or however long thinking about what's on my voice mail or what's in my mailbox. I have to know it's a one-sided correspondence, and I'm the one side. Agreed?"

"Agreed."

"Good."

John sighed. Not one of those weary man sighs, but the sigh of a kid who doesn't have a clue about what to say next. Finally he said: "I was still hoping that maybe you'd change your mind and come up for the Seder."

"Is this some really subtle way of trying to get back with me that I'm not getting?"

"No," he said softly.

"Okay. Then let me tell you about me and holidays. When I started at Ivey, I spent Passover with the rabbi and his family who lived three towns away or with one of the girls whose families actually practiced Judaism, as opposed to just being Jews. And for all the American holidays and Christmas and Easter, I was with Tatty, either in New York or their other two houses or with other friends. The same thing at college and J-school. I always found someplace to go.

"But no matter where I went, I was always so envious. Even when it was a dysfunctional or twisted or some-kind-of-awful family—like Tatty's, with her father so drunk he took a nap at the table with his cheek on his roast goose—I was jealous and resentful that I wasn't part of it. Even if I was a regular, I was still a guest. I had no unconditional right to be there. All of which is a way of saying that aside from loving you, I loved your family. I appreciate the invitation and your persistence. If I went, I would be envious. And I bet I'd even be angry, because this was something I wanted and couldn't have."

"You never acted angry or envious," John said.

"One of my talents is knowing how to get asked back. It's only when you're part of a family that you have the luxury of behaving badly. So many times in the last—I don't know—five or six years I tried to get my father to come for some holiday, any holiday, Saint Swithin's Day for all I care. But he was always with some woman or other who couldn't know he had a twenty-something daughter. And Aunt Linda and Uncle Sparky go to his family for all the holidays and they're nice people, but there's no chemistry, even though they're Italian. I asked Linda and Sparky to come over once for a Seder, but Aunt Linda called at the last minute and went *cough-cough, I have a bad chest cold* so I wound up with four quarts of matzo ball soup and pounds of roast chicken and five people from the Weinberg Home for the Aged because I'd volunteered and they all turned out to be ex-communists who were still having doctrinal fights with each other."

"You had all of them in your apartment?" John asked.

"Yes. The food was in the kitchen and when I cleared, I put the dirty dishes in the bathtub so it wouldn't look messy."

"You never told me that."

I was so tempted to go into the story about how one of the men stood up and started shaking his knife at a tiny cotton ball of a woman, a Trotskyite. I was getting so comfortable with the normality of the conversation that I pushed the blanket off the top of my head. Except this was what I'd told him I didn't want to do. "John, I find myself falling into the friendship trap."

"Can I ask you, Amy, what's so terrible about that?"

"Because it's over."

"You know, you're the one who called me that time, asking if we could reconnect." Although John occasionally blew up, most of the time, like now, his anger was low-key. "You're the one—"

"I know. Let me explain. I was having a really bad night. I'd just broken three ribs and I was in pain and probably scared. Whatever."

"Why didn't you tell me, for God's sake?"

"What would you have done? Come over and been very kind and taken me to the emergency room. And then what? You and I are history. I took myself to the emergency room." I was so tempted to say, *And I met a cute doctor who really came on to me.* Instead I said, "John, I wish you nothing but happiness. If I accused you unjustly about that woman at the Mahler concert, then I'm sorry. And now it's time to say good-bye."

"Did you ever see yourself being married to me?"

"I didn't allow myself a marriage fantasy too often, but when I did . . . Yes." Then naturally I asked: "Did you see yourself being married to me?"

"Yes. I guess so. But then whenever I took a step toward you, you took a step back—"

"Good-bye, John," I said, and very gently hung up the phone.

Chapter Fifteen

John wouldn't call again, I was positive of that. But just in case, I threw on my running clothes and sneakers and rushed outside. Another gorgeous day, not that I could see it from my apartment. To celebrate, I began to run as soon as I hit the park, daring any rib to slice through a lung and stop me. Once I didn't drop dead, I did my obligatory nature check. Okay, the daffodils had done their bit for New York, and now their heads drooped from shriveled necks. They'd been supplanted by tulips and those giant pink and purple pom-pom flowers that grew on bushes. That was pretty much it for me and botany. As for zoology, I saw a cardinal, pigeons, and too many dogs wearing bandannas.

As I veered onto a bridle path, I must have shifted into runner's high. For me, it was never exhilaration, but the ultimate dumb-down, a blank mind, free of productive musings such as *Is John calling at this precise minute? He wouldn't believe I'd get*

*out of the house so fast. Now he's thinking I'm deliberately not
answering. Is he about to slam down the phone swearing never
to call me again? If he remembers our relationship at all, will it be
as two wretched years in an otherwise lovely life?*

As I cooled down back in the apartment, I realized my torso
hadn't accordioned, which meant my ribs were still intact. I ate
breakfast, one of those practices that will, one day, be the subject
of a column in the Science section of the *Times*, where someone
will report on a study that runners who eat while still breathing
hard and sweating into their pineapple cottage cheese survive, on
the average, ten fewer years than runners who have a modicum
of self-control.

Minutes later, I was washing the conditioner out of my hair
while musing that since John had been so clear about being just
friends, he was probably on his way to a big-time commitment
to *La Belleza* or someone else. With that, I thought I heard the
phone ring. I willed myself to believe it was one of those phantom calls that occur when one is emotionally in extremis and
also in the shower. Trying to distract myself, I thought about
Steve Raskin. Sharp-witted, nice, plus that solid building-trades
body that carried itself as if it knew its way around.

This did nothing to stir me up about Steve. It did get me to
ruminating about John. Two years, and I'd never tired of him.
Part of it was his look, the gold skin, the brown hair potentially
perfect but usually mussed up from his running his fingers
through it all day as he read or worked in the editing room. And
his smile was lovely, though too broad for Manhattan: the well-
adjusted smile of a happy suburban childhood. His body was
fine, with thighs like rocks. But it was his chest and arms that
got me, solid—*Come on*, I'd say to him, like a girl with her first
boyfriend. *Let me feel your muscle.*

John was always warm. We could come back from an hour-long romp in new snow, undress each other, and he'd put his arms around me. The temperature of him, and his unflinching ability to wrap himself around me and heat me, no matter how cold I was, made me feel not just secure, but treasured.

Of course it was more than his temperature, his personal normal of 99.6. It was his ardor. John was one of the rare, highly sexed guys who didn't bring his mother along into bed. No *Do what? Are you kidding? Blech!* No dash to the bathroom a second and a half after ejaculation. In other words, he had no no-no's. Neither was there *Look what I'm doing, Mommy!* naughty-boy shit. No tedious attempts at Kama Sutra positions 147 to 152—*It's the left leg that goes around my neck.* No request for a threesome with a Rottweiler.

Sometimes he'd say a few words. *You're beautiful.* Or something raunchy that got me higher and hotter. But he was, blissfully, not a blabbermouth. I didn't have to deal with lines that sounded as if they'd been culled from a multiple choice list: *I want to kiss-suck-lick-bite your tits-clit-tongue-ear.* True, no *I love you.* On the other hand, his cock was his cock and I didn't have to call it Joey.

The second I got out of the shower I checked the phone and discovered the phantom phone call had been an actual one. I punched in my code, 1920, the year the constitutional amendment guaranteeing women's suffrage became law. Although the message was a letdown, i.e., not from John begging me to go back with him, it at least had some interesting potential. "Hi, Amy. This is Freddy Carrasco. If you get a chance, give me a call. I'm home. I'll leave this message on your voice mail at work also."

Quickly, I pulled on panties so I wouldn't feel self-conscious and dialed Freddy's number. "Hi. Amy Lincoln."

"How mad at me are you?" He sounded bright and snappy, just like at the press conference.

"Give me a hint, Freddy. What am I supposed to be mad about?"

"You didn't get the scoop."

"I told you right from the beginning, *In Depth* wouldn't run a story like this."

"Well, just in case, I wanted to apologize about, you know, leaving you out of the loop. I know I owe you big-time. I mean, when the only reporter who'd speak to me was a guy from one of those Martians Eat Baby newspapers, you went out on a limb for me."

"You don't owe me, Freddy, but I'm glad things worked out for you."

"You know Moira, my father's press person? She said to tell you she was sorry about the mixup at the press conference—your having trouble getting in—and that if you'd like to do a story on me and my father and the rest of the family, she'll do everything she can to make it happen."

"Thanks for passing along the message," I said, a little too cheerily, as if I, too, had caught the Bowles's happy-talk virus.

"Sure thing!" He sounded abnormally ebullient for someone born and raised in New York. Even the worst news—*Fifty people were accidently ground into cement this afternoon*—had a positive spin when spoken from the West Coast. Not that Freddy shouldn't feel happy, but considering the short time since Thom Bowles had acknowledged him as his son, it didn't seem sufficient to account for a disposition transplant. "Things are going well with you and your father?"

"Great!"

"What do you call him?"

"We had a wonderful talk about that. He said that at this

SUSAN ISAACS

point he could understand that I'd feel more comfortable with
Thom, but he hoped that someday I would feel close enough to
him to call him Dad."

Had someone been in the room with me, I would have rolled
my eyes. Instead I just took a deep breath and said, "That's great.
Where is he now?"

"New Hampshire." Ten months before the Democratic primary, nearly all the candidates were spending serious time in that
state. "Everyone thinks either Kerry or Dean, the two New
England guys, will take it, but Thom says because of the environmental stuff up there, he's the natural candidate. I'm meeting
him this weekend to campaign in South Carolina."

South Carolina? That was such a lost cause to a left-of-center
like Bowles that I couldn't believe he was even wasting his time
down there. To ask his newly acknowledged, out-of-wedlock
son to campaign with him was probably a quick way of halving
the single-digit number he might conceivably pull in a Bible Belt
state. Why would Bowles do that?

Because it didn't matter. Keep the kid happy. Keep him part
of things. Keep him quiet. Although Freddy Carrasco might be
a plus in a Latino neighborhood, Thom the Tree-hugger would
only take Freddy down to South Carolina if he'd already
decided the state was a lost cause, but for some reason couldn't
wiggle out of a commitment to appear there. "I hope you'll have
fun campaigning" was all I could think of to say.

"Just one question," Freddy said. I was now holding the
phone between my chin and shoulder and dressing, so I could
get out and get to the office by nine, a dubious possibility. "Ms.
Maller has been conferencing with my father's lawyer. Thom
wants to set me up to take care of graduate school. And then
some. He's being really, really generous. But I'm a little nervous
because Ms. Maller—I know she's a friend of yours and I don't

286

want to put you on the spot—turned down the other lawyer's first offer. She said she could get more, but the last thing I want my father to think is that I'm being greedy."

"I really don't know what to tell you, Freddy. My guess is she wants to protect your interests in case your relationship with your father turns out to be . . ." Forget diplomacy, but I did the best I could. ". . . less than what you hoped for."

"You know, I have no worries in that area. We're so comfortable with each other. And it's amazing how much alike we are. Weird things, like we both get a real candy craving late in the afternoon." What could I say to Freddy? So did 85 percent of the American public? "Neither of us could get over it," he went on, "that we deal with it the exact same way, by having a cup of coffee instead! So as far as Thom Bowles and I not getting along . . . it's almost like saying I don't get along with myself."

Sometime in the 1950s, our Revered Founder bought the ugliest building on Union Square, a four-story, Romanesque rodent's nest. He named it the Optimus Publications Building. The plural, Publications, suggested the great man had once hoped to put out several boring periodicals rather than just one. Although he never was able to accomplish this—the newsstands then, as now, sagged under the weight of magazines no one wanted to read—he did deserve some credit: *In Depth* had been a going concern since 1951 and was even rumored to be slightly profitable.

But a few years more into the fifties, the square had grown too sleazy to be credited even with rough charm. One decade later it was still worse, unless you liked to watch street crime. The seventies brought salvation by, of all people, farmers. Four days a week, they set up a greenmarket in the square to sell what they grew and made. At first, having heard rumors of avant-garde lettuces, a few hip chefs and restaurateurs dropped by. They were followed by small bands of foodies seeking clever little upstate cheeses. By the late eighties, so many affluent New Yorkers were elbowing one another aside to get at the cranberry catsup that there wasn't any room left for drug traffickers.

It wasn't just the moveable feast. The shaky buildings surrounding the square were shored up, their facades dermabraded back to the gruff brick reds and pearly white stone of their youths.

Pretty soon, the area became the darling of architecture critics and the neofuturists. Perhaps unaware of this reverence by the intelligentsia, the public liked it too. So in addition to being a sometime farmers' market, electronics store haven, and quirky boutique venue, the square reverted to what it had once been in the nineteenth century, a place to hang, to demonstrate. An Americanized Speakers' Corner. In any case, our Revered Founder's real estate investment, for which he'd probably paid in the low thousands, turned into what was now worth millions.

Usually, I got down there between noon and one for lunch. Although trendy and increasingly upscale, life in the square reminded me of life in the projects. Living in midtown as I now did was to live in a world of relentless movement, pedestrian and vehicular: people shopped or raced to and from offices or in and out of performances at Carnegie Hall. Tourists double-timed it to get on line early at theme restaurants that had zero to do with New York and ate fifteen-dollar bacon chili cheeseburgers served by waiters dressed as carhops.

In the square though, as on the Lower East Side, the pace was slower, the sidewalks grittier. People didn't just rush from building to building. They had street lives. The blend of publishing and food people, gallery owners and demonstrators, farmers and housewives reminded me of the Lower East in that it was an amalgam. Not stereotypical New York City Melting Pot. More like a stew, in which the meat and carrots and potatoes mixed, but remained discrete ingredients. In the low-income projects, near-poor and working-class Latinos and Jews and Asians and blacks and Italians got along tolerably well, and sometimes formed fast friendships. But the individuals did not assimilate into beige Americans who could pass in Nebraska.

This day, however, there was no homey feeling for me. My article on the Democratic left hung over my head, my very own miasma. Like most professional ideologues, the people I'd just spent hours interviewing considered themselves important, their mission urgent. They lived to be heard. A reporter from *In Depth,* of course, was the perfect audience, though most would embrace an editorial assistant from *In Style* if that were the only journalist available. In any case, from nine-thirty until two-thirty, I'd traveled the left all the way to Z from A. I'd gotten an earful from everyone from ancient Marxists to younger-than-I antiglobalization warriors.

Out in the square, I tried to put aside all I'd heard. I took a deep breath and smelled everything from sweet potato fries to distant doughnuts. Being that it was a greenmarket day, I bought up a pygmy baguette at one stand and a small blob of goat cheese at another and smeared together a sandwich. But no, I couldn't unwind. I strolled around, taking tiny bites, attempting to distract myself by eavesdropping, but the only two conversations I managed to overhear concerned new thoughts on roasting venison and Dick Cheney's worldview, two subjects I preferred not to think about. I gazed at a vegetable display, a rainbow of beets, but my mind kept snapping back to my article.

The war in Iraq had focused the left in a way that their standard causes—racism, human rights violations, environmental degradation, anti–World Bank and IMF—had failed to do. What

I'd noted during the day of interviews was that after the requisite howls about Bush's unilateralism and the administration's often lame excuses for going to war, the lefty Democrats seemed to be moving toward the anti-Americanism of their Euro counterparts.

They were also embracing, with unseemly eagerness, the Europeans' anti-Israel stand. As they saw it, the problem in the Middle East was Israel. If Israel could be obliterated, all would be peachy in the region. The Palestinians willing to commit mass murder by blowing themselves up (in spaces not unlike Union Square) were, to them, heroic. Given that intellectual construct, it turned out to be a mere hop, skip, and jump from blaming a sometimes odious, often obnoxious right-wing Israeli government to blaming Israel to blaming Jews. I threw away the rest of my lunch and went back to the office. I realized my smoldering Zionism was about to catch fire. While a journalist can have political convictions, political passions were to be avoided.

Except I couldn't. "I want to change the focus of my Democratic left piece," I told Happy Bob.

This time I got his indulgent smile, an upturned curve of the lips that blessedly did not expose his teeth. "Change it to what?" he asked. "Or should I say, to whom?"

"The left's anti-Semitism."

The smile's curve straightened out a little. Now it said: *You poor, benighted (Jewish) fool.* What he actually said was: "There's a difference between being anti-Sharon and being anti-Zionist. Both are a far cry from anti-Semitism." For added emphasis, he expelled a short blast of gas.

That normally was a guaranteed conversation stopper, but I was determined to have my say. "Listen, Bob, I can't tell you how many of the sources I spoke to—mostly in academia, I admit—are using Jews as the scapegoat. They've picked up the European attitude. More and more, what they're saying on the campuses and in the lefty think tanks is that the Jews of the world, all twelve or thirteen million of them, are to blame for the Iraq war, and also that their so-called agenda is the cause for the misery of not only the Palestinians, but for the plight of over one billion Muslims."

"This isn't new," Happy Bob said. "The French—"

"I'm not talking about the French and the Germans. You're right. That's old. This *is* new because it's Americans who are talking the talk. I spoke with Henry Hobart, that political science guy at Ohio State. Mr. Big of the lefty-anarchist circuit. I'm telling you, he could have been quoting from the Protocols of the Elders of Zion."

"Amy, I'm not in the mood for hyperbole. What I *am* in the mood for is objective analysis, as you well know. There is a legitimate case to be made that the Palestinians' plight—"

"I know. But if the left is talking about plights, how about the plight of women in Iran and Saudi Arabia? Is that situation—which happens to be a scandalous human rights violation—the fault of the Jews too?"

Happy Bob scratched his crotch thoughtfully. "A couple of misguided academics do not a movement make."

"It's more than a couple of academics. Anti-Semitism has always been the ideology of choice for the third-rate. What's bothering me is that countries that have descended from first-rate to second-rate, like Germany and France, are signing on. We are no longer preeminent: Blame the Jews. And now it's come here. The lefties have been cut out of the Democratic Party since Clinton, and now they're making a big noise to get attention: Blame the Jews. That's my story. Out of all the causes to embrace, kids at Harvard and the other Ivies have been carrying signs with a swastika superimposed over a Star of David: Blame the Jews."

"Blame Israel."

"No. Blame the Jews."

"It can be a paragraph, Amy. Not the article."

"Bob, listen—"

"I did. Or do you want it to go from a paragraph down to a sentence?"

Maybe I was feeling vulnerable, considering the morning had begun with John's call and with me, basically, saying, *Good-bye forever and this time I really mean it.* So when I got home and saw the large padded envelope with Rose Moscowitz's return address, I was determined to face whatever was inside. Except I couldn't. Instead I set it on my one foot of kitchen counter, took out a beer from my minirefrigerator, and drank it slowly, my eyes never leaving the envelope. God knows what I anticipated: an explosion, a rubber-banded wad of bills with a note saying, *Don't bother me again,* or a selection of weird materials that would prove my maternal grandmother was Boca's most prominent victim of multiple personality disorder and the Nice Rose I'd met had been one of her lesser entities making a rare appearance.

It was either one more beer standing up or open the envelope. I finally chose the latter and peered inside. Lots of photographs and a folded piece of stationery, the paper palest lavender with deckled edges. *Dear Amy, I went through several shoe boxes of pictures. (I still hold on to the belief that someday I'll get organized.) I came up with these of Phyllis, both before and after the Véronique changeover. I had these copies made so you could keep them. Whenever I could, I put an approximate date on the back and noted who else was in the picture with her. Hope you are well. I look forward to seeing you again. Love, Rose.*

I stuck my hand into the envelope and closed my eyes like a kid reaching for a present in a grab bag. I got Mama Véronique and her boys. One of those awful posed pictures arranged by someone with the emotional intelligence of a fruit fly. The three were on the couch, Mama in the middle looking straight into the camera. The boys—somewhere between seven and eleven, I guessed—were in three-quarter view, their lips planting a kiss on each of her cheeks. Herself staring into the camera with the blank expression of a patient waiting for the ophthalmologist to flash an eye chart onto a wall. Her sons didn't seem to look like her. Both had round heads and flat features, so it looked as if she were being kissed by two Caucasian pumpkins.

Between my therapy at Ivey-Rush and the library of self-help books I'd read over the years, I recognized I was being a tad mean-spirited, especially about the pumpkin heads, a.k.a. my half brothers.

So I called Tatty, figuring she could do the mean-spirited stuff, thus permitting me to be benevolent, if not objective. Also, if I started looking at the pictures not as photographs, but as a Rorschach test, she would have no hesitation in telling me I was going off the deep end. We had a five-minute debate about who would come to whose apartment. I don't know which one of us won, but I got to go to Tatty's and she got to order in sushi and Japanese beer.

Luckily, Preshie and Four had gone someplace else to drink for the evening, so we had the apartment to ourselves. We knocked off the sushi in less than fifteen minutes and went into her bedroom, the place where we'd had most of our serious talks since 1987, when we were fourteen.

The room was the same as it had been back then, with a white, six-armed chandelier decorated with hanging crystals and porcelain roses. Her bed was a family heirloom—an odd size, as if custom-made for one very fat person. It was covered with a pink, red, and white quilt, the mostly floral patches sewn into a pattern of wreaths. When we first became best friends, we'd sit on the bed cross-legged, facing each other. But by the time we were sixteen, we developed a simultaneous, unspoken embarrassment about being on the same bed at the same time, as if that would propel us into a lifelong lesbian relationship. So during Christmas vacation of our third year, Tatty had stretched out on the bed. I'd taken to pulling up a Windsor chair with a red-and-white cushion that always reminded me of the pot holder I'd made at a Police Athletic League after-school program when I was about eight.

"Find the one where she's leaning against what's his name, the husband, with the background that looks kind of Tuscan, although it could be Toledo," Tatty ordered.

"If you're talking about the city in Spain, it's To-*lay*-do. Toledo's in Ohio."

"It so happens there is a famous painting by El Greco that's called *View of Toleeedo.*"

I said: "No. The painting is called—"

"Shut up," Tatty suggested politely. She turned onto her side, unscrewed the finial of her bedside lamp, and removed the shade. I handed her the photograph of my mother and Ira Hochberg, which she studied in the harsh light of the bulb. "I think I'm getting her style," she said. "Suburban gypsy. Or maybe suburban artiste. Long Island *Moulin Rouge!* Her jacket's Dries Van Noten. Those sandals are Manolos from five or six years ago." I leaned forward to check out the picture again. I could barely see the sandals, much less identify them, but I had no doubt Tatty was right. "But you see all those long chains she's wearing," she continued, "with all those shitty little charms hanging from them?"

"Yes," I replied.

"I'm not saying she didn't pay a reasonable amount for them, but it looks like she went out and bought a handful at one time.

See? They're all the same length and different textures." I nodded. "I never really trust people who pay a fortune for clothes
and then scrimp on accessories. Either you love beautiful things
and are willing to pay for them, or don't bother. Wear one really
great chain, not four or five mediocre ones. *You* don't think in
those terms because you deeply don't care whether you're wearing Manolos or a seventy-five-dollar copy. It's not that you don't
have a sense of style, well, a vague sense of style, but you could
live happily ever after with an entire wardrobe in which nothing
is hand-stitched."

"Sad, but true."

"See, what Phyllis-Véronique does is pick stuff that's bla-
tantly recognizable. I mean, even you'd recognize that her jacket
is a Dries."

"Sure." No.

"So." Tatty took a deep breath and let it out slowly. She was
about to deliver her analysis. "She wants to be seen as artistic or
having flair, but even more she wants to be seen as having
money. But whether she's in your Toledo or my Toledo or in
Siena or wherever, she will never look either chic or genuinely
artistic. She looks like what she probably is, a suburban woman
married to someone who can afford to keep her in Manolos, but
who can't or won't keep her in great, antique gold chains. Or
even great, new gold chains."

I went through the photos quickly, the way someone would
search for a certain card in a deck. "Okay," I said, "let me give
you my analysis. It sort of complements yours. There isn't a single picture in all of these in which she's smiling." I handed over
a photo of my mother and a man standing in the middle of a
bunch of cactus and desert flowers, the flora so balanced in color
and size that it screamed *Landscaped!* rather than murmured
Nature. The two were holding hands in the way that suggested

the photographer had said, *Hold hands*. To their left was a three-tiered fountain with an ostentatious display of water.

"Who's this again?" Tatty asked.

"He's the husband between Chicky and Ira. Look. You can't see her features all that well, but there's a slight upturn in her lips." Tatty held it up to the lightbulb, squinted, then nodded her agreement. "In all those pictures, from girlhood to the very recent ones—with Ira and the kids at Disney World—this is the closest she comes to a smile. Did you notice that?"

"I bet she has lousy teeth."

"She doesn't have lousy teeth."

"How do you know?"

"Because her parents would have seen to it that she got braces or caps."

Tatty opened the door of her nightstand, took out a buffer, and began to shine up her nails. "Then she *can't* smile. She's Botoxed."

"She wasn't Botoxed when she was twelve. There is a real sad look about her throughout her life." It must have sounded like a compassionate statement, because Tatty gave me one of her slit-eyed looks. "I'm not getting sentimental about her, and don't tell me I'm reading stuff into the picture."

"You're reading stuff into the picture."

"I don't think I am, Tat. It's not sentimental to come to the conclusion that somebody's a depressed person and probably has been all her life."

Tatty shook her buffer at me as though it were her finger: no-no-no. "It's sentimental to make her the victim of some psychological thing. There's just as much chance that she's a born malcontent. Nothing she has pleases her."

"Maybe she thinks she's somehow unworthy, so instead of being happy about what she has—"

"She was a bitch to run away from home and never tell her parents that she was alive for *years*. She was a double bitch, if it's true what your father said, about lifting that ring and letting him take the rap for it. And she's a bitch cubed for taking off and leaving you. I mean, I know I found Grandma Lil more amusing than you did, but I would never in a million years consider leaving her in charge of a child."

"I think my mother hurt so much that she could never face coming back. I think the enormity of what she did hit her at some point, and it was so unforgivable in her own eyes that she couldn't imagine me being able to forgive her."

"You're looking for trouble, Amy." Tatty, right or wrong, was never uncertain.

"I'm looking to understand."

"You're looking for a mother. And you know what? You found her. She's alive. Leave it at that."

Back at home, getting undressed, I played the *There have been worse days in my life* game, remembering Chicky going off to prison for the third time, glancing back at me. His lips made a big smile, while his eyes filled with torment. I remember trying to break away from the social worker and a bailiff to reassure my father. They each grabbed an arm and held me back, so I screamed, "Don't worry, Chicky, I'll be fine." But my voice went from scream to screech. His strong, handsome features collapsed into grief.

Worse days. Toward the end of her life, whenever I visited Grandma Lil, she showed no recognition that there was another human being in the room. An aide helped me get her into a wheelchair and I took her into a dayroom. It was filled with winter light and pathetically cheerful people trying to be magnetic enough to keep a parent or a spouse with dementia in this world. They dreaded the inevitable, their turning into dehumanized lumps of human tissue like my grandma.

She'd sat in that bright room, the woman who'd coached me on the only proper way to blow one's nose in public. Now she was in public, grunting and turning bright red with constipation. *Grandma? Want me to take you to the bathroom?* But she didn't hear my voice. All she heard was the inner command ordering her to shit.

Worse days? There'd been all those nights of sleeping with guys so bad I didn't even want to be promiscuous with them. But I did because they got a little too demanding, a little nasty. For that particular week or month, being an assertive, don't-fuck-with-me woman was too much of an effort for me.

I recalled being at Harvard and trying for the dean's list while working three part-time jobs, and being so nauseated with fatigue that on many nights, my final thought was *I hope I don't vomit in my sleep and choke to death.*

But if this day, which had begun with the hope of hearing John's voice, was not the worst, it was a real stinker. The *Can't we be friends?* business indicated there was a woman in his life with whom he was more than friends. And I sensed he'd called me in the first place because his colossal curiosity, the quality that made him such a good documentary maker, had to be satisfied, not because of any profound desire to hear my voice.

And then there was the Freddy conversation, hearing him so elated about being a son, yet sensing something wasn't right. Except maybe it was jealousy: Why had he had the guts to confront a lost parent and I hadn't?

And my work. The left's cozying up to anti-Semitism was upsetting. More than upsetting. Scary. The day had gone from bad to terrible talking to Happy Bob. God knows I was not one of his pets, like Gloria, but this had been the first time in all my years at *In Depth* I'd understood that if I didn't play the game better, I could be one of those print media journalists who wound up in the public relations office of some not-for-profit organization calling former colleagues who'd phone back at seven-thirty in the morning or nine at night praying to get her voice mail.

Having to be happy in front of Happy Bob not only made me angry, it outraged my sense of fairness. Why couldn't ideas fly on their own? Why did they have to be accompanied by a smile or a *tada!* of charisma announcing their importance? What burned me was that at least one out of three suggestions of mine that he'd quashed wound up as cover lines on *Time* or *Newsweek* within six months. Alas, even I knew I couldn't wave them in front of his face saying, *I told you so, asshole.* Suddenly it was clearer than it ever had been that my livelihood was dependent on someone who did not like me.

All right, the day hadn't been a complete washout. There had been the nice note signed *Love,* and the photographs from Rose. And I had an old friend like Tatty to rely on. I should be grateful.

But who knew if Rose would be around for the long haul? And even when someone turns out to be a treasure, if she's in her upper seventies, how long could the haul be? And Tatty: I was aware that our long conversations in her flower-chandeliered bedroom wouldn't go on forever. She would remarry. She was one of those women to whom men liked to give engagement rings. She'd find somebody else, create a third wedding cake for herself, then throw herself into being Mrs. Whoever with just enough time off from marital togetherness, baking, and social responsibilities to fit in a biweekly girls' night out. Or lunch. *How about lunch next Tuesday?* she'd ask when I called to say, *Hey, I really need to talk to you.*

Now, though, she had been available, and I needed to take her warning seriously. Okay, she wasn't thoughtful, never had been, but one of the reasons I loved her was for her ridiculous conviction that she knew all that needed to be known. Thinking never got in her way. Nevertheless, Tatty's talking off the top of her head had always been informed by a gut understanding of what made people act the way they do. *She's alive,* she'd said about my mother. *Leave it at that.*

I finished the worse-days game but still, all I could offer God was a précis instead of a prayer. I figured I'd be up all night, turning my pillow over and over for a new cool spot, breathing in, then out to the count of seven as I willed different parts of my body to relax, trying not to think about the day I'd had.

Instead, I thought about what I'd said to John that morning: *I loved you. I lost you.* I ruminated on the words, hearing them echoing like dialogue from an early John Cusack movie. Now they were an epitaph. I felt my nose filling up the way noses do before a good cry, but before I could reach for the corner of my blanket to dab my eyes, I was asleep.

A good night's sleep, it turned out. When I woke up, I brushed my teeth, pulled on my running clothes, and got into the elevator deciding that I would not suck up to Happy Bob. I would, however, attempt more than civility. I would be courteous and maybe work my way up to being cordial. *Hiya, Bob!* I'd say the next time he clomped into my cubicle without asking if he could come in. I wouldn't smile because he'd know I was faking it. But I would show no fear. The only problem was, I was afraid.

Chapter Sixteen

From the computer monitor, the three sentences I'd typed of the article I didn't want to write stared me down, daring me to try for a fourth. That's when I realized my anger with Happy Bob was getting in the way of my work. Unfortunately, I knew what I had to do: clear the air. To remain employed at *In Depth,* I needed to be viewed as what I was, a better-than-competent journalist and political analyst, not as a perpetual pain in Happy Bob's undoubtedly hairy ass.

I picked up the phone, but didn't press nine for an outside line. This was a rehearsal. "Bob," I addressed the dial tone, quieter than a whisper, "I'd like to clear the air." Good opening, I congratulated myself. The only problem was that I needed a middle and an end. All that came to mind was dialogue like *Go fuck yourself, you flatulent, faux-macho jerk.* I tried harder, but the only words I could get out were: "Since you're paying me not just for writing skills but my expertise, why the hell do you say

X is Y, or X is no big deal, when I tell you X is significant?" Just as I added "You egomaniacal cocksucker," my second line rang.

"Amy, Bob. Come down to my office."

Dragging myself down that long corridor, I barely thought about the twenty-eight thousand dollars in still-outstanding student loans I would now be unable to pay, or the likelihood of winding up, at age almost-thirty, as a contributing editor to a political website hurtling headlong into bankruptcy. All I could imagine was John one day picking up a copy of *In Depth,* leafing through it, and noticing my name had fallen off the masthead. Would he think I'd quit? Or would he guess I was fired and say to himself *What's wrong with them to fire someone with her talent? Or, God, did I do the right thing! What a loser.*

Happy Bob was on the phone as I walked in, but he made a shut-the-door motion with his index finger. Then, as he was wrapping it up, he jabbed the same finger downward to tell me to sit.

"Amy," he said as he put down the receiver. Here it comes, I thought, the *Maybe you'd be happier someplace else* speech. "Why is it that whatever I ask from you, I always get an argument in return?"

Considering his question, I decided an argument might not be the best response. Sweat began to glaze my skin inside my polyester knockoff of an incredibly cool Calvin Klein white cotton shirt. I tried to recollect whether, in my usual rush to get out of the apartment, I'd forgotten deodorant. I sat silent so long I began to worry that Happy Bob would think my nonresponse was hostility. But I couldn't think of what to reply that would make him back down, maybe even rethink me. Finally, independently of any consciousness on my part, my mind got disgusted with my inaction and began to speak.

"I think one of the reasons I became a writer was that it

allowed me to edit myself," I told him. "That's not one of my nat-ural abilities." I noticed I'd interlaced my fingers. My hands looked like those of a child about to pray. I pulled them apart. Of their own volition, they fell onto my lap Grandma Lil–style, palms down and neatly arranged, the right covering and perpen-dicular to the left. "You know I grew up in a pretty rough part of the city?" Happy Bob nodded, probably wondering on what bumpy road I was going to take him. "It was not a neighborhood necessarily known for its reflective souls. Early on, I learned that taking time to think before talking was guaranteed to make me the loser of any argument. Even now, all these years later, my response to a challenge is to argue it away, not say, *Hmmm, let me reflect before I speak*." I waited for him to say something about not being interested in excuses, but instead of speaking, he cleaned under the nails of his left hand with his right middle fin-ger. "I know I can shoot from the hip. But I hope you realize that I recognize not just your experience, Bob, but your authority."

He peered up from his personal grooming. "Really? You don't act as if you do."

"That recognition and respect doesn't mean I'm not going to fight for my ideas."

"Did you ever think," he said slowly and a little too evenly, "that your verbal street-fighting skills are a bit too confronta-tional for *In Depth*?"

"I'm thinking it now." He managed a small non-tooth-displaying smile. "Look, I wish I had a smoother style. I'd like to be able to wow you with wit or brilliant observations. It would be nice if I had some quirk, like wearing a monocle, that would make me a legend at the magazine: *Oh, that Amy Lincoln is so deliciously eccentric.*"

"How about a combination like good writing and noncom-bativeness?" he suggested.

I recognized I had an invitation to agree with him. That meant that within seconds, I had moved from the verge of unemployment to more stable ground that would not necessarily shift and throw me off the magazine. "How about good writing and an automatic ten-second time-out before I speak?"

He paused long enough to give my stomach time to churn a couple of times. "All right," he said slowly. "We'll try that. I don't object to discussion, you understand." He waited. So I nodded. He gave me such a broad smile that I was able to glimpse a new brown spot on his upper right canine. "In fact, I encourage discussions."

"So can we discuss whether I can have two paragraphs on anti-Semitism rather than one?"

Happy Bob's smile diminished only slightly as he said: "Two short paragraphs."

In graduate school, my concentration was in magazines, mainly because I realized that anyone who took two hours to compose an opening sentence was probably not suited for work on a daily newspaper. So I surprised myself when I finished my article at four o'clock that same afternoon. I read it. I reread it. It seemed okay to me, but not wanting to ruffle a single one of Happy Bob's feathers, I took it down the hall to Gloria Howard's office. "I know you're busy," I said, "and I know I should go up the chain of command—"

"But you don't want to," Gloria observed. Except for the pencil stuck behind her ear, she was as perfectly groomed and ladylike as ever. She wore a dark blue skirt, a white blouse with a simple ruffle of the sort John Adams would have admired, and a blue and ivory herringbone jacket, the bones coming from teeny herrings.

"Could you give this a fast read and let me know if it's coherent?"

For an instant, I thought I saw Gloria's eyes darting back and forth, as in *Trapped!* That's when I decided the only way she would allow herself to get stuck is if she was willing. "Have a seat," she murmured, her eyes already whizzing down the first page. Although she was not the neat freak I was, with piles of paper obsessively straightened until all corners were aligned, she was orderly, with her department's work separated into a rainbow of manila folders.

"It's fine," she said. "I like the anti-Semitic stuff. You know what I mean. I like what you've written about it. If I have any criticism, it would be to expand that part of it and drop something . . . probably the quote about America becoming a pariah among nations. That's old."

"Happy only allowed me two short paragraphs on the anti-Semitism. The reason I wanted you to check it is because I pushed him too far. He got so seriously pissed that I'm going to have to be simultaneously agreeable and serious for a couple of weeks. Maybe even a month. The thing is, I need to get out and do background for another story. So if you say this is okay, I'll sneak out tomorrow morning and hand this in late afternoon. On the other hand, if you say it seriously sucks, I'll keep working."

"It doesn't suck at all," Gloria said. "Go and do . . . whatever it is you have to do."

"You're making it sound much more intriguing than it is," I said, a little too perkily.

"I don't think so," she retorted. "Ten dollars says it's something I hope to hear about someday. In any case, good luck tomorrow morning."

If I got into the passenger seat of a car and saw that I was the driver, I'd get out and take the subway. Not that I'd ever had an accident. But I didn't learn to drive until I was twenty-two, and that was only because I figured I'd need a license to rent a car for work. Until then, my attitude toward driving was similar to what my attitude toward sex had been when I was eleven: Doing it would make me crave more, and more again, and I'd wind up another scrawny hooker in thrall to the pimp of Avenue B, a guy with a diamond in his nose and a belt buckle that was a three-inch-high Knicks logo in brushed gold.

Getting a driver's license had seemed equally perilous. Such temptation! Like my father, I would develop a passion for other people's cars. On a holiday from boarding school, lured by a silver Porsche stopped at a red light, I would begin the sad spiral downward from scholarship student to compulsive carjacker.

Of course, I knew it wouldn't be a Porsche that could set me off. Ever since I'd left the projects and discovered a level of luxury far beyond Nike sneakers, I'd been nervous that one day the barrier between me and criminality would collapse under the weight of my desires. I longed to be the casual owner of sumptuous goods. *Oh yeah, right, the third drawer has my cashmere twinsets. I know the boots feel like velvet, but they're actually suede, from the skins of aborted Turkistan calves. Those pillowcases trimmed in hand-crocheted lace? Aren't they sweet? My great-grandmother—I think—sent them home from Brussels the summer she went on her grand tour.*

I ached for luxury. Since heisting a couple of prime ribs for dinner didn't appeal to me, I pictured myself keeping up the family tradition of thievery by stealing cars. Best to be ignorant of them. Nevertheless, once in journalism school, I recognized that in America, if not in New York City, adults drive cars. I learned the basic how-tos from some temporarily smitten guy in my magazine writing workshop, who took me home to his parents' house in Tenafly, New Jersey, every weekend and gave me all sorts of lessons in his father's Jeep Cherokee. A year and a half later, after Tatty and I spent a weekend in her Jaguar practicing three-point turns and parallel parking, I passed my test. Since the hottest car *In Depth* would spring for was a Dodge Neon, my propensity for felony was never tested.

The next morning, in a Chevy so gray it blended into the sky and the pavement, I drove to Long Island and parked on Main Street in Shorehaven. The *Shorehaven Sentinel* took up the first floor of a building that, according to the black-painted directory on the glass front door, was also home to Hudson Gaines, D.D.S., and Rosenthal-Lipsky Investments, Ltd. I realized a woman behind the counter at the *Sentinel* was giving me the eye, but for moments I just stood outside, reading the door, unable to make my hand open it.

I kept thinking how much better John would be at a gig like this. Most often, the people I spoke to for a living were people who wanted to get their points of view across to the public. As for any others, once they started talking, I had the strategic skills to get from them what I wanted to know. My charm, such as it was, had always been in presenting myself: likable, friendly, but not gabby, so people felt comfortable talking to me. John's charm was in making people believe he was interested in them. That was because he actually was. When he'd volunteered to help me, I should have said, *Go to the local newspaper in Shorehaven and find out whatever you can about Véronique and Ira Hochberg.*

When I finally made it through the door, I spent a couple of minutes convincing a woman behind the counter, Ms. Nature Girl—no makeup, no bra, gray frizzy hair—that I wasn't interested in placing an ad, despite the *Sentinel*'s low rates. I tried to get across the idea that I was deserving enough to get to see the editor-in-chief, Sandy Garfunkel. Ms. NG said she'd never heard of *In Depth* and Sandy probably hadn't either.

Sandy Garfunkel, when at last I got to meet her, turned out to be a woman with respect both for *In Depth* and makeup. She didn't look painted, but it was clear she knew which end of an eyeliner pencil was up. She was one of those small, thin-thighed, supertoned types who could be any age between thirty-five and fifty-five. Her office was as well taken care of as she was, all blue and white, like a design on an antique Chinese bowl. "I'm honored," she told me, taking her seat in a tall striped chair behind her desk. "Unless *In Depth* is doing a story on the decline of the suburban weekly."

"Not at all. I just used my being at *In Depth* as a door opener, although it would sadden our publisher to know how few doors it actually opens. I'm here doing due diligence for myself." Generally, journalists are pretty quick at figuring out if someone is a straight shooter or a liar, so by the almost imperceptible nod of her head, I sensed Sandy had determined I passed the truth test. "I recently found out I'm related to a family in Shorehaven. I know I could probably knock on the door and say, *Hi, I'm Amy Lincoln,* but I figured a little background couldn't hurt, just in case they're the town psychotics. In journalism school, we were told that if you need a quick take on an area you're not familiar with, talk to someone on the local paper."

"Sure. Would you like coffee or something? There's a Starbucks two blocks away and an independent coffeehouse across the street. I can send Nell, the one in front." We both chose coffee with whole milk and Equal and agreed to split a muffin, so I felt we were virtually soul mates. "Who's the family?" she asked.

"Véronique and Ira Hochberg. They have two sons."

"Sure, sure, sure." She had a line of small white animal figurines about two inches high, elephants, camels, and the like, and she spent a couple of seconds rearranging them in what I guess was supposed to be a circus parade. Since she glanced my way right after that, I smiled at their adorableness, although I wasn't sure whether I was supposed to be admiring them because they were cute, for their artistic worth, or for how expensive they were. "Ira owns a big lighting fixture store," Sandy went on, "and he's a pretty steady advertiser. If not for that, I wouldn't know him. He's not active in the community. As far as him being the town psychotic, I don't think so. Let me be open with you and ask for . . . I guess you'd call it reciprocity. In exchange for the information, do I have your word that even if Ira turns out to be your long-lost father or whatever, you'll keep everything I'm telling you under your hat?"

"Absolutely."

"The best way I can describe him? He's someone you don't want to get stuck with at a cocktail party. Unless you play golf." I shook my head. "That's the only thing I've ever heard him talk about, other than business. A couple of years ago he called me to announce he'd been elected chairman of the rules committee at his golf club."

"Front page," I said.

"He thought so. He made it pretty clear that he viewed his appointment as a major accomplishment, if not actually front page. In a kind of half-kidding way, I offered to send over a photographer and get some shots of him on the putting green. Guess what?"

"He said yes and you ran it."

"Right. So bottom line on Ira is that he's a little full of himself, what with his wanting photo ops and talking endlessly about golf. But he doesn't seem to be a bad guy. Just a boring guy."

"And what about Véronique?" I asked.

"Is she French or something?" Sandy asked. I shrugged.

"She's on a committee to bring back a small theater to Shore-haven that did a lot of Shakespeare. It closed a long time ago, late sixties. Besides the bandshell and the library, that was the town's claim to culture."

"Did she organize the committee?"

"No, she's just on it. We ran a couple of pieces on it and if her name wasn't Hochberg, which I noticed only because I was proofing the article, I wouldn't have paid attention."

"Did you meet her?"

"No. I'm sure we ran a photo. If you want, I can find it." As I was saying no thanks, Nell, Ms. Nature Girl, came in with the coffee, muffin, and a surprising number of paper towels, as if a spill of *Exxon Valdez* proportions were inevitable. When she left, Sandy said: "As far as Véronique Hochberg goes, you now have the sum total of my knowledge."

"And the two sons?" I took a bite of muffin—either intensely seasoned bran or bland pumpkin. "I think they're elementary or middle school age."

"If they were superstars at academics or sports, I'd probably have heard of them. Same thing if they were deep into delinquency. In a community this size, sealed juvenile records don't mean you don't know what's going on. But I never heard of them. Nearly all my business with Ira is on the phone, but the couple of times I've seen him he's never whipped out his wallet and shown me pictures." Sandy took a couple of sips of coffee, and then put down her paper cup on a small saucer-size plate. "Actually, we have a fair number of interesting people in this town. The Hochbergs are not among them."

For someone who was not an ace behind the wheel, I had an amazing ability—well, amazing to me—to read maps. During the fighting in Afghanistan and the war with Iraq, I could have been one of those CNN generals standing next to a floor-to-wall map with a pointer in my hands. Give me a few seconds and I'd not only be able to present the best off-the-main-highway route from Karbala to Kirkuk, but also remember it a week later. Likewise, after a couple of minutes with a Greater New York road atlas, I could have been named official cartographer for Shorehaven.

I got off Main Street, which seemed to be a half-mile-long exhibit of pizza places and nail salons separated only by a hardware store, shoe store, bank, or gift shoppe featuring fat candles embedded with flowers. The residential areas nearest the center of town were middle class, with plastic tricycles temporarily abandoned by schoolchildren in front of single-car garages and odd objects stuck into spring green lawns: gnomes, frogs, bald eagles, though sadly, no flamingos.

As the neighborhoods became more prosperous, metal, plastic, and inflatable things disappeared from the grass. So did sidewalks and, eventually, streetlights. The Hochbergs' house was in a section called Shorehaven Manor. That part of town was as upper middle class as it is possible to get without being actually rich. Still, the plots of land looked pretty small to me. At least they were far from the acreage of the estates in which a couple of my friends from Ivey had lived, and not close to the Orensteins' house in suburban Connecticut, with its hill of a front lawn and forested backyard.

The houses themselves, however, came close to being grand. There were huge, red-roofed Spanish villas, massive, beamed Tudors, impressive brick Georgians with Tara-like white columns, often so close to each other that someone might be able to read the vintage of the bottle of sauvignon blanc on her neighbor's dining room table. As I neared the final left turn to chez

Hochberg, Shorehaven Manor felt cramped to me, as if an entire kingdom's aristocracy had been squished into ten acres.

I made my turn and drove around the block slowly to check out 48 Knightsbridge Road. A Tudor. Maybe Véronique Hochberg's devotion to the Bard of Avon was such that she'd bought it as a constant reminder of his genius. The upper part of the house was the predictable white crisscrossed with dark timber beams. Perhaps the first floor was some pre-Elizabethan style that I didn't remember ever seeing before, but it was part brick, part roughed stone, so it looked as if the builder had run out of one material and simply continued with whatever the next truck brought in.

As far as the landscaping went, I couldn't judge. It was grass, a couple of trees, and a lot of bushes with small red and pink flowers. Not labor intensive. To me, gardens were either the big Botanicals in Brooklyn and the Bronx, or like Dr. Orenstein's — lots of flowers that bloom at different times of year to attract butterflies, and, way in the back, a vegetable plot surrounded by a homey little fence to keep out deer, rabbits, and other vegetable-eating Connecticut creatures.

Coming back from my trip around the block, I parked the car across the street and a few houses down from the Hochbergs', then took out the road atlas and my cell phone in order to look lost in case there were suspicious neighbors. Not that I saw any. Knightsbridge Road was quiet enough to seem devoid of life. I felt like an interloper who had dropped in from a parallel but populated universe.

With all that suburban silence, I stared at the dark wood door of the Hochbergs' Tudor and tried to imagine myself standing before it, ringing the bell. I would hear footsteps. The door would open and my mother would be standing right there. In a bathrobe? In what Tatty had called her suburban gypsy style, some brilliantly striped Missoni outfit and hoop earrings? Maybe she'd recognize me because I looked like Selwyn's sister. More likely, having been tipped off by Rose that I was alive, well, and in investigatory mode, she wouldn't have to ponder, *Hmmm, who is this person on my doorstep?* She'd had a ninety-seven average. She would know.

Except maybe it wouldn't be her at the door. Ira could be an easygoing entrepreneur who didn't get off to work until eleven o'clock. Or he might have a regular morning golf game. I pictured him looking like an aging playboy in a lighthearted thirties movie, dressed in knickers and one of those hats that looked like a tumescent beret with a pom-pom.

Perhaps the door wouldn't open at all. They might have an intercom. I'd be waiting for the door to open, but instead I'd hear a disembodied voice, *Yes, who is it?* What could I answer? Amy Lincoln? Would she come racing down from her bedroom or out of the kitchen, open the door and stare at me, whimpering, *Oh my God, Oh my God,* and then enfold me in her arms? Would a tinny voice rage through the speaker, *If you don't get the hell out of here I'm going to call the cops*?

I put the seat back as far as it could go and rested my feet on either side of the steering wheel, the ultimate in un–Grandma Lil posture. The truth was, I still had no idea about what my mother was like. Okay, impulsive, strong-willed, and, at least in her behavior toward her own mother, anywhere from cool to nasty. But although the more I knew of Rose, the more I liked her, she herself wouldn't win any prizes at the International Warmth Competition. True, she'd been welcoming to me, but maybe she and Selwyn could have been unloving toward Phyllis—or even worse.

I leaned forward and turned on the ignition for a second so I could open the window. Even though the day was gray, the smell of new-mown grass and the friendly chirps of birds on the quiet street made it seem lovely outside. The breeze had a chill, but I still felt enveloped by spring. The real reason I couldn't figure out my mother was because I knew my father.

Chicky was midway between good-looking and handsome, like a really attractive actor playing a likable hoodlum. Except with my father, it wasn't an act. It was him. Likable and somewhat crooked. Uncomplicated too, largely because he hadn't the brains to be complicated. He had been loving to me, far better than anyone else who had known him could have imagined. And if he was telling the truth and he'd taken the rap for my mother so that I'd have an appropriate parent to bring me up, then he was also a profoundly good man.

But that didn't explain Phyllis + Chicky = ♥ 4-ever, even though that ♥ endured less than two years. I could certainly understand a girl from my mother's background falling for Chicky the Hunk, Chicky Bad Boy, and having a hot romance with him. I could even imagine someone like her falling so head over heels for his sweet sexuality that she'd run off with him for a few days. Even a few weeks. But longer? Marry him? Live in a rat-infested tenement? Get pregnant by him and actually have the baby?

My own sexual career had begun when I was fourteen. In all those years before I calmed down, the guys I hung with were definitely not all Harvard material—unless that category included guys who could hold up the bursar's office at gunpoint. Certainly among those who actually were Harvard material—or Harvard students or Harvard faculty—there were some who were ill-mannered, misogynistic, or downright mean. But out of all these losers I'd fooled around with, probably 30 to 40 percent of the total, there was none with whom I would have plighted my troth, much less lived with rats.

I guess the pop-psych diagnosis for my mother would be self-hatred. By her slumming, she was punishing herself. That didn't explain, however, why she was punishing her parents, too. And if she was so down on herself, how come she was able to break from me and Chicky and run off with—if the rumors Grandma Lil heard were right—a bodyguard? True, he might have been an utter delight, but he also could have been a dumb slab of beef packing a Smith & Wesson.

I could understand why she didn't go back to her family, assuming they were not monsters. She was terrified that Chicky could convince a lawyer or a friendly fellow criminal that his was a bum rap and they should see that justice was done—*right, and here's her address in Brooklyn*. Or that one day, Lillian Lincoln would show up on her doorstep and hand me over, shitty diaper and all: *I don't want her and besides, she's yours.*

A glance at my watch. Almost eleven. I had to get back to the city, return the car, and show up at work to hand in my article, then hang around in case an editor had any questions. So if I was going to act, it had to be soon. Down the block, I saw a woman about my age or a couple of years older walking, or rather, being pulled by, a huge, hairy brown dog.

I put down my feet, pored over the atlas again, and had a conversation with no one on my cell phone. Dog and woman were coming closer. Okay, I thought, going up to the Hochbergs' door wasn't a great idea because doors can be slammed in faces. Police can be called. So what was the best way to approach my mother? Follow her? It might work, but what if she intended to spend the entire day reading *Coriolanus* or cleaning out her closet? What if she was agoraphobic and never went out?

And suppose she came backing out of her garage? Could I follow her? I knew detectives and investigatory reporters did that in movies: *Make sure you stay four car-lengths behind.* What if she was a terrific driver, taking turns at eighty miles an hour, while my car went out of control and crashed into a garden-supply center? Or what if bad driving was genetic and she led me on an eighty-mile journey out to the Hamptons at thirty miles an hour?

White woman near my age was schlepped by young brown dog past the car. She didn't even see me. I had been surprisingly calm until then. I don't know whether it was because I'd seemed invisible or because I knew all my thinking wasn't getting me any place and the clock was ticking. Suddenly I became agitated. Within seconds, I went from agitation to fear. I only realized how frightened when I heard myself whimper.

I started the car and drove past my mother's house again. Then, still too unhinged to be ashamed of myself for being such a loser, I drove on to the city.

Chapter Seventeen

I didn't even have to wait to get on the Long Island Expressway before being overcome with shame. Shame because I'd spent sixty-five dollars on a rental car, cut work, and accomplished nothing except learning Ira Hochberg liked golf. Shame because I, the make-an-outline, plan-ahead, neatness-counts kid, had driven to Shorehaven and gotten information, free coffee, and half a muffin from the editor-in-chief of the local newspaper, then hadn't a clue about what to do next.

Back at *In Depth*, I made it a point to be seen, going to the library and making ostentatious notes, punching the soda machine with the heel of my hand, and other idiocies to establish in my colleagues' minds the notion that I'd been around all day. Naturally, I also felt ashamed for doing this. Subterfuge was unnecessary because staff members were in and out of the office all the time. As long as your articles were up to standards and you didn't miss deadlines, nobody gave a thought as to whether you were reading Federal Reserve stats on household debt service or going to a shoe sale at Saks. Still, I couldn't get past the need to display what a splendid worker I was, just the way I had in elementary school, when I walked around with a backpack twice as heavy as it needed to be to impress my teachers with my willingness to cripple myself for knowledge.

The national editor, the guy who stood between me and Happy Bob, wanted a few changes in my piece, so I didn't get out of the office that night until eight. It took me forever to walk home because I was so deep in unproductive thought about what I hadn't done in terms of my mother and what I ought to do. I caught a reflection of myself—gray boot-cuts, blue shirt, black sweater, hysterical hair in need of cutting—in the window of a large drugstore. Clearly, I was staring at a display of Huggies diapers and Thermoscan ear thermometers, except I was clueless as to what had made me stop walking, how long I'd been standing there, and what I'd been thinking about.

It wasn't until I was home, reheating the two slices of thin-crust pizza I'd picked up on the way, that I had my first productive thought of the day. Freddy Carrasco. The master of the Confronting a Long-Lost Parent game. Maybe I could learn something from him. Okay, our circumstances were not the same. His father was famous, my mother was not. His other parent had died, while Chicky was very much alive, albeit not a constant presence in my life. What I sensed in Freddy was that he'd tracked down—or stalked—Thom Bowles because he was looking for love. Admittedly, there was also money at the end of Freddy's rainbow, but I didn't think that had been his motivation.

For a few minutes, I mulled over trying to get more information about my mother from Chicky, but I knew him well enough to understand I'd gotten all I was going to get. The more I asked, the more willfully forgetful he would become.

I opened a Sam Adams and chugged down about a third of it while asking myself: What did I want from my mother? Love? Probably, though my head understood what my heart didn't, that someone who had run away from me twenty-eight-plus years earlier wasn't likely to want to hold me close and croon lullabies. Besides, she knew where I was. If she wanted to get into the lullaby business, all she had to do was call. But listen, my heart told my brain, she doesn't know what to expect. Maybe she can only imagine you wanting to get even.

Freddy hadn't confided in Thom Bowles's handlers that he was looking for love. Bowles had every reason to think Freddy was a nut job or an extortionist. What had changed his mind— or at least his behavior? A call to his lawyer from Freddy's lawyer, Mickey Maller? A warning from his advisers to love his son or lose the Latino vote? Or was I afflicted with the curse of journalists, uncontrollable cynicism? Wasn't it possible that upon seeing this child born from his youthful love, Thom Bowles's heart had melted?

Halfway through my first slice of pizza, I decided to track Freddy down. In a day so short on results and long on questions, maybe I could get some answers. But how could I elicit his help? Not by being vague. I could let him know we were in the same boat, tell him my story, and ask what he would do in my place. No. I'd already stepped over the ethical line by recommending a lawyer to Freddy; I still had to deal with people on the Bowles campaign staff throughout primary season and, in the unlikely event Thom Bowles became the Democratic nominee, beyond. I couldn't be a confidante of his son.

Having finished off my pizza, I was debating between another

beer or a sugar-free, fat-laden ice cream bar that had the pleas-
antly minty flavor of Elmer's Glue. It occurred to me then that I
could call Freddy, ostensibly to find out how things were going,
and simply start asking questions about what he'd been thinking
all the times he'd tried and failed to talk with his father. Maybe
he'd say something that could help me.

I opted for the ice cream bar and called Freddy's cell phone. I
closed my eyes for a moment to marshal my resources to deal
with the New Freddy, throwing off sparks of vim and cheer.

"Hello," he said. Forget vim and cheer. He spoke slowly,
heavily, sounding as if he could use an electroshock treatment.

"Hi, Freddy, Amy Lincoln. How are you doing with all the
fried chicken and bougainvillea, or whatever they're serving up
in South Carolina?"

"I'm back in New York."

He might as well have said good-bye. He showed not a hint
of desire to talk. However, this was not an unheard-of situation
for a journalist. "Was Thom on one of those in-out trips, just
make a speech or whatever?"

The silence was so long I was able to finish half the ice cream
bar. "Amy, anything I tell you . . ."

"Totally off the record. You know that, Freddy."

"I feel like the biggest asshole in the universe."

"Well, you're not. What's going on?"

He did some of that audible breathing that depressed people
do before speaking. Finally he said: "It's like this. I met him at
Teterboro. He has a private plane for the campaign. Anyway, he
said something about he has to do some reading on the trip
down but we'd have some time together once we got there. So I
figure, that's okay. I even brought along a book I'm reading.
About ENIAC." He paused. "It's considered the first electronic
computer."

I said "Uh-huh" to let him know I was listening.

"Thom has his own office, room, whatever, on the plane. He went in there. His people kept going in and out. Moira especially, and one of his pollsters. And the guy who's his administrative assistant in the Senate but who's on a leave of absence for the campaign, Yancey Wilson. Do you know him?"

"Yeah."

"He's a little—I don't know. Strange. He stares at you and kind of squints and doesn't look away even if you look him right in the eye."

"He does that with everyone," I explained. "He's trying to get people to think he has supernatural powers. The ability to read minds or see people naked. But for what it's worth, he has a good reputation in the Senate. He's too odd to be liked, but people on both sides of the aisle seem to trust him." I walked to the sink to get a glass of water to dilute the taste of Elmer's. I couldn't figure why Freddy would have more than a nodding acquaintance with Yancey Wilson. "Did you have any dealings with Wilson?" I asked.

"Kind of."

"Freddy, you sound less than happy. What's going on?"

"It's Thom. I mean, everybody except me was going to the back of the plane to talk to him. He was supposed to be doing some important reading, but he wasn't alone for more than five minutes during the whole flight down."

"Maybe he shouldn't have used the word *reading*. Very often candidates do business on planes, catch up on phone calls. Even though Thom Bowles comes from a wealthy family and has made money on his own, he's not bankrolling his own campaign. Fund-raising is a huge part of what these guys do."

"Pretty soon after we landed, he said, 'If you need anything, anything at all, speak to Yancey.' I thought that was pretty nice, but the whole time we were down there, the only time I saw my father was during public appearances. Before audiences and any meeting . . ." His voice trailed off and became a sigh.

"Any meeting in which there was someone who might be Latino?"

"Yes."

"So where did Yancey Wilson fit into this?"

"I guess he was what they call my minder. Thom didn't have his campaign bus down there, just a bunch of cars for the staff. So, a couple of times I asked Yancey if I could sit with Thom. You know, when there were twenty-minute, half-hour drives. And every time he'd make some excuse."

At first, I couldn't conceive of someone on Yancey Wilson's level being assigned as a hand-holder. That was a job they'd give to some engaging, cold-blooded kid just out of college. Then I realized that the Bowles campaign viewed Freddy as both an asset and a potential liability. If for any reason he became disenchanted with his father, or with how he was being treated, Freddy had become enough of a public figure in his own right that when he railed against Thomas Bowles, people would listen. He might be a one-day wonder, but his mouthing off might be enough to make some voters have doubts about the candidate.

"Did you ever get to see your father alone?"

"The final ride of the day, after a talk at a junior college on the way to the airport. Thom said he was so sorry, blah blah blah, about not being able to spend any time with me. This is what pisses me off: My mother was a very smart woman. Thom's a very smart man. Why doesn't he give me credit for inherited intelligence? Why does he think I'm so fucking dumb that I don't realize that his treatment of me means one thing?"

"And what's that, Freddy?"

"That he has no feelings for me. That I was a big problem, or at least could have been, so the best thing to do was to pretend to give me what he thought I wanted. Love."

I heard a sniff and realized he was trying to keep from crying. "I'm so sorry," I told him. "Look, there's always the possibility that Thom is a guy who can't walk and chew gum at the same time, that the mere fact of you is too much of a distraction during a presidential primary campaign. Maybe once this is all over, which I think it's safe to predict will be sooner rather than later, he'll be more himself."

"The truth, Amy. Does being more himself mean that even though I'm an adult, he'll consider me his son?"

"I don't know. Obviously he knows you are in terms of paternity. But Freddy, if what you're looking for is a family, a place to belong now that you don't have your mother, I can't say whether it will be with Jen and April and Brooke and Thom. I just don't know."

"Do you think he was just using me?"

"I'm a reporter, Freddy. I'm cynical by nature. So if you want a reassuring answer, I'm not your girl. On the other hand, having had a checkered childhood myself, I can only tell you I understand your need for family. You might not get it with the Bowles clan. Public people often have limited abilities to sustain private relationships. You're a great guy and whether it's with the girlfriend you have now or with someone else, you're going to have a fine, deep relationship. You're going to be part of a family. Trying to get love from a United States senator can be like trying to get blood from a stone. Even if something oozes out, it's not real blood. Freddy, you're a great guy. You deserve the real thing. Go for it."

✈ ✈ ✈

Since Preshie had spent most of Tatty's childhood either drinking, recovering from hangovers, or getting dried out, much of Tatty's upbringing had fallen to the household help. Even as a toddler, my guess was, Tatty could be imperious. In any case, nannies came and nannies went. The cook and the housekeeper, however, stayed put. They were the ones who taught Tatty her skills. Besides her business of creating cakes, Tatty grew up to be a homemaking genius. She could iron a pleated tuxedo shirt, unclog a shower drain, cook sauces from béarnaise to zabaglione, and, in minutes, whip up a round tablecloth with matching napkins on a sewing machine.

Since my intelligence was mostly linear and hers visual, in our friendship I was the designated reader/thinker and she was the aesthetician/shopper. At one point, shortly before John and I parted, I'd casually handed Tatty twenty dollars and mumbled something about needing a new shower curtain. If, in her near-daily shopping expeditions, she saw something she liked, she should buy it for me. She'd stared at the twenty-dollar bill with incredulity and annoyance. *Impossible,* she'd sniffed, but I knew she'd view it as a challenge.

The day following my conversation with Freddy, she called me at work to announce she'd finally found a king-size sheet imprinted with flowers like the ones in those seventeenth-century Dutch still lifes. She said she'd be over between seven and eight to take measurements against my shower curtain liner.

"This is really pretty," I told her. "I can't believe a sheet like this could be on sale for $11.95!" The dark green, almost black, of the background emphasized the beautifully detailed flowers, making them appear illuminated from behind.

"It's decent for a shower curtain, if one's taste runs to florals. But seriously, Amy, can you *believe* someone would actually put this on a bed?"

"You know the answer to that."

"Bed linen should *always* be white. No exceptions. You know that, but you don't really care. That's the pity of it. I'd rather spend a night walking the streets of a foreign city filled with purse snatchers than sleep in a hotel on peach-colored sheets. That happened once, in Venice, at the Cipriani, except there were no streets to walk. And get that stupid smile off your face, like *Oh, she's exaggerating for a change.*" We pushed furniture aside. Then we laid the vinyl shower curtain liner over the sheet. Tatty knelt down and attached it with paper clips. "Pins leave hideous holes," she said. "Would you please get down here and help me? Oh, before I forget: Don't worry, you won't have to deal with the curtain blowing around."

"I'm not worrying."

"You wouldn't. When I sew up the hem on my machine, I'll put in drapery weights so the curtain stays out of the tub." We finished the paper-clip business and she started marking where the curtain holes would go to match up with the liner's. "I want to get married again," she said suddenly.

I looked over to her, but all I could see was the top of her head, bent over the curtain. "You want to get married again as a general proposition?"

"If that means do I know who to, the answer is obviously no." She switched from sidling around on her knees to sitting cross-legged on the floor. "I don't even know anyone right now that I'd want to go to a movie with, much less have a baby or two."

Pleased at this chance to get off my knees, I leaned back against my couch and stretched out my legs. "This time," I said slowly, massaging my knees, "I hope you won't go looking in bars. The last two—"

"I know what you're going to say. You've made this point a thousand times before, so don't even bother—"

"I'm going to bother. Unless you want to wind up re-creating your parents' marriage and having cocktails every night from six to ten, you need a new source of manpower." Tatty screwed up her mouth so it looked as if she'd just eaten something she was going to spit out. She made a move to shift her position and start marking shower curtain holes again. Still, her butt and the floor remained in contact, so I kept on. "The other problem is this. Even if you don't wind up with someone who's a major alcoholic, if you marry one of the *Aren't I sophisticated downing seven martinis even after they ran out of olives?* guys, you run the risk of getting a mean drunk. To be brutally honest, your father's an okay drunk. I know you get upset when he gets sloppy and drips shrimp cocktail sauce onto his tie. But you had one husband who got into fights with waiters and another who wrecked furniture. If you wind up with another big drinker, you and your children could be risking more than a potential black eye."

"Every guy who drinks isn't a drunk. You know that."

"Of course I know that. But so far, you've had two out of two. Even if that's too small a sample for any poll, it's a statistic to be concerned about when you're talking on a personal level."

"There are hundreds of nice guys in bars," Tatty said, loud enough to show she was angry.

"Tatty, there are hundreds of guys, nice ones, in other venues, too. Go to tennis matches, car things—you're always saying you want to go to a Jaguar rally. So go. Listen, you and I both know that you could stand on the corner of Park and Seventy-second and within the hour get two marriage proposals. Men like you. Not only like you, they want to marry you."

"I know." She took up the hem of the curtain, removed a paper clip, then placed it back about an eighth of an inch from where it had been. "Sometimes I think it's a mistake to cook for them. It makes them happy and comfortable. Other times . . . you know."

"Damaris dough?" I asked. That was how we'd always referred to her parents' wealth. She nodded. "Well, you have a choice. Tell the next potential husband that you're going to renounce every cent of any money you inherit so you can be judged on your own worth."

"That's not funny."

"Or you can deal with the fact that someday you'll be really rich and start thinking not just what money will buy but what it will do."

"Charity?" Though not as bad as her father, Tatty tended to believe charity began and ended at home.

"Yes, charity. Or like thinking about the fact that you didn't earn this money, that it's been handed down to you and you're the steward. Tat, you're thirty. You'll be making choices in the future: Do I want to not save a dime and spend it all on Valentinos and Chateau Latour? Or donate the whole bundle to the Costume Institute at the Met or some other cause?" For a fraction of a second, she looked intrigued. "Do you want to marry a rich guy and spend his money and save yours? Do you want to marry a middle-class guy, like a teacher or a Legal Aid lawyer, and use your money to live a little better than you might on his salary? There are so many interesting ways to live if you just stay away from the men who don't have the capacity to stay sober. Then there's only one way to live. Your life will revolve around his drinking."

"What about you meeting someone?" Tatty asked. "More than half the people you deal with in your job are men. When are you going to push yourself a little, try to get John out of your system?"

Just hearing John's name spoken about three feet from my

bed made me sense him with disturbing clarity. Small details: the shadow of his beard by the end of the day, the incredibly soft skin between his wrist bone and thumb. It took some time before I could speak. "Soon. Maybe I'll give that lawyer, Steve Raskin, a call. He's pretty attractive. Smart. Seems genuinely nice. I told you about him. He's the one there's nothing wrong with."

"That's not a ringing endorsement."

I got back on my knees again to signal that we still had shower curtain holes to mark. "Right now, I couldn't get it up for a ringing anything. He'll be okay. Or someone else will be. But men don't throw engagement rings at me the way they do at you. So it will take longer. I just hope my ovaries still work by the time I meet Mr. Acceptable. If I do."

"And what are you going to do about your mother?" I'd already told Tatty, at unfortunate length, how I'd chickened out in Shorehaven.

"I don't know yet. I've thought through a hundred different scenarios—"

"After you say, *I'm Amy Lincoln,* what are you going to say to her?"

"I'm not sure. That's part of what's holding me back."

"What's the other part?" Tatty demanded. "What else is holding you back?"

"I guess fear."

"Of what?"

"That I'll see that she's a fucked-up mess and that I'm doomed to be just like her."

"Why do you think you'd be like her?"

"Because I'm not like my father."

"So?"

"So, I'm probably like her."

"Why? You're the logic queen, but you're not making sense. You're you, not her. She's a high school dropout and a first-class bitch. You're not. You're not going to abandon your children."

"How do you know, Tatty?"

"Because I know you. Now stop thinking about all that nature-nurture shit. Stop thinking like a person who works for a magazine like *In Depth*. Forget depth. It gets you no place. If you want to meet her or confront her or whatever, you should think like you work for . . ." Tatty closed her eyes. She was concentrating. Her knowledge of media did not extend far beyond *Vogue* and *Pastry Art & Design*. "Think like you're the person at the *New York Post* who cuts out stories because they're too tasteful."

On Saturday, Tatty met a new man. Not in the bar. In a restaurant supply store. She was looking for a wooden-rim sieve and he, newly separated, for pots, pans, dishes, and glasses. His name was Troy, he was a textile conservator at the Brooklyn Museum, he was six foot two, forty-one years old, and still had most of his hair. She wouldn't have asked, but I told her to go out with him—that I'd have our Saturday night George Cukor film festival on my own.

Since Tatty only liked movies with great clothes, I postponed Cukor, took *My Fair Lady* and *Les Girls* back to the video store, and rented *Radio Days* and my old favorite from adolescence, *The Sure Thing*. I wound up loving the clothes in *Radio Days,* to say nothing of the movie. And watching *The Sure Thing,* I realized I'd seen it so many times over the years that I'd memorized most of the dialogue. In it, John Cusack finally learns that all the babes are nothing compared with his ultrasmart and somewhat anal-retentive traveling companion. I'd never been able to remember for long the name of the actress who played ultra-smart/anal retentive because the girl in that role was always me.

I went to bed, mouth still puckered from all the popcorn I'd eaten, and was on the edge of sleep thinking that if, as predicted, Sunday was glorious and warm, I'd call Steve Raskin in the morning and see if he wanted to do something outdoorsy. Maybe go to the Bronx Zoo. Sports? He didn't look like a runner, but maybe he played tennis and . . . I sat up and turned on the light. A glorious warm day. Where would Ira Hochberg be? On the golf course. And okay, my half brothers, the pumpkin heads, would be home from school, but hopefully they would be typical kids and would be playing baseball, diddling video games, or plotting how to get past the porn-blocking software on their computer.

Which meant my mother might be alone with nothing to do but meet me.

Whoever had last been in the Civic I rented to drive to Shorehaven that Sunday had either worn an aftershave heavy on the musk or had sex in the front seat. I pulled up to my mother's block on Knightsbridge Road and parked on a different corner from earlier in the week. It was only a little after eight, but since I wasn't sure of the customs regarding tee-off times, I figured early was better. I rolled down all four of the car's windows to demuskify the car and once again went into my road atlas–cell phone tableau vivant.

On my way out of the city, I had picked up the *Times* and the *Washington Post*. However, in order to read them without having passersby wonder, *How come that woman sitting in that green Civic is reading the paper there instead of doing it at home?* I would have had to position it on my knees, which would prevent me from looking out at the doings around chez Hochberg.

By nine o'clock, the only action on the block involved the neighbors walking one or another variety of retriever and shuffling down driveways in robe and slippers to fetch plastic-bagged Sunday papers. I realized about ten minutes later I did not have the temperament for detective work. It was so boring. My choice was to roll up the windows, listen to NPR, and inhale musk or keep the windows down and silently recite Hamlet's soliloquy, the Gettysburg Address, the preamble to the Constitution, the Twenty-third Psalm, and then move on to R.E.M. lyrics.

By the time I got to *promote the general welfare,* I was out of the car. Either the Hochbergs were know-nothings or someone in the family had already brought in the newspapers. If I didn't do something, my day could be interminable. Would I have to wait for Ira to peruse every ad in *Newsday* before heading off to his club? I did not want to have to deal with him. I wanted to meet her alone.

Casually, I strolled down to the middle of the block. My eyes went right-left-right, up and down, again and again, looking into the windows of the colonials and Tudors to see if anyone was looking out. No one was, it seemed.

And there I was, at the end of the Hochbergs' driveway, looking at a garage that did not have any windows. I was surprised. I'd simply assumed all suburban houses had windows uselessly high up on their electric garage doors. On the other hand, the absence of them was somewhat comforting since I would not have been able, except via ladder or pole vault, to peer through a pane of glass at least six feet above the ground. Figuring I looked suburban enough in khakis, pink shirt, and well-aged loafers, I moved closer, crossing the strip of lawn that was no-man's-land between the Hochbergs' Tudor and the hacienda next door. I went slowly, trying to appear like a girl in the 'hood searching for a key or some small possession in the grass.

What if she glanced out her window and saw me? My mouth went dry. My palms became wet as I imagined the nasal shriek of a police siren as Nassau County cops, summoned by my mother—*She's stalking me, Officer*—leaped from their patrol car, guns drawn. Or called by the neighbor in Casa Perlmutter, in which case their guns would remain holstered and they'd simply spray Mace.

My hope that there would be a window on the side or the rear of the garage was soon dashed. So I had no way of knowing if there were two cars or one, if Ira was sitting in the kitchen or standing in a sand trap. I retraced my slow steps over the lawn and made my way back to the car, regretting that I hadn't brought along a Styrofoam container of coffee, like detectives in movie stakeouts.

A look at my watch made me groan—fortunately, not loud enough to disturb any neighbors. Nine-twenty. The good news was I didn't have to go to the bathroom yet. The bad news was I could be stuck on Knightsbridge Road anywhere from five minutes to eight hours. I might have put the car in drive and gotten the hell out of there at that moment, except, while reaching into my handbag to feel around for a random Tic Tac, I came up with a pen. I reached over to the passenger seat and grabbed one of the eighteen thousand sections of the *Washington Post*. In the narrow margin, I began to write: IF I CALL & SHE ANS & I ASK FOR IRA, WILL THNK AMY? MAYBE Y MAYBE N. IF Y, WHAT CAN HAPPEN?

I started imagining the police siren once more, but I took a deep breath and forced myself to write again: IF SHE THNKS IT'S ME, I CAN DENY/HANG UP/ADMIT IT'S ME. WHICH??? PLAY BY EAR?

IF SHE THNKS ME, WON'T NECESS. KNOW I'M IN CAR 4 HOUSES AWAY. ON OTHER HAND, MAYBE KID OR IRA HIMSELF P/U FONE. IN THAT CASE

I never got to that case. A mechanical noise interrupted the suburban quiet. I glanced at my mother's house. The garage door was rising. I turned on the engine of the Civic and somehow remembered to put the car into drive. I waited and within seconds, the rear of a dark car emerged. Someone—no, two people were in the back. I was about to creep up to follow it, but then I realized the car might turn and face my way. Yes, there was the front of the car. A woman driving. No one in the front passenger seat.

The car backed up onto the road and drove toward me. Fortunately, I was momentarily paralyzed, because any obvious move might have made her look my way. She didn't. Her eyes were on the road as she passed me and turned left. Within seconds I did some kind of turn, three-quarter, U, God only knows what, but now I was behind her. A Volvo, dark blue. Even though I'd never thought about her behind the wheel, I felt slightly disappointed that she had such a stolid car. One block, two blocks. Not that I expected a Maserati, but . . .

She pulled into a driveway so quickly I didn't have time to slam on the brakes. I kept going at about twenty-five miles an hour right past her. A boy, one of the pumpkin heads, I realized, got out. She waited while he moseyed up the path toward the front door. The house was like an oversize fairy-tale cottage with a thatched-looking roof and sides of old stones. The boy's hands were in his pockets. His shoes dragged along the stepping-stones. Obviously, the hip walk for the under-ten set. By the time he must have reached the door, I was on the next block, hiding out in someone's driveway, waiting for her to back out. I kept looking back and forth, from the Volvo to where I was. A face suddenly appeared in a window of the house whose driveway I was in. A man in his mid-forties in a white T-shirt was staring at me, wondering why I was there. What the hell was I going to do? I smiled, waved at him. As I began backing out, he finally waved back. But had I lost sight of my mother's Volvo? I looked down the cross street left and right, then finally, as I begin to pant frantically, I realized she was still where she had been.

I gripped the wheel to keep my hands from shaking. If this had been happening in Manhattan, I could have handled any-thing—almost anything—with barely a blink of an eyelash. Ditto for any other city, Chicago, Madrid. But in the suburbs I felt like a foreigner who, with every uncertain movement, every effort to blend in, feels as if she's inviting the attention of an entire populace who will not like her.

As it turned out, this was not a car chase to write home about. She was a better driver than I, but that was no contest. Still, though she didn't signal for any turns, I managed to follow far enough back to feel safe. The other thing she didn't do was look in her rearview mirror. She appeared intent on driving and, as far as I could tell, was not having any conversation with whoever was in the back.

This time she didn't pull into a driveway, just slammed on the brakes in front of a modern redwood house that looked as if it had traveled to Long Island from Marin County and, for some reason, decided to stay. The back door opened. The other pump-kin head emerged from the car. Actually, both of them looked like nice kids. This was the younger one, chubbier than his brother, his round head echoed by a round belly, the kind of sweet-faced fat boy who shows up in TV news segments on the perils of fast food.

Now she was alone. For an instant, I recalled the standard movie maneuver in which a car passes the car it's been following, then cuts it off, forcing the driver to slam on the brakes: Taking cover behind fenders, cursing, and gunfire often ensue. I knew such cinematics were ridiculous, so I simply started following her again.

For a few minutes, I concentrated completely on the driving. When she turned, so did I. We pulled onto a main road, a wide boulevard with traffic lights and what looked like uninteresting stores. She passed a traffic light, green. For me it turned yellow. Then, just as I got to the corner, red. Quickly, I looked one way, then the other, saw no one, driver or pedestrian. I ran the light.

About two miles down the road, she stopped for a red light. I could have pulled up next to her and gotten a glimpse, but I was too afraid some biological ESP would murmur, *Véronique, that's your daughter over there.* And speaking of being afraid, I suddenly realized she could be on her way to the club to join other golf widows for a three-bloody-Mary brunch. Okay, I might be able to get past a guardhouse by smiling and saying, *I'm Dr. Cohen's guest,* except the Honda Civic would not be much of a help. Mentally, I was still at some country club, wishing I had worn dressy pants instead of khakis, when she made a quick left. The light was changing. Cars were speeding toward me, but I gunned the gas and, a couple of seconds later, pulled into a parking spot six or seven cars away from where my mother's had pulled in. It was the parking lot of . . . I looked up at the sign . . . the Gold Coin Motel.

She got out. Still petite, but then, most girls don't grow much after age sixteen. Skirt on the short side, boots on the long side, and a black turtleneck tucked in to display a small waist. Not age appropriate, but from where I sat, she looked surprisingly good. No bulges, no jiggles. I didn't get to see her face because her back was to me. She was hurrying, almost running, to get to the motel entrance.

I checked out my watch. A little after nine-thirty. Fine. If she was going into a local motel for the usual reason, I figured I'd have time to go and get a cup of coffee. And maybe even read the papers.

Chapter Eighteen

Maybe I'd been too harsh in my judgment. Why adultery necessarily? Other things could be going on in that motel—brunches, conferences. It was, after all, April. Maybe Bring Back the Bard was having a Happy Birthday, Shakespeare gala. I glanced at the rearview mirror.

Then I realized: Of course, the Gold Coin Motel. It was part of a cheesy travel chain, one of those approved by *In Depth*'s accounting department. All the Coins I'd ever stayed in looked like this one: two or three stories covered with quarter-inch brick siding and a faux-slate roof. It was supposed to evoke the glamour of an estate from the Gatsby era, but not even the most unreconstructed yokel could be conned into such a belief.

From Manchester, Vermont, to Miami to L.A., there were two types of room: cheap but overpriced, and cheaper. The former had a four-poster bed made out of some mystery material the color of maple. In all the rooms, the bedspreads exuded an odor of chemicals from their biennial dry cleaning. The lounges at the Gold Coin were just as predictable. Bartenders, dressed butler-style, served a house red, a mélange of merlot and Juicy Juice. Mixed drinks were set down on paper cocktail napkins imprinted with birdbath-shaped champagne glasses. *Here you are, madam,* a cocktail waitress in a black dress and a white apron would say when she handed over one of the Coin's large, luxe drinks, 100-proof smoothies with names such as Cotillion Raspberry and Hunt Club Lime.

The Gold Coins' coffee shops, if I remembered correctly from the 2000 primaries, featured a gold lamé cloth draped over tables on which the breakfast buffet—composed mostly of small boxes of expired cereal and petrified scrambled eggs—was spread. I could not pass a Gold Coin anywhere without recalling the gelatinous, rotting green grapes concealed beneath a thin layer of honeydew in what the room service menu referred to as *Our Sumptuous Fruit Medley.*

Would a group devoted to Shakespeare be willing to celebrate the Bard in such a setting? To imagine that was beyond my powers of fantasy. So I tried to picture my mother chairing a brunch for some cause: pro-gun-control, anti-war-in-Iraq, or anti-gun-control, pro-war. Or perhaps she was attending one of those sales that took place in C- hotels and that I kept seeing advertised in newspapers: *10,000 paintings all framed including large landscapes for over sofas one day only!* the ads would proclaim. Or *Miles and miles of genuine Oriental rugs!*

I turned the car around and backed into a space across from where I'd originally parked. I wanted to see my mother through the windshield when she left the motel, not as a small figure reflected in a rearview mirror. Also, this way I was directly across and a few cars down from her Volvo. Thus situated, I studied my cuticles for a while. Once that thrill was gone, I phoned the motel's front desk. "You know," I began, "I suddenly remembered I'm supposed to go to something in the conference room at the motel. Anyway, I *think* it's at the Gold Coin. But I'm not sure. Do you have anything scheduled this morning?"

"Uhhh," a hungover voice on the line said. "Let me check." I waited, and waited some more. "Uhhh," the voice returned at last, soft, so as not to make a headache more painful. "We don't have anything on today. Not till Tuesday. Uhhh, North Shore Quilters Guild."

I decided that while I waited, I ought to stick to my Sunday schedule. Newspaper reading might be tranquilizing, or at least a comfortable routine. I picked out the parts of the papers I usually read, then placed them in my customary order of preference. Having gotten sorted out, I stacked the excess five pounds of newsprint neatly on the floor in the rear.

As always, I began with the news. This time, though, planes, trucks, a passing crow, and the thud of my heartbeat kept distracting me. I found myself having to go back over the same few paragraphs. No matter how many times I read what Senator Inhofe was supposed to have said in a closed Armed Services Committee hearing, the information refused to penetrate my consciousness. So I abandoned any attempt at substance. Instead, I checked out the employment section to see what writing jobs were being offered in Washington, hoping to see *The New Republic will double your salary! Become a columnist today!* I didn't. Then I looked at the *Times Magazine*'s food page. It featured some disgusting soupy thing with whole shrimp. The accompanying photo was so high-resolution it showed the little buggers' bulbous shrimp eyes, as well as their antennae. It seemed more a lesson in evolution—From Insect to Crustacean—than dinner. I closed the magazine, divided the newspaper sections back into *Times* and *Post*, and set them on the passenger seat.

I was then free to gnaw the knuckle of my thumb and glance continuously from motel to Volvo. After a few minutes, against my will, my eyelids drooped and closed. It was as if a drain had suddenly opened and my energy was running out fast. I tried to open my eyes again, but it was too enervating. I leaned back against the headrest. Just a five-minute power nap. But almost instantly my head jerked forward as I contemplated the varieties of head lice from other rental car drivers who'd similarly laid back their weary heads for an I-can't-go-on moment.

How many times would I have to shampoo before I'd feel sure that my hairdresser wouldn't get nipped? Stop this craziness! I ordered myself. There aren't any lice. This isn't about lice. This isn't about shrimp eyes. This is about your mother.

I calmed down, or at least the back of my head gradually stopped itching so badly that I wanted to claw at it. But reality was worse than imagining an entire corps de ballet of lice doing pirouettes. My strength was nearly gone. I glanced down at my legs. They looked the same but felt so weak I doubted they could support me. If I got out of the car, they would turn from flesh and bone into a substance resembling diaphragm jelly. They'd give way and I'd wind up three and a half feet tall. Frightening, this weariness, because I was a strong person. I knew it. My life had proved it.

So what was wrong with me? Maybe throughout the years, to stay strong, I'd locked away my mother in a small jail cell located on the farthest border of my consciousness. She couldn't get to me from there. To be sure, I understood intellectually that she had to be a major factor in my psyche. Ergo, I couldn't be all strong. When the person genetically wired to care for you says, essentially, *Fuck it, I don't want this job,* you're never going to be 100 percent.

But in locking her away in that cell, had I indeed protected

myself? Or had I simply given her time to grow more dangerous? Could this whole confrontation gig wind up breaking me
instead of making me whole? Except for the total of two and a
half years when Chicky was out of prison, I'd gone without
love. Okay, that's how the cards were dealt. While I wouldn't
recommend my childhood to anyone, it was a better hand than
some kids got. Still, I was beginning to understand that to my
young mind, I'd been abandoned by both parents—my mother
by taking a hike, my father by his refusal to stay out of the slammer for long. No matter how much strength I believed I had—
and proved I had—it could be that surviving that lonely life had
made me not just vulnerable, but fragile.

Fragile? Fragile was looking good. I was so wiped I didn't
have the strength to extend my arm, turn the key in the ignition,
and get the hell away from the Gold Coin and my mother. Take
it easy, I soothed myself. You'll feel better in a minute. This is
totally psychological. But five, ten minutes later I was no
stronger. Okay, my head understood that at some point I would
find the wherewithal to start the car and escape. Yet my body
knew I was incapable of doing it any time soon.

Or maybe whatever action I took wouldn't matter. My
mother would stroll out of the Gold Coin in an hour or a
minute, catch a glimpse of me, know precisely who I was, and
chuckle to herself knowing she had won. With just one glance,
she could see that she was stronger. Always had been, always
would be.

It wasn't even five minutes later that the electric double doors
at the motel entrance parted. Out she came. Alone, but that
wasn't proof of anything. If one is an adulterer, one does not
depart the site of the assignation arm in arm with one's
inamorato. She was dressed as before, short skirt, high boots,
black turtleneck. This time, though, I could see her face. Not the

eyes, because she was wearing sunglasses with overlarge tortoiseshell frames that were either avant-garde or retro-hip; I'd have to ask Tatty. I thought back to that single black-and-white photograph of my mother I'd studied throughout my life: hidden behind other sunglasses, her mouth chalky from that early-seventies lipstick that made her lips appear the color of pearls.

Here she was in color. How come I hadn't noticed her hair earlier? Probably because she'd worn it up. Now it was loose, down to her shoulders, with layers of cascading curls, a passé profusion of twirly hair seen nowadays mostly in hookers' wigs. As she emerged from under the overhang at the entrance, I could see its color, a striking dark red that emphasized the pallor of her skin. As for the rest of the face, from a distance it appeared heart-shaped with a pointy chin. Not a witch's chin: It was the sweetheart face of a silent film star.

She was walking slowly with a slight side-to-side ungainliness. Arthritis? Sex-soaked panties? General klutziness? I couldn't guess because even thinking required more energy than I possessed. Oh God, I prayed, give me just a few minutes of strength. But there was no surge of vigor. I could only stare, so mesmerized by her approach even my autonomic nervous system—breathing, blood flow, and the like—seemed suspended.

Yet each of her steps toward me brought a new revelation. A Vuitton drawstring sack, the absurdly large kind, spacious enough to hold a bag full of groceries or a couple of dachshunds. Fishnet panty hose rising above the high boots. Her legs were young, her face not quite. What looked like gullies of dissatisfaction had dug themselves from her nose down to the sides of her mouth. Her lips were purplish black, a wild color for a pale redhead to wear. It wasn't until she came within fifteen feet that I realized she was so close, in seconds she could simply get into her car and drive off.

That galvanized me. I turned on the ignition, put the car in gear, my foot on the gas, and drove six feet. Then I slammed it into park. Now the Civic was making the top of a T with my mother's Volvo, blocking her exit. *No, no,* she gestured from her distance, waving her hand. Then, from ten feet away, she pointed over and over with her index finger: *My car. That's my car.* Then her thumb told me, *I'm pulling out.* Was her rust-colored nail polish meant to go with a lipstick other than the one she was wearing? Or was it an outré touch?

I turned off the ignition and got out of the Civic. I took my eyes off her only to locate the lock button on the car's remote. Dropping the keys into the pocket of my khakis, I stood where I was, about five feet from where she'd frozen the instant she looked me in the eye and knew.

"I'm Amy. We need to—" As I said "talk," her head jerked from right to left. In a far corner of the lot, on the other side of the motel's entrance, she spied an elderly man putting a suitcase into the trunk of his car.

"Get away from me!" she blared. One hell of a powerful voice, like a quarterback calling an audible. Her Bring Back the Bard affiliation made that line from *Lear* spring up: *Her voice was ever soft, gentle, and low—an excellent thing in woman.* The man glanced up from his trunk. Maybe he didn't think her voice was all that excellent. Maybe he hadn't heard the words themselves. Or if he had, he may have decided this was one catfight he could pass on. When she realized Trunk Man would be of no help, she pivoted and started to run away from me, down the row between the lines of parked cars.

Not running exactly. Not in those high-heeled boots. Not when she was way into her forties and competing with a practiced runner still not thirty. Two strides and I was beside her. I grabbed her upper arm. Slender, but no muscle tone, all flesh. "I know this must be hard for you," I told her. "But if we don't talk now, we'll have to talk at Knightsbridge Road." A little incentive, Chicky would call it, although the fussy might call it blackmail. "We can all talk there. You, me, and Ira and the boys."

"Let go of my arm!" I kept my grip. "Now!" Perhaps chez Hochberg that was her scary voice. *Don't mess with Mom. Sorry, Véronique, sorry.* It certainly wasn't scary to me. Nevertheless, I realized that in playing rough with her, I had pushed her to be tough in return. "I understand," I said. "I don't want you to feel threatened. I apologize if I came on too strong." Her response was to raise the arm I was holding on to and try to bite my hand. "Are you crazy?" I squawked.

"Let go of my arm," she demanded. It was a fairly even tone for someone who had just gotten through baring her teeth. "I don't like to be threatened with physicality."

What do you like to be threatened with? was the response that came to mind. I suppose it disappointed me that she'd used a pissy word like *physicality*. I'd expected better. "No running," I told her. She nodded, just once. "I don't expect a relationship," I went on. "What I do expect from you are answers to my questions this one time." Again, one nod. "Full and complete answers. Not nods, not nos and yeses."

"Fine," she exhaled. I couldn't tell if she was trying to sound bored or if, when she wasn't yelling, she spoke in a flat, unemotional tone. "This one conversation only. I don't want you driving out here every—"

"I have no intention of doing that," I said. "But for the record, I make the rules for this discussion."

"And if I don't abide by them?" In the spring sunshine, her pale foundation clung to her skin a little too passionately, emphasizing spiderwebbing on her upper lip, enlarged pores along the sides of her nose.

And if I don't abide by them? she had said. A response between snide and snotty. In all my imaginings of meeting her, I'd considered feeling fury, mortification, disgust, or even surprise tenderness, and I'd been prepared for powerful feelings on my mother's side as well. What else could be expected after all these years, after the sundering of the most basic bond in nature? Yet so far, aside from her lame call for help, all that seemed to have been stirred up in both of us was a moderate-to-high level of crankiness.

"We can't talk comfortably standing out here in the parking lot," I said. "Let's go get a cup of coffee someplace so we can sit down."

She sighed, a long breath let out slowly through slightly parted, dark purple lips. Ordinarily, that was the nonverbal announcement *I am passive-aggressive.* On this occasion, however, I had to consider that she was truly at a loss for what to say. Consciously or not, she was buying time. Finally, she glanced toward the motel entrance: "There's a coffee shop in there."

But her lover might be in there having a postcoital grilled cheese sandwich and would come to her rescue. "Not in there," I said.

Another long breath, although this one was exhaled through her nose. "There's a patisserie in a little shopping center. They have a few tables. You can follow me in your car"—with a little too much patience she raised an eyebrow—"unless you think I'm going to floor it and escape."

"I'm sure you won't. The patisserie will be fine."

She waited until I moved my car before walking over to the door of hers. I noted her skirt didn't look right. The side seam had relocated itself between her hip and spine, indicating either a rotating waistband or that in the motel, the skirt had been hurriedly pulled on and zipped. These are the details that get the

attention of some of my colleagues, embed journalists, after too
many nights of Gold Coins and Courtyards by Marriott, too
many days of hearing their assigned candidate making the same
self-deprecating jokes at the same point in the same stump
speech. The real news for that segment of the fourth estate often
became a sighting of the campaign manager coming down to the
bus with a shirttail poking out obscenely from the top of his zip-
per after an alleged breakfast meeting with a field organizer.

I wondered if my mother knew I was an associate editor at *In
Depth*.

Perhaps the citizens of Shorehaven were sleeping late, had
sworn off croissants and brioche as high-carb criminals, or were
enraged at Chirac, de Villepin, and all things French. Aside from
the woman behind the shelves of tarte tatin and Paris-Brest, my
mother and I were the only people in La Petite Patisserie.

My mother chose the table farthest from the counter and sat.
"If you want something, you have to go up there and tell her.
There's no table service."

"What would you like?"

"Nothing." That was pretty much what I was in the mood
for, but I went up and ordered a café au lait and a *langue de chat*
as rent for the table and also because *la vendeuse* was one of
those intimidating French women with a large nose made solely
for derogatory sniffs and those small shoulders and miniboobs
that made Americans look like Brobdingnagians. As I stood at
the counter, I had an urge to toss off the order in French. I spoke
it pretty well. At least French people now and then told me how
nonterrible my accent was, though apparently I sounded as if I
came from a region they did not. But since most of my life has
been spent covering my ass, I didn't want to risk the counter
woman saying *Pardon?* as if she could not understand my order
of a *langue de chat*. And if my mother was enough of a fran-

cophile to have chosen Véronique, I didn't want her explaining, in Parisian French, what kind of cookie I wanted.

On second glance, walking back to the table, I began to see why my mother's style was suburban gypsy. The little skirt, high boots, and turtleneck were all basic, except for the fishnets. But she wore at least a half dozen bracelets on her right wrist in varying shades and textures of gold, woven, twisted, high-gloss, matte. A few were decorated with semiprecious stones. One looked like a watch, but what I thought was the face turned out to be, as I came closer, an emerald-cut citrine about the size of my cookie. Her earrings were, disappointingly, the usual diamond studs, that rite of female passage that comes after the bat mitzvah and wedding canopy and before the funeral. Hers were sizable enough that if she wore them daily, her ears would resemble a beagle's by the time she was sixty. When I sat down at the small, round table, she slid her chair back to increase the distance between us. With her slightest move, she jingled.

She pulled back the cuff of her sweater to get a look at her watch. It, too, was gold. It wrapped around several times, as if it had been modeled on the Slinky. Her wrists were much smaller than mine. Although we were about the same height, side by side we probably looked like Barbie and a Cabbage Patch kid. "This can't take longer than twenty minutes or so," she told me, not looking directly into my eyes. "I have to pick up my sons and bring them—"

I reached into my backpack and handed her my cell phone. "It will take however long is necessary. You can apologize for being unavoidably detained." Maybe I was ODing on adrenaline; my nerves were aquiver like a plunked tuning fork. Still, I sounded amazingly like a person who has her wits about her.

"I have my own cell phone," she replied, but didn't reach for it. She wasn't exactly hostile. More like someone resigned to an unavoidable delay at an airport. For a few seconds I just stared at her, my cell phone in one hand, coffee cup in the other. After nearly thirty years of studying my own face in the mirror, from admiring my gift for making cross eyes as a kid to agonizing over zits to the daily application of makeup, I knew it well. Now I kept searching for something of myself in her face.

Her eyes were green, but of an intense emerald color that comes from contact lenses, not nature. My hair was brown with red highlights. Hers was the dark red found on Irish setters and Titian's women, as well as in two-step, three-hundred-dollar coloring processes in salons such as Beauté. Her skin was porcelain. Mine wasn't dark, but over the years of playing sports and working as a flagman during college summers, I had grown permanently ruddy, in the manner of white trash girls in *Gone With the Wind* who went without bonnets. So we shared a five-foot-three gene and maybe a couple of coloring genes. But I could find no other likeness.

She adjusted her bracelets to her satisfaction, then asked: "Well?"

"Tell me something about your life now," I said.

"I thought you wanted to know about—"

"We have a deal. My questions get answered. I know what I'm doing. I don't know if your mother mentioned it, but I earn my living as—"

"Whatever. My life? I'm married, but you know that. Ira has a successful business. Lighting fixtures, indoor and out, and lamps. He also has the contract to maintain fixtures for all Nassau County's governmental buildings. And for the Diocese of Rockville Centre, which is quite a coup for someone named Ira Hochberg. What else do you want to know?"

"You have two boys?" This phrasing was in lieu of my asking, *Besides me you have two other children?* Instead of anger for forcing her into a conversation she didn't want to have, or fear that I'd drop in on Ira and read aloud from *Phyllis Moscowitz: The Adolescent Years,* the only emotion my mother displayed was annoyance. Sighs. Now and then compressing her lips together in an expression more intense than pique but less than disgust. She shifted around in the small, woven café chair. Her annoyance threw me. I was so used to going through the world getting myself liked. *Isn't Amy Lincoln adorable and feisty and wonderfully down to earth?* Or something like *And so bright. Harvard!* My mother, however, seemed to have a natural immunity to my charm. Maybe worse, she didn't seem to hate me. Still, I tried a smile. "Are you a full-time mother?"

She was trying to turn the rings on the left hand with her pinky. I noticed what I assumed she wanted me to see: Besides the wedding band, she wore a ring with two diamonds slightly larger then M&Ms. "What does the term *full-time mother* mean?" she asked.

"That you're at home raising your sons rather than working outside the home."

"Then yes, I'm a full-time mother. I thought you wanted to know about me back then." I probably should have said, *Wow, what a beautiful ring!* She said: "Are you asking me all this to soften me up or do the questions have some point?"

"To soften you up." I tried one more smile, my broad one that shows a hint of dimples. In response, she reached down to the depths of her giant handbag and after a few seconds retrieved an inch-long enamel box with a minuscule paisley design, opened it, and popped what looked like a little mint into her mouth. "Okay," I said, "let's get on to the information I'm really interested in."

"Is that a cappuccino?" she asked me.

"A café au lait. Can I get you something?"

349

"One of those. And a chocolate croissant." I walked back to the counter and in a few moments came back with her order. She lifted the plate up to nose level, sniffed, then turned the pastry around, as if she had to do a 360-degree examination. Then she lifted the croissant, not between two fingers, but by clutching it in her fist. With her mouth open wide, she ripped off about a third of it and chewed with something less than delicacy: lips smacking, mouth making *chomp, chomp* sounds. I was so startled because Rose, her mother, had been well mannered. One of my dubious legacies from Grandma Lil was hypervigilance when it came to table manners, no matter how archaic or stupid they might be. If someone passed a creamer without offering the handle, they got an immediate minus five. Clutching a croissant as if it were a leg of fried chicken was beyond the pale. I remembered that the first time we'd gone out to dinner together, John had made me inordinately happy when he'd broken off a bite-size piece of roll, buttered it, and popped it in his mouth.

"What attracted you to my father?"

"What do you think?" She ran her tongue over her top front teeth, presumably to mop up any chocolate or stray crumbs.

"I believe I was pretty clear before. I want all my questions answered."

"He was . . . Do people still call him Chicky?" I nodded, expecting she would ask me how he was or what he was doing now. "He was a rebel," she said. "A car thief. Did you know that?"

"Yes. What else is there about him that made you willing to run away from home?"

"Frankly? He was a great fuck. Of course, that's by a teenager's standards. Does that"—she opened her mouth and widened her eyes in mock astonishment—"shock you?"

"Do I look shocked?" I sipped my coffee. It had cooled but still had that wonderful bitter French bite. "You stayed with him for a considerable amount of time. He told me you were living under fairly hellish circumstances, with a rat—"

"I will not under any circumstances talk about that!" The woman behind the counter seemed unnerved by my mother's outburst. She edged closer to the cash register. My mother demanded: "How the hell can you talk about a rat in a place like this?"

"Let's move on then. You married him, at least in part, because you thought you were pregnant. You weren't. How come you stayed?"

"I can't remember. I was a kid."

"Why didn't you go back to your family? What was there about your parents that was so terrible you couldn't—"

"They were boring. Okay? I know that doesn't sound like a big deal. But just try living with it. More than boring. Suffocating. And incredibly pretentious. My father would give me endless lectures. He'd sit in his chair in the living room and keep trying to get me to sit too, but I would never give him the satisfaction. He'd blab on and on about my getting some goal in life. Oh, and that I needed to do something after school, like being a candy striper. Or collect dollhouse furniture. His big thing was that I should join a group of nice, young people and take long bike rides. Like out to Montauk Point. He hadn't a goddamn clue as to who I was. And worse, he didn't care. He knew what he wanted in a daughter and it was never me."

"And your mother?"

"A five-foot-seven cube of ice. A cube that fancied herself an intellectual. I don't think there was one time in all my teenage years that she said, 'Véronique, you look great.'"

"Your name was Phyllis then, right?"

"That's not exactly a brilliant deduction. My mother or someone told you."

"But boring parents . . . Is there anyone who got through

adolescence without thinking her parents were boring or stupid or crass or snobbish? Was there anything else about them?"

"Like what?"

"Were they abusive to you in any way?"

"Emotionally abusive." She bit off another hunk of croissant with the same sound effects as she had the first. She washed it down with her coffee, a surprisingly silent operation. "*Completely* unloving. Nothing I did was worth anything to them. I mean, even if I had taken up stamp collecting for him or let her take me to orchestra concerts, it wouldn't have been enough for them. The fact of my collecting stamps or going to concerts would have made stamp collecting and concerts the wrong thing to do. Maybe it doesn't sound like a big thing now, but believe me, I was *dying* in that house. If I'd been forced to stay there, I would have committed suicide. You know why? Because eventually they'd break me. They'd turn me into them. And I'd rather be dead than be that way."

"I hope to have children one day, so now I'm going to ask you some medical information. Not a lot. Rose can give me the family history."

"Rose? Are you and *Rose* best friends now?"

"I met her. We've exchanged a couple of letters and phone calls."

"Are you planning a round-the-world trip or a Fifth Avenue penthouse with your inheritance from Rose?" my mother asked. "Because if you are, you should know she loves the boys, absolutely loves them. And what she has isn't serious money anyway."

"How was your pregnancy with me?"

"What? You want the truth? Terrible."

My heart was so heavy it sank into my gut. "Why was it terrible?"

"Because he couldn't even afford a doctor. I had to go to a clinic up at Bellevue. It was like being in hell. Sometimes there weren't even enough chairs for all the women, and most of them . . . It wasn't their first baby. They would bring their other children with them and they kept screaming at the top of their lungs. And most of them were dirty. I know that's not politically correct to say, but that's how it was."

"Was I born in Bellevue?" She nodded. "Forgetting about the clinic for a minute, how did the pregnancy go medically?"

"All right."

"No problems during the nine months or with the delivery?"

"No. Normal. Okay?"

"What about your other pregnancies?"

She put her cup back down on the saucer a little too vehemently. "What does that have to do with you?"

"It's part of your medical history."

"They were fine. No problems."

"Were there any miscarriages or anything like that?"

She shook her head. "Does Chicky still have all his hair?" she inquired.

"Yes." Unfortunately, not all his teeth, but I saw no reason for me to mention that. "Have you had any medical problems? Diseases? Operations?"

"Why don't you ask Rose?"

"You seem to have less than a close relationship. You might not want to confide in her."

"I'm fine. Nothing is wrong. I had a hysterectomy two years ago, but that was all about fibroids. And I'm on antidepressants, but who isn't?" She took her napkin and polished up the citrine on her bracelet.

"When did you decide to leave Chicky?"

"I don't know. I mean, I knew right from the beginning that

I'd want out in a year or two. He was never going to make a decent living. He had a few friends who were, well, I guess they'd be called connected. I'm not talking about godfathers. Lower-level guys. But they were fun. I was just a kid. I guess I was attracted to their flashiness. You wouldn't *believe* what some of the girlfriends looked like. The men were like Chicky but different. Oh, they liked him because everybody did. But when you hung out, you could see they had no respect for him."

"You mean, they wouldn't want him for a colleague."

"The highest up he was ever going to get was chauffeur. Not that I ever wanted to be married to someone in the Mafia, but even if he'd been hanging around with guys who owned clothing stores or travel agencies or something, he'd still be driving. Do you know what I mean?"

"I'm assuming you're saying he lacked a certain entrepreneurial spirit. But when did you decide to leave?"

"After he went to jail. I was living with his mother. You knew her, right?"

"Of course I knew her. You left me with her and she brought me up. That was most of my childhood, because Chicky kept going off to prison."

"Look, don't blame me for leaving you with Lil. You were crawling then. Every single time I got down on the floor, you'd crawl over to *her*. You were happier with her than you were with me. To be perfectly honest, I couldn't bear it there. It was like living in hell, having to listen to her talk about Jackie Onassis's clothes, like she knew something about fashion. There were cockroaches. All over the place."

"Did you run off with someone?" I asked.

"Yes, a diplomat. I only stayed with him a couple of days. Then I went off on my own. First to San Francisco. But then I left. It was a really bad scene in Haight-Ashbury by then."

"Where did you get the money to travel?"

This time she centered the two diamonds in the ring with her right thumb and middle finger. "I had a little money saved."

"From selling the five-carat diamond ring?" If I hadn't grown up in a neighborhood where kids routinely stared down other kids to establish primacy, I might have been cowed by the look she shot me. Her eyes, rimmed with brown eyeliner that had been expertly smudged, narrowed. Her white skin flushed a pink that wasn't pretty. Her nostrils dilated too, but I sensed that was for effect. "What's wrong with my asking about a stolen ring? He served the time for stealing it."

"I don't like to think about it."

To reinforce my primacy, I took my spoon and pointed it at her. "Well, for the next few minutes, your job is to think about it. After that, you're free. In terms of the ring, you have absolutely nothing to worry about. The statute of limitations ran out by the time I was six. There's no good reason not to talk."

She crossed her arms tightly over her black sweater. "Why should I have anything to worry about?"

"You don't, unless you're not straight with me. Then, we can start discussing the fact that you never got a divorce from my father. That means you've entered into two bigamous marriages. That guy in Arizona or wherever and the one you're in with Ira."

For a second, I thought she was going to give back the two-thirds of the croissant she'd already eaten. She looked sick. Her eyes, which really weren't all that pretty except for the green sheen of her lenses, grew huge. "You promised me, you *swore* if I spoke to you this one time you'd never bother me again."

"What can I tell you? I come from a criminal background." Clearly, from the looks the patisserie lady was giving us from behind the counter, it was obvious we weren't out for a mother-daughter kaffeeklatsch. Our volume was too low for her to hear us, but I decided to change the video she was watching. I rested my chin in the palm of my hand and smiled at my mother until my cheeks could rise no higher. Then I sat back. "Believe me, I don't want to have to see you again or deal with you again. But I do want the truth."

"You want to hear what you want to hear, not the truth," she said.

"So what happened? You were in the jewelry store looking at rings. You pinched me, I started screaming my little lungs out, the ring went into my diaper. Then what? You got out of the store?" She shook her head up and down: Yes. "I see. You think I'm wired," I observed. "I'm not. But okay, this is just for me. You can give silent answers."

"I was a different person then. A young girl. I was living in slum conditions. I never got more than two hours sleep a night between you—I don't hold it against you or anything. You were a baby. But after Chicky went away I had to sleep on a terrible convertible sofa. I could feel the bars underneath. Lil wouldn't give up the bedroom. Anyway, go ahead. Ask what you want to ask."

"You showed the ring to Chicky after you took it?" She nodded. "Did he want to take it back or send it back?"

"He didn't know what to do. As usual."

"When did the cops come?"

"That's not a yes or no answer."

"When did they come?"

"On the fourth day after."

"They had a search warrant?" I got a yes on that. "Obviously they didn't find the ring. Where did you hide it?" She pointed to herself in the general area of her solar plexus, although I assumed that was not where she'd stashed it. "Did they take him away then?"

"The next day. They came back."

"But by then," I said, "you told him you'd hock or sell the ring and use the money for a lawyer for him. Did you cry?" The look she gave me showed that if she had any physical courage, she'd throttle me on the spot. Instead, she rubbed her hands together, then sniffed the tips of her fingers. I had no idea why. "Did you cry?" I insisted. Yes, she nodded. "So you said you had to stay with me. Who could separate a mother and baby? And since the authorities were looking at him as the perpetrator anyway, he might as well keep denying it. There was no ring. No proof. Right? Anyone could have taken it. You'd get him the best lawyer in New York and everything would be fine. Did he tell you where to fence it?"

"Yes, but I didn't go there. Most of the guys Chicky knew weren't much smarter than he was. I went to the one I told you about before, who was connected."

"How much did you get for it?" She wasn't answering. She shook her head with an unnecessary ferocity, although it did make her curls bop back and forth. "This is the deal," I snapped. "I ask and you answer." She held up one finger. "One thousand for a five-carat diamond ring?"

"It wasn't a quality stone," she whispered.

"When he was charged and then convicted, didn't he tell anyone that it was you, not he, who'd stolen it?"

"*Not he,*" she repeated. "I feel sorry for you. You need to make sure I don't forget you went to Harvard. Anyway, he told Lil. But he said to leave it because a little girl needs her mother. Naturally, she made my life a living hell."

"Why didn't you just run after you took the ring?" I demanded. "Why did you let him go off to prison? If you'd run, they wouldn't have suspected him."

"But then I'd have had to spend the rest of my life worrying about a knock on the door during the night and opening it and seeing the cops. This way, they wouldn't look anymore. They had their robber."

"You took off when I was ten months old?"

"Something like that. With the man in the diplomatic corps." The bodyguard from the Maldives. "I went off with him, but I didn't want to be tied down. That's when I hitched to S.F. A thousand doesn't go that far, and I knew I had to save it. Then I came back to the city. I lived in the Village. What else do you want to know?"

"What was I like?"

"You were all right. You know. A baby," she said quickly, brushing off the subject.

"Give me some incidents. Is there anything you remember?"

"Look, I wish I could oblige you. No, really I do. It must have been hard on you not having a mother, but trust me, you really preferred Lil. Frankly, I was fucked-up beyond belief. You were much better off without me. If you need me to say I'm sorry, I will, but the truth of the matter is that I had to get out of there just to survive. I admit it, I was an unfit mother."

"So you don't remember anything about me?"

"Not really. First of all, I was in a state of turmoil. And second of all, it was better, healthier for me to forget you. There was no way I could go back without getting into big trouble for abandonment. And Chicky might've made a big stink about me being the one who did it. So it was better to blank out the past."

"You never thought about me or missed me?" I was mortified at begging, but I just wanted one small gift from her. Anything.

"You know, you're putting me in a very uncomfortable position. You're forcing me to hurt you. The answer is no, I was so glad to be out of there that the relief drowned out anything else that might have come up. And after that, I just forgot because I started another life."

"What do you know about me?"

"Just that you went to Harvard. My mother started going on about you but I cut her off. Trust me, she's dangerous in her own quiet way. The only reason she's taken you up is because she wants a do-over. I wasn't the child she wanted. There was never a minute of my childhood that I didn't know that."

"Did she mention to you what I do or—"

"Look, you can call me the biggest bitch in the world, but I don't care. I don't want to know. I have family now. That's my life. My whole life."

"All right," I said, "so let me tell you something about my life." Her knuckles rapped nervously against the little café table, like a judge demanding order. "Stop the knocking. This will take less than a minute. All through the years, I understood I was different from my father, Lil, Aunt Linda. I had brains. I had ambition. I had a relentless work ethic. So I figured if I wasn't like the Lincolns, I had to be like you, whatever you were. I imagined you as smart. I thought you were probably wild but courageous, in a fucked-up way."

"What is this, a soliloquy or something?"

"No. A soliloquy would be when a character is talking to herself, without a listener—within the universe of the play. I have a listener."

"I don't have to take this shit from you."

"You do. For another thirty seconds or so. The one thing I didn't have to imagine about you is that you were morally defective. That didn't take imagination. It was so clear from what you did. I was afraid that if things got rough with a husband or with a child, I was doomed to do what you did: take a walk. Oh, one last thing. The best part of my life has been this last half hour."

"What do you mean, the best part of your life?"

I stood, reached into my backpack, and retrieved a twenty from my wallet. I carefully smoothed out the bill on the table. "Because," I said, right before I turned my back on her, "I learned I'm nothing like you."

Chapter Nineteen

Perhaps to celebrate the joy of spring, Chicky wore an azalea pink rayon shirt with a wide band of green around the collar and across the pocket. Since the first three buttons were open, he was able to display both his chest hair and a new, braided gold chain. "Eighteen carat," he confided so softly that only about half the patrons of the Royal Athens diner could hear him.

"Really nice," I said. "I guess if you're talking jewelry, it means you don't want to hear any more about my mother."

"Amy babes, listen, from the minute I heard Phyllis ditched you, I knew someday you'd decide, *Hey, I gotta find her.* So I'm glad you did what you had to do and it turned out okay. Personally, I wish she'd've dropped dead in agony in 1974. That's after you were born in '73, because she had to be around for that. But in '74, it would've been great if she died screaming in pain with no medicine before she copped that ring. Anyhow . . ." He hooked his thumb under the chain and lifted it so it could better catch the light. "You see some guys and they look like they're gonna choke to death in their chains because they're so tight. You know why?"

"Because the guys gained weight?"

He stuck out his lower lip and rocked his head back and forth weighing that possibility. "Yeah, maybe. But most of the time it's because they're cheap. They buy it just long enough so it'll close. I'll say this for Fern, when she gives, she gives good." Then he winked at me. "Remember what I used to tell you about my mother? *Lil's got quality with a capital K.* Well, Fern gives quality with a capital Q."

Fern, however, was not generous with a capital G with my father's allowance, so I ordered my usual dish of ice cream. He had his usual malted. For a few minutes, we became unnecessarily intent on eating, me scraping the spoon across my scoop of peach for minimouthfuls, he taking sips and swishing the malted around his mouth thoughtfully, like an oenophile checking out a burgundy.

"Chicky, listen, I need to talk a little more about my mother. I know you don't want to hear it but—"

"S'okay. When was it? Oh, I remember. When I got out after serving my time for that Lincoln Continental business: I had this girlfriend, Cindy Lou. She always used to say, 'Chicky, I gotta ventilate.' That meant like getting it off her chest. So I get what you need to do. It's okay. Talk about her, that . . . I know you're grown up, but you're still my kid. So I won't say what I want to call her even though you know what I mean."

"I don't blame you," I told him. "What's such a relief for me is that having met her, I see there's nothing in her to love. I can't whip it up to hate her for what she did to me because I look at myself now and think, *You did a pretty good job raising yourself whenever Chicky wasn't around. You turned out okay.* But I do hate her for what she did to you. Stealing the ring, conning you into keeping quiet by saying she'd hire the best criminal lawyer."

"Amy, what can you do? Shit happens. More times than you ever know."

"I agree. There are times shit is unavoidable. Floods. Earthquakes. Getting caught up in some horrible political situation." Bosnia came to mind but I wasn't sure whether Chicky would have heard of it. So I said, "Look at Iraq. For years, hundreds of thousands of people were murdered. They couldn't say, *Hey, I don't want to be tortured and murdered by Saddam, so I'll keep out of his way.*"

"Yeah. Like with Hitler. I get that."

"But what happened to you was avoidable. If my mother had just hocked the ring and run off, everything would have been okay. The police would have known it was she, not you. She could have disappeared. She *did* disappear. How long do you think they'd look for her? And you wouldn't have gone to prison. Chicky, think back. You were holding down a good job as a mechanic back then."

"It wasn't so good. Mostly Fords. Crap cars, except some of them look nice."

"It was a good job because it was honorable work. You recognized it was your responsibility to support your child. Don't put down what you did. It takes training and intuition to be a mechanic. I couldn't do it. The job wasn't going to make you a millionaire, but you had a right to be proud of it. I hate her because once you served that first sentence, you were never able to hold a job again. I know how hard you tried, but I think that besides betraying you, she caused you to be injured in a way you were never able to recover from. You're a good man, Chicky, and what she did was more than bad. It was wicked."

My father made two fists; when I'd been little, he'd try to lighten any dark mood by saying, *Put up your dukes, kid.* Though the only thing either of us ever punched was air, he inadvertently taught me self-defense was not just acceptable, it was necessary. I put up my dukes. Chicky landed a fast left hook about an inch away from my chin. Then he sat back. "I don't know about her being wicked. Whenever I hear that word, it's with witches. Who knows? Maybe that's what Phyllis was, someone who came into your life just for the fun of fucking it up. But this is the thing, babes. No matter what she did and how bad her leaving was for you, it would have been worse if she stayed."

"I know that now." I planted my spoon into the half scoop of ice cream that was left and watched as it slowly keeled over. "I worry about you a lot, Chicky."

"Don't worry. I'm fine. Fern's not such a dog. Most of the time it's pretty good with her. She can cook and we get out a lot. You should see us do the Latin dances! Salsa, merengue. And if God forbid she got run over by a truck tomorrow, I hate to say it, but there are other Ferns in the world. You don't need to be worrying about me. I'm too old and I've been in the slam too many times to do something dumb again that would put me back in."

"Good. That's a huge relief to me." I paused. "Chicky, I'm about to hit thirty."

"Isn't it funny, me with a thirty-year-old kid?"

"It is. But I've got to face facts. My clock is ticking and I don't know if I'll ever meet the right guy. Except I do want a family."

"Kids?"

"Kids. Or kid. It's important to me that they know you. And speaking of family, I need you in my life."

He made right angles with his thumbs and index fingers to frame his face. "Here I am."

"I'd like you to find something to say to Fern so you don't have to sneak out to meet me. I wish I could see you more than every few months. I want to be able to call you without saying I'm Amy from the Probation Department."

"You think I haven't tried to think up something? See, the big problem is she thinks I'm thirty-six. Plus even if I say I gotta meet my cousin Amy or my niece Amy, she wouldn't believe me in one million years. You know how they say *I'm at a loss*? Well, I'm at a loss. I'm in a situation with her. I got it pretty good, for me. I'm no bargain. I'm a lazy guy. I admit it. I'd rather live off a Fern and get my wake-up coffee in bed and have fun than haul my ass to some job at eight o'clock in the morning."

"Chicky, I'm sure you'll find something to tell her."

"I'll work on it," he assured me.

"Did you ever consider the truth?"

He shook his head vehemently. Then he paused midshake and leaned against the back of the booth, smiling. "The truth?"

"Stranger things have happened."

"I don't know about that. But I'll tell you what, Amy. I'll think about it."

The gingerroot Tatty picked up from the street cart was so long and thick it looked like the branch of an ancient tree. "A ginger wedding cake?" I asked. It was a Thursday night in Chinatown. The narrow streets were packed with people seeking long beans, golden elephant rice, and the odd pig part for the weekend.

"It's his second marriage. He adores ginger and he's very very rich, so she adores ginger, too. She's twenty-three. Anyway, they want it tiered, with traditional white icing. Snore. But they love the idea of decorating it with crystallized ginger and gold foil and icing—all swags and bows and sparklies. Garish in a tasteful way. Like them." She hefted the root in one hand then sniffed it. "Lovely. This is as fresh as you could get in Peking."

"Beijing."

"Who cares?"

"Apparently they do," I replied. "Oh, I think that store with those little embroidered purses—the ones you can use for evening bags—is right around the corner. They're about four bucks. I've been thinking about getting one in turquoise because it would be weirdly wonderful with that purple silk dress."

"Do you have some big event?"

"Not even a little event. Although Steve Raskin, the lawyer with nothing wrong, has definite big-event potential. But since we're down here, I figure I might as well go for it."

"You're a wild spendthrift," Tatty observed. She paid the street vendor for the ginger. There was a three-second flirtation between the two of them as he stuffed the root into an orange plastic bag. As we walked to the turquoise purse store she said: "I have to admit, my heart sank when you said, 'I saw my mother.' I also have to admit I almost fainted when you told me that at the end you put down a twenty-dollar bill and walked out *without getting change.*"

"I'm a different woman. Seriously, I feel that way. I'm *Amy Lincoln, the Sequel.* I've exorcised my mother. My soul is out of her clutches. I know it sounds very *The Devil's Advocate,* but I feel lighter. Frolicsome."

"Frolicsome? That's the first time I ever heard someone say that word. It's only in books. I bet there are a million words nobody's ever said out loud. Wait." I waited. "I have one! Peripatetic. I think that's how you say it. But I forget what it means."

"It describes someone who moves from place to place."

We strolled into a huge Chinese general store, meandered

past a table piled high with packages of rice noodles, walked down the aisle between incense and incense burners and canned fish, then up the stairs. "Did the turtleneck your mother was wearing have very wide ribbed cuffs, about six inches long?"

"I know I'm a perpetual disappointment to you, but I didn't notice." We'd been together for almost a half hour, and Tatty had said nothing about the man she had met. "Why aren't you telling me about Troy the textile conservator?" I asked.

"He's fine. You know I went out with him Saturday night. Right? Right. Well, I saw him again on Tuesday. The parents were out, so I asked him to dinner. Extremely simple, no elaborate presentation. So don't think I was trying to seduce him with salmon in puff pastry with citrus beurre blanc. Just grilled vegetables and Arctic char with caramelized onions and raisins."

"That's all?"

"A napoleon filled with strawberries and whipped cream."

"Isn't a napoleon puff pastry?"

"Yes. I had some in the freezer, so don't think I cooked all day for him."

"You cooked all day for him," I said.

"I swear I didn't. I arranged flowers for an hour. Then I had my hair and nails done."

I spotted the silk purses down the aisle and headed toward them. "So is he in love with you yet?"

"No," Tatty said. "Don't look so surprised. He left without trying to sleep with me, even though he's a hundred percent definitely not gay, because we did some good kissing and it was . . ." She straightened her index finger and poked it toward the ceiling a couple of times. "I thought his restraint was wonderful. So Age of Chivalry."

"How was his . . . ?" I mimicked someone glugging down a drink.

"For your information, he had one small single-malt scotch neat and two glasses of pinot noir with dinner."

"Practically a teetotaler." We reached the purses, small silk envelopes wrapped in noisy cellophane. I couldn't find the turquoise, so I decided bright orange would be fine with dark purple. Tatty took one in black, white, silver, and some sick-looking beige that could have been left over from an old ladies' underwear factory. "Listen, Troy sounds like an interesting guy—potentially decent. I like that he didn't want to rush you to bed without knowing you well."

We looked around for a cashier, couldn't find one, then decided to try downstairs. "I'll tell you what else was good," Tatty reported. "He didn't get all wide-eyed at the size of the apartment and two minutes later start asking me innocently what my father did for a living. We talked the whole time. About textiles—Fortuny mostly. And growing up in New York versus growing up in Des Moines. Did you know Halston came from there, too? And his marriage and my marriages. He wore a wonderful pair of old cordovan loafers, just the least bit scuffed, so they didn't look like someone just polished them, which is always awful." She pulled open the drawstring of my backpack and found my Altoids. "While we're on the subject of men," she continued, "are you going to be stupid and hold off Steve until after the 2004 election? Because that's what you said in 1999 about 2000. Trust me, you can fit a new boyfriend and a president in the same year."

"I know. And maybe it's not Steve. Except I just don't know where else to begin."

"Take your own advice. You hate hanging out in bars and clubs, so that's out. Go places. Call everyone you know, which is about one million people, unfortunately mostly Democrats. Say you're available. You want to get fixed up."

"I don't."

"If Steve doesn't work out, then yes you do. The sooner you meet someone who can make boring intellectual conversation about PCBs or PBS, the quicker you'll get over you-know-who." We waited in line to pay for our purses. "You need someone in your life for the long haul."

"That doesn't necessarily mean a husband, Tat."

"Don't you think I know that? I just happen to enjoy getting married. But on nine-eleven, remember, Roy and I were separated? The first separation, before we went back for those five months. I woke up late, as usual. So did the parents, also as usual. And then we heard what happened. . . . You know how it was. We were shocked beyond belief. Panicked. We felt what everybody else felt. I called you and couldn't get you and finally you called me. Once I knew you hadn't gone down to the Trade Center to interview someone or whatever, I relaxed a little. Well, not relaxed. I was less terrified. The parents and I sat in front of the TV watching it happen over and over. All of a sudden D started shaking." Without mockery, she imitated a person with quivering arms and head. People stared. She didn't notice them. "I never told you this because I didn't think you'd believe it. No one who knows him would. But he was so broken up. He knew lots of people who worked down there. He understood some of them probably died terrible deaths. M went and sat on the arm of his chair and I got up and sat on the other arm, and we took his hands and just sat there holding hands a long time. Finally he said, 'I am so grateful to have you both in my life.' And, believe it or not, as appalling as my parents are and always will be, I felt the same way about them. Amy, it's time to find someone who will feel that way about you and you about him."

"John called me almost right away that morning. I was

amazed he'd gotten through and amazed that . . . I seemed to be his first call. But I didn't appreciate—"

"John's over," Tatty said. "I wish I could make it different, but I can't."

"I know."

"You've got to move on, Amy. Find yourself a place in the world."

"I know that, too."

"Give that Steve a chance." I nodded. "Promise me to give him a fair shot." I nodded again. "Amy, say it."

"I'll give Steve a fair shot. Now please, leave me alone."

All night I kept waking and discovering myself on my left side. Besides worrying about my ribs breaking again, I recalled I'd heard something years earlier about how too much sleeping on your left side can squash your heart out of shape. Naturally, I preferred worrying about this for about fifteen minutes each time I woke rather than turning on my computer and finding out it was pure idiocy.

By morning, I was so groggy I stood before the medicine cabinet not knowing why I had opened it. As I got ready to run, yawning, pulling on my socks, tying my sneakers, I marveled at Tatty's genius for oversimplification. For her, finding a soul mate was on the same level of difficulty as cooking pasta al dente. Not only had she ordered me to get out to find true love, she also wanted me to do it in a presidential election year.

That was part of what was so seductive about romantic comedies, I decided. Work never interfered with the play of love. From Katharine Hepburn to Jennifer Aniston, women were shown at their jobs, but whatever they did rarely took longer than fifteen seconds of screen time. They had enough freedom not only to meet a Cary Grant or Hugh Grant—a snap in itself in New York—but also to have escapades and adorable misunderstandings on the road to romance. I, for one, loved what I saw in those movies so much that I believed in them more than in my own experience.

In the elevator, I bent over to stretch my lower back and hamstrings. A Mr. Appropriate might come along sometime in 2003 or 2004. It could already be that I'd met him—Steve Raskin. But there would be no Mr. Right until I stopped thinking about John every day. I stood straight and set my jaw at a brave angle, hoping all that body-mind theorizing had some value.

Not being able to see weather from my apartment, I discovered when I got outside that it was a fine spring morning. That day, Central Park South was scented not only with its usual horseshit and exhaust fumes, but with apple blossoms or bluebells or whatever sweet, intoxicating flower bloomed in mid-April. The air was velvet on my face.

The park was jammed with walkers and runners, so many that it slowed me down to a trot. I wove between slowpokes while keeping watch for the legions of runners faster than I. The crowd was understandable. Who could fight going out on a morning like this? Even the most inert would pull on shorts and a shirt to run their annual four-hour mile.

If my life were one of those romantic comedies, what a delightful scene this would be: Running with my hair flying beautifully, I would collide with a stud with an IQ over 150. At first the two of us would be combative, throwing clever insults. Then we would stomp off in different directions. Two scenes later, we would meet on the way into someone's campaign headquarters. The rest of the movie would consist of antics, arguments, and a bittersweet parting. Then we'd realize we were madly in love and meant for each other. But I couldn't sustain such a fiction, not when what I found myself doing was eyeing the male runners coming toward me to see if one of them would turn out to be John.

Of course, I'd planned exactly how to deal with him should the situation arise. I'd say, *Hiya, John,* and keep going. There was no way I would be at a loss upon seeing him any place because I'd imagined every possible scenario.

On the slim chance he'd call again, I would hang up after a courteous *I'm sorry, no more conversations.* I already knew the nod I'd give him—less than forty-five degrees up, then down—along with a self-possessed, no-teeth-showing smile if I ever ran into him and he was with a woman. Dignity, that's what I'd offer him. No wisecracks, no hostility. I kept searching the crowd.

While it is true that Manhattan can sometimes seem like a small town, the people you most often see are your periodontist's receptionist, your best friend's aunt, and Darren Kaminsky from fourth grade who could squeeze his palms together and create monster fart noises. So while I ran past an ex-*Times* reporter who had taken an early retirement package, I did not see John Orenstein.

I wanted so badly to see him. Immediately after that thought, I found myself slowing down so as not to work up the usual cascade of sweat that would be flowing for a half hour after I'd stopped running. Then, without even asking myself, *Are you crazy?* I exited the park at West Seventy-second and jogged to John's building. For a microsecond, I suppose I entertained such familiar, humiliating fantasies as 1) John would be living with a woman, probably *La Belleza*—though that would mean he'd be at her place because there wouldn't be room for her clothes in his apartment. 2) Unlike me, who could see neither sky nor sidewalk from my place, he had a view of both, and seeing me approach his building, he would call the doorman, order him not to let me up, and, if I grew insistent, to call the cops. 3) He would let me come up and then, without offering me even a glass of water or a seat, he'd tell me, with slightly more pity than disgust, never to call or come to his apartment again because he was sure I wouldn't want any—he'd search for the right word—*unpleasantness*.

"Hi," his doorman said. I doubted if he had any idea how long it had been since he'd last seen me. But maybe he studied acting at night. "Can you *believe* it, how beautiful it is today? Is he expecting you?"

"I'm not sure." I was uncomfortable with this misrepresentation, i.e., lie, because I didn't want the doorman, a nice guy who reminded me of a young Mr. Magoo without glasses, to catch hell from John.

"Go on in," he told me. "I'll call and tell him you're on your way up."

When the elevator door opened, the aroma of coffee from four or five competing pots seemed to invite me in. I stepped into the hall. John was already outside his apartment door waiting. He'd pulled on jeans and what looked like yesterday's T-shirt. As I walked down the hall I could see he hadn't yet combed his hair, much less shaved. He looked like one of those tough-beard guys in razor blade commercials. I was scared: Any second he would demand I get out. I slowed, not wanting to hear him say it, and nearly tripped as the inner sides of my sneakers merged for an instant. No, he wouldn't order me out because he wouldn't want to be nasty. That wasn't his style. And bickering in hallways wasn't his style either.

Then I was before him with not a thing in my mind to say. He said, "Hey, Amy." My reflexive reply should have been *Hey, John*, but the words wouldn't travel from brain to mouth. I stayed where I had stopped, a foot away from him, staring up into his lovely light brown eyes. I'm sure I was slack-jawed by then, and since I was considerably shorter than he, the fillings in my bottom teeth were no doubt on display. Probably I was standing pigeon-toed as well, thus offering a top-to-bottom portrait of utter idiocy.

Random responses flitted through my consciousness. I could throw myself at him. Or how about saying: *This is a terrible mistake. I apologize,* then turning and running down five flights of stairs. Or he would say *Good-bye* in a voice so icy that passersby a half block away would shiver. Except none of that got started because I could neither move nor speak.

"Amy."

I think I said something elegant, like "Huh?"

"Are you okay?"

"Yeah. Guess what? I met my mother."

He reached for my hand. It was so comforting that I automatically stepped toward him, stood on tiptoes and kissed him. No big wet thing. More like a healing touch.

"I'm so sorry," he whispered.

"Me too."

His eyes filled with tears. As they started to overflow, he wiped his nose on the sleeve of his T-shirt. Only when his cheeks became wet did he comprehend he was crying. Then neither of us knew what to do until John finally said: "I was so tempted to call you so often. But each time, I kept hearing myself telling you how we were over for good. I couldn't stand hurting you again. I don't know. Maybe it was more that I didn't want you to say, *Listen, I gave you a chance. You blew it. Now I'm involved with someone else.*"

"I tried that. It didn't work. The only one I was involved with was you."

"Do you want a frozen blueberry waffle or do you want to go out for breakfast?"

"Is that from the same package you bought a year ago?"

"Yes. Remember? We shared that one waffle and we both spit it out, so there are three more left."

I waited in his living room while he took a fast shower and dressed. I could have gone into the bedroom and talked over the sound of his electric toothbrush, but I held back. Maybe I was afraid of spotting someone else's hair clip.

Holding hands, we walked south on autopilot to our customary breakfast/brunch place. When we stopped for a light on Broadway and Ninety-third, I inquired: "We're not doing friendship here, are we?"

"No." Maybe it was his nature, maybe it came from doing so much editing for his work, but one of the things I loved about John was that when it came to matters emotional, he was both direct and succinct.

I drew his hand toward me and held it for a moment against my chest. "I'm having this big internal debate," I explained. "I'm too overcome to cry. Except if I don't, maybe you'll think I haven't changed at all and that I'm holding back my feelings because crying would be an attempt to evoke sympathy and I'm afraid to appear vulnerable."

The light changed and as we stepped into the street, John said: "Relax. You don't have to cry for me."

"I don't want you to feel I'm shortchanging you anymore. I'll give you all the great, traumatic moments of my childhood. If you ask me to stay for a day, I'll stay for a year."

He smiled. "I like that."

"Let's make a deal," I said. "If you feel I'm hiding my emotions by pulling back just let me know."

"Deal." We walked in silence for a moment, then he said: "So we're together again?"

"She wasn't your lover, was she? The Mahler woman."

"No. She was my producer. I'll take you to PBS to meet her."

"I'm sorry."

"Okay. Now, any other conditions?" I glanced up, possibly on the verge of giving him a dirty look for being snide, but I saw he'd simply asked a question. His brows were slightly raised, waiting for an answer.

I shrugged. "I don't know. I can't see this as a negotiation. Either we're going to work or not. All I ask is that after a few days or weeks, if it doesn't feel right to you, tell me."

"All right. And you tell me."

"John, we both care about each other so much. With that caring, I know there's a desire not to hurt the other person. But if it's not as good as you want it, dragging it out won't help. It would be more of an injury than a favor."

"Fair enough," he said. "Are you waiting to tell me about your mother until we're sitting down?"

"Yes."

"How did you break your ribs, for God's sake?"

For two more blocks, I filled him in on my ribs, the simultaneous adorableness and undesirability of Dr. Shea D'A, and the nonpublic story of the happily-ever-after reconciliation between Freddy Carrasco and Thom Bowles. I didn't mention the lawyer who had nothing wrong with him. John told me about a proposal from the History Channel for a three-part series on the Ottoman Empire, which he was dying to do—except the money was more suitable for a kid's allowance than a professional's fee.

We sat across from each other in a truncated, two-person booth at the Doughnut Hole, a place that served breakfast from five in the morning until two in the afternoon, when it closed because the owner needed time to read, although John and I had always preferred to believe it was a CIA front. "I hope you're planning on paying for this," I told him, "because all I have is my key."

He patted his pocket. "Thousands in unmarked bills."

There was only one waitress at the Doughnut Hole, an ox of a woman who always wore a T-shirt, white painter's pants, and a cross nearly large enough for Calvary. She shuffled over to our booth in her customary rubber beach thongs and, as always, asked: "What do you want?" There was no saying *the usual* because every customer, whether a rare tourist who wandered in or a seven-day-a-week regular, was treated like a stranger who was about to make some irritating demand. The owner, a tall man with the posture of an apostrophe, grilled, fried, and toasted, but never said a word to the waitress.

"Small grapefruit juice and poached eggs on buttered whole-wheat toast," I told her. Now, as about half the time, the right side of her upper lip twitched in either disgust or an Elvis imper-sonation. "I'll take my coffee now, please."

"A large OJ and waffles," John said. "Nothing else on the plate." His saying that insured there was only a 60-percent chance that his waffles would share the plate with hash browns, bacon, or white lumps the waitress insisted were grits. "I'd like my coffee now as well."

By the time the coffee got to us, I'd had time to tell John all about tracking down and meeting my grandmother Rose Moscowitz. Then I recounted, in detail, how I'd finally met my mother. When I got to the part where I blocked off her Volvo, our knees came together. For the same instant, we rubbed knees, shins, and calves and went mutually mindless, aware only of each other's touch. Rationality returned a moment later. Both of us sat straight, pressed our spines against the backs of the booth, and returned to the conversation.

"I always thought that if I heard one more person use the

word *closure* I'd become homicidal," I told him, "but that's what I got."

He put his hands on the table and took mine. "No closure for us. Okay? Only open-sure."

For a minute I didn't say anything because I didn't want him to feel pressured, but then I thought, *Screw that*. "Most of my life I was so proud of how I was able to fit in any place. In the visitors' room at the prison, at an Ivey alumnae tea, in any smoke-filled room. And then with our breakup and everything else, I realized that fitting in every place wasn't all that great if you didn't have one place to belong."

"That's what you want?"

"That's what I want." I hesitated because I was sure my next sentence would make him pull a twenty out of his pocket, smooth it down on the table, and walk out. Well, I decided, better now than in six months or a year. "I want a family. I hope that will turn out to be a husband and kids. If not, it will be me and a kid or two." I figured mentioning a dog might be the tipping point. "I want a place where I can hang my hat."

He squeezed my hands. "I've got the place to hang it." *What does that mean?* I was so tempted to say. So I said it. "It means that I want what you want," John told me. Then he took a deep breath, a sip of water, took both my hands again and added: "Marriage."

"To me?"

"Do you know someone better?" I thought we were having a staring contest, but we both became grinning fools. "Do I have to ask formally?"

I started to cry, but as we were still holding hands two tourists at the counter gave each other an *Aren't they sweet?* look. "Before you can ask anything formally," I declared, "you have to tell me something." I took a napkin, dabbed my eyes, and blew my nose so delicately I would have made Grandma Lil proud.

"Tell you what?"

"The three little words."

"You say them first, Amy."

"Why? For my own good?"

"For your own good."

I leaned over the table toward him and he leaned toward me until our heads were nearly touching. "I love you, John."

What did I expect, that he'd get up, laugh uproariously, say *The joke's on you. Now that you've said it, I'm leaving?* Maybe, but he said: "I love you, Amy. Will you do me the honor of being my wife?"

"Yes!" We said *I love you* a few thousand times more and then I told him the honor was all mine.

Acknowledgments

I sought information from the people listed below. All were courteous and helpful. I thank them and hope they will understand that on the occasions when their facts did not fit into my fictional universe, I chose credibility over truth.

Alvin Bragg, Jr., Paul Budline, Samantha Zises Cohen, Michelle Cottle, Joe DeBari, Jonathan Dolger, Dennis Farrell, Jacqueline Garber, R. T. Hawkes, Robert M. Kaye, Susan Lawton, Tamara Lipper, Joal Mendonsa, Daniel D. Mielnicki, Stephanie Moore, Sara Nelson, DeeDee O'Hearn, John Peterson, Sheila Riesel, Allen Salkin, Maggie Sandoval, Daniel Summers, Bernice Wollman, and Susan Zises.

Thanks to Elizabeth J. Carroll for her splendid research and for opening the door to boarding school for me.

I learned so much from the staff, faculty, and students at the Taft School. I appreciate their warm welcome and their sharing knowledge and memories of boarding school with me. Particularly, I am much obliged to Suzanne H. Campbell, Eleanor Gillespie, Massiel Santos, and Clayton B. Spencer.

I love libraries, particularly the Port Washington (New York) Public Library and the New York Public Library.

I am enormously grateful to the fine people at my publisher, Scribner, including my editor, the brilliant and gracious Nan Graham, as well as Susan Moldow, Pat Eisemann, Alexis Gargagliano, and their colleagues.

Owen Laster, my ace agent, is unfailingly shrewd and kind. It is comforting to be represented by such a fine man.

My assistant, Ronnie Gavarian, is awesomely gifted, as knowledgeable in gemology, music, and cake decorating as she is in Internet research. She's also funny, insightful, and hardworking. I was blessed from the day she agreed to take the job.

The following people made generous donations to Long Island charities in exchange for having characters in this novel named for them or for a friend or relative. I hope they enjoy their other selves: Barbara Axinn; Sandy Garfunkel; Robin Ziegelbaum for her mother, Margaret Jane Maller; Joan Bernhard in her maiden name, Joan Murdoch; Matthew Schwartz; Mary Sloane.

So much of what I know about contemporary popular culture comes from my children and in-law children, Elizabeth and Robert Stoll, Leslie Stern and Andy Abramowitz. It is a joy to learn from them.

Naturally, I must hail my muses, Nathan and Molly Abramowitz.

I dedicated my first work of fiction to my husband: *Elkan Abramowitz, the best person in the world.* This is my tenth novel, and he still holds the title.

About the Author

Susan Isaacs, a former magazine editor and political speech-writer, is the author of nine novels, including *Long Time No See, Red, White and Blue, Lily White, After All These Years, Compromising Positions,* and *Shining Through,* and one nonfiction title, *Brave Dames and Wimpettes: What Women Are Really Doing on Page and Screen.* She lives on Long Island with her husband.

© Elizabeth Stoll